Venetia spun the chair to face us and laughed up at her mother, the tone girlish and excited. Almera Gordon grabbed her daughter beneath the armpits and lifted. And Venetia Gordon came to her feet.

I felt the breath go out of me in a whoosh. The sweat on my skin, chilled by the air-conditioned air, seemed to freeze. A silence fell upon us, deep and heavy, as if we were immobilized by a shock of lightning in our midst.

Almera stepped back, holding her daughter's hands. Venetia slid her left foot forward, her socks scraping the floor, sounding loud in the total silence. Her right foot followed more sluggishly, meeting the left. I could hear the grunting of her breath as she struggled. Her eyes were looking at her feet, her head hanging forward, hair straggling over her face. The left foot moved forward again. Venetia Gordon was walking. Two steps later, the girl's legs began to shake. "Catch her," Almera said.

Hands shot forward and caught the girl. Babbling broke out.

"My God, what happened?"

"Did you see that?"

"She walked."

I stood away from the group, watching.

"It's a miracle, is what it is. It's a miracle," Almera said. "My girl is walking. And that healer praying for her is what done it."

The crowd grew around the wheelchair, the excitement drawing other employees to look and listen. Quietly, cold to my marrow, I walked away.

I had no idea what had just happened. I didn't believe in miracles. But...what if I was wrong?

GWEN HUNTER

DEADLY REMEDY

MIRA

ISBN 1-55166-669-3

DEADLY REMEDY

Copyright © 2003 by Gwen Hunter.

Visit us at www.mirabooks.com

Printed in U.S.A.

To Joy Robinson
Best friend then,
Best friend today,
Best friend always.

ACKNOWLEDGMENTS

Though I drew on Chester County, South Carolina, and its hospital blueprint for inspiration and information, Dawkins County, its citizens, its employees, its hospital and patients are entirely fictional. I have tried to make the medical sections of *Deadly Remedy* as realistic as possible. Where mistakes may exist, they are mine, not the able, competent and creative medical workers in the list below.

Laurie Milatz, D.O., in SC
Susan Prater, O.R. Tech and sister-in-love, in SC
Susan Gibson, O.R. Tech, in SC
Marc Gorton, Registered Respiratory Therapist, in SC
Robert D. Randall Jr., M.D., in SC
Tammy Varnadore, R.N., in SC
Tim Minors, Paramedic, in SC
Barry Benfield, R.N., in SC
Cindy Nowland, R.N., in SC
Jason Adams, M.D., in SC and FL
Dan Thompson, R.N., in SC
Earl Jenkins Jr., M.D., in SC
Eric Lavondas, M.D., in NC
And especially J. Michael Glenn, M.D., in FL, without whom this book would never have made it to print on time.

As always, for making this a stronger book:

Miranda Stecyk, my editor
Jeff Gerecke, my agent, who wisely told me to write a medical book
My writers' group for all the help in making this novel work. Thanks for bleeding all over its bits and pieces: Dawn Cook, Craig Faris, Norman Froscher, Misty Massey, Todd Massey, Virginia Wilcox.

_____ Prologue _____

I never put much stock in omens and portents, but that strange August Wednesday had been rife with them, according to Miss Essie, who knew more about such things than I ever would. Temps went from typically hot and muggy to oddly cool and wet as a Canadian front blew through. And the appearance of sun-dogs and a double rainbow on the heels of a nasty summer lightning storm, together with the screaming crows perched high in the trees, were portents enough to have the older woman muttering to herself and banging pans in her kitchen.

When I stopped by on the way in to work, I tried reminding her that the rain was a welcome relief, drenching the overheated earth and straw-dry crops still in the fields, making a dent in the awful drought we had been suffering and bringing cooler weather. Miss Essie was having nothing of it. When I left her, she was casting dark glances at the sky and talking to God as if He had made a mistake somewhere and needed her advice to fix things.

I, on the other hand, reveled in the sudden return to fresh air and temperatures in the eighties. Delighted in the vision of brilliant rainbows on one horizon, framed against furious purpled clouds. Loved the sun-dogs— weird refracted spots of light to the left and right of the sun on the other horizon. It had been breathtaking for all of fifteen minutes just after the storm passed. Now, as I left Miss Essie's and drove in to the small rural ER of Dawkins County, South Carolina, they had faded. The sun-dogs had vanished. The rainbows were little more than broken curves low in the sky. And the black crows that alighted in the topmost branches of the white oaks in the woods between Miss Essie's home and mine were not a harbinger of death and change. No matter what Miss Essie said.

Omens. Portents. Hogwash.

Simply a prism of sunlight refracted through rain-mist on one side, and sun-dog-forming mile-high ice crystals on the other. Science. Meteorology. Just big black birds, celebrating having lived through the wind and lightning, flapping their wings and calling out to other birds. Nothing more. Though ice crystals in August *were* rare. After all, this was the South. And crows usually didn't make that much noise.

Still, I had experienced enough of the religiously weird recently and I wasn't buying into any more. I had helped put the Reverend Lamb of God behind bars and seen his TV station shut down. And lived to tell about it. I wasn't going to listen to spiritual nonsense, no matter what happened in the heavens.

At 6:00 p.m., I pulled into the doctors' parking lot of Dawkins County Hospital, where I worked under contract as an ER physician, and knew instantly that it would be a busy night. The surrounding parking area was filled with cars and trucks, many with yellow emergency lights affixed to the roofs. Three county ambulances, two rescue squad vehicles loaded with equipment, a fire truck and a crowd of milling people met me. Hot time in the old town tonight. Busy? Yes. Kaleidoscopes and rainbows? Definitely.

Omens? Portents? No way.

1

STORMS AND MISERY

The storm started three brushfires and kept the rescue squad on its toes, though the rain put the flames out before extensive damage was done. Fire wasn't the reason why my ER looked like a major disaster area. The bus accident on I–77, about nine miles from the hospital, had a far greater impact. And lightning had hit the hospital, resulting in minor damage to the surgical department and bringing out the rest of the county crews and volunteers.

I spent half an hour treating minor burns, cuts and scrapes so my boss could head home. We usually switched shifts at 7:00 p.m., but I owed the hospital some time. Together, Dr. Wallace Chadwick and I moved patients in and out and cleared the backlog of victims before he left for the night. It was good to get the place emptied out and start with a clean slate.

While the nurses changed shifts and the security guard made rounds, I settled in. Ignoring the weakness in my healing back muscles, I picked up my bag, abandoned earlier under a desk chair in the nurses' station, and headed up the hall. On the way I took in a brisk earful from Trisha Singletary, the nursing supervisor called in to help deal with the mess. She was shorter than I, cute and buxom, and had a way with men that bordered on the mystical.

"It's mostly over now, but Dr. Rhea, you shoulda seen the smoke. I was clocking in when it hit—the lightning, I mean. It shook the whole building, made the lights go out. Knocked a hole in the last surgical suite, up high near the ceiling, and let in rain and leaves. Ruined any pretense at sterility. There's smoke damage in two rooms. Thank God they weren't doing the procedure in either one."

"Someone was cutting at the time?" I asked as I led the way to my call room. It was calmer in the ER but I didn't know how long that might last, and I wanted to drop off my overnight bag, make sure the call room had clean sheets and towels.

"Dr. Haynes was assisting Statler with an appendix on a seven-year-old with muscular dystrophy. Statler was closing and the lightning hit. Lorella Smith—you know her?"

I shook my head, tossed my bag on the bed, checked the room for cleanliness and decided it was fine. Locking the door behind me, we started back to the ER.

"Well, she's an OR tech, and she said she jumped outta her skin when it hit, and landed on a tray of sterile instruments. Statler started cussing and Haynes slipped and fell on the anesthetist's equipment. Lights were out about twenty seconds before they came back on. And to make it worse, Lorella said she saw a bat fly through."

"A bat." I would be careful not to mention that part to Miss Essie. It would surely feed her omen talk.

"It musta found its way into the eaves from outside and been sleeping there till dark, then got knocked out of its place by the lightning. Now it's inside. The kid's okay, and the maintenance crew has a tarp over the hole.

The fire started by the lightning was put out by the rain, but fire crews are here to make sure nothing is still hot in the walls.''

As she spoke, a fireman in full protective gear, heavy coat, boots, gloves, helmet tucked under his arm, approached. Trisha slowed, preened and stuck out her chest a bit, though her impressive bustline didn't require any effort to draw the man's attention. He slowed, too, smiled, and after a moment met her eyes.

"Miss Trish. You gonna be at McDowries Bar and Billards Friday? They got a deejay with shagging." The fireman's dark eyes held hungrily to Trisha as he mentioned the state dance of South Carolina.

"That divorce finalized yet?" she asked archly. Trisha was perpetually looking for a man, but her standards were well known in the area. Married men were not a part of her social calendar.

"Last Monday. I'm a free man." They both kept moving as the flirtation continued, turning and walking backward in the halls.

"I may be there." She flipped back an imaginary strand of hair, touching her neck in the process, the motion unconsciously sexual. "You can buy me a drink to celebrate."

A wide grin split his face. "It's a date."

"Well, I wouldn't go that far. But you catch that bat, I might consider dancing with you."

"Not my job, gorgeous. But speaking of bats…" The fireman pointed past us at a dark corner just ahead.

Trisha jumped and stared, then shivered. A dark form moved in the corner, turning its head as we neared.

"Lordy, I hate bats. I'll get the cops after it now. When's this backwater county gonna get us an animal control officer?'' she demanded of the fireman. But he was gone.

"Close the fire doors to the other wings,'' I recommended, "and trap him here. And be careful. A small percentage of bats carry rabies.''

"Well, ain't that just fine and dandy,'' Trish muttered. "A big strong man all dressed out to save me and he can't kill a single little old flying rabies factory.''

I grinned. The recently divorced fireman had passed up an opportunity to play knight in shining armor to the damsel in distress. If he had visions of dancing Friday night with his Miss Trish, I figured he was in for a disappointment.

My beeper went off, the code in the little LED window displaying the ER extension followed by the numerals 911. "Got an emergency, Trish.'' I half jogged away from her. "If it stays quiet, I'll spring for pizza for the ER crew around nine. Join us if you like.''

"Beep me if you need help,'' she said. "Oh, and we got a whole bunch a' new agency nurses starting tonight, so things may be a lil' chaotic.''

"Little chaotic?'' I said to myself as I rounded the corner to the ER. The emergency scanner crackled with coded general information, and the ambulance scanner with more specific info, reporting on a patient being brought to the ER, code three. I had a sixteen-year-old female quadriplegic with a severe headache, shortness of breath and blood pressure that was sky-high. My best guess from hearing the paramedic's report was autonomic dysreflexia, or toxic hypertension. That was a dangerous condition in a quadriplegic, sometimes resulting in hemorrhagic stroke, respiratory shutdown and death.

"From the address, I can tell it's Venetia Gordon.'' Anne, one of the ER nurses, commented.

The ability of a nurse to tell a patient's name just by the address was not particularly unusual in Dawkins. The rural county had around fifty thousand residents, according to the last census, and just like any business, we had our regulars. "We got an old chart on her?" I asked. I wanted to see the original report on the cause of the girl's paralysis, and a breakdown of everything that had happened to her since.

"She was in the ER last week," Anne said. "UTI from a permanent catheter. But the original accident happened six months ago, down in Lancaster County. Two-car MVA on a back-country road," she said, referring to a moving vehicular accident—medspeak for a car wreck. "They flew her out from the scene to CMC in Charlotte. Except for a minor infection, you'll be flying blind."

"Lovely. Ask the crew where the spinal break occurred."

When the scratchy words came back at C4, I sighed. Vertebrae were named and numbered from the base of the skull to the tailbone, with cervical vertebrae at the top. The lower the number, the greater the amount of paralytic damage. Damage at C7 would have left Venetia's upper body under her own control. At C4, things could get dicey.

I told Anne what I would likely need in terms of meds and equipment, and asked her to get respiratory therapy down here stat. If this girl crashed, I wanted help getting her intubated and on the ventilator. There was an old saying, "C3, 4, 5, keep you alive." My patient was barely in the safety zone. Anything could happen with spinal damage at that location.

Anne nodded, writing nothing, remembering everything. She was a medium woman in every way except her memory. Medium-length medium-brown hair, medium height, medium weight, medium disposition. But her memory was phenomenal, as I was learning. Tell her once and she'd remember forever. And she was really great in an emergency, which was a good thing, as the other RN on duty tonight was a newbie, fresh out of nursing school and likely useless. She'd get good eventually, but for now she needed watching so she didn't kill somebody. Coreen was her name. Dark-skinned and brown-eyed, petite as a model and twenty years old. So fresh-faced and innocent she made me feel ancient at twenty-nine.

Venetia Gordon, still with the healthy-looking limbs of her preaccident life, was wheeled in, strapped to an ambulance gurney. She was breathing fast and shallowly. Not much air was being exchanged.

The girl was on 100 percent oxygen but her color was poor, an ashen blue shade that told me her lungs were shutting down. I looked at the monitor sitting atop the stretcher as the EMS guys moved with her: blood pressure 230 over 145. Pulse 72. I bent over her head, moving with her as she was swept into the cardiac room, and checked for papilledema of her optic nerves. They looked fine, no swelling that might lead to blindness if not corrected. "What is her O_2 sat?" I asked, referring to the oxygen saturation level.

"Eighty-four percent last time we checked the pulse-ox," a voice answered, referring to a device that clipped onto a patient's finger and measured both pulse and oxygen levels.

"I want ABGs, repeat O_2 sat, and Catapress PO," I said, ordering the same tests and drugs I had mentioned to Anne only moments before. I told them the dosage and stood back as the EMTs lifted the patient and moved her to the ER stretcher. "How long on the ABGs?" I asked no one in particular. My attention was on the patient's ragged, shallow breathing. There was a look of panic in her eyes, a mottled appearance to her skin.

"Beth?" Anne asked the lab tech.

"Fast. Maybe three minutes."

ABGs referred to arterial blood gases, which would tell me how well or poorly Venetia's lungs were working. I bent over the patient and positioned my stethoscope on her chest. While not much air was moving, there didn't appear to be any fluid buildup. Her skin was damp and cold, not feverish. Not pneumonia, then. Symptoms matched classic toxic hypertension. At least, so far.

"Get me an EKG after you get the ABGs back. Family here with her?"

"I'm her mama. Almera Gordon."

I turned away from the sight of the lab tech drawing blood gases to the soft voice, and found a timid-looking woman, mousy brown all over, wearing sturdy matronly shoes and a sturdy matronly skirt, her hair pulled back in a tight bun. She would have been unremarkable in every way, except for her eyes. They were wide and a vivid deep blue, almost lavender, fringed around with odd double lashes, thick and lustrous. Her entire demeanor may have been subdued, but her eyes claimed something else about her, a hidden strength, some powerful determination. I nodded at her. "Tell me what was happening when this started."

Mrs. Gordon checked her watch. "At 6:00 p.m. I got her outta the bath. The water temp was jist warmer than tepid, and she wasn't in for very long," she said, anticipating my next question. Quadriplegics were not supposed to spend much time in heat, which could cause all sorts of weird things to happen. "I dried her off, got her halfway dressed in pj's and swung her to the bed."

"Swung? You have a transport sling?"

"On movable tracks, but we usually keep the system set up between the bathroom and bed. It makes bathing her jist so much easier," she said in her drawn-out mill-hill accent.

I nodded my understanding.

"O_2 sat on the pulse-ox is 82 percent, Doc. BP 242 over 147," Anne said.

I checked my watch. "Blood gases?"

Beth put the result strip in my hand. Venetia's pH was 7.053, her CO_2 at 74, and her O_2 at 52. Not good. Her oxygen saturation levels matched the results for the pulse-ox. Bad all around. "Go on," I said, addressing Mrs. Gordon.

"She seemed to be having trouble breathing. And she said her head was hurtin'. I checked her blood pressure and it was 190 over 120. Her eyes looked kinda funny, like she wasn't seeing so good. So I called the EMS."

"You checked her blood pressure when?"

"About 6:20."

"The call came in at 6:24, Doc," an EMT said.

"Blood pressure is still rising," Anne said.

Panic bloomed in the dark-brown depths of Venetia's eyes. She was using accessory muscles to breathe; her shoulders lifted and the sternocleidomastoid muscles of the neck and the very upper chest stretched with effort, all the movement the girl could make to force in air. With her breathing so bad, she didn't speak, but I understood her fear. "Venetia," I said, leaning over her chest, "is your head hurting?" She nodded once. "Is your vision blurred?" She nodded again, the movement spastic and jerky. "Do you have a throbbing in your neck, right here?" I asked, brushing the skin over the carotid where the baroreceptors measured pressure in the carotid artery. Venetia nodded shakily.

"I'm going to get your blood pressure down so your headache goes away, okay? And your breathing should ease at the same time." She managed a nod, lifting her shoulders slightly. Besides the desperate breathing, it was the only motion I had seen her make. "Bag her. Give her another Catapress. Get me a Nipride drip ready."

"Nipride is ready, Doc," Coreen said, her voice steady and composed.

I raised my eyebrows. "Thanks."

"And I got another line going," she added, indicating the IV line in the patient's right hand.

The respiratory therapist moved into place beside Venetia's head and put a tight-fitting, blue plastic mask over her face. She attached an ambu bag and pumped the large balloon; 100 percent oxygen began to fill the girl's lungs.

"Do you understand what's happening here?" I asked Mrs. Gordon, not taking my eyes from the girl.

"Not to say," she said softly, which meant "not really" in the local lingo.

"Injuries to spinal cords can be tricky things. Venetia's was six months ago?"

The woman nodded, her eyes on her daughter with a single-minded intensity. "Six months ago next Monday."

"Do you know if she had any sacral sparing?" I asked. When the woman looked blank, I asked, "Does she feel anything anywhere on her body? Heat or cold? Pain? Pressure sensations?"

"No. Nothing. My baby don't feel nothing," she whispered. "Dr. Danthari, her neurosurgeon, said she won't never feel no more than she does now. It's at C4. She had a lot of swelling at the site and it caused more damage than he expected.''

Spinal cord injuries often resulted in strange reactions, depending on the location of the injury. Even though there are only seven cervical vertebrae, there are eight pairs of cervical nerves. Injuries on the dorsal spine will cause one type of sensory loss, while injury to the lateral spine will cause other types, depending on which pair of nerves are affected. I had once seen a patient with a spinal fracture at C7 who had lost his intrinsics, which were responsible for abduction and adduction of the fingers and his ability to key-pinch—meaning that he was able to flex and extend all of his fingers or make a fist, but not able to pinch his car key or move his fingers from side to side.

I really needed to know what kind of injury Venetia had received, but there likely wasn't time to get a call through to her neurosurgeon. I told Anne to call Dr. Danthari, just in case, to cover my backside. She ran to the phone at the nurses' desk.

''Her blood pressure is very high, and swelling may be what we're seeing here. The original injury could be causing pressure on the part of the lower brain that controls blood pressure, much higher than C4. The high blood pressure could then slow down her ability to breathe.''

Mrs. Gordon bit her lip, her almost-lavender eyes filling with tears. ''I don't want her on no ventilator. She don't want to be on no vent.''

I checked the BP on the monitor. It was down a bit. I smiled at the woman. ''We'll avoid that if at all possible.'' I wasn't closing any doors, not on a patient who seemed fully aware of what was going on in the room. This was no brain-damaged person without the ability to interact with life. This was a vibrant young woman with a future ahead of her, especially if modern medicine made some small leaps in the next few years.

"We got a living will. It's in the van." The timid voice sounded suddenly firmer.

The room seemed to go still. If her breathing deteriorated further and she was not put on a ventilator, Venetia Gordon could die. I crossed my arms over my chest and glanced quickly at Anne.

"Would you get it so we can make a copy?" Anne said, reading my look.

"Yes. A'course." The timid woman reached out and lovingly touched the unfeeling toes of her daughter before she turned and moved away on her sturdy shoes. Almera Gordon was a sudden inconsistency—loving her daughter, yet willing to let her die.

Checking my watch, I said, "Get the Nipride going. I want that pressure down." I bent over Venetia's chest again and listened. If I couldn't get her stabilized, I might have to initiate a legal battle to keep a sixteen-year-old girl from dying. Slipping the stethoscope around my neck, I left the room and checked the administrative call sheet for the night. I wasn't letting this girl die without a fight.

"Nipride's going," Coreen said through the open door.

Rolanda Higgenbotham was on call for the night. Good. Rolanda was a take-charge, no-nonsense woman. I motioned Anne to the side. "When you get that living will, fax a copy to Ms. Higgenbotham and call her with the problem. I may need to intubate. And this is a minor. We may need DSS or a judge." Department of Social Services would remove the girl from her mother's custody and have her receive lifesaving medical treatment. There wasn't any doubt about it.

Anne nodded, her eyes troubled. Whatever we did with Venetia, it was legal trouble. To allow a mentally healthy minor die was impossible. To ignore a legally correct living will was a nightmare. It would be a mess both legally and emotionally, no matter what I chose to do. But I had made my decision already and everyone around me knew it, except Mrs. Gordon and her daughter.

"Pressure is dropping," Coreen said from the room where Venetia Gordon struggled, fighting the headache pain caused by high blood pressure. "It's 204 over 136. O_2 sat is up to 90."

"She's breathing easier," the respiratory tech said. "Bagging isn't as stiff."

It was too soon to feel relief, but I felt a surge of comfort anyway. Leaving the room, I called Dr. Haynes, Venetia's medical doctor, and filled him in. The man was sleepy, as though I had interrupted a post-fire, post-surgery, post-embarrassing-spill-in-the-OR nap, but he instantly knew which patient I was dealing with, listened to the litany of symptoms, and then recommended admission. "Mrs. Gordon will say no. She always does. But offer it anyway. And call me back if you can't get the pressure down. She and Venetia saw a lawyer about a living will. It's pretty airtight." He yawned hugely, the sound making me sleepy. "We'll have to get DSS involved to get the girl on a vent. I'll come in and help you with the mother. She's a handful."

"Thanks. If you don't hear from me, you'll either find her admitted or sent home."

I was holding a pair of latex gloves, and absently folded them and stuffed them into the pocket that held my reflex hammer, a Maglite flashlight and a small collection of other medical junk I usually found myself carrying when at work.

"Pressure is 198 over 130, pulse 81, O_2 sat at 92." Coreen looked up at me through the door, her eyes bright with excitement. For a newbie, she was doing great. And she was young enough and inexperienced enough to still find the medical successes exhilarating. There were compensations for the lack of experience.

Venetia's mom stood by the copier while Anne made copies, then folded the original papers that could end her daughter's life and slipped them in her purse. Returning to the cardiac room where Venetia lay, I stood to the side where I could view both the mother and daughter without moving my head. Drinking a cup of coffee I scarcely tasted, I watched Venetia's color return to pink, her BP continuing to drop, her O_2 sat rising.

When Venetia could draw enough air to speak, she said, "My head feels a little better." I nodded at her, pleased.

Mrs. Gordon sat through the procedures with tightly clasped hands and a strained face, body rocking slightly, silent, staying out of the way, but with her lips moving, her eyes tight on her child. I figured she was praying. There was no doubt she loved the girl. The living will was a mystery.

Forty-seven minutes from the time Venetia was wheeled into the ER, I asked for a repeat ABG. The results were good enough for me to turn down the O_2 and tell the respiratory tech to stop bagging her. At an hour and fifteen minutes, Venetia was sitting up, strapped in the bed to keep her from slipping down again, laughing and telling knock-knock jokes to the respiratory therapist. Her pressure was stabilized. Her breathing was dang near normal. The respiratory therapist was satisfied with her blood gases, her O_2 sat, everything. The threat of fighting a legal battle while trying to save a life had been neutralized, just that fast.

I poured a couple cups of coffee and motioned Mrs. Gordon into the office the contract doctors used when working ER duty. It was little more than a closet, but it did have chairs and a desk and a new print hanging on one wall, depicting the Charleston Battery under attack by hurricane winds.

"Venetia is going to be fine," I started. And then wished I could take back the words as Mrs. Gordon's face twisted in grief. Venetia was paralyzed. Fine was relative. I took a breath and started over. "You called 911 quickly enough for us to catch and treat Venetia's condition before it went too far. You did well, Mrs. Gordon."

The woman nodded her head, still biting her lips. Her vivid lavender eyes were tear-filled but steady.

"She developed a disorder called autonomic dysreflexia, or toxic hypertension. It's a condition, not uncommon in quadriplegics, caused by stimulation of the autonomic nervous system by something as simple as a urinary tract infection. It could have happened just by moving her from the tub, if her catheter got a slight yank. You understand what I mean by autonomic nervous system?"

When Almera shook her head no, I said, "That's the part of the nervous system that controls automatic things like breathing and heart rate and blood pressure. In quadriplegics, it can be affected by many things. The blood pressure goes up fast and to frightening levels, and if not treated, can result in stroke and death. We have her stabilized at the moment, but I called Venetia's medical doctor and Dr. Haynes recommended that she be admitted overnight, to monitor her better.''

The woman's face grew hard. Her hands, which had gripped one another repeatedly during treatment, began to work on each other again. The skin was rough and reddened from what appeared to be constant abrasion. ''No insult to Dr. Haynes,'' she said steadily. ''He's a good man. But my girl's seen enough doctors. Can't none of them fix her. A few say she could maybe get some feeling back. Maybe get some use of her arms. Maybe. But can't not a one of 'em fix her. And I'm not making her stay in any hospital any more than I have to. Not unless you say she'll die tonight without it.''

I shrugged, uncomfortable with the statement. Venetia could die at any time. Sometimes toxic hypertension could hit so fast, a five-minute wait for an ambulance might be the difference between life and death. It wasn't likely. But I had to consider the possibility.

When I said this to Mrs. Gordon, her face hardened again, a mask of frustration that I understood. ''You're jist riding a fence like all the others. Make sure you cover your backside so I can't sue. Well, you ain't got to live with a sixteen-year-old who can't move to even scratch her nose. A little girl who has lost everything. Who wants to die so bad I can hardly keep her alive.'' The tears that had threatened for the last hour finally fell in a steady stream. I forced myself not to look away. ''You ain't got to pay the bills for every overnight stay in a hospital, or listen to the bill collectors hound us on the phone. Venetia's got a one-million-dollar lifetime limit on her health insurance and a probable life span of sixty years.'' She sniffed hard. ''I'll be broke and dead long before then.''

Disconcerted, I looked away for a moment. "You're right."

Mrs. Gordon's eyebrows went up. Her hands, which had continued kneading one another, stilled. Our coffees sat untouched on the desk between us, a curl of steam lifting from each.

"She initiated the living will?" I guessed suddenly.

"'Bout drove me nuts till I took her to a lawyer. She wants to die. Can't stand the thought of living like she is. Tonight, jist now, is the first time I seen her laugh in six months." Almera Gordon fished in her neat handbag and pulled out a small, thin pack of Kleenex. Delicately she blew her nose.

I remembered the knock-knock jokes the girl had been telling. Had the freedom from extreme fear temporarily reversed extreme depression? I waited until Almera had put away the pack before resuming speaking. "It's easy for a doctor to get so caught up in potential medical problems that we forget the realities of time and cost." I focused on her bright tear-filled eyes. Her skin was mottled and flushed with the effort of controlling the crying jag. The tissue she still held was already crushed and wilted. "I'm sorry. I know this is hard for you, but we sometimes have to save patients against their will."

The woman's eyes dropped, but not before I saw tears gather again. She took a shuddering breath.

"Mrs. Gordon—"

"Call me Almera."

I figured that meant I had passed some test in her eyes and I nodded my thanks. "And I'm Rhea." I leaned across the desk toward her. "Almera, Venetia could get this condition at any time. Once a patient has had toxic hypertension, it's easier for them to get it a second time. The next time, it could come on her so fast that you wouldn't have time to get an ambulance to her before she had a stroke or expired."

"Died."

I nodded. "Died." This woman wanted plain talk. I could give her that. "But it isn't likely that it will happen again tonight, any more than it's likely to happen any other specific time. She's as stable as I can get her in an ER."

"I'll be taking her home then. I followed the ambulance in my van." Almera stood, straight-backed and resolute, opened the door and stepped out into the hallway. I accompanied her, leaving the coffees on the desk. "I'll stay up tonight watching her," Mrs. Gordon said. "I can check her BP every half hour if I need to." She paused, looking up at me, her face once again hard, eyes calculating. As if to challenge me. "We have an appointment with a faith healer tomorrow. I ain't missing that for nothing."

My heart fell. I opened my mouth to say that was foolish. To tell her they were all charlatans. Fakes. To tell her that in a few years medicine would have a cure or at least a good treatment for people in Venetia's condition. But I remembered the tears in Almera's eyes and her worry-roughened hands, and kept my mouth closed. The words strangled there. Right now, medicine couldn't provide the kind of help Venetia needed. And the Gordons needed something to give them hope.

I settled on, "Would you call us in the morning and let us know how she's doing? We'll be here till seven."

"I'll do that. And thank you, Doctor."

"Rhea," I said again. But she shook her head.

"Doctor. And you're a good one. You talk to people."

With that, she turned her attention to her daughter and getting the girl strapped into her specially made wheelchair. I stood under the covered ambulance bay and watched as they loaded her up, the gray panel van situated against a backdrop of vibrant fuchsia clouds and a dying scarlet sun. It was eight-thirty and growing dark, the sunset seeming alive in the dusky sky. I looked up. Not a rainbow to be seen. The cool temperatures wouldn't last. By morning it would likely be back in the high nineties. For now, the false fall was blissful.

Coreen stood beside me as the van drove off, her wispy brown curls shaded rosy in the light. "They used to go to my church. Now they stay home. Watch TV preachers." The Gordons' van turned onto the road in front of the hospital and moved slowly away, the brake lights glowing.

In the distance, an engine revved, the whine high and growing shrill as it approached. Headlights rounded the far curve. It was another panel van, this one vibrant as the sunset, flying up the hill. Foreboding gripped me.

"That thing's moving too fast," Coreen said. "It isn't gonna make the—"

The van, silhouetted in the orange sun, made a hard left in front of the hospital. Tires squealed. Its headlights flickered. All at once, the van seemed to lift and topple then rolled and disappeared off the road into the ditch. The sound of it hitting earth and the telephone pole was like a bomb going off. The pole splintered and flew up into the air. An instant later the impact was over. And I was moving.

2

PSYCHEDELICS AND VERTIGO

Behind me, Coreen shouted into the ER for someone to call 911, her voice muting as the doors closed. I still had my stethoscope around my neck and latex gloves in my pocket. I sprinted down the road toward the ditch, pulling the gloves out as I ran. A latex tourniquet fell from the latex fingers and I grabbed it, gloved quickly and wondered what the heck I thought I could do without equipment. In the dark. I had one Maglite, a thin tourniquet and a rubber hammer for checking reflexes.

Behind me, I heard the sound of doors bursting open, voices following. I was a runner, and easily outdistanced the ER crew, reaching the hole and stopping. My heart was banging in my chest. I was sucking down air like a drowning victim. From below I could hear the tinny strains of Led Zeppelin playing. The sound of someone screaming.

The van, painted in psychedelic, sixties shades with a Day-Glo orange sun, was still, lying on its driver's side, up against the hill, steam billowing from the ruptured radiator. The smell of gas was strong. Inside it was dark as pitch.

I skidded halfway down the muddy hill on my rump

and heels, Maglite bouncing, providing no illumination at all. I landed with a spine-jolting drop on the side of the vehicle. Slipped as my mud-slicked soles caught on the pitted metal. Crawled over to the open sliding door.

Farther down the hill, in the brush, something moved, catching the last rays of the sun. But when I glanced up, there was nothing there but a piece of paper propped against a tree. From inside the van, the screaming changed pitch.

I shined the thin beam of the Maglite inside the gaping door. The utility pole's base was rammed against the windshield frame, the van's front bucket seats tight against it. The screaming grew labored. Then I spotted her. Wedged between the pole and the passenger seat, hanging by the restraint belt.

I found a clear place to land and dropped, ignoring the twinge to my injured back. I crouched to keep from banging my head on the van side, over my head, and I experienced a moment of vertigo adjusting to left and right turned into up and down.

There were two bodies in the mangled front cab. A broad-backed male was in the driver's seat, crushed between the utility pole's base and his seat. His head drooped out the driver's window into a pool of gas. Gray matter and blood slimed together with a rainbow hue of gasoline.

I remembered the double rainbows after the storm. "Not an omen," I said, the words lost beneath the heavy guitar of Led. "Not an omen."

As I made my way to the man, his seat broke and fell, held in place only by the seat belt and his limp body. Across his newly exposed back, shiny silver letters glittered on a black T-shirt. *Choo-Choo. God's Gift to Spee-*

dos and Women. He was way beyond my help. Still I checked his pulse. None.

The woman beside him, hanging from the passenger seat, gurgled. Her screaming softened, quieted to an arrhythmic grunting. With the beam of my tiny Maglite, I checked her over.

In my first glance, all I saw was blood. Blood everywhere. In her kinky, brown hair. Smeared into her ashenbrown skin. Even showering over me. She had a ruptured artery, somewhere. But I couldn't tell where in the dark, with her hanging from the seat, tangled in the belts and the twisted metal.

Led Zeppelin paused to change melodies. In the sudden silence I could hear her mewling moans, and other sounds from the back of the van. Other victims? I didn't have time to look. Frantically, I held my hand over my face to shield me from the spurting blood and bent.

And I saw it. The twisted, shattered left leg, caught between the telephone pole that was wedged against the place where the windshield used to be and other lengths of contorted metal. The leg was crushed. The popliteal artery severed.

The leg—already effectively amputated—had to come off. She had to get to the OR fast. But first I had to stop that bleeding, and my skinny latex tourniquet was next to useless for this. Led Zeppelin started to grind again.

Choo-Choo had a belt. I reached around in front of him, unbuckled the inch-wide leather strap and pulled, but nothing gave. Choo-Choo was a big man, and I clenched the Maglite in my teeth to free both hands, bracing myself against the moaning, now gasping, patient at my back. It took six pulsing beats for me to free the belt. When it suddenly loosened, I jerked, banged my head on the van side.

Above me someone said, "Holy crap!"

Another voice, more hesitant, said, "Dr. Lynch?"

"Get me some light!" I yelled as I whipped the belt free and threaded it around the woman's thigh. "A handful of scalpels. A bone saw. Some big surgical clamps. A couple paramedics. A stretcher. Heated blankets. Someone page the bone doc on call. Get him here fast! And someone cut off that music!"

I yanked the belt tight. The jets of blood slowed to a pulsing flow. I pulled tighter, making a fulcrum of my arms and hands, grunting with the effort. The bright-red flood became a thin trickle.

No one had joined me in the van. I was still alone. I used my light to find the tape player and reached through the beam to cut it off. My lab coat was stained red with blood in the faint light and stuck to me like a second skin. Looking down, I understood the mild expletive when the nurses saw me from above. I looked as though I had showered in blood. A victim in a slasher flick. I punched off the tape. Blessed silence surrounded me, punctuated by moans from beside me and from the back of the van. I pulled off the bloody lab coat and tossed it out the opening above me. I was still bloody, but not quite so dramatic looking, my movement not restricted by the wet cloth sticking to me.

The smell of gasoline, vomit and burned rubber filled my nostrils. I checked the woman's pulse. It was fast and my watch was too coated with blood to take an accurate count, but I guesstimated about 150. Her respiration was fast, too. Shallow. I checked her over as best I could. Her right arm was wedged between the seat and the door, canted at a weird angle, wrapped in what looked like brown terry-cloth towels. I couldn't see her hand. Her left arm dangled toward Choo-Choo as if in supplication.

Her pupils were equal and reactive. Her airway was open and she had no other obvious injuries. She was unconscious, head hanging. I couldn't reposition her in case of spinal injury. Until I had equipment, I had done all I could. I turned to the back of the van.

My unsteady beam of light fell on a bloody, blond face and staring, lifeless, blue eyes. A child. She was naked. Armless. And smiling. And then, with a quick intake of breath, I realized it was a large doll. Like the old-fashioned walking dolls, or a mannequin.

Clutching it was another girl, only a bit larger. This one stared, too, with wide horrified eyes, pupils tiny, constricted with fear. Lips parted. Crouching, I crawled over to her and she withdrew into the space behind the back seat, repeating the monotone phrase, "No, no, no, no." Pause. "No, no, no, no," over and over again.

"It's okay." I said, crawling past a ruptured suitcase, clothes spilling like tendrils of intestines, over scattered piles of books with spines bent and ripped and packages of unidentifiable stuff, around a bench seat still bolted in place. "I'm a doctor. I'm here to help." Careful to keep my bloodied arms out of the Maglite's beam, I reached her. Settled in beside her, in the tight space behind the bench seat and the side of the van. Floor? Up and down were meaningless in the dark. My only ambient light came from the van's open back door swinging slightly above us.

I didn't try to take the bloody doll from her, but gently touched the girl's fisted hand. It was cold. "I'm a doctor. My name's Dr. Rhea-Rhea. What's yours?"

"No, no, no, no." Shuddering breath. "No, no, no, no."

"Can you tell me if you're hurt?"

"No, no, no, no. No, no, no, no."

Her pupils didn't change in the beam of my flash. Tightly constricted. Gently, I slipped my fingers around her wrist and estimated her pulse. Slow. About 60. Her respiration was fast and shallow. Weird. Drugs?

I upped her age, now that I was close, to late teens. I could see no obvious signs of bleeding. The blood was only on the doll. I touched it. Dry. It was paint. The doll had been drenched in red paint that flowed down its body like blood.

I tried to communicate again as my hands ran over the young woman's limbs, searching for breaks. "My name is Dr. Rhea-Rhea," I repeated, using the name my young patients called me. "I'm a doctor. You understand? What's your name?"

I found a deformity on the woman's arm, a bump on the radius like a fresh break or a poorly set old one. When I applied pressure, she didn't pause in her running "no" monologue. No reaction. But when I touched what looked like a huge hematoma on her upper leg she flinched. Blackened teeth fanged at me in anger.

Reaction to pain. Good. It made me think the arm deformity was an old one, but it didn't make me happy about the leg. A bruise there could mean a break of the femur with a tear in the femoral vein or artery. She could bleed out fast. At this angle and lack of light, I couldn't tell.

"I'm a doctor," I tried again.

The litany paused. Stopped. Slowly the girl's head twisted to me. The eyes focused. "Doctor?" It was a little girl's voice, high and quavery, like Dolly Parton might have sounded as a child. But the eyes were old. Wounded. The effect of the combination was eerie.

"Yes. A doctor. What's your name?"

"Healing hands. Healer."

"Well, yeah. Sorta," I said. "Where are you hurting?"

She closed her eyes, smiled, and seemed to go to sleep. Not pass out. Just go to sleep. She had to be stoned, probably on several different classes of illegal meds at once.

Above me, I heard clattering, then grunting. In the distance, I heard the sound of sirens. "Thank God," I muttered.

Standing up as straight as I could, I moved back to the side door, open overhead. A powerful light dropped in and I caught it, the beam momentarily blinding me. "Got it. And I need new gloves," I said shortly, putting the light on the edge of the bench seat, the beam focused on the girl in the passenger seat. I couldn't remember having asked for gloves and I needed them badly. The pair I was wearing were a slimy, bloody, muddy mess.

Coreen's dark-skinned face appeared beside mine at a strange angle. She had to be lying on her stomach on the van's side. "I got you gloves, Dr. Lynch, several kinds, but I forgot what size. Small?"

"Yes." The word sounded bitten off. She held out a pair of blue, heavy latex gloves. "What about the orthopedic surgeon? What's his ETA?" I asked. It sounded more like a demand.

"Half an hour at least. He was at dinner for his wife's birthday. In Ford County."

I dropped my head for a moment, then turned quickly to the girl in the passenger seat. Just from here I could tell she wouldn't last that long. And the smell of gasoline was growing. An explosion was possible. I was going to have to cut.

Nothing sterile. No light. No anesthesia. No techs to help. I had often called myself a meatball doc. Greet 'em, treat 'em and street 'em. Or slap temporary solutions on a patient until the specialists could take over. Tonight was going to be different. Battlefield amputation.

"I'm gonna need that saw." My voice was coarse. I snapped the filthy gloves off and tossed them, replacing them with clean, thick gloves.

"Trisha's gone for it, Doc. But there was a fire in the OR. She said things have been moved around a lot. She said finding the saw may take a while."

I cursed.

Coreen grinned down at me. "I reckon you could. But it's a pretty funky place for that kinda activity."

I couldn't help it. A bark of laughter escaped me. And a short giggle. I took a shaky breath. Grinned up her. "Thanks. I needed that."

"Anytime. Paramedics are here. And the equipment and stretcher are here, too."

Coreen was doing well, not panicking, not falling apart in the emergency. I was pleased. I took a deeper breath. Steadied myself. Flashing blue and red lights strobed down from the road above me. Sirens silenced their wail, leaving the sound of voices and the clank of doors and equipment. The cavalry was here. Too bad Dudley Do-Right was in Ford County. I could use an orthopedic surgeon on a white horse to rescue me from the butcher job I had waiting.

"Yo, Doc. Nice set a' wheels you got here," a paramedic joked as he lowered himself inside. It was Buford Munsey, called Buzzy for the buzz cut he had worn all his life. Buzzy could handle anything. I was glad he was here. "I like the decor," he said, looking around quickly, taking in the victims, the tight space. "That just off-the-showroom-floor scent. Almost as much as I like your scrubs. Nuevo bloody?"

"Cute, Buzzy," I said, feeling more of my tension melt away.

He bent and inspected under the bench seat blocking the space. "I need some clippers!" he yelled. Then turning to me, he asked almost conversationally. "What'cha got, Doc?"

I quickly filled him in. In seconds I had lights and another body in the van with us. The van's back doors were wedged open, and the chanting girl and her bizarre doll were strapped down, carted off up the hill to the road and the nearest ambulance. Now we had to free the girl trapped in the front.

Everyone rearranged in the crowded space. Huge pliers-like cutting shears were handed down and muscles bulged as the bench seat was cut loose and tossed out the back of the van. More supplies were passed down. Blankets. I piled them on the side-door panel under my feet.

"I can't see how we can get her out without an amputation," I said. "See what you guys think." I stepped aside and let the experts at the girl. "And if you can't get her out, that means I have to amputate. Here. Now. And you get to play surgical techs. So I suggest you find me another way and fast."

With the light, I decided where to layer heated blankets and packed them around her torso, her other leg, even up around her neck and ears.

The paramedics went to work again. They unstrapped Choo-Choo and handed him back, kicked his seat loose and out of the way, then maneuvered in the rest of the equipment.

The girl's breathing had changed. It was suddenly deadly fast.

"Doc, this arm's trapped between the utility pole and the outside of the van," Buzzy said. "Even if you get the leg free, the arm's not gonna be free. And the leg's not trapped against the seat and the dash, it's between the dash and the pole, as if the leg went through the window at impact and got stuck. Even a wrecker isn't gonna get this thing separated anytime soon. Look.''

I bent around him and saw what he was saying. With my small flash, I hadn't been able to tell what trapped the lower leg. But now I understood. The girl was indeed stuck. The smell of gas grew stronger. My patient moaned. Vomited. Buzzy caught her head and supported the girl's cervical spine as he turned her face and cleared her airway.

I broke out in a hot sweat in the confined space. ''Get the jaws in here. See if you can cut the pole or van struts to get her loose. I refuse to amputate two limbs.''

''Jaws are on the way,'' he said as he slipped a cervical collar around the patient's neck and a nasal cannula into her nostrils. The soft hiss of oxygen came to me.

The jaws I wanted were the Jaws of Life. Like a huge jack mated with pry bars, it could be wedged between layers of twisted metal and turned on. The pneumatic engine forced the pry bars apart, separating most anything made of metal. Pneumatic cutters finished off the work.

Overhead, thunder rumbled.

''Oh, great. Just freaking lovely,'' I said.

''But Doc, the working conditions are the best part of the job,'' Buzzy quipped. ''My contract lists working in lightning storms as a benefit.''

I laughed again. I couldn't help it. I loved these guys.

''Doc, we can cut away the seat and you can lay her onto a stretcher, if that would work better.''

I bent and studied the girl lying on the arm of the bucket seat, held in place by the shoulder strap. The bucket seats appeared new, unlike the bench seat, which had likely been original equipment, simply bolted in to the metal floor and held up by rusted legs. "Can we lay just the seat back and use the stretcher as a worktable?"

The EMTs agreed and began to prepare the site for me. The seat rolled back, giving me more room. My patient moaned. "At some point, I'm gonna need you guys to pull on her to provide some separation in the joint."

I inspected my equipment laid out on the stretcher shoved against my hip. A handful of disposable scalpels in sterile paper envelopes. Clamps. Sterile gauze in four-by-four-inch squares. Several pairs of sterile gloves, size six and a half. My size. Sterile drapes, which were a nice touch but not much good. Someone had brought bottles of Betadine and normal saline for irrigation. Wonderful! I hadn't thought to ask for that.

Buzzy had opened out one sterile drape and arranged the instruments on it. I glanced at his hands. Sterile gloves over trauma gloves. I nodded at the package of sterile gloves. "Open them?"

A bit clumsily, he took the package and peeled it back, exposing the beige of the sterile gloves. I took one by the cuff and pulled it out, slipped one hand in. Then the other glove. With the double gloves, my hands felt as if I was wearing matching rubber garden hoses.

Below me, the other man, an EMT whose name I couldn't remember, was inserting a large-bore IV needle into the patient's cephalica vein near the elbow. A bag of fluids dangled from the busted-out passenger window. Ringers Lactate. Standard fluid for major trauma.

I stuck my head out of the van, through the open side door over my head. "What about that saw?" I shouted.

Coreen held a cellular phone to one ear. Turning, she shrugged helplessly. "The lightning hit the room where they do the orthopedic procedures,'' she said. "Things are a mess in there because there was another fire in the wall and they had to rip out all kinds of stuff to put it out. Trisha says she can't find anything.''

I rotated my neck twice before I ducked back inside. My muscles were aching from holding my head at an angle. In the front of the van, there wasn't enough room for me to stand upright. Sweat and the girl's blood had mired on my skin.

Outside, I heard a familiar voice. Local police captain Mark Stafford, my some-time boyfriend. I felt some of the tension go out of me again. "You okay in there, woman?" he shouted.

"I'm fine. Thanks for asking," I shouted back. "Now leave me alone. Can't you see I'm working?''

I could hear him chuckle. His head bent through the overhead open door. His expression changed fast at the sight of me. "Rhea?''

I looked down at my bloody clothes and knew instantly he was thinking of the last time he saw me covered in blood, the day I was stabbed and he rescued me. "Not mine.''

"Good.'' And he was gone.

An excited voice called from outside the van, "It looks like we can get this arm free, Doc!''

I glanced through the opening where the windshield once sat. Boots stood on the side fender, a face at another angle near them. Vertigo hit again. I closed my eyes. Opened them, focusing only on my patient.

"Position one light at the top of the knee, one at the bottom," I instructed, "and open several of the scalpels and lay them on the sterile drape. Good. Now, listen close. I'm going to go in from the medial side. Find the severed popliteal artery. Clamp it off. Find the popliteal vein, clamp it off. Then y'all are going to pull on the patient and create a space between the bones of the lower leg and the head of the femur so I can cut through the joint where the patella, femur, fibula and tibia all meet. Then get her out of here. Understood?''

They glanced at each other. "Piece of cake," Buzzy said.

"No problem, Doc," the other EMT said, not to be outdone by Buzzy's bravado.

"We got a BP?"

"Blood pressure 95 over 60," a female EMT said. She leaned in through the passenger-side window, working on the patient. "Pulse thready and weak at one-ten. Hooking up heart monitor now..." She drew out the word as if waiting. "Got it. Sinus tach rhythm. Putting the monitor where you can see it, Doc."

"I got an IV," the EMT at my feet said.

"Open it wide. And as soon as it's open, start me another one."

"Yes, ma'am. Coming up."

"Sure you can't get the pole away fast enough to save me doing this, here?" I asked one last time.

"No can do, Doc," the woman said. "Sorry."

"Me, too. Open that Betadine and pour it over the knee," I told Buzzy. "More. Good." I bent and sliced the skin at the inside of the patient's knee. A thin line of blood appeared.

3

UNHOLY GLEE

Sweat trickled down my spine like a warm, slow-moving snake. "Open a package of four-by-fours. Then get over here and swab the incision so I can see what I'm doing."

"I can do that, Doc." I looked out the windshield into Anne's face. She was wearing sterile gloves and a layer of mud. Beside her stood a cop she had pressed into duty as a table, holding a sterile drape with clamps and packets of various things on it. She tore a package and stretched in, leaning across the hood of the van as she pressed a wad of gauze into the incision. I cut deeper. Blood flowed, trickling out past the makeshift tourniquet of Choo-Choo's belt.

Moving with a series of swift cuts, I fashioned a flap of skin to cover the site. Working deeper into the tissue, I finally found the popliteal artery. The patient moaned. Jerked weakly.

"Jeez. She's coming to," a voice muttered.

"Great," I murmured under my breath. "Just freaking great." I clamped off the artery. The last of the bleeding stopped. I could not administer anesthesia at an accident site. I glanced at the heart monitor. Rate 150 and increasing. I had to ignore the pain element. "Okay, boys and girls, let's go after the popliteal vein," I said.

Quickly, I found the vein and clamped it off. I paused. Looked out the windshield. "Bone saw?" Anne shook her head. Rain had started to fall. Her hair was sparkling with raindrops, as was all the once-sterile stuff on the drape.

I checked my patient. Breathing. Pulse at carotid fast and thready in the emergency lights. But the monitor was slowing. She was unconscious again. I looked back out the window and asked, "You guys got anything I can cut bone with?"

Instantly, as if someone had been expecting the request, a hand shoved through the broken windshield. In it was a hacksaw. The blade was slightly rusted, dirty. "You got to be kidding."

"It'll cut through most anything, Doc."

I studied the saw. It was barbaric. I could feel a dozen pairs of eyes on me as I stared at the blade. "Anne, wipe down the blade and pour some Betadine and sterile saline over it." As she wiped and sloshed, I said, "Okay, guys. Lift and pull." Arms reached under the patient. Bodies braced themselves. My patient moved. "More that way," I directed with my chin. Took a deep breath. Rotated my head on my aching neck. My back, the muscles still weak where I had been stabbed, protested. I felt something pop deep in my own tissue. Ignoring the discomfort, I bent closer.

A small space appeared in the incision as the bones separated. "That's good. Harder." The space widened. Again, I began to cut.

It seemed to take hours. My fingers and biceps began to cramp. Stopping, I massaged my hands, saying nothing. As I stretched my fingers, I could feel the crust of drying blood crack on my arms and torso.

In the silence, I heard a mild curse, followed by an odd tone. "Doc, you better look at this."

I glanced up to where the EMTs had been working to separate the patient's trapped hand from the wreckage. The terry-cloth towel I had thought was brown had once been white, but now was thickly crusted with dried blood. From its stiff folds came a lower arm. One with no hand.

The stump was ragged and inflamed, stitched with black thread in jagged sewing stitches, not proper surgical stitches. Thin, serous fluid leaked from the incision like tears.

"A homemade amputation..." I breathed. "What the... Get the cops in on this."

In the background, I heard someone calling for Captain Stafford. I heard Mark's voice before I blocked it all out and went back to work. The angle was impossible. I'd have to finish with a scalpel.

I dropped the bloody saw on top of the used scalpels and stretched my hand. It was frozen in a death grip. I'd never liked orthopedics. Never liked cutting on people.

"You done in there already?" a new voice asked. "I coulda stayed home."

I looked up. It was Bernard Mayfield, the county's newest orthopedic surgeon. Tall enough to see over heads through the windshield, lithe and loose-limbed, he stood in the now-pouring rain, his big hands in his pockets, a wicked grin in place. "And I'm never quite so messy when I work. Maybe I should take lessons."

"Don't go giving me a hard time. If you'd been at home watching *Jeopardy* instead of out for dinner, I'd never have had to do this. And I didn't steal your equipment,'' I grunted, finally straightening out my cramped palm.

"No? You find such unusual uses for my toys."

A few months earlier, trapped in the unfinished orthopedic surgical suite, I had found a box of specially modified surgical tools and used a few of them to stop some men who were chasing me. When Bernard got to town a few weeks later, his unique tools had been confiscated by the police and held as evidence. Bernard had not been a happy man. He hadn't let me live it down. "I didn't touch your things," I said. "This time. But when you see your surgical suite, you might wish I had simply borrowed your stuff." I made a fist and stretched to stop the cramping in my right arm.

Bernard's eyebrows went up in question. "How's that?" Rain trickled down his face. He shook his head to whip the droplets away.

"Your new suite got hit by lightning and then had a fire in the walls. My guess is that you'll be doing surgery in the obstetrical suite. And your stuff has been scattered all over. Trish couldn't even find me a bone saw."

Bernard's face fell. I gave him back his wicked grin and picked up another fresh scalpel. Preparing to finish the amputation, I paused. "And you'll be cleaning up more than my nasty work. Take a look at that wrist." I nodded toward the girl's arm, now wrapped in a padded field dressing. "Someone did some homegrown surgery. Doesn't look to me like they made any effort to plan for a prosthetic device." I held the scalpel up, let the beams from the multiple flashlights dance along its edge. My grip on the handle was weak.

"How come every time I have anything to do with you, I have these kinds of problems?" he sighed, peeling back the dressing.

"Omens," I grunted, bending over my work. "Portents. I'm a virtual lightning rod for them these days. Ask anybody."

With a grunt, I made a final cut, folded over the flap of skin and clamped it into place. Standing, I threw the scalpel on the pile of used tools and backed away. Dried blood crackled across my body, feeling like ants crawling. "Get her out of here," I said as I peeled off my too-tight gloves and tossed them, too.

EMTs and paramedics swarmed around me, one taking the used equipment and bundling it safely out of the way, another releasing the seat-belt straps, still others grabbing and easing the patient free of the wreckage and the seat that had been her surgical table. As they worked, Buzzy field-dressed the stump.

I squeezed through the press of bodies and ducked out the back doors of the van, into the steady downpour. Instantly, I sank up to my ankles in a mire of mud, gasoline and rain. Mark met me there, wearing his business face and his cop rain gear. "I need a statement from you."

I looked at him openmouthed, then spread my arms as if displaying myself for inspection. As I moved, the muscles of my back wrenched, releasing tension in a spasm of pain. Rain trickled, softening some of the dried blood crusted on my arms and torso, down the long length of my legs. I looked like something from a movie about the walking dead. "You have got to be kidding," I finally managed to say.

His eyes raked down me. Widened. He looked abashed, his mouth clicking shut.

Cops. Men. No sense of timing. "You can cross-examine me later," I said shortly. "First, I have a shower and a change of clothes waiting for me." Turning, I grabbed my balled lab coat from where it had fallen on the top of the van, stepped around Mark and slogged up the boggy hill, back toward the hospital. I stretched my shoulders and rotated my head on its stiff pedestal as I climbed. Mark marched beside me.

"And then?"

"And then I have patients to get stable. And then, sometime around ten, maybe, I'll be free to talk to you," I said stubbornly.

A gust of wind splattered down on us. My neck was in agony, my barely-healed back muscles screaming. I had pulled something major. I moved, still stretching, down the length of the street. It was lined with emergency vehicles and wreckers of all kinds, flashing lights, radios crackling. Suddenly Mark laughed. "I have take-out from Sottise."

I groaned, and pulled again at shoulders so stiff I wanted to cry. Sottise was a French restaurant, recently opened in Dorsey City. The source of nourishment and pleasure for my fast food–poisoned taste buds. Mark had figured out my weakness for the restaurant's fare and used takeout on a regular basis to twist me around his little finger.

I looked down at the blood draining to the roadway in the warm, streaming rain, blackened in the flashing lights. Bloody rain dripped off my nose. "You are a cruel, evil man. Okay. Meet me in my room in twenty. I'll eat and you ask questions."

"People will talk."

"Let 'em. I'm starving."

Unexpectedly, he asked, "Bad in there?" His tone, almost gentle, unnerved me.

I paused, turning my face into the summer downpour. I had always loved walking in the rain. Running in the rain. Sitting in the rain. It battered my body as I stood there, face to the sky, washing me clean of sweat and the girl's blood. Soaking me to the skin. If I was crying, I couldn't tell. No one could. "Yes. It was," I said simply. "Real bad."

"I nearly freaked when I saw you all covered in blood."

"I know," I said softly.

"I never did get all your blood out of my jeans."

My eyes popped open. They met Mark's green ones, dark in the rainy night. "Why was my blood on your jeans?" I asked.

"I carried you to the ER. Made a mess."

I hadn't known that. I hadn't remembered that he had carried me the night I'd been stabbed. The incident had driven a wedge of silence between us; we had been unable to talk about it much.

"Go shower," Mark said gently, touching my rain-wet face. "I'll meet you shortly."

Without another word, I turned and squished in my soaked shoes to the ER. Beside the outer door was a splotch of freshly sprayed neon-yellow graffiti. It looked half-finished, as if someone had interrupted the artist. Not bothering to study it, I entered, went to the nearest laundry cabinet and wrapped a sheet around me, hiding the rain-diluted blood from patients and their families. But as I walked, a trail of bloody water dripped thickly after me, squished out of my shoes, followed me toward the trauma room and my two accident patients.

Anne sat at the nurses' desk in fresh scrubs, her hair still wet. "Order pizza," I said. "Whatever anyone wants." I pulled a bloody twenty from a pocket and tossed it on the counter. She looked at it distastefully. I didn't blame her.

In the trauma room, there were dry nurses, a portable X-ray machine and a tall, damp man bent over the girl I had cut on. "We're okay in here, Rhea," Bernard said, looking up from the patient. "I'll take care of them both until you can get cleaned up."

"You are a gift from heaven," I said, already backing out of the room.

"Yes, I am. Go."

I stood fully clothed under the scalding spray, letting the stream wash away the gore and the spasms and the charley horses in both legs. Letting it take away the stiffness in my neck and back and hands. Wishing it could also take away the sounds the girl had made as she became conscious during surgery. Gurgling. Gasping. Mewling like a kitten being drowned.

I had pretended I hadn't heard. But I had. Every painfilled groan.

When the tears hit, I fell against the shower stall and slid to the floor. Shaking, sobbing in long tortured sounds.

The explosion of emotion was short and hard. Over almost instantly. Leaving me gasping and shuddering. Lying on the bleach-scented tile, my head thrown back.

I had done the best I could. I knew that. I had to get her out of there. Gasoline fumes could cause an explosion, no matter how much rain there was. A ruptured artery. A crushed and mangled leg. It had to come off. No one but me to do it. I had done the best I could for her. And it hadn't been enough. She had lost a limb. Two limbs.

Someone up there had it in for her.

Kneeling, then standing, I ripped off my soggy clothes and tossed them to the floor, slipped out of my running shoes and left them in the stream of the shower to continue to rinse as I washed my hair and scrubbed my body clean, ignoring the tears that came and went as I washed. I used a stiff brush on my watchband and crystal, down the length of my arms where blood crusted most thickly, a rough rag on my body and face. Finally, long minutes later, I felt clean.

Leaving my shoes to drain, I toweled off and smeared almond-scented jojoba oil all over me, dressed in clean scrubs and left the bathroom door open to let it air out. In my small call room I pulled clean socks over my feet, grabbed a comb and stood over the sink. Stared at myself in the mirror.

Short black hair curled over my ears and into my low collar. Black eyes, olive skin. Too tall and gangly to ever appear womanly, at least by southern belle standards.

"I did the best I could," I assured myself. But tears welled again, and every time I blinked, I saw a scalpel slicing through muscle, a saw hacking through tendon and bone. "I did the best I could."

And though it was true, the knowledge didn't make me feel any better. Tears fell again, dripping like water trickling from a fountain.

A soft knock sounded on the door and quickly I wiped the tears away. Mark stuck his head in and entered without asking. He left the door open a respectable three inches, though my room was down one corridor from the nearest nurses' desk. Anyway, anyone who saw him walk down the hallway would form opinions about what we were doing based on the worst possible scenario, no matter how far open he left the door.

Dr. Lynch and her boyfriend having wild sex on hospital grounds. Dr. Lynch and the cop doing it on the stiff sheets in the doctor's call room. Dr. Lynch and her cop beau having wild, screaming-monkey-sex on the floor of the call room.

The fact that we had never engaged in any kind of sex, wild or otherwise, would not factor into it. But frankly, I didn't care. I was too tired and hungry to cater to gossips.

Mark fed me some wonderful sole and veggies with an herbed white sauce, and plenty of creamed potatoes with sage, parsley, chives and what tasted like bits of crab, and crusty bread. Literally fed me. He put me on the bed, leaning me against the wall, an adjustable table pushed up under my breasts, a plastic fork in his right hand, knife in the other. He didn't eat. Simply fed me, his flecked green eyes on my face. A tender look in them.

When I finished the entire meal, he tidied up, crushing disposable containers, wadding up plastic bags, wiping my lips with a rough, brown paper napkin. Then he turned me around on the bed, pulled me between his straddled legs and began to massage my shoulders. When I groaned, he asked, "Feel better?"

"Heaven. Oh, God, that feels good. A little lower. Oh yes. Harder."

When he chuckled, I knew what he was thinking. "Let 'em talk. I don't care."

"There was no one at the desk when I passed," he said. "You don't have to worry. No one knows I'm down here but us."

"Okay. So I was a little worried. Lower on the right. My whole right side got into a cramp during the amputation. Yeah, that's it." Captain Mark Stafford of the Dawkins County Sheriff's Department had great hands. I told him so.

And his touch changed. Slowed. Beside my ear, his

breathing deepened. I smiled and let myself rest back against him. A single tremor ran down his legs.

The phone rang. At his expletive, I chuckled, moved out of the embrace and answered. "Lynch."

"Place is filling up, Doc. And Dr. Mayfield is ready to go to OR."

"On my way." I hung up the phone.

"Good," Mark said, letting me see the lie. "This was getting entirely too cozy."

"Downright improper," I agreed, rising and hunting for a fresh lab coat in my bag. I hadn't packed one and would have to use the dirty spare hanging on the back of the doctors' office door.

"I need you to see that mannequin. And tell me everything you can about the way the van looked when you first got to it, where each person was. Where everything was before your EMTs shoved it all around."

I considered his words. "You're treating it like a crime scene," I said slowly.

"We found a stash of pills and what looks like marijuana in a side panel, with more taped to the underside of the bench seat. Enough to fall under the category of possession with serious intent to sell. And three guns. Loaded. One was tucked into the waistband of Choo-Choo's jeans—it had the safety off. You could have shot yourself pulling off his belt."

I slowed, thinking about the dark and bloody interior of the van. "Lovely," I said.

"We also found some knives. Four, at last count. One was sharp and bloody, like it could have been used to cut off the girl's hand. And I want your opinion about the girl with the missing hand. Mayfield agrees the procedure wasn't done in a hospital."

As we walked to the ER, I shared with Mark the moments when I first reached the van. Told him what I remembered of the interior and what I thought about the amputation of the girl's hand. It wasn't much. My head was too jumbled with images left from the meatball surgery to remember much else.

"There was a flash of white," I said at last. "I keep thinking about it. A flash of white at the back of the van when I first got there. And later, when I checked the girl in the back, I noticed that one of the back doors was open and hanging a crack."

"And?" he asked. Mark didn't prod or question or suggest, but I could hear the interest in his voice.

"And I think there may have been a fourth person in the van before I ran up. I think he left. Or she left. And hid in the brush."

Mark sighed. "With all the rain we just had, I don't think there will be any tracks left, but I'll have some of the guys look anyway. Thanks, Rhea."

No one said anything as we passed the nurses' desk. No one even looked up. But this was a small rural hospital. Everyone knew everything about everyone. And I was sure Mark and I would be on the front burner, gossipwise, within the hour.

When we arrived back at the ER, Mark left to write reports and I went to the office and reached behind the door for the spare lab coat that was usually left hanging on the hook. Besides being dirty, it was too big, but it would be better than nothing. My hand scraped the bare wood of the door. The lab coat was gone. Momentarily irritated, I went back to work in just clean scrubs.

My first patient was the other girl from the accident. She was still holding the weird doll, gripping it tightly, crushed against her chest. I looked over the patient's chart as I studied the pair. The girl, still in a cervical collar, had given her name as Na'Shalome, no last name, a birth date that made her twenty-three. She was tiny, blond and blue-eyed. Pupils still constricted. Her vitals were normal. Her skin was dry and warm. Someone had collected a urine sample and drawn blood, so I wrote orders for a urine drug screen, a urinalysis and a few basic blood tests. Remembering the hematoma on her leg, I checked to make sure Bernard had ordered and read the X rays. Because they were all negative, I sat down beside her on the stretcher and removed the uncomfortable cervical collar.

"I'm Dr. Rhea-Rhea. Can you tell me how you're feeling?"

Her eyes stared at the far wall. She pulled the doll even tighter to her. The doll was about four feet in height, painted as bloodred as it had looked in the dark of the van. Naked. A dime-store dummy someone had chopped up.

One of the legs was missing, and had been replaced with a length of black steel, scarlet ribbons and flowers, all held together with black electrical tape. A length of red tubing was tied low on the leg, securing a beat-up bunch of silk roses, and twined up the steel to disappear into the anus of the doll, hot-glued in place.

The left arm was a tree branch painted red and green, the right was a length of metal that looked like coat hangers and chicken wire. The steel leg and both "arms" were twined through with silk and dried flowers, leaves, herbs, beads and ribbons. Bloodred body, head and hair.

The doll's eyes were blue, just the same shade as Na'Shalome's. Oddly, they seemed to follow me as I got off the stretcher and walked across the room. The effect was weirdly chilling.

"We decided it's a voodoo doll," Coreen said from behind me.

"No. You decided that. I still think it's something from New Orleans Mardi Gras," Anne countered.

"Witchcraft," Coreen insisted.

"Which isn't the same thing as voodoo."

"It's evil. You can feel it," the younger nurse said.

"It's a party decoration."

"Voodoo."

"Orgies, maybe."

"Oh yuck!"

"You'd rather voodoo?" The good-natured argument ended when I handed the patient's chart to Coreen. The two nurses, both dressed in borrowed-but-clean surgical scrubs, left the room to go to work.

I privately thought the doll looked like a New Orleans-style float decoration. For years my mother had pulled me out of school to take in Mardi Gras, both in New Orleans and in Lafayette, Louisiana. Long drunken parties with gal-pals and too many men. When I was younger, I had loved it all, my mother being so gay and wild and happy. Men looking at her with desire. When I got older, I refused to go with her to Louisiana. Not that she cared. By then her drinking problem had reached the point where she didn't think too much about anything. Me included. Or perhaps, best to say, she thought about me least of all, a bottle most of all.

I spent ten minutes more alone with Na'Shalome, talking to her. Telling her I was a doctor. Finally, just as I was about to give up, the word *doctor* seemed to penetrate and her eyes turned to me. Tiny little pupils, empty lifeless eyes, focused unblinkingly on mine. No words, yet instantly I knew she understood that I wanted to examine her. Wanted to lay the doll aside for a moment.

Gently, I took the doll and tugged once. She let me put the doll on the foot of the stretcher. Listlessly, Na'Shalome watched as I cut away her clothes.

She wouldn't let anyone else touch her. Didn't want anyone else in the room with us. The girl tensed up and pulled away when Anne entered the room to assist, so I handled her myself. And as I cut away her clothes, I discovered why.

There was evidence of broken bones, fractures that had never been set properly. Along her inner thighs were old burn marks, the perfectly circular scars of cigarette burns. Higher, on her belly, across her breasts, were other scars, less clearly defined. But I knew what they were. Signs of abuse. Torture. Not recent. But old scarring, the result of prolonged misery. I had seen enough of it in Chicago, where I did my ER residency.

Na'Shalome. No peace? A name she chose for herself to describe her inner soul? Her young life?

And the other girl? The one in the OR having two amputations cleaned up. Would she also show signs of abuse? Had the amputation of her hand been done by the same one who had so abused this girl? Visions of escape came to mind—two, perhaps three, young women running out to a highway, flagging down help, the old hippie, Choo-Choo, a savior stopping to let them in his van, then fleeing at a high rate of speed. Someone racing after. Perhaps even now outside. Waiting to take them back.

Or another scenario... I had never seen Choo-Choo's face. Had he been the man who had tortured her?

When I had Na'Shalome cleaned up and dressed in a soft hospital gown, I gave the doll back to her. Eyes still on me, she took the mannequin in her own doll-like arms and held it close. I left the room. As I did, I heard her speak two lines, so low I wasn't sure I understood.

"Hands of evil maim and kill. Hands of healing do Lord's will."

I looked back quickly. She repeated the odd phrases in a singsong voice and smiled.

Horrid glittering eyes, terrible slash of smile. Expression so lifeless she might have been dead. I had no idea why, but my gut twisted beneath her stare. The words *unholy glee* came to my mind. I was certain Na'Shalome knew what I was feeling. And it pleased her.

4

DEN ETIQUETTE AND DOG SPIT

I admitted Na'Shalome based on her positive urine drug screen, evidence of abuse and the massive hematoma on her thigh, along with an OFW—old folks work-up—to Dr. Bokara, a new doctor in town. She was originally from India, and had the most stunningly smooth skin I had ever seen, limpid brown eyes and black hair so dark it seemed to throw black sparks. She moved with a grace I envied, spoke with a lyrical accent and wore long, beautifully patterned, flowing silk robes over latex calf-length pants and what looked like a latex jogging bra. She was everything I never would be, summed up in one word. Feminine.

And I really liked her. On the day we met she told me to call her Boka, because her real name was unpronounceable to an American. I had tried a few times, thought I did pretty well, but I must have left something out or mangled it obscenely. All I did was make her giggle and peer at me through her spread fingers.

We had eaten lunch together once at a nearby Chinese restaurant, hers strictly vegetarian, mine chicken. I figured she must have been Hindu, but she didn't seem to mind when I ate things that once breathed and clucked.

Boka came in to see the patients I described to her on the phone, believing, I think, that it was a joke on the new doctor. She spent a few minutes evaluating the OFW, an elderly nursing-home patient who'd suddenly become disoriented and fallen in the hallway, ordered some tests for the a.m., and then went in alone to see Na'Shalome. When she came back, she looked profoundly distressed, her dark eyes hooded by kohl-darkened lids, her mouth tight.

"What do you think?" I asked as she flowed around the desk and settled on a rolling desk chair.

"Think? I think she needs a great deal more help than I could ever give her. That child has been savaged."

"I thought so, too." I leaned my elbows on the high desktop and let the half wall hold me up as I held my left toes behind my right knee for warmth. My paper-slippered feet were cold in the air-conditioned hallway.

"I am calling DSS to take a look at her," Boka said suddenly, reaching for the phone and dialing as if from memory, her red lacquered nails stabbing the numbers. "I don't care how old Na'Shalome says she is. That girl isn't more than eighteen. Perhaps as young as fifteen. She will need a great deal of counseling to make it through what was done to her. Perhaps detox also. She has at least three classes of drugs in her system. Opiates, benzo and amphetamines."

She paused as if listening to a recorded message. Quickly, she identified herself to the Department of Social Services message machine and recited a beeper number and the ER phone number where she could be reached, her usually mellifluous voice sounding tight. When she hung up, she looked at me, her expression still severe. "There are good reasons for total orchidectomy and penectomy. The man who did this to her deserves nothing less.''

"Surgical castration?'' I asked, amused.

"Eunuchs are not unheard of in India, though the practice of castration has been outlawed. I saw one once in Delhi, on vacation with my husband. Of course he, or perhaps I should say she, was a creature created for the pleasure of another, and perhaps against her will. But I thought then that such a fate was deserved for any man who tortured children.'' A sudden twinkle appeared in her eyes. "My husband was horrified to hear me say so…but intrigued, as well.''

I laughed at her expression. "Liked finding out that his darling delicate wife had teeth and claws? Turned him on?''

"Remi has always loved cats,'' she said primly, drawing her nails across her lips.

I laughed at her and she laughed back before her eyes darkened again. "What was done to her…to Na'Shalome…is unspeakable.'' Boka looked at me, her eyes so hard I couldn't read them. "She may need reconstructive surgery to correct the scarring on her vaginal walls.'' I flinched. "There is inflammation there, too, but she is so scarred over I can't see what causes it. I will be asking Michelle Geiger to take a look at her.

"Eunuchs.'' She said again, her dark eyes flashing. "Perhaps without anesthesia.''

For a woman who looked so gentle and delicate, and who didn't eat meat, Boka had a nasty view of criminal justice. I liked it.

The rest of the night was spent with a SOB—a patient with shortness of breath, a MVA with five victims, all hoping for auto and disability insurance settlements but having no injuries I could find; four children, all with viral symptoms; and the excitement of cops and the hospital security guard playing at animal control, cornering and catching the errant bat in a fishnet. The instinctive fear most humans had of bats made that a comical interlude. I got little sleep, but woke at 6:00 a.m. before the wake-up call came from the ER. I hadn't dreamt, but I came awake with visions of blood spurting, and the wet, hot feel of it beating against me, drenching me.

I dressed, stuffed my feet into my wet, gasoline-scented running shoes and looked in on Na'Shalome and her friend. The multiple amputee, who had been unable to give the nurses her name and was admitted as Jane Doe, was stretched out on the mattress, amputated wrist and knee supported in the air with orthopedic traction to relieve the probable swelling. She was asleep, breathing the slow cadence of the deeply drugged. I slipped in and studied her for a moment. She was fine-boned, a light-skinned African-American. I hadn't remembered her race, being too concerned about the body beneath the skin. I had never really seen her face. She was pretty, even with slack, drugged features.

In the darkness she looked about twelve. Broken. Lost.

A wisp of the anguish left over from last night drifted through me. I wondered if Jane Doe would hate me someday for saving her life at the expense of her leg. Or would she pull an Oprah moment and find some way to celebrate her handicapped life? I had never figured out how anyone celebrated a traumatic injury.... Oprah was either really charismatic, able to convince people it was possible, or I just didn't get the whole "Oprah lifestyle" thing. Likely it was the latter.

Unable to stop myself, I finally stepped close to the bed and lowered the covers from the girl. Her breathing didn't change. Slow and steady. Almost peaceful. I lifted her gown. Old scarring met my eyes. Round cigarette burns across her abdomen. Down into her pubic hair.

In Chicago's Miami Valley Hospital, where I did my internship in emergency medicine, I had seen the torture sometimes inflicted on cocaine whores. Torture that the women willingly accepted in order to get the drug they craved to survive another day. I had also seen the kind of torture adults committed on children.

This looked like that kind of torture—sexual, dominant, cruel beyond reasoning. Surely committed over a long period of time. A childhood of pain. I dropped her gown, lowered the sheet. Smoothed the folds over her. Jane was still asleep. Deeply. I left her room.

Na'Shalome, by contrast, was wide-awake, buzzing with energy, sitting in the dark in the hospital bed, knees raised, her eyes glued to the television bolted high on the wall. The sound blared, the light flickered in action-movie speed. Her fingers were snapping, her toes moving to the same TV beat, her concentration complete. Even the wedge of hallway light that crossed her face as I entered didn't draw her attention. Across the room, propped on her bent mannequin stand in the corner, was the strange doll, her blue eyes on me in the dim light. I ignored the doll, watching the patient.

On the adjustable table pulled up beside the bed was a leather drawstring bag and five smooth stones laid out in a cross. The stones were rectangular in shape with rounded corners, letters carved into the center of each. I glanced at them and then stepped closer to the patient.

When Na'Shalome finally noticed me, I was standing beside her bed, observing up close the hyper twitches, snarls and snaps. An addiction just entering the withdrawal stage. By tonight, she could be a howling maniac, ripping at the sheets, fighting the nurses, needing restraints. For now, she had abnormally fast reflexes. Na'Shalome scraped the stones off the table and dropped them into the bag before she focused on me.

She recognized me and spread her lips hard in a parody of a grin, her poor dentition black in the darkness. Her pupils were noticeably less constricted. The drugs wearing off? Beneath the drugs what would we find? Psychosis? Schizophrenia? Ignoring me, she turned her attention to the TV.

As I left the room, I heard her murmur in her little-girl voice, "Hands of evil maim and kill. Hands of healing do Lord's will."

But when I looked back, she was still focused on the TV screen; she stared, mesmerized, snapping her fingers in an uneven cadence. I left the hospital just after 7:00 a.m., a bit unsettled, yet not able to identify the underlying dilemma that left me feeling so weird. As I walked out the ER doors, I saw a maintenance man trying to scrub the neon graffiti off the outside wall. He wasn't having much luck.

After putting on a stack of CDs, volume on low, I fell into bed, my sheets lank and slick, long unwashed. Arlana was spending the summer with a cousin in New York, and my house had not been cleaned in weeks. Miss Essie's great-granddaughter Arlana was part friend, part decorator, part housekeeper, and she ran my life with an iron hand and loads of pithy wisdom that kept me on my toes. Without her, I had quickly digressed into a slovenly uncaring woman with a very disordered house. Mold grew on the tile in my bathroom, dirty sheets cradled me. The dust on the furniture was so deep I could have hidden a body in it, the smell of the sixty-year old bungalow I recently purchased was anything but pleasant, and dust bunnies moved across the floor with the slightest wisp of air. Okay, I wasn't exactly the best housekeeper in the world. Arlana would be back in town in two days. I had forty-eight hours to clean and disinfect.

I'd think about Tara tomorrow.

Several hours later, I rolled out of bed and pulled on an old T-shirt and sweats. Hitting the button on the coffeemaker, I settled in at the computer for a bit of research. Witchcraft. Voodoo. Weird dolls. Sexual torture. In the background the CD player hummed with an eclectic mix of music, Liz Phair, the Beatles, Pearl Jam, Santana, Counting Crows and Jimi Hendrix. I had a new collection of Latin CDs I had never listened to, but the rich, heavy music didn't fit my mood like the slightly bizarre mix I was playing today. This musical blend seemed to fit the kind of search I was doing.

After an hour spent with the practitioners of Wicca, tarot, witchcraft, alchemy and voudon, which was an odd spelling for voodoo, I was left with the belief that humanity was a species easily influenced and shaped. And while I was surprised to discover that there were still myriad forms of witchcraft practiced today, most appeared to be slick forms of advertising for love potions, spells to snare a man or punish him for leaving, to make a rival sicken and die, and voodoo dolls for sticking pins in. Silly stuff. Nothing I found led me to understand the red-painted doll from the accident.

Just about the time I finished with e-mail, the computer politely telling me goodbye, the dogs bounded through the too-small doggie door and into the living room where I had the computer set up. To the sound of Hendrix's nasty guitar, I roughhoused with them on the living-room carpet, which needed a good vacuuming, and let them lick me for all of twenty seconds. I'm not much for dog spit, but dogs need to lick the dominant member of the den. It's part of den etiquette, their way of saying, "Hi, Big Dog! We love you! We respect you! We follow all your rules even when they don't make sense! Please wear our scent so you'll recognize us when we've been away from the den for a while!" So, once a day, after they've missed me, I let them lick my chin, and then I roll them each over and scratch their tummies, my way of saying, "Okay. Y'all are still part of my den. I'll still take care of you." People, I didn't always understand, but dogs made sense.

They were large dogs, mixed breeds, mother and son. Belle was part setter, part Lab, with long beautiful black hair and golden-brown eyes. I found her on the side of a road, giving birth in a graveyard. Abandoned. Pup was part Belle, part yellow lab and part monster. Less than a year old, he already weighed in at eighty-five pounds and he was still growing, a short-haired yellow giant.

Pup was actually Marisa's dog, and he missed her almost as much as I did. My best friend in the world had received a traumatic injury to the brain last winter. She had been in a vegetative state for several weeks, until I managed to get her the medical help she needed to begin a recovery. That recovery had been complicated by pregnancy.

After the birth of her twins—a boy and girl, each weighing less than six pounds—Marisa had gone back to Duke for more rehab therapy, leaving me pretty much alone in rural Dawkins County. Pup and I were forming a bond based on mutual abandonment.

Dawkins County was huge, with more horses, cows, and pigs than people. There was only one movie theater—and it had only two screens—a church on every street corner, and two small country radio stations. The closest public radio stations were in Charlotte, North Carolina, over fifty miles away. I survived Marisa's unintentional defection because of cable and Internet access, and the knowledge that she would be home soon. But I had begun to suspect that I was lonely.

I had never been lonely before. I wasn't sure what it was supposed to feel like.

"Run?" I asked the dogs before I became too maudlin. Of course, they went nuts. *Run* was their favorite word, next to *treat* and *French fry*. While I changed into shorts and laced into clean running shoes, attached my phone to my waistband along with a water bottle, they warmed up by dashing madly from back door to front, around the bend in the hallway, up and down, claws clicking madly. I warmed up a bit more slowly, stretching and pulling at muscles that still felt the strain of the amputation in cramped quarters. My back muscles felt oddly weakened, and I extended the stretch slowly. Then I snapped on Pup's leash and led them outside.

"Pasture," I said, telling them which way we were going. The dogs bounded beside me, Belle running in the perfect heel position, her nose just back of my left thigh, even without a leash. Pup, clumsy as a clown, tripping over his snowshoe-size feet, ran on his leash beside her, nose to the air sniffing madly, yellow ears flopping forward. He was so awkward, the only reason he could keep up was because his legs were so long and the few smooth paces he made covered so much ground.

After the rains, the earth was mushy, making speed difficult. The cooler temps had died, smothered in humidity that blanketed the Piedmont of South Carolina like wet wool. Stifling and hard to breathe, the damp air covered me in a fine sweat in the first five minutes. But I loved being outdoors, blowing off some of the strain of the night before, working my legs into a rhythm that matched lungs and heartbeat, the pulse of blood. And the dogs needed it, testing the limits of their territory, taking in new scents, padding hard, tongues lolling and happy.

After a five-mile run through the cow pasture and farm that made up one boundary to my neighborhood, we turned across the creek into Miss Essie's, hoping for supper. Miss Essie was Marisa's former nanny, current live-in housekeeper and cook, and a dear friend. I'd known her forever.

Knowing instantly where we were going, Pup strained at his leash, hoping that Marisa was home, and I snapped the woven strap loose, letting him have his freedom. His excitement was comical whenever we'd head to Risa's. His disappointment when he discovered that his master wasn't there might have been funny, too, had I not always felt the same way. A little bit lost.

Both dogs bounded ahead, barking and yelping, alerting Miss Essie that we were coming to visit when I was just coming out of the woods. She met us on the back deck, her purple shawl loose in the heat, her smile wide. Miss Essie seldom met me on the back porch. I figured she was lonely, too. After checking me over to make certain I was appropriately attired in bra, T-shirt and decent shorts, she nodded once in approval. "Stop and pick some of that purple basil," she demanded. "I got tomato sandwiches on five-grain bread. You hungry?"

"Ravenous!" I said, my stomach growling.

"Then get you some that borage and that clove basil, too. And a handful of lettuce for a salad. Door open," she instructed, returning inside.

I picked the basil, the purple plants higher than my waist, the leaves papery and dry-feeling. The clove basil was beside it, the paper marker with its name in pencil, long faded by rain and sun. But I was learning which plant was which, tutored by Miss Essie whenever we ate together. I didn't much care for borage, the leaves a little prickly for my taste, but I loved the three varieties of lettuce, and I harvested some chives, some marjoram, a stick of rosemary and some thyme while I was at it, cutting the stalks with the scissors kept on the deck. The scent of Miss Essie's raised beds made my mouth salivate.

Over the sandwiches, the bread so fresh it was still warm and moist from the oven, and tomatoes still holding the day's sun, we talked.

"I hear from Miss Risa today. Her talkin' gettin' better."

"When is she coming home?"

"When they let her," Miss Essie said shortly, standing and filling my tea glass. There was a sprig of mint floating in the bottom. She then added a helping to my salad bowl. Miss Essie worked when she was upset about something. "Them babies is growing fast. She say they sleeping the night through." Miss Essie fussed with the lid on the sweating tea pitcher, turned her plate a quarter turn. I waited.

"Rheaburn and RheaLynn, they rolling over, playing with they toes. That service Dr. Cameron hire for helping with Miss Risa every day, and the nurse that take care of them at night, so's she can sleep…"

"But you aren't there to help," I said, my tone soft.

"It jist ain't right, Dr. Missy Rhea, her all alone at the rehab place, them babies with strangers."

Personally, I agreed, but this wasn't the time to say so. "She'll be home soon." I didn't add anything about the English nanny expected to join the household. No point in bringing up another sore point with Miss Essie. "And Risa is great with the kids. After all, she had you to teach her."

Miss Essie made a harrumphing sound, half pleasure, half disbelieving snort. She knew what I said was true, however. Marisa might always have problems with her speech, but she had no problems in the motherhood department. It was a treat to watch her with the babies, competent, relaxed. Her best self, as if she had never suffered an injury to her brain.

With nothing else to do, Miss Essie plopped back into her chair. Fidgeted with her shawl, fussed at Pup who tripped over something in the mudroom and sent mops scattering.

"What's the matter, Miss Essie?"

The older woman focused on me with a furious intensity. "She say you gone get that English woman to come be a nanny to them babies. Say you got to handle some Visa, though why you getting her a credit card I don' know." I looked away. So much for sore points to be avoided. "And them babies don' need no *nanny*. I know all they is to know 'bout babies. I raise her, din' I? Drink yo tea."

Obediently, I drank some tea and set my glass down. Miss Essie promptly filled it. Fretted with her dress, rearranged her shawl. "Marisa is just trying to save your back and your sleep, Miss Essie. She knows you could handle the babies. But she wants to protect you."

Miss Essie snorted, glared at me. "Ain't so old I can't take care a' two babies. Ain't nothin' but trouble coming you get that woman over here." She touched her dark-skinned temple knowingly. "Trouble. Mark my words."

5

JUST MAKE SURE SHE CHEWS BETTER

I drove in to work that Thursday evening with the windows rolled up and the air conditioner on high. Though I had showered and changed, the air was still sticky and hot, plastering my skin with sweat. Even at nearly 7:00 p.m., the temps were in the high nineties.

On the way in, I passed the softball field used by the Mount Zion Free Will Holy Evangelical Church of God. A huge tent had gone up in the field, just on the outskirts of Dorsey City—DorCity to the locals. Beige billows and poles and guy-wires were everywhere, the tent sides roped up to allow in the scant breeze. Rows of chairs lined the tent, tables clothed in gold fabric stood against one canvas wall, and camper trailers of the sort used by carnies were circled in one corner of the old pasture. Parking was roped off and small crowds of people milled everywhere. I didn't see any carnival equipment like that used by small traveling carnivals. No small Tilt-a-Whirl, no kiddie roller coaster, no undersized Ferris wheel or bumper cars. But whatever the tent held, it was drawing a crowd.

When I got to the ER, I settled in and took a report from Wallace Chadwick, the doctor getting off shift.

There wasn't much to tell. The ER had four patients, one with strep throat who was signed out and leaving, one with a laceration needing stitches, one sexually active fourteen-year-old with a case of PID—pelvic inflammatory disease—and one patient who had been admitted.

"Not much for me to do," I said.

"That'll change," he said, white teeth flashing under the fluorescent lights. Raising his hands high, palms to the front like a TV preacher, he said, "I prophesy that you will have a wild and wonderful and *very* active night. Call me in if you need me." His hands dropped in theatrical flourish.

"You telling my future? I got Miss Essie on my case already, now you?"

"Simple arithmetic, my dear Watson," he said, applying his best fake-English accent, his milk-chocolate-skinned face crinkling in amusement. "Add together the following, if you please. Temps in the nineties, plus humidity at 100 percent, plus gospel music in the highest decibels, plus over a hundred people outside in the heat, plus one tent meeting—" he paused for dramatic effect "—plus one faith healer." He hoisted his bag and faced the door, but spoke to me over one shoulder. "And what do you have? Think about it, Watson!"

I sighed. "A couple dozen DFOs and a few MIs?" I asked, remembering the tent and the crowd. DFOs were "done-fell-outs—" as in "Doc, she jist standing there one minute, and the next she done fell out." MIs were myocardial infarctions, or heart attacks. Generally somewhat difficult to determine from DFOs on initial examination. Almost all DFOs and chest pains were worked up as possible heart attacks, a long, expensive, time-consuming process.

"Splendid, Watson! Give the lady doctor a Kewpie

doll! Don't forget the heat prostration, drunks and other assorted mischief, and all the traumatic events you might want to see. I am postulating seven of each,'' he added, holding up a finger.

"Are you referring to fights and violent altercations?" I asked, putting on an accent and pretending to clean a pair of learned specs, entering into the spirit of the exchange.

"Indeed I am, Doctor. Though of course, I do hope I am wrong."

"I believe that your math is right on target, Holmes." I dropped my own English accent. "Thanks for the heads up. I passed the tent on the way in. I thought carnival but didn't see any rides."

"At least you won't be facing multiple traumas from a ride spinning off and killing ten, injuring twenty. Only a couple dozen difficult-to-diagnose chest pains and dehydrations. And you already have an ambulance standing by at the meeting."

"Thank God for small favors."

"Oh, and have you seen the work of our graffiti artist?"

"I saw a half-finished one outside the ER last night."

"Well, he got inside and spray painted the hallway outside the OR while you slept. All his signs are half-finished. Weird stuff."

"Maybe he's stoned out of his mind," I suggested.

"Or doesn't speak English," Wallace said. "See you in the morning. Cheerio!"

Wallace and I worked twelve-hour shifts. He generally worked 7:00 a.m. to 7:00 p.m., I generally worked the graveyard shift, though my contract was soon up for negotiation and I might bargain for different hours. I hoped tonight would not be a literal graveyard shift.

Faith healers in the South have long enjoyed a high reputation and drawn huge, sickly mobs, especially those patients with illnesses difficult to treat or diagnose. Repeated attempts by the press to expose healers as charlatans and frauds only seemed to increase the size of the trusting crowds. Some healers offered hope and redemption and healing of the wounded soul. Some offered much more, promising to heal physical illnesses. I remembered Mrs. Gordon's claim that she was taking her daughter to a faith healer. I hoped the healer in town was not one of the more virulent frauds, and that Venetia Gordon's mother was not taking her daughter to tonight's meeting. The heat would only exacerbate the girl's condition.

I quickly stitched up the small laceration and signed the last patient out of the ER, keeping an ear out for the scratchy rumble of the 911 dispatcher on the county scanner, and the even scratchier sound of the ambulance scanner. With little to do, I sat in the break room and had my first cup of coffee of the night, listening to the nurses talk about a book they had passed around and loved, and catching up on the details of Trisha's love life. I was working with the same nurses from the night before, and I took a gentle ribbing about traumas and amputations and the bloody accident scene from Coreen and Anne.

Two of the new nurses from the temp agency wandered up while we were talking about the accident scene. They identified themselves as Fazelle Scaggs and Julio Ramos, and poured themselves a cup of coffee. "Sorry I missed that one," Julio said of the van wreck, no trace of a Hispanic accent in the words. "Sounds like it was fun."

"Fun?" I said. "You call that *fun?*" The nurses all laughed. "Medical people have a sick sense of humor if that was fun."

"Makes a great story, Doc," Trish said, eyeing Julio. He was slight of build, blond and blue-eyed, with olive skin. The contrast between the blond hair and the dark skin was attractive, though not traditionally Hispanic. It was clear that Trisha liked what she saw, and she followed him with her eyes as he and Fazelle wandered up the hall later.

"I never saw him when the new nurses came on last night," she said softly. "My loss." The other nurses laughed.

Until just after 8:00 p.m. the county was silent, giving me hope that tonight, at least, I had dodged a bullet.

At eight-fifteen, I got my first DFO from the tent meeting, an elderly woman with high blood pressure. By nine-fifteen I had four more, most in various stages of dehydration, drunkenness and religious fervor. Oddly enough, one woman who arrived just wanted to share with someone—anyone—it didn't seem important who—that she could walk for the first time in three years without pain. She did a little dance for me, and had her pupils not been slightly dilated and her blood pressure just a bit too low for her bulk, I might have agreed that it was a miracle and not some drug-induced temporary aberration. Instead, I cautioned her to see how she felt in the morning, and suffered a censorious look in reprimand for my own lack of faith.

At 10:00 I had my first true MI, a forty-year-old with crushing chest pain and PVCs—preventricular contractions—on the rhythm strip curling out of the heart monitor. The lab did an EKG and drew blood, and the nurses prepped the patient for clot-busting meds and called in medevac to ship him to a cardiac center in Columbia, the state capital. While they worked, the EMTs told me about the meeting.

Carla, a stout woman in her thirties with dark roots and highlighted hair, shook her head. "Doc, I been to a dozen a' these things over the last few years. Ain't seen one like this. No rolling in the aisles, no dancing in the streets. Just a bonfire going in the field nearby, an old man walking through the crowd waving a burning bunch a' herbs, and the healer praying and quoting scripture. And some strange stuff happening. Strange stuff. And I ain't all that religious."

I looked up from the chart on which I was writing orders. "What kind of strange stuff?"

Carla looked up at her partner, Gus, and shook her head again. Gus grinned. "Carla's afraid I'll convert her and she'll have to give up sleeping with married men and drinking hard liquor. And the healings going on tonight are making her think twice."

I put down the chart, checked on the nurse's progress with my MI patient and returned to the desk. Quietly I asked, "Healings?"

"You remember that motorcycle accident victim from last March? SUV crossed over the centerline and hit him head-on? Guy went through the windshield?" Gus said, leaning his long body against the desk as he filled out the paperwork from the ambulance run.

I hadn't worked that day, but I remembered the story. Somehow the man's bike had risen up at impact and carried him through the SUV. Rider and bike were a snarled mess in the back of the sport-utility vehicle when emergency workers arrived at the scene. The SUV driver, who had been stinking drunk at the time, was decapitated. The EMTs had been forced to cut the biker from the wreckage, some of which had been part of the driver. The accident had been talked about extensively for weeks, a macabre and bloody joke told the way only a jaded paramedic can. "I remember."

"Biker had a busted knee, shoulder and pelvis. Reconstructive surgery was a success but left him with a permanent limp. Well, he got up and walked tonight. No limp." Gus looked down at Carla meaningfully.

"And my next-door neighbor's aunt said her arthritis is gone. Totally," Carla added reluctantly. "But that don't mean I'm coming to church with you. So don't ask," she said to Gus. He just grinned again, but then I'd seldom seen Gus without a grin.

"And?" Gus asked.

Even more reluctantly, Carla said, "And…there was this patient we picked up a couple times in the last few months. Myasthenia gravis so bad he can hardly blink his eyes. End-stage thing. He left the stage blinking. Waving his arms. Not looking tired at all. 'Course, he'll probably pass out on the way home and be dead by the weekend, but he looked a lot better when he walked off that stage."

"And that don't even touch on the last three people I saw go to be prayed over. One had fibromyalgia, one had some kind of retinal disease—" Gus ticked off on his fingers "—and the other was deaf. I asked him how his hearing was when he passed us afterward, and he heard me. Every word."

"So how do you explain all the drunks I've been seeing, coming right from the tent meeting. And the MI in there?" I nodded to my patient, who was ready for the first dose of retavase—a version of TPA, tissue plasminogen activator, the strong medicine that might give his heart a chance to heal. "Faith healer didn't fix him right up?"

"Yeah. Right!" Carla said. "What about them?"

"Drunks just need an excuse. We watched four or five make repeated trips to their cars in the parking lot. And the faith healer didn't pray over your patient,'' Gus said smugly. "He was in the back of the crowd. Never got close to the podium.''

I shook my head. "Well, he needs all the help he can get. We'll be flying him out of here in the next couple of hours.''

"We'll ask the healer to pray for him when we get back out there,'' Gus said.

"You ask her. I'm staying at the back of the crowd, like I'm supposed to,'' Carla said, her mouth in a stubborn line.

By eleven-thirty, the MI was long gone, already at the heart center and showing improvement, according to a phone call from his admitting doctor. I had also treated three MVA victims and several more DFOs, and admitted two patients to rule out probable heart problems. All of them had been to the tent meeting, which had ended in a tangle of traffic and a shower of sparks as a drunk driver ran into the dying bonfire. It was a pretty busy several hours for the small ER where I worked. We had six rooms and eight beds, and most stayed full from tent-meeting victims.

My last patient from the tent meeting came in at eleven forty-five. She was the one I had feared for all along. Venetia Gordon.

Her mother brought her in by POV—her personally owned vehicle—and ran through the ER doors shouting for help. Venetia was having trouble breathing again.

The nurses had the girl on a stretcher in the empty cardiac room in seconds, and had results of pulse, blood pressure and oxygen saturation readings in only seconds more. Venetia's condition was both strangely similar to and vastly different from the previous night. Her O_2 sat was low, her lips blue, and the look of panic in her eyes was extreme, but her blood pressure was normal. This wasn't a case of toxic hypertension, yet Venetia was suffocating.

Quickly, I checked her airway. Little air was moving in or out through Venetia's mouth. I thought I heard a faint whistle as she struggled to breathe. "Has she been speaking?" I asked her mom.

"No. Not since we stopped at McDonald's after the tent meeting. I fed her—she likes Quarter Pounders—and then we headed home. But I could tell something wasn't right. What's wrong with her?" Mrs. Gordon's voice rose as she fought panic.

"Venetia," I said loudly, placing myself in her line of sight. "Are you choking?"

The girl managed a nod.

"Are you choking on food? Is it stuck in your throat?"

Again she nodded, her eyes focusing on me with desperate fear.

"Help her!" her mother said. "Help her!"

There was nothing I could say to that. Rather than reply, I reached up and pulled the adjustable light over Venetia's face to recheck her airway. I couldn't see any obstruction in her mouth or the back of her esophagus. But the soft wheezing seemed to worsen. I pulled my stethoscope out of my pocket and listened to Venetia's lungs, which sounded fine. Whatever was lodged in her throat was somewhere between her mouth and her bronchial tubes.

Suddenly the slight wheeze stopped. Venetia rolled her eyes at me, her irises dilating in panic, begging. Whatever was blocking Venetia's airway had shifted. Over the cries of Mrs. Gordon standing at the foot of the bed, I bent forward to her mouth and listened. No air at all was moving in or out now. A hot sweat broke out down my spine.

I yanked the back of Venetia's stretcher fully upright. "Hold her," I said to Coreen. Without asking why or how, or anything else that might have been a distraction, the young nurse grabbed Venetia's shoulders and braced her body forward.

"What are you doing?" Almera Gordon asked, her voice quivering in fear. "I don't understand."

Letting the bed down to fully horizontal, I crawled behind Venetia and gripped her around the middle, just at the base of her rib cage, and fisted my hands into the notch below her sternum for an abdominal thrust. Three quick, hard thrusts later, the sound of air blasted from Venetia's lungs. Anne opened the girl's mouth and pulled out a hunk of half-chewed hamburger.

"Oh," Almera whispered. "Oh, my."

Anne tossed the chunk of food at the foot of the bed as I repositioned Venetia's head. The teenager sucked in a single loud breath, then jerked her head forward and breathed deeply several times, the sound like ripping flesh. Tears streaked her face. She gulped. Coughed. Breathed again.

Repositioning the back of the stretcher, I stepped away, watching her color quickly pinken. My heart was still racing. I raked a wrist across my brow, shoving my too-long bangs off my forehead.

Turning to Mrs. Gordon, I smiled and said, "She's going to be fine." The woman closed her eyes and shuddered. "Just make sure she chews better."

"Mama?" Venetia said, her voice quavering and rough. "Mama?"

I looked at my patient. Her eyes were huge, staring

down at herself. Her arms were lifted off her lap. Slowly, she lowered them. Lifted them.

"Oh!" Mrs. Gordon said, tears falling. "Oh my God!"

Venetia, who'd had no reflexive movement only twenty-four hours past, was holding her arms in the air.

A shiver shocked down my sweaty body. A far-off roar slammed into me, like the sound of an ocean wave just before it crested over and dragged me down. Beneath the clamor I could hear the tinny voice of Mrs. Gordon, praising God.

After the Gordons left, I ambled to the old county map and looked for their address. I found it in a faded crease, the name of the street almost rubbed away. Mother and child lived only a few miles from my house, through the woods, as the crow flies. I remembered the girl raising her arms, lowering them, over and over. I could still see her face, filled with wonder as she watched them move. I could still hear her mother praising God, a God who had never done anything for me or mine. And yet…

Though Venetia had not been able to rotate her wrists tonight, the girl had reflexive response in both arms when I tapped her with my reflex hammer and stimulated various nerve nexus with my thumbs. When we covered her eyes and placed hot and cold rags on her skin, Venetia could differentiate between temperature. And she could feel pain. When I pinched her, she felt it, and she claimed her arms were aching like a toothache, with a vaguely electrical sensation running through her muscles.

It was weird, and I didn't much like weird. I was a scientist, trained to look for problems and solutions. Reproducible results. That was science. Doing the same thing over and over and getting the same results every time. Like my MI patient. A clot had lodged in his heart. We started meds that broke down clots. He would have a fast heart cath, a stent or two placed in his cardiac arteries to open them fully, and in a few days he would be sent home, maybe needing further meds or even surgery, but he was already feeling better. The medicines had done what they were supposed to do and started him healing. That was science.

Omens and portents were not science. And I had a patient who was exhibiting some unexpected and sudden improvements. Without science.

"Anne?" I asked as the nurse passed by the bleached-out map. "Do you think I could get a copy of Venetia's original accident report faxed over here?"

"Sure. I'll call and ask. We'd need a signed release from her mother, but I don't think that'll be a problem. Want me to handle it?"

"Please. And thank you. See it gets put in my box?"

"Will do."

With nothing else to do and too many weird thoughts I didn't want to have, I ambled up the hallway to check on the two patients I had admitted from the night before, Na'Shalome and the Jane Doe with the multiple amputations, one of them my responsibility.

Na'Shalome's door was cracked open, the room was empty and rank-smelling, the light off but the TV blaring and bright, her covers rumpled. The doll was no longer standing in the corner. As I shut her door, I spotted neon letters spray-painted on the varnished wood surface. When I touched them, they were tacky, as if freshly painted. The graffiti designer had struck again. If Na'Shalome had not been trapped in the van or been under the watchful eyes of nurses when the first graffiti appeared, I might have thought she was the painter.

I studied the design on Na'Shalome's door. It wasn't English, yet the forms were similar to letters, perhaps Russian or German. They didn't form words, just a pattern of shapes, half-familiar, as if I had seen them somewhere once. "Have you seen this?" I called to a passing nurse.

"Yeah, he—or she—got three doors on this hallway, Doc. I called housekeeping. If they catch the paint while it's damp, they might keep it from setting permanently."

"You know what it is?"

"Looks like those Japanese tattoos the kids are getting. Why?"

"No reason." Japanese. That was one I hadn't considered. I knocked and entered the next room, where Jane Doe was. It too was dark, and smelled odd—a fetid, unwashed scent. Music blared, some kind of unpleasant New Age melody, harps and bells and what could have been a bagpipe. A candle burned on the adjustable patient table.

Startled at the sight of an open flame in a hospital setting, I stopped in the doorway. As my eyes adjusted, I saw the doll, propped on the bed with Jane. Kneeling beside it on the bed was Na'Shalome. Sitting across Jane Doe's body. Straddling the girl.

Over the sound of the repulsive music, I heard Na'Shalome's voice, chanting, a singsongy melody like a monk's chant, but with a hard edge. Caustic.

I stepped into the room. And saw that the Jane's arms were bound, held in the air by Na'Shalome. Something glittered in the air beside her.

"What are you doing! Nurse! Call security!" I shouted.

Na'Shalome whirled and looked at me, the movement so fast I didn't see her turn. Her eyes, black in the darkness, stabbed me. "Get out!" she screamed. "Get out!"

6

DREAM-FIGHTING

I slept hard the rest of the night and woke wrapped in the call room's rough sheets, tangled as if they had fought me and won. The room was hot, the AC not working well enough to dissipate the body heat I had generated in my forgotten dreams.

I fought my way off the mattress, peeling the sheets and my wrinkled scrubs off me. Standing under a cold shower, I felt the water shocking my overheated body, as bits of the dreams returned, a montage of images, all underwater. Twisted strands of kelp, the feel of them grasping me, holding me. The need to breathe. The sudden loss of vision as underwater currents stirred the silty bottom. The far-off sight of my mother's face, dead. Drowned.

I turned up the shower temp to hot and scalded my chilled body, gasping with the sudden change. Childhood nightmares had often been about drowning.

My mother had drowned, all right. In the bottom of a bottle of Jack Daniel's Black Label. A voluntary death. Suicide by liquor.

Bringing the temperature to bearable, I forced the dream-memories away and focused for a moment on the night before. Na'Shalome. I recalled the sounds of her ranting as she was dragged off Jane Doe and carted to her room, sedated against her will, a security guard stationed outside her door.

Contrary to what I thought I had seen, Na'Shalome had not had a knife. It had been only the flash of hallway light along the bars of the orthopedic traction system. Shoving the thoughts away, I dried, dressed in jeans and T-shirt and left the hospital, waving to Wallace on the way out. I didn't stop to speak, as he was frowning angrily and I didn't want to be trapped by a tirade. He was staring at neon letters on the wall just inside the ER. The artist had been busy, and Wallace looked mad to see his ER defaced.

On the way home, I slowed as I passed the site of the tent meeting, canvas walls closed fast against the early light, the parking lot deserted but so clean it appeared to have been swept, ashes of the bonfire still smoking. It looked innocuous and harmless and unimportant. But Venetia had moved her arms....

Back home, I changed again, this time into running attire, dark-purple shorts and jogging bra with a T-shirt I could tie around my waist if I got overheated. Dressed, I stretched out muscles tightened by dream-fighting. The dogs ran in highly charged circles around me, yelping, playing tag, knocking me over twice and finally making me laugh. The laughter made me feel much better and I sat on the floor, scrubbing the ears of both dogs as I laced up my running shoes and avoided overeager tongues. Snapping the leash onto Pup's collar, we three left the house, entering a world of steamy heat and damp, dew-drenched, dripping greenery.

On the narrow back stoop was a dead mole. It had not been there only moments before when I entered the house. My first thought was more omens and portents. Voodoo stuff. A quick anger rose in me.

I stopped, pulled the dogs away from the freshly killed animal and studied it. The mole was large and well-chewed about the neck. I had seen something like it before, but couldn't place where. Then, to the side of the steps I noticed tracks. Cat tracks. I suddenly understood the import of the mole. Not voodoo. Of course not voodoo. I felt just a bit foolish.

"Great," I said to the dogs. "Looks like a stray is leaving presents. You two be sure to chase away any pesky cat you happen to see. You hear?"

Belle ignored me, doing her business beside the largest oak in the yard, marking the huge slab of broken boulder at the oak's base. Pup pulled on the leash, his face heading toward the pasture where we had taken our last run.

Instead, I pulled him a different way and moved out at a fast walk along the creek, through the woods, to the Gordons' neighborhood. Running easily, not pushing muscles that still felt slightly sore and stiff even after warming up, the dogs and I slipped through the woods of late summer, startling squirrels, attracting the attention of a stray hawk. All sorts of trees grow wild in the Piedmont of South Carolina, oak, maple, sweet gum and cedar, wild cherry, pecan and walnut, swamp hickory with its broken and curling bark. Even the rare chestnut and elm, and along the banks of streams, birch and willow.

Of course, there were things to avoid, too: patches of poison oak, poison ivy, poison sumac, clouds of mosquitoes, ticks that fell from trees carrying various rickettsial diseases, and the occasional rabid animal, which was why I carried a cell phone in summer, to report the location of any animal that was acting strangely. And then there were skunks. Never forget the presence of skunks. But even with the possible problems one might encounter in the woods, I loved to run there. Loved the cooler temps and the sound of birdcalls and the way the forest soothed my raw soul.

I stretched into the run, feet pounding on the hard ground. Beside me, the creek gurgled like a happy infant. The dogs ran as though their hearts were made of steel, tongues hanging from their mouths. Sweat beaded on my skin and ran in uneven rivulets, drenching my clothing. Without breaking stride, I pulled the shirt off and tied it around my waist.

When we reached the neighborhood I thought was Venetia's, I checked street signs and oriented myself, pulling Pup along, whistling in the breathy way I had to keep Belle near. The neighborhood was newer than mine, most of the small homes built in the sixties and seventies, some with the modern look of high, square windows and low-pitched roofs. Others were split-level or ranch style with decorative shutters and front porches, some with fences, some with garages, all with well-established yards and plenty of heavy, crowded greenery.

It was not yet eight o'clock but was steamy hot, and we were interlopers in the area. Other dogs barked, warning their owners and the dogs farther on that a stranger had appeared. We set up a cacophony on the quiet street, but no worried-looking human with shotgun in hand appeared. Instead, we passed other joggers, two bicyclists and numerous walkers. All smiled and spoke, seeming perfectly at ease with the presence of a lone woman and two huge dogs on their paved streets.

I found the Gordons' house by recognizing Almera's specially built gray van with its hydraulic wheelchair lift sitting in the front driveway. I slowed my pace, studying the brick house. Its overgrown yard and shrubs were in need of trimming, and the trim work was in need of a fresh coat of paint. The house wasn't in disrepair. It didn't look abandoned, just in need of attention, as if its owner had been out of town for a while. Or involved with other interests.

Feeling a bit like a stalker, I turned the dogs and increased my pace. We made it back home without meeting any myriad problem animals and I set the dogs free to romp the last few hundred feet along the creek that meandered behind my house.

They must have read my mind, or smelled bacon, because instead of playing they headed to Miss Essie's at a dead run. I followed at a slow walk, taking stock that I was indeed wearing a heavy jogging bra and pulling my T-shirt back over my head, making sure that my running shorts were long enough to be discreet. Miss Essie was firm in her opinion that no woman should ever leave home without the essential clothing needs. I had shown up not too long ago without a bra, thinking myself covered enough with dress and jacket, both lined and made of dark fabric. Big mistake.

But it wasn't Miss Essie who stepped on the back deck and watched me approach as I came out of the woods. It was Cam, and my heart jumped in excitement. Marisa might be with him.

"She's still in Raleigh," he shouted through cupped hands, as though he was reading my mind. I tucked my disappointment back inside and nodded to show him I'd heard. Cam rested against the house, one foot braced on the brick at his back, crossed his arms and waited for me.

Dr. Cameron Reston, long and lean with muscles one didn't know he had unless one touched him, or saw him shirtless. Black-eyed, black-haired, teeth so white they were blinding, and a rakish quality that made me think of the heroes in the Regency romance novels Marisa had read back in high school. Cam had gone to medical school with Marisa and me, then on to a residency in neurosurgery at Duke, where he still had a few years of specialized training to go. A black belt in more than one form of martial arts, a great dancer and conversationalist, Cameron Reston had a way with women that was near-legendary. And he was one of my best friends.

His dark eyes sparkled at me as I approached, taking in my sweat, my limbs still tight from the run, and looking his fill. I lifted an eyebrow when I was close enough to be heard. "Finished yet?"

"I'll never be finished with looking at beautiful women."

I snorted. I wasn't beautiful and I knew it. My mother had told me so often enough, and the mirror didn't lie. Oh, I wasn't ugly, and I did have great legs, but I was no beauty. Cam grinned, dimples appearing in his five o'clock shadow. "Did you fly all morning after working all night?" I asked, censure in my voice. Cam wasn't reckless, but like all doctors, he thought he was bullet-proof when it came to the long hours he put in.

"Guilty."

Cam owned a single-engine Cessna and routinely made the trip from Duke to Dawkins County with Marisa, bringing her and the twins home between stints at the rehab center. He tossed me a towel and pushed Pup off his waist. I ran the towel down my arms and legs, conscious of Cam's eyes on me as I moved. He had a way of looking at a woman—any woman, all women—that made them acutely aware of themselves. Even women who were nothing but friends. It wasn't anything that he consciously did. It was just Cam.

"What are you in town for?" I asked, managing to sound nonchalant in the face of his regard.

"To help Shirl move in. She's bringing up a van from Atlanta and needs muscle. I thought I'd just kick back a couple days and relax in the country."

"When? I can pitch in," I said. Dr. Shirley Atkins, a mutual friend and Cam's most recent love interest, was moving to nearby Charlotte, North Carolina, after finishing a two-year placement at the Center for Disease Control.

"Sometime in the next day or two. I already volunteered you. We can party, go dancing."

"Your favorite dream, two women on a dance floor."

"Close," he retorted, a glint in his eye.

I tossed the damp towel at him and he caught it, five thousand dollars' worth of childhood orthodontia flashing in his olive-skinned face. "Miss Essie's bringing out maple-syrup-cured bacon and eggs, grits and fresh biscuits. Down, Pup. Can't you train this dog? Are you hungry?"

"Haven't bothered. And I'm ravenous."

We all sat on Miss Essie's back porch for breakfast, the dogs in well-behaved, panting lethargy beneath the table, hoping for dropped table-scrap treats. Marisa was the prime topic of conversation, with Cam alternately teasing us and filling us in on details of Risa's progress, which was limited.

"You can't expect much more improvement," he said finally to Miss Essie. "With the kind of invasive trauma she suffered, we're looking at a very slow, measured improvement or even a plateau."

"My Missy Risa still got a ways to go yet before she get to any plateau," Miss Essie said stubbornly, pouring more coffee. "You be seeing. Them two babies a' hers be bringing her back to herself more and more."

Cam glanced at me, a doctor-to-doctor communication, and shrugged fractionally. Patients' families and caretakers needed any hope and reassurance they could get. For Marisa, however, Cam and I had become family, too, straddling the doctor-patient-loved-one roles with differing success rates. Cam could still find that once-removed space required in doctor-patient relationships. I couldn't, at least not without some preparation. Like Miss Essie, I wanted reassurance. Cam didn't offer much.

The heat seemed to smother me as I sat, watching Miss Essie and Cam and thinking of Marisa. Thinking too of the still-numb place along my spine where muscles and a few nerve endings had been cut by a sharp blade wielded by an angry man. I had been to my share of rehab in the last few months, and the improvement had been sporadic. I was still taking iron and prescriptions to bolster my body's red blood cell count.

Nightmares about the event persisted, and I still felt the phantom pain from the blade as it cut me. I felt the breath of the man as he propelled me down empty hospital hallways, a scalpel slicing my back, rivulets of my blood leaving a trail for Mark to follow. I could still see his face, feel the heat of his blood on my skin as he fell toward me and died. That death had stopped an epidemic and resulted in the Reverend Lamb of God going to prison.

Breaking my thoughts, Cam said quietly "She's never going to be what or who she was, Miss Essie. We have to accept that."

"You be acceptin' anything you want. I still got the Lord on my side," Miss Essie said, chomping another bite of bacon. "This family done suffer enough misery 'thout giving up hope and thinkin' the worse. My Miss

Marisa coming back to me, her whole self. You be seeing.''

"Got any more of that delicious bacon, Miss Essie?" Cam asked, turning the conversation to more neutral ground. "And coffee?"

"You changing the subject, I know what you doin' and don't you pretend I don't," she said, heaping four more strips onto Cam's plate. "And you had enough coffee. You need to sleep shortly. Leave that pot alone," she slapped his hand away from the carafe. Cam winked at me, stole my nearly full cup and drank it halfway down.

The phone rang while she was speaking, and Miss Essie pulled a cordless from a pocket of her purple apron.

"Cordless phone, Miss Essie?" I said, surprised. "You?" Miss Essie was not exactly a forward-thinking woman, preferring to live in the comfort of the past. She worked her own garden, baked her own bread and cooked her own meals. I didn't especially want any of that to change. If Miss Essie entered the twenty-first century, I might have to eat more fast food. Totally selfish, I know.

"I got a family a' three to take care of now," she said between rings. "I'm learning new things to make our life easier. I even signed up for a computer course in DorCity. Keep that English nanny-woman out the way." She stabbed the phone with a gnarled finger. "Hello."

I smiled into my coffee. Marisa had arranged with Shirl to have her Auntie Maude come from England in the fall and be nanny to the twins, a move that was sure to upset the long-standing balance of power in the Braswell home. Shirl's Auntie Maude spoke several languages and read several more, having worked all over the world with the British Home Office. Marisa wanted Auntie Maude to help raise her kids, to read to them and teach them to speak with proper little accents, now that she herself had lost much of her power of speech. But Miss Essie had been Marisa's nanny, and was insulted that Marisa thought she needed anyone else to fill the role.

"No, Miss DeeDee, she ain't back home yet."

I sat up at the name. Miss DeeDee was Marisa's aunt. She was also the one responsible for Marisa's injury.

"She still in that rehabilitation hospital…. Don't you be taking that tone with me, ol' woman. I know them peoples at Silver Lakes lets you talk on the phone mos' anytime you want, but you still crazy."

My eyebrows went up. Cam laughed into my coffee cup, smothering the sound in a slurp. His black eyes glittered with hilarity.

"I still praying for you. But you done let the devil get the bes' a' you. Take you down the wrong path. And till you repent a' yore sins and get right with the Lord, you ain't welcome to come back here and you ain't welcome to talk to my Miss Marisa….

"No. I tellin' you how it is. You don' pay my salary no more, I can speak to you how I want and how you deserve…. You want my respect then you got to earn it, same as any other body."

I laughed softly through my nose. Miss DeeDee Stowe still wielded great power in Dawkins County, even from her sealed room in the luxurious Silver Lakes, the psychiatric hospital where she was undergoing treatment for committing murder and hurting Marisa. But it seemed as if the deference still offered to Miss DeeDee by so many no longer lived in Miss Essie's heart.

"No, you can' talk to her neither. Yep, she here. But I ain't puttin' her on. No, I ain't asking her if she want to talk to you."

I shook my head. I didn't want to talk to Miss DeeDee, either. I was enjoying the one-sided conversation too much. And Miss DeeDee unnerved me. She had tried to injure me once, too, and yet still demanded the polite manners of Southern etiquette.

"No. I ain't got nothin' to give you. You ain't getting my Marisa's phone number from me, and not from Dr. Missy Rhea." Miss Essie pushed back from the table, holding the phone in the crook of ear and shoulder, plucked my cup from Cam's fingers and began loading dishes on a tray. "I tell her to hang up on you if you call. Slam the phone right down. We got nothin' to say to you."

I laughed behind my hand. For the first time ever, I was hearing Miss DeeDee Stowe—of the Charleston Stowes, of seafaring riches and fame—get her due. And it was a fine thing. Cam was enjoying the show, too, saluting Miss Essie with my cup, stolen back from the tray.

"Hol' on, old woman." Miss Essie punched the mute button on the side of the phone and nodded toward the woods, stealing the cup back again. "Cam, you walk Miss Rhea home. I got a few things to say to Miss DeeDee what ain't polite. No reason you young people should sully your ears with it. Go. And take them blame dogs. Lordy Moses, they ain't nothin' but something else to trip over and I got some mighty brittle bones at my age. Git."

We got, Cam jumping from the low deck, hands in his jeans pockets, me in my running clothes, now dry but still a mite ripe, as some of my patients would say. Miss Essie took back ranting the moment we cleared the deck, her voice fading as she reentered the house with the load of dishes. "I tole you, you ain't talkin' to my Miss Marisa.... You done give up any rights to them twins when you hurt my baby.''

"God, that woman is amazing," Cam said. "I could never stand up to that old biddy. And I never heard anyone else do it, either."

"Miss Essie's been with the family for so long she's part of it. Heck, she runs it! Marisa's taken to calling the house Miss Essie's, did you know?" Cam nodded. He knew. "Maybe Miss Essie just finally had enough of Miss DeeDee."

"Maybe. And maybe they both just got old enough to be totally honest with each other. I'll be in town for a few days," he said, changing the subject. "Let's take in that new Mel Gibson action flick. Maybe hit a club in Charlotte, do a little dancing."

"I haven't danced since I broke up with John," I said, uncomfortable with plans that almost sounded like a date.

"And John danced like he had two wooden legs. Me? Now, I can dance," he said, placing one hand on his stomach and holding one in the air as if leading a partner, moving his hips and feet with sensual grace. His jeans-clad legs moved in a tight circle in the narrow path to the creek.

I had seen Cam dance, watched him with numerous other women, all of them beauties. He danced as if Latin blood flowed in his veins instead of royal English blueblood. "I think the proper medical term is multiple prostheses," I said primly.

"*I* think the proper term for John's dancing is CUHB," he spelled. "With a Corncob Up His Butt."

I tried not to laugh and failed, fighting the combined emotional reactions of amusement and the bittersweet memories of being with John Micheaux. John hadn't been the most graceful man in the world, it was true.

And I had called off our engagement recently enough that the pain was still fresh.

Cam and the dogs and I entered the woods, the shade cool, the sound of the creek trickling across stones. The dogs bounded back and forth, playing tag. Overhead, a mockingbird called, its series of notes reminding me of Miss Essie and her one-sided conversation with Miss DeeDee.

"So, we going to take in a movie? Dance a bit? Just as friends." He rolled his eyes at me. "You can buy your own liquor, since I won't stand a chance of getting lucky."

I laughed again, equally relieved and disappointed. Cam was a scamp. And he had told me many times I was his only female friend. He'd slept with all the rest.

"Unless maybe you changed your mind?" he teased.

"Not a chance," I said, lifting my nose in the air as if smelling something foul in his suggestion. "I want a one-woman man."

"Never met one. Even John is dating again."

The words hit me hard, the air whooshing out of my chest. John and I had been together for over three years before he let me know our life together would not be the one we planned and I left him for it. My steps faltered as I approached the creek. "He is?"

Cam jerked to a stop, took my upper arm in his grip. "You didn't know?" We stood on Risa's side of the creek, the air wet with creek water and humid heat, Cam's eyes on mine. "Ah, Rhea, I'm sorry. I thought you knew."

"No." I lifted my chin. "But I'm not surprised." I pulled away and stepped on the stones, easing my way over to the other side instead of jumping the three-foot width as I usually did. Carefully, I kept my back to him. "It's been over a year since I left. Who?"

"What?" Cam looked up, suddenly distracted. "Wait, I see you got a cat now, too," he said, changing the topic. "Very domestic of you. You're becoming a real country girl, Rhea. Next thing I know, you'll be driving a truck."

"No cat." I paused and let him catch up with me, stopping our forward progress with a hand on Cam's arm. I was tall for a woman, and on the uneven ground I stood nose to nose with Cam. "Who. Is. John. Dating?"

Cam turned red, the flush starting at the base of his neck and moving north. He kept his eyes on my house instead of on me, pulling his arm free as he answered. "One of the Larouche twins."

I laughed again, suddenly relieved. "Larouche? Oh my." I willed his eyes to meet mine. They didn't. "Sally or Boopsie?"

"Boopsie," he said drolly, fighting a smile. "Thank God. Though no one gets by using that old nickname anymore. These days, she's Gabrielle Larouche. Her mama makes sure we all remember that."

"Is Mama Larouche a happy camper again? Got another doctor-type for her youngest. Not a neurosurgeon, of course, but a man with a pedigree and an M.D. after his name. How does it feel to have Mama Larouche's claws out of your nape?"

"Very freeing." He turned me back toward my house. "That woman was still calling me at all hours, asking me to join the family for holidays and weekends."

"You asked her daughter to move in, as I recall. Domestic bliss, I think you called it," I reminded him.

"Yeah, well, a man can only stand so much prattle."

The thought of John with Gabrielle "Boopsie" Larouche was suddenly freeing for me, too. Except for a short few weeks just after Christmas, we had been apart for over a year, ever since I came to Dawkins County. It was time to let go.

"Thought I saw a cat! And she's a beaut!"

I followed Cam's pointing finger to the big rock beneath the even bigger oak near my driveway. On top, tail curled around her feet, sat a cat. She stared serenely into the distance, the half-gnawed dead mole at the base of the rock. I eyed the cat narrowly, but she seemed unperturbed by my irritation and Pup's barking as the big clumsy dog ran round and round the rock, yelping in frenzied warning. She looked quite regal—gray and brindle-striped, long-haired, maybe part Persian, and bloodthirsty, of course.

"I love cats," Cam said.

"Good. Take it with you. Cats don't like me."

"This one may have chosen you." He gripped my arm and pointed. "She left you a gift. Pup! No! Come!" he commanded. The huge canine whuffed at him and came running, to sit at Cam's feet.

The cat turned glowing yellow eyes on us as if measuring our reaction to the sight of her. "Well, maybe I don't like cats," I said. "I certainly don't like dead moles."

"You ever had a cat? And dead moles mean less live ones beneath the ground making trails all through your lawn."

"No. And I don't want one. A cat," I clarified, pulling my arm out of Cam's grip. Like ten-year-olds, we had been grabbing and tugging on one another for the whole of the trip back to my house. It was annoying. "Look, I'm tired. I need to hit the sack for a few hours, and then I have to work tonight."

"Call in sick and we'll catch that action flick."

"Yeah, right. Me, call in sick. When is the last time *you* called in sick?"

"When I had the 'both ends flu.' But then, I didn't have me in town to keep me company." He leered suggestively.

"Later, Cam. And take that annoying cat with you. I don't like things that stare at me."

7

BUT HE WAS HEALED

I woke early in the afternoon, feeling out of sorts and uncomfortable. Third-shift workers often feel weird, wired, unconnected with the rest of humanity. Permanent jet lag. I assured myself that I was reacting to the hard hours, not to the combined effects of Venetia, the amputation, the tent meeting and Cam. I wasn't very convincing, even to myself.

A distraction was needed to calm the multiple voices in my head all assuring me that I was worthless, troublesome and occasionally too interested in men who were uninterested in me. Staring through the living-room window, I considered doing some lawn work. I wasn't a homey sort of woman, and had no desire for housework. My interest in and knowledge of lawn care was even more deficient. But I was intelligent, and had collected enough gardening magazines and surfed enough gardening sites on the Internet while I was recuperating from the stabbing to feel I had a handle on the subject.

I had hired a lawn-care crew to test the soil, fertilize, seed for drought-resistant grass in the few sunny places of my lawn and shape beds for shade-loving plants. There were rows of bedding plants under a tree in the front yard, with drip irrigation on a timer keeping them alive until I found time to stick them in the ground. They had been there for six weeks. Hardy little things. I figured that was a good thing.

But instead of lawn work, I pulled on my slightly ripe jogging clothes and took the dogs for a second run. As I worked up a fast sweat in the hot, humid air, I looked at my feelings dispassionately. I accepted that Cam Reston was charming, tempting, sometimes overwhelming. He was my friend. He was also trouble, jumping in and out of bed with so many women it made me dizzy to try and keep track. I didn't want Cam. I wanted a one-woman man. If such as thing had ever existed.

After three miles, I began to feel better, the endorphins kicking in and giving me a needed lift. I ended up at Mark's house, pulled across the street by the dogs, who scented out the freshly charred steak and veggies roasting on Mark's backyard grill.

Belle and Pup played with Mark's dogs, while the two humans, tired and worn and guilty of working too many hours, ate and drank wine and watched the sun move west. Mark was soothing. Mark was calming. Mark had great hands that worked the tight feeling out of my shoulder muscles while a second steak charred on the outside, to rare perfection on the inside, on his grill.

Of course, nothing is perfect. I discovered that Mark had taken up cigar smoking. Still, the scent wasn't as bad as I might have feared, and he assured me he smoked outside, never in the house, and then only rarely. As a doctor, I couldn't approve. But Mark was a miracle worker with a propane grill, mesquite chips and garlic-marinated venison steaks wrapped in bacon. It was hard to be censorious when my stomach was growling.

And if a small voice deep in my psyche whispered that

I was once again mourning John, I was able to ignore it. John had Boopsie Larouche of the massive boobs and gene-created blond hair, blue eyes, and hips made for child rearing. John had what he'd always wanted on some level. A woman without a mind and goals and desires of her own.

At six-thirty, the heat still so high I glistened with sweat, I jogged back across the street, showered, changed into scrubs and took off for the hospital.

Passing the tent meeting on the way in, my BMW was slowed to a crawl by the crowd waiting to turn into the parking lot. The bonfire blazed with a cloud of smoke, the Friday-night worshipers milled about in agitated confusion and the tent walls were turned back in a welcoming loop secured with ropes. I had a bad feeling already.

I was met in the Dawkins County Hospital ER by Ronnie Howell, a brittle diabetic, a repeat patient I had come to know over the last year. Wallace had labs waiting that showed Ronnie's blood sugar was over 900. Normal blood sugar was under 125.

The thirteen-year-old-kid was severely acidotic, and his ammonia level was well above normal, meaning that his sugar had been high for a long time. Long enough to be deadly. Ronnie was in bad shape, his lungs and kidneys threatening to shut down. Wallace and I discussed treatments before he left.

Ms. Howell, a single mother with dyed, dark auburn hair, a tattoo of a rose on her neck, the thorny stem passing between her generous breasts and out of sight, and multiple silver earrings in one ear, was distraught.

"It can't be," she kept mumbling, her mascara-rimmed eyes wide. "It can't be." Can't in mill-hill talk was "caint," with the accent on the third word in the sentence. It caint *be*. It caint *be*.

But it could. And it was. "Ms. Howell," I said gently. "Tell me what happened."

The woman turned shocked eyes to me. Her skin was damp and pale, and I led her to a chair in the room where Ronnie waited, his body flaccid and drained. Behind me a nurse started a second IV line to administer an insulin drip. A respiratory therapist stood ready in case the kid coded. "Ms. Howell?" I prodded.

The woman blinked, her eyes on the child. "But he was healed," she said slowly. *"Healed."*

Suddenly, I thought I understood. I shook her, my hands less gentle than they should have been. "Tell me what happened," I demanded.

After a moment her eyes lifted and settled on me. Her irises were green, flecked with red, as if the pigment in the iris had flaked off, exposing the retina beneath.

"I took him to the tent meeting."

A slow burn started somewhere beneath my skin. I was right. I wanted to howl.

"The preacher prayed over him." She blinked, the odd green-red irises vanishing and reappearing. "I had faith," she said, as if assuring me of her holiness. "He was healed."

"And you took Ronnie off his insulin," I said, fighting disgust.

"Yes."

I took a slow breath, the passage to my lungs restricted by a barricade of anger. "Ms. Howell. I have two things to say to you. One—as of today, there is no cure for the kind of diabetes Ronnie has. Never has been, miracle or not. Two—DSS might have something to say about you taking your child off his insulin. Especially if he dies."

Her eyes widened, her pupils opening in shock. "Dies?"

It was cruel; I didn't care. I shoved her out of the way and went to work. Behind me I could hear her mumbling, "I had faith. I did."

The nurses started an insulin drip on Ronnie while I called Boka, Ronnie's regular physician. Dr. Bokara admitted him, ordered labs and promised to be by shortly. The kid would have repeat glucose levels every hour until further notice, interspersed with regular chemistry panels, ammonia levels and blood gases. He'd be a pincushion, but we might save him. And perhaps—just maybe—it wasn't too late to save his brain function.

Hours later, Boka and I sat in my office, her flowing silk a medley of fuchsia, rose and teal draped across her limbs. I had never seen Boka sweat. Or even glisten. Across the desk from her, I felt artless, crude and unfeminine in my scrubs, hair uncombed, no makeup.

"That woman needs to be horsewhipped," she said, one red nail tapping on the desk. "Boiled in oil."

"Tarred and feathered?" I supplied.

"Exactly. She took Ronnie off his meds. *Off his meds!*" she repeated.

I nodded. "She took him to the tent meeting."

"Stupid!" The lacquered nail pounded on the desk. "Beyond reason! Are all the people in the South so asinine?"

I was Southern, but didn't take offence. "Heck yeah," I said in an accent that would have done a drunken hunter proud. "It comes from that there shrinkin' gene pool. My mama *tole* me not to be marrying my first cousin. 'Cause a' her marryin' *her* first cousin or something. It keeps us

all family, is the way I'm thinkin'. And family is a good
thing. Right?''

Boka's tinkling laugh was a reward, as the irritation
slid from her features. "I don't mean to sound as though
I really believe that, you understand. I'm simply frustrated.''

Her painted nails fluttered over her face, pushing back
strands of hair that had worked themselves loose from
the braid at her back. I could imagine Mark's reaction
should I attempt the same maneuver. Some women had
that essential femininity at the ready. Some of us didn't
have it at all.

"He may have brain damage from this episode," Boka
said softly, echoing my earlier fears, twirling strands of
hair around her braid. "I really like that child. He is so
bright. He paints, did you know?" When I shook my
head, she continued. "The most beautiful watercolors. He
brought me a hibiscus that had this lovely pearly sheen
washed across it.''

"You calling in DSS?"

Her dark, expressive eyes steeled. "I had to. No
choice. What that mother did was negligent at best. Child
abuse at worst. He's hyperreflexive on the right side. He's
still acidotic, and his sugar is still over 400. I don't like
what I am seeing.''

The phone on my desk buzzed and I answered. I had
a DFO and an OFW, both from the tent meeting. The
faith healer was clearly in full swing. Coming in by ambulance was a SOB in a COPDer—a shortness of breath
in a patient with chronic obstructive pulmonary disease.
I love med-speak. So much information in so few letters.

"I won't keep you," Boka said when I hung up. "I
have a husband and a good video on." She rose with

languid grace and preceded me down the hallway. "Call if you need me."

The patients tonight were different from the patients of the night before. It wasn't anything I could put my finger on, but they just didn't seem quite right. They seemed sluggish, somehow. Unconcerned with their own physical conditions. The OFW was singing hymns and smiling at the ceiling, appearing to be suffering from senility, though her fifty-something-year-old daughter assured me that she was usually as sharp as a tack.

The DFO was suffering from chest pains, but all he could do was tell me about the woman preacher. He had a generous amount of belly fat, thin limbs, little hair on his head and copious amounts on his body, and a funny-looking EKG lead on the heart monitor. I ordered a cardiac work-up on him. He seemed happy.

The COPDer was the most obvious. Patients with chronic obstructive pulmonary disease have lungs that can best be described as leathery, injured by years of cigarette smoking, or working in a chemical plant or cotton mill, lungs exposed to toxic fumes or cotton fibers with every breath. Instead of moving with elastic grace every time they breathe, the lungs are stiff, especially as the patient exhales.

Anytime COPD patients come into contact with any chemical or allergic irritant or bacterial or viral infection, their lungs fill with fluid and the new condition is negatively affected by the preexisting one, which means that they suddenly can't breathe. The carbon dioxide builds up in their systems, putting a strain on their kidneys and their entire metabolic processes. They actually begin to suffocate.

"I'm Dr. Rhea," I said, glancing at the chart. "You are Martha Stone?"

"Yes. I am. And I'm having a little trouble breathing, Doctor."

"Do you smoke, Martha?"

"Used to. Three packs a day. And I worked at the mill. Secretary to the big man," she said proudly, "for thirty-two years."

The human body has a specific, encoded series of reactions to the feeling of being smothered. In the early stages it is panic. A medical doctor expects to see a cold sweat, fast shallow breathing, faster than normal heart rate, pinpoint pupils, shakes. Patients grimace with the effort of holding it all together, eyes wide, mouth open as they fight for air, using the sternocleidomastoid muscles of the neck and the very upper chest to expand the chest muscles and force apart the ribs so air can enter. Pure panic. Then, as CO_2 builds up, they become sleepy as carbon dioxide narcosis sets in.

The lab tech stuffed a blood gas test result into my fist as I studied Martha Stone. This patient smiled at me, though her relaxed lips were a frightening shade of gray-blue. Her pupils were slightly dilated. Her oxygen saturation level was at 70 percent and her CO_2 level was at 97. She wasn't fighting. She wasn't panicking. She wasn't becoming somnolent. She was dying right before my eyes and yet she was oriented, alert and calm.

I wrote orders and knew I should probably go ahead and intubate. Martha needed to be on the ventilator if her CO_2 levels rose any higher. She was actually past borderline. Yet I held off. Nurses and the respiratory therapist rushed to start additional IV lines, and breathing treatments of drugs that would relieve the symptoms.

I remembered the patient from the night before. The woman who was pain-free for the first time in ages. She had danced for me just to show me that she could. And her pupils had been slightly dilated, her blood pressure just a bit too low for her bulk. Were the people at the tent meeting being given some kind of drugs?

I gave additional orders and stood back to watch. Martha smiled at me, a satisfied smile I could see through the blue plastic of the mask and breathing tube used to administer drugs directly to her lungs. No panic at all.

Over the scanner, I heard another ambulance announce departure from the tent meeting. Another SOB on the way in. I didn't like the way this was heading.

I found the EMTs who brought in Martha Stone. They were lounging together at the nurses' desk, leaning against the extra-tall vertical length draped across the horizontal surface at the top, filling in the paperwork for the run. Mick Ethridge and Buzzy Munsey.

Mick and Buzzy had been on-again, off-again partners for the last few months, ever since Mick passed the paramedic exam. Mick was a wiry twenty-one-year-old milltown kid with an accent so broad he added vowel syllables to almost every word. Buzzy, laconic and in his mid-thirties, was an experienced paramedic. Both had been around long enough that I could read them easily. Neither had dilated pupils. Neither looked especially lethargic. "What's going on at that tent meeting, guys?" I asked as I slapped on latex gloves.

Buzzy shook his head. "Ain't never seen nothing like it."

Mick nodded. "There's people getting up and walking. A blind lady says she can see. And she was blind, I know. I brought her in one night for chest pain. And she says she can see! Described the tent and everything."

"Beats all I ever seen," Buzzy said.

"They passing out drugs over there? You see any

pills? Any drink? Anything?'' I could hear the anger in
my voice, a low controlled hum of suppressed fury.

The two shared a look I couldn't decipher.

"I'm getting patients with dilated pupils. Slow heart
rate. Lower than normal BP. Is there any way they are
on something?''

"Only thing I saw was the communion wine,'' Buzzy
said. "And they get only a sip of that.''

"I tasted it. It's bitter as all get out, but it didn't do
anything to me. Look at my eyes. I'm normal.''

"Mick, you ain't never been normal, boy. Not since
the day you was born.''

I interrupted the banter. "I'm getting a UDS on the
patient you brought in. If it's positive, you might want
to be tested, too, Mick.'' His scraggly eyebrows went up
as I turned and left.

I was angry. I was sure someone was giving my patients drugs, but I couldn't prove it. And if some small
devil's advocate part of my brain was insisting that I was
actively looking for problems because I was spooked by
Venetia Gordon's improvement, I was able to ignore it.
I ordered the urine drug screen to test for six specific
classifications of illegal and prescription drugs. There
were hundreds of other drugs that could cause the effects
I was seeing. The test could only pick out a few, but it
was all I had. Even large hospitals seldom tested for more
in-house. Other drug testing was sent to reference labs. I
added a written note that the urine and the patient's blood
should be held for further testing. The lab would do that
anyway, but I wanted it documented.

My other SOB came in, blue and struggling to breathe,
a faint tinge of panic on her features. I directed that this
one be put in a separate room. If one of them crashed, I
wanted plenty of space to work.

As the EMTs brought her in I saw movement behind me. A flash of gray, slightly hunched. Turning, I saw a child in a hospital gown, dishwater blonde, slight of build, furtive eyes. It was Na'Shalome, her intense gaze on me through fallen, oily strands of hair. She stood at the far edge of the nurses' desk, her body curved into the desk, fingers clawed into the top as if seeking protection from an avalanche.

I had contrived somehow to forget about the patients, one of whom I had mutilated, both the victims of torture. Wondering how she had gotten free of the restraints and sedation, I smiled. Na'Shalome showed her teeth at me, part grin, part feral snarl. I managed to hide my reaction to her expression and went back to work.

For two hours, I battled breathing problems in repeat patients. Most of them had preexisting lung conditions, and yet none had positive urine drug screens. The longer I worked, the madder I got. All but one patient had come from the tent meeting, and all the ones from the tent meeting wanted to tell me about miracles while they struggled to breathe. I wanted to tell them to go jump in a lake, that their precious miracle worker was making them sick, but I didn't. It wouldn't have helped and I couldn't prove anything. Not a thing. Whatever the people at the tent meeting were doing, they were doing it in such a way that the victims didn't even notice.

About eleven, I found a free moment to pour a fresh cup of coffee and dialed Mark's mobile. When he wasn't working, he usually went to bed about that time, and if I hadn't been so angry, I might have waited until morning to call. But I was hotter than the coffee.

"Yeeeellow," he said, sounding wide-awake.

"Scarlet. Vermilion. Crimson and cerise," I said, reining in my temper and playing my part in the silly phone game.

"Somebody bleeding all over you again, or is that the color of your temper?"

"Correct on the latter. I'm pissed." The word was crude, but it correctly denoted my state of mind.

"Ouch."

"Someone's practicing medicine in this county without a license."

"Who?" he said, instantly dropping into cop mode. A phone rang in the background, a second voice spoke. Without asking, I knew Mark was at the Law Enforcement Center, working late, like me. I remembered the smell of the grill, the taste of venison. He must have been called in to work on a case. It happened often.

"The miracle worker in the tent meeting." Even I could hear the derision in my voice on the words *miracle worker*. I drank some coffee to steady myself.

"Can you prove it?"

I didn't want to answer that one. "No," I said finally. "But I've got a lot of patients coming in acting weird."

"Is that a medical term?" Mark was laughing.

"Don't laugh at me. I have a problem and it's getting serious. I have patients coming in with decreased blood pressures, dilated pupils, and acting happy."

"Hmmm. That happy part sounds dangerous."

My lips turned up in unwilling amusement. "Okay, so it sounds silly. But seriously, Mark, I think something odd's going on out there."

"You got Saturday night off?"

"Yeah, why?" I asked, then thought instantly of Cam and dancing and of Shirl and moving and felt guilty.

"Let's go get us some religion."

"You mean go to the tent meeting?"

"Undercover," he whispered, laughter hidden in the breathy syllables.

"So I can't wear my scrubs and lab coat and you can't wear a windbreaker with the word police silk-screened on it?"

"You got it, babe. I'll pick you up at six-thirty. Wear something cool but rednecky."

"I can pull that off."

"I keep hoping." The phone clicked dead, with me trying to figure out what I had said that left him laughing. And then it hit me. *Pull that off.* I meant the redneck look. He meant the clothes. "Cute," I said to the phone, dropping it back in its cradle and rising to freshen my coffee.

"Healing hands."

I turned quickly and found Na'Shalome in the doorway. Her pupils were more normal-looking, but her skin was still pasty, sheened with oily sweat, circles beneath her eyes so dark she looked bruised. Under her gown, I could see bandaging across her abdomen. Boka had said she wanted to call in Michelle Geiger, the county OB/GYN to do reconstructive surgery. Had that been done already?

Down the hallway, a determined-looking African-American nurse strode toward us pushing a wheelchair. Na'Shalome focused on my coffee cup. A grimace of pain twisted her face. "Hands of evil maim and kill," she chanted so softly I could hardly hear. "Hands of healing do Lord's will."

Uncertain what to say, not knowing much about religion except what I picked up from Marisa over the years, I came up with, "Yes. They do. Sort of."

Her eyes flew to my face. Wild emotions roiled beneath the surface of her skin. Surprise, fear, even hope.

"Yes?" she whispered. She looked about to faint. I reached her just as she listed forward. "Healing hands," she moaned as I caught her one-handed, sloshing coffee over us both. The nurse reached her just in time, sliding the wheelchair beneath the girl's legs.

"Thanks," I said.

"You're welcome. This one's a handful," she said, strapping the girl into the wheelchair and positioning her feet.

"Demanding?"

"Nope. Just got the wanderlust. Dr. Geiger won't be happy we let her get away again. She's going to pull out her stitches."

"When was the surgery?"

"This morning. Anesthesiologist had a hard time keeping her down. You gotta warm blanket?"

Remembering the constricted pupils in the back of the van, I wasn't surprised. The girl was probably floating on a sea of illegal drugs. Leading the way to the warmer in the corner, I opened it and handed her a warm blanket.

"They found all kinds of scarring. Fibroids. Several chocolate cysts. Dr. Geiger said one looked like an eyeball," the nurse said, swathing her patient in the heated length of cloth and heading back up the hallway to the medical/surgical floor.

"Really?" I said, intrigued, following. Chocolate cysts were fluid-filled cysts containing their own blood supply and the patient's DNA. Often, the cysts had formed elements inside—hair, teeth, and I had heard of an actual eye being found inside.

"Yeah. Dr. Geiger saved one ovary, but had to remove everything else. Now the kid's spiking a temp."

"That's a shame. They called in DSS?"

"Yeah, but she has no ID and she ain't talking. We're

guessing her age at about seventeen. DSS took one look at her and called the cops.'' The nurse rolled her eyes. "She especially ain't talking to them. Come on, baby-girl, got to get you back to your bed."

I watched as the nurse pushed her charge up the hall-way, Na'Shalome's head tilting far to the side.

I was sitting when Mark entered the ER long after midnight Friday night. He was dressed in standard after-hours police-work clothes: jeans, T-shirt, windbreaker with POLICE emblazoned across the back, and his badge and gun on his waist. I lifted an eyebrow in question when he poured a cup of tarry coffee and sat in the break room with me.

"This is worse than LEC coffee," he said.

"Can't imagine why. Its only been cooking on the burner since seven or so. Should be just about perfect."

"You got time to drink a cup with me and take a look at something?"

I nodded to the table between us and my full cup. "I can make time."

"Ever seen anything like this?" Reaching into his windbreaker he extracted a book and slid it across the table to me. "It was in the van the other night."

The book was thin, about the size of a regular hardback book, but bound in soft, supple leather that begged to be touched, black on one side, white on the other. No title marred the surface, but both front and back were em-bossed. The white side was embossed with a tree growing inside a three-ringed circle, the depressed areas stained with green dye. The black side was embossed with a dead tree, one that might have been lightning-blasted. There was no circle around the dead tree, and no staining that I could see.

I stroked the surface, the leather worn but still in good repair. I opened the book from the white side and flipped slowly through the pages cover to cover, white side to black. "Oh," I said, after a few moments. "I see what you mean."

The book was strange, unlike anything I had ever seen. Half of the pages were ordinary white paper and black printing. The other half, the one that opened from the black cover, was on black paper, printed with white ink. The book was printed as if it were two books, the black paper printed upside down if the reader opened the book from the white side. I flipped several pages, reading a passage here and there.

It was a book of magic. Two kinds of magic.

The white pages were Wiccan magic, which I recognized from my short magic search on the Internet. It was earth magic, full of herbs and blessings and messages about reaping what one sowed. Some of it didn't entirely clash with messages I heard from the pulpit when I attended church with Marisa, stuff about love and forgiveness and treating everything in nature with respect. It seemed pretty innocuous.

The black pages were something else entirely. Where Wicca warned its users about misuse of power, the black pages were about blood magic, about blood sacrifice, about death and taking power over others. About retribution and murder. There were graphic illustrations in white ink on the black paper. In many, red ink had been added to show the flow of blood into vessels or onto altars, or over the head and body of the murderer.

I kept my face expressionless as I turned pages, reading a bit here, a bit there. It was gruesome stuff. Spells to stop your enemy's heart or clog his bowels or bring him boils. Spells to kill livestock. Spells to kill children in their sleep.

The paper felt slick. Oily. I had an urge to wipe off my fingers, though when I paused and inspected them, the skin was fine.

I turned to the front of the black pages looking for publication data—publisher's name, copyright information. There was nothing. Nor was there anything in the front of the white pages. I closed the book, slid it back across the table to Mark and surreptitiously wiped my hands on my scrub suit before picking up my coffee cup. "Nasty. Never seen anything like that."

"Do me a favor. Take it. Ask Miss Essie what she thinks about it."

"No way." I sipped my coffee. It tasted vile. Even worse than usual. I stood and rinsed the cup and the pot, found grounds in the cabinet and made a fresh pot as I talked. "She'd skin me alive if I brought it into her house. She nearly whipped the skin off my back when I was a kid and I brought a pack of tarot cards into her house. Miss Essie does not hold with evil in any form. You want her to see it, *you* take it to her."

Mark sighed. "I figured you might say that. Tell her I'm coming by, then. She can beat me if she wants."

"Why Miss Essie?" I asked.

"Miss Essie knows stuff," he said with a shrug. "She was one of the people who got rid of the root back in the sixties."

Thinking, I stood with my back to Mark and watched fresh coffee flow out of the coffeemaker and into the pot. The root was a Southern term. It meant root doctor, root medicine. It referred to a practice of medicine and religion brought over from Africa and blended with Christianity. It was also called voodoo in some circles, though there was a distinct difference that I had never bothered to learn.

I had seen evidence of the root in my short time in Charleston. I treated a man who claimed someone had put a root on him, meaning someone had hexed him, and he had died. I never did figure out how or why. His postmortem had been nonremarkable. In his case, the root could have been poison. The root could have been superstition. But whatever it was, the root was dangerous to some people. And they didn't necessarily have to believe in the root to be affected. My patient had not been a believer until he lay dying, his women wailing around him.

I hadn't known that Miss Essie had been involved with the root in Dawkins County. But as I stood with my back to Mark, I realized that I hadn't seen any evidence of the root, and hadn't even noticed that till now. If Miss Essie had gotten rid of the root in the county, then Miss Essie was a powerful woman indeed.

"Rhea?"

"Miss Essie got rid of the root? Here?"

"Yeah. My mother told me about it. Miss Essie and another woman ran the root practitioners and the main root doctor out."

I turned to Mark. "I'll tell Miss Essie you're coming by to see her. But I suggest that you keep that book out of her house. Is that book why you're up so late?"

"No. Not really. We had a stabbing over near the old Killian Mill. Pretty strange stuff, so I stayed around."

"Strange?"

"Yeah. Hinky." He grinned. *Hinky* was Mark's word for weird. It was clear he had enjoyed whatever had been hinky about the stabbing, but he didn't offer explanations and I didn't pry. Cops think the weirdest, most gruesome things are interesting and I had learned over the years not to ask too many questions.

Out in the hallway a patient limped by, trailing a splatter of blood. Mark looked at the patient and back to me, shook his head and stood. "Later, girl." He left, abandoning his cup for someone else to discard.

After Mark was gone, while the nurses were checking over the patient, I washed my hands again, this time under hot water, trying to clean the feel of the magic book from my fingers.

There were things I hadn't told Mark. Things about my past. For a while, my mother had played around with all kinds of magic. And none of it had been good.

I got plenty of sleep that night, a night without patients or dreams that I could remember, and woke at six-fifty feeling refreshed. The air was cool, the humidity was low for a change, and I was in a pretty good mood until I got home. Then it crashed fast. I had forgotten about Arlana coming home.

When I drove up to my yard, I found four piles of laundry on the driveway. One pile was sheets. One was towels. The other piles were whites and colored clothes. The back door was propped open, and as I idled in the drive I saw another towel fly through the air. Pup, rolling in the pile of damp towels, looked up happily and watched the towel fly, his huge tongue dangling to the side of his open mouth.

The cat, who seemed amused by all the activity, sat on the big rock, tail tip twitching. Moving slowly and feeling not a bit brave, I cut the engine and got out. I could hear the sound of the vacuum cleaner in the far reaches of the house. The scent of bleach and Pine Sol wafted from the back door.

Belle rose from the shade and padded over to me, her

head deferentially low, tail wagging slowly. I knelt and ruffled her dark hair, rubbing behind her ears the way she liked. Belle seemed to sigh in pleasure, lifting amber eyes to mine in happiness. "Arlana's home, huh?"

Belle whined softly, giving my chin a single lick. Pup swiveled and rose in a motion worthy of a Hollywood karate master and loped over, tripping once over a fallen twig. He raised up and rested his paws on my shoulders, looking down at his mama as if to say, "See what I can do?" I shoved him down, rubbed once on his head, and stood straight.

Squaring my shoulders, I entered my house. The sound of the vacuum was in the living room. Without speaking to Arlana, I moved into my bedroom, changed quickly into navy shorts, T-shirt and comfortable sandals, grabbed my extra-large laundry bags and ducked back outside. "Chicken," I whispered to myself.

I gathered up the laundry, stuffed it into the bags and then into my toy-size BMW, and took off. I could buy some time by making a laundry run, picking up a few groceries and stopping by Miss Essie's. "Chicken," I said again.

I reached Miss Essie's about nine, carrying in the only bag of groceries that might suffer from the heat. She had seen me drive up, waved me to the back and opened the door, leaving it cracked. "Morning, Miss Essie!" I called, closing the door behind me. Depositing the groceries in the mudroom's secondary fridge, I carried in a bag of blueberries. They had been on sale, ninety-nine cents a pint, and Miss Essie loved to make blueberry pie. I loved to eat blueberry pie, fresh out of the oven. With ice cream. Miss Essie and I got on perfectly where food was concerned.

When I reached the kitchen, I held out the bag. "Blue-berries!"

Miss Essie turned from the sink and fixed me with a hard stare. "You ain't cleaned that pigsty you live in since Arlana been gone?"

"Uhhhh."

"Don't you *uh* me. She call about six and say she drop by to leave you a present from New York, and she 'bout *fell out.* Place dank and dirty and smell like them dogs. *Nasty,* is what she say. Got *mold* in the bathroom." Miss Essie snatched the bag from my fingers. Slammed it on the kitchen counter.

"I know you mother din' do much toward teaching you the way things suppose to be done, her having her little problem and all. But I know Miss DeeDee done taught you when you go to work for her. I knows you know how to scrub and mop and vacuum."

"Miss Essie—"

"Don' you Miss Essie me neither." Her finger shook toward my face. "My Arlana say that place so nasty a pig wouldn't live there. You ain't even give that place a *lick-and-a-lie* since she been gone. *And* she say you got a *cat.*" Her head made an indignant jerk at the word.

"I don't have a cat," I said quickly, hoping to stave off anything worse.

"Arlana say you do. You got a cat, you leave it outside. Make it mouse for you," she instructed. "You don't let it inside where it can walk all over the counters and tables. People say cats is clean. But they walk on they litter box and then on the countertops. Uh-uh. They ain't clean. They be walking all over with salmonella and Ecoli all over they feets."

I wasn't about to argue. She had a point. And my house *was* a wreck. So I stood there, mute, giving her time to finish running me through the fire of her anger. There was no stopping Miss Essie when she got riled, and she was most definitely riled. Her purple shawl was off her shoulders, draped over a kitchen chair, a sure sign she was heated, hopping mad.

Her movements ragged with rage, Miss Essie opened the bag and pulled out the six pints of blueberries, dumping them into the waiting colander. "I shamed of you, girl." With a sharp glance she looked me over to see if I was wearing a bra, checking to see if I had transgressed further. "Hmmph," she said, running water over the fruit. "You hongry?"

"Yes, ma'am," I said meekly.

"I got some fresh yeast bread and homemade fig preserves I put up last night. Behind you." Her head jerked toward the built-in bread basket. As I reached for the rolltop she speared me again. "You gone apologize to my Arlana?"

"Profusely," I said. "And pay her well."

"Uh-huh."

I pulled out the loaf of bread and the wooden bread slicer, a loaf-shaped cradle with slots in the sides to measure off perfectly shaped and sized slices, found the serrated knife Miss Essie used to cut bread, a fine knife from Germany that probably cost more than some third world countries made in a year, and settled myself at the kitchen counter for a breakfast snack.

"Cam gone to tinker with his plane, then do some flying. He gone crash in that thing one day."

With the change of subject, I knew I was forgiven. "This jam is great, Miss Essie."

"Ain't jam," she said sternly. "Them fig preserves. Jam be something else entirely, though I don' 'spect you young peoples know the difference. Buy that trash off the shelves in the store. I put me a slice of lemon rind in mine.''

"It's good," I said through a mouthful. "Miss Essie?"

"Hmm?"

"You know anything about witchcraft?"

8

YOU SHAMED A' BEING OLD?

Miss Essie turned quickly from the sink, her eyebrows meeting together in the middle. "What you say?"

"I had this patient who came in the other night. Accident victim. She was drugged out. Had this doll with her."

As I described the doll, Miss Essie cut off the water, dried her hands and joined me at the counter. Her eyes on me, not missing a word, she poured us both coffee and settled onto a tall, padded stool.

"You say it painted? Like blood?"

"Yes, ma'am. And twined all over with beads and flowers."

She sipped, added cream and a spoon of sugar. Stirred, sipped, thinking all the while. "Painted like fresh blood or old blood?" she demanded.

"Fresh blood. Arterial."

Miss Essie nodded, her grizzled head moving thoughtfully. She drank again. I drank, too, the coffee far superior to the tarred caffeine from the ER coffeemaker. "She say anything to you?"

I thought it was a strange question. "She said several things."

"Anything that seem out of place. Mysterious, maybe?"

I remembered the odd chanted words and paused as they resurfaced in my mind. "'Hands of evil maim and kill. Hands of healing do Lord's will.' Something like that."

Miss Essie put down her coffee cup, her eyes holding mine. "Say that again. Jus' like she say it."

I repeated the phrase, with the odd inflection the girl had given it each time, the accents even on each syllable.

Miss Essie drew away, sitting back in her tall seat. Reaching over, she took her purple shawl, this one crocheted in lightweight summer yarn, the strands silky and carefully knotted. The shawl seemed to glisten in the morning light. She shook it out, placing it around her shoulders. Then she stood and went back to the sink and the blueberries. I waited as she rinsed the fruit, lifted the stainless-steel colander, letting the water run out. She shook the colander, spraying the sink lightly, then put it on a towel to drain. She wiped the sink and counter and came back to me. Her eyes were troubled.

"Some things is bes' not looked into too deep. Powers and principalities. Things a' darkness. This one a' them things."

"I don't understand."

"Spells. What she saying a spell. That doll, it one a' three things. Ain't none a' them good. All a' them a danger. Evil is evil, one way or another." She pulled her shawl tighter around her shoulders as if she was suddenly cold. "And that all I got to say."

I drank my coffee, waiting her out. Miss Essie puttered around the kitchen neatening things, pulling the silver, china and the tableware from the dishwasher, putting them away.

"Don't you think I need to know?" I said finally, after giving her time to think. "If she was spelling me..."

"I don' think she spelling you exactly." Miss Essie raised up, one hand on the counter, her gaze far off.

"Why not?"

"'Cause a' the doll."

"So? You said it could be three things."

Finally she nodded. "I tell you. And if that girl do anything else that don' look right, you tell me. We got us an agreement?"

I had already slid perilously close to breach of patient confidentiality. What was another inch? I nodded.

"That doll, it sound like a toy."

"How can a toy be dangerous?"

"Anything be dangerous it be used in the wrong way."

I could see her point. I liked sugar and fat, but if not used in moderation, they became dangerous.

"If it a toy, like I think, then it dangerous to the chile's soul. If it ain't a toy, then her soul may be lost already."

I felt a sudden chill as the AC blew cold air up from the floor. "Why?"

"'Cause if she ain't playin' then she done took the nex' step. And she made that doll one a' two things. One is a hub. That be a focus for blood spells. Spells that control somebody who done hurt to her, or a focus for spells to control someone she want power over. The other thing it could be is a gateway."

Miss Essie turned away from me, standing with her back to me, gripping her shoulders over the purple silk shawl. Not working. Just standing, rocking slightly, as if thinking deep thoughts.

"What's a gateway, Miss Essie?" I asked softly.

She seemed to come back from a long distance, her eyes gradually focusing on me. Her back straightened, her shoulders stiffened. "A gateway be a portal to the spirit world. A place for spirits to come and go, like a doorway."

Because she seemed so serious I didn't laugh, though nervous laughter bubbled inside me somewhere. But I still felt cold, as if her words had chilled me even more than the air-conditioning.

Omens. Portents. Hogwash, whispered some steady, logical part of me. "Evil spirits? Like in possession?"

"Any spirits. Not all spirits evil. Some jist lost. Some tryin' to decide whose side they want to be on in the heavenly war. Some even friendly to mankind. But some..." Her voice trailed off, her eyes still strong on mine. I sipped my cold coffee.

"I know you don' believe. I know you think all life is jist flesh and bone, germs and viruses, mankind and nature. But they's some things can't be explained away by all that. Some things jist strange. This one a' them, I'm thinking."

"Supernatural stuff." The very words seemed to calm me. Hogwash...

But Miss Essie nodded slowly.

"I thought if you believed in God, you couldn't believe in supernatural stuff."

"If you believe in God then you do believe in supernatural stuff. You make a choice to worship God and not dabble in things bes' left to him to take care of. This one a' them things, I be thinkin'. Dangerous things. I be prayin' about it. Taking it to the Lord. I be prayin' over you, too, even more than usual, les you get lost, too."

I nodded. I knew Miss Essie prayed over me often. I didn't think it did much good, but it didn't seem to hurt. "Miss Essie, Mark Stafford has a book of magic he wants you to look at later today. I told him to bring it by the house, and that you would look at it outside."

Miss Essie nodded, her expression strange, as if she saw something far away that I couldn't see.

"You know I don't believe in magic," I said gently. "Charms and love potions and voodoo dolls, hexes and juju."

"You a docta," she said, still looking away, speaking slowly. "Doctas din' believe in zombies neither till somebody figure out that makin' a zombie possible. Find the recipe what use blowfish poison. Doctas got to know *how* something work afore they accept that it work. They is trash magic like you talking about, and then they is *magic.*" Miss Essie looked at me hard, her black eyes like old polished stone. "Magic a fact, even if mos' of it in the mind of the believer and the rest be root and herbs and poison for the brain. Fear and poison. That kind a magic can kill...or be an excuse to kill."

Fear and poisons. That was psychology and medicine. Those I could understand. Suddenly, magic didn't seem quite so weird, if you left out the part about hubs and gateways.

"You go on back home now. Take your groceries out the fridge and go." Miss Essie made little shooing gestures with her fingers, her eyes suddenly focused and sharp again. "I take care of Mark Stafford. You go back and offer your mose sincere apologies to my girl, and get to work gettin' that pigsty clean."

I groaned.

"Um hum. You be groaning all right. My Arlana gone take off a layer of flesh with her tongue-lashing. You be wise, you be brining her a present and paying her real well, too."

"A present?" That was a great idea. A bribe to slow

Arlana's temper. I had never thought of that. "Like what?"

"My girl like jewelry. And them gold hair things, but they cost a arm and a leg. Get her some earbobs, the dangly kind. Gold. I like her in gold." She shooed me again and I left to make a quick trip back into town to the jewelry store, hoping my yogurt and goat cheese wouldn't go bad before I got home.

I stopped at the DorCity Gems and Jewels and bought Arlana a pair of earrings, fourteen-carat gold, because I remembered the stench of the bathroom before she got to it. They dangled like Miss Essie suggested, each with tiny sapphires on the end of a dozen gold chains. I spotted a pair of gold hoops, tiny thick things, which I liked. I had never worn jewelry, except when John and I were engaged; the huge, heirloom Micheaux emerald had weighed down my finger, the heirloom earrings and brooches and necklaces feeling cold on my skin.

On impulse, I bought the earrings and forced them through the nearly sealed holes in my pierced ears. They looked good with my shaggy, short, sooty hair. I waited while the dangly earrings were gift wrapped, then I went next door and bought a card, tucking a hundred-dollar bill into it. I figured Miss Essie would approve. Arlana deserved the payment for cleaning my pigsty.

Arlana let me off easily, at least from her point of view. She was standing in a cloud of dust when I arrived home, her dark hair wrapped in a silk scarf, the vacuum cleaner still roaring. I came in and started putting away the groceries, the dogs winding anxiously around my feet and between my legs, threatening to flip me over. They had picked up on the aura of anger in the house, and couldn't decide whether to protect me or run and hide beneath the bed.

Arlana was younger than I by more than ten years, but there was no doubt that she was the stronger personality. Said more simply, I was scared to death of her in a righteous temper. The way the dogs were acting, I figured she was feeling justifiably angry today and that I would suffer for it.

I was finished with the groceries and had started on the sinkful of dishes when the vacuum cut off and the pad/slap of rubber flip-flops moved up the hallway. She didn't say anything, just stood behind me, wordless. Waiting. The dogs curled beneath the table, Belle whining softly.

I washed, scraping dried food off the plates, the new cheap ironstone clinking dully, envisioning Arlana, arms akimbo, a scowl on her face. After a few moments of the terrible silence, I couldn't stand it anymore, dropped the rag into the hot water and turned. Her gift sat on the high counter between us, the card propped so she could spot it.

She was staring at the card, head back, slender hips canted, petite breasts shoved aggressively against the dirty T-shirt she wore, nostrils flared. Without looking my way, she said, "This house so bad even the dogs know it dirty." I said nothing; she was right. Arlana's eyes stayed on the gift. "It bad when I first come here. It worse now. It don't get this bad all by itself." Still I said nothing. Arlana shifted on the pink flip-flops. They squeaked slightly on the dirty floor. "You had to work to make it this dirty. And I *ain't* you maid."

I nodded, picked up a drying rag and twisted it to give my hands something to do. "I'm a pig and an ungrateful friend. I deserve to be flayed alive, boiled in oil and served up as shish kebabs.'' Her expression didn't change. "I'm sorry. I really meant to clean up before you got home.''

Face impassive, her head nodded to the counter. "That a bribe? Think you can buy your way outta the mess a' this house?''

"God, I hope so.''

Her lips twitched.

"Because only mercy and a kindhearted woman will save my backside.''

One delicately arched eyebrow lifted. "What in the box?''

"Jewelry. Gold. And a hundred-dollar bill in the envelope.''

"Real gold?''

"Yes, ma'am.''

"Hmmph,'' Arlana said, doing a fine imitation of Miss Essie. "I ain't feelin' merciful or kind. I'm feelin' dirty and abused and mighty unhappy.''

"Would it help if I said I really am ashamed and embarrassed. That I know I'm a slob. And I don't deserve your friendship and the way you take care of me.''

"No. It would not.''

That didn't sound promising, but Belle quit whining and thumped her tail on the floor. I took a chance on Belle's senses and went again for humor.

"Okay, so I won't say it.''

Arlana fought a grin and lost. Finally flicked a glance my way. "Fourteen-carat?''

"With real sapphires on the end of little gold chains. Cost me an arm and leg.''

"You gonna help me get this place clean?''

"I'll clean all day. And I already took the clothes to the laundry.''

"You a filthy pig, you know that."

"I know that. But I didn't do it to abuse you. I did it because…" I realized I had no good reason for not cleaning. "Because I'm a pig."

"Long as we got that straight."

"I'll finish the dishes, clean the cabinets and then come help you."

"You finish the dishes, clean the cabinets with bleach, and then you mop this floor with bleach and Pine Sol. That cat been all over this place."

"I don't have a cat," I said, unable to keep the exasperation out of my voice.

"Well, it got you." She nodded to the antique table, over the tops of Belle's and Pup's heads. The long-haired cat was stretched out on the table, huge front paws milking a heavy piece of pottery that held peaches. Her yellow eyes were on me. The cat was so big, she stretched across the kitchen table, looking wild and vaguely like a young bobcat. The dogs hadn't chased her off. They didn't seem to mind that an intruder was in the house.

"I don't like cats," I said to the feline interloper. She yawned, clearly bored.

"It left a dead rat on the back stoop. It done claimed this place. It done claimed you. Bes' thing you can do is get it shots and give it a name. It home." Arlana finally reached forward and deigned to open the card, which she read, face slightly averted.

"Get!" I said to the cat, flapping the drying rag at it. She ignored me, the tufts of hair at her ears twitching, tail tip working as if amused.

"Nice card," Arlana said, tucking the hundred-dollar bill into her shorts pocket. "I done pick out a name for that cat. Selicia Stone. 'Cause she look like my friend Selicia, all that wild hair and streaks and all."

"You named her, you take her." I walked closer to the cat and she yawned again.

"She yours. You bes' buy a litter box and some cat food." Arlana ripped into the paper on the small gift box.

"How'd she get in here anyway?" I reached out a hand and ran it down the cat's side. She didn't jump up and run or claw me. Instead, she closed her eyes and purred, the sound like a motor on idle. A big motor. Her fur was softer than I expected, darker and longer hair on top, delicate and downlike beneath.

"She come in with the dogs through the doggie door. Belle seem to like her fine. Pup bark awhile till I tole him to shush. Ohhhh." Arlana held the earrings up to each ear, turning sparkling eyes to me, a smile at last lighting her features. "Oh, I like. I got me some blue contact lenses I can wear with my blue dress and I look *fiiiine* all got up!"

I grinned at her, and her face crunched down into a scowl. "But you still a pig."

"Oink."

Arlana laughed and slipped the jewelry back into the velvet box, closed the lid and walked/slapped the few steps to me. She hugged me. Hard. I was surprised. Arlana wasn't the touching kind. For that matter, neither was I, but I hugged her back. "I'm glad you're home," I said as she released me.

"Me, too. New York still a place full a' depression and sadness, and it stinks like exhaust. Them peoples got to have lungs blacker than a coal mine."

"You decide how you intend to spend the rest of your life?"

"I ain't around you more'n ten minutes and you already harping on school. I start nursing in two weeks."

I sighed and returned to the sink.

"And don't you go on about me bein' a decorator. Can't make but twenty thousand the first year as a decorator with a four-year education. Can make over fifty thousand as a nurse with a two-year degree. I can decorate on the side if I got the mind."

She was right. But then, Arlana was far smarter than I about life and living and important decisions. "Okay. Do I need to go sign for your loan?"

"Okay? That it? You been gibber-jabbering on about decorating school for six months and more and all you got to say is okay?"

I looked over my shoulder at her. "I know when I'm beaten."

"Well, praise the Lord." Arlana flapped down the hall, Pup at her heels, chasing the flip-flops and stumbling over his big paws. I plunged my hands into the hot water and scrubbed gunk off a plate. The soaking had done some good, old food sliding off the stoneware. The cat jumped and landed beside me, sticking her paw into the pile of bubbles and swatting them. I dried my hands and pulled her away, exposing her belly. The fur there was a lighter shade of brindled gray. "Arlana," I called.

"What?" she yelled from the front of the house.

"Selicia Stone is a Steven Stone!"

She poked her head back into the room, her scowl back in place. "I hope not. He be spraying all over this place."

"Even if he's neutered?"

"Maybe not then. Steven Stone? After Marisa's husband?"

"No!" I said, startled. I hadn't even thought about Marisa's soon-to-be-ex-husband. The cat rolled back into a less submissive position and swatted at the bubbles again. "Something else, then."

"There a deejay in Ford County name a' Steven Stone.

He a good-lookin' man, I hear. Good name. But if he mine, I call that cat Stoney." She pointed at the cat curled on the counter. "Stoney, you start marking your territory in this house, I take off what left a' your manhood." And she was gone again.

As if he understood the threat, Stoney the cat rolled off the cabinet and leaped to the floor, padding regally to the dog bowl where he drank with delicate motions. Belle, looking bored, watched him move. It seemed as if I had a cat. I didn't need another animal. Didn't want another animal. Tail twitching, Stoney sauntered off to explore.

I cleaned till I was sneezing with dust and the skin of my hands ached from strong cleansers. I scrubbed, mopped, dusted and disinfected till the house was pronounced livable by Arlana. It was nearly six when she called a halt to the process, handed me some salve for my irritated hands and a gift-wrapped box. She plopped down on the living-room sofa, newly vacuumed and plumped, and watched me.

"What's this?" Squishing a bit of salve onto my hands and rubbing it in, I took the wingback chair beside the sofa. She passed me a cold Coke, popped the top on her own Diet Coke, and waited. I remembered, somewhere in the long day, that Miss Essie had said Arlana had a gift for me. I opened my own can, drank and lifted the present. For its size, it was heavy.

"Mama Essie say you never celebrate your birthday. Not ever. I say that a sin. Life meant to be honored and your birthday specially. Open it."

I never told people my birthday. I wasn't raised with birthdays being important. My mother had spent so much time in a bottle that gifts weren't expected and holidays

weren't celebrated. I stared at the box. It was wrapped in
bright red and blue paper, a curly tuft of ribbons tying
the paper closed at the top. Slowly, I tore the paper, the
sound suddenly loud in the house. My birthday hadn't
been celebrated since I broke up with John and moved
from Charleston to Dawkins County. Almost two years
ago to the day, he had gifted me with the Micheaux emerald and pearl earrings in their heavy baroque settings
and a small brass telescope. I had returned the Micheaux
jewelry, but I still had the telescope. I had just dusted it
and put it back in place on my kitchen window ledge.
Like the earrings, it was antique, heavy with the work-
manship of two centuries.

Beneath the paper was a small, pale jewelry box, gray
as Stoney's underbelly. I opened the box and found a
jeweled pin inside. A gold lion lying with front paws
crossed, two emerald green eyes staring right at me. It
could have been a gaudy bauble, but was saved by the
simple fact of its delicate design. The lion's lines were
traced with fine strokes, the muscles of the thighs seeming to quiver as the light hit the gold. I blinked away
tears.

"You tole that man a' yours that your birthday this
week?"

"No," I said firmly. There was no point in arguing
with Arlana that Mark was not my man. She had decided
that Mark and I were a couple destined for the altar and
nothing would dissuade her.

"You shamed a' being old?"

I snorted through my tears and wiped my nose on the
back of a wrist. Hands shaking, I pinned the brooch to
my T-shirt. "No. I'm not ashamed of being old. I'm only
old to a child like you." This time it was Arlana who
snorted. "I'm just not ready to enter the gift-giving stage

of a relationship yet. Before last August, Mark and I weren't exactly speaking."

"Because he found out about John," she prompted, drinking her Diet Coke, long neck moving with the motion of swallowing.

"I told him about John. Mark wanted…well…he wanted more than I wanted at the time."

"Say it like it is," she said with pursed lips and arched eyebrows. "The man wanted to do the dirty deed and you wasn't ready."

I hid a smile behind my Coke can and ignored her comment. "And then when Christmas came, John and I were talking and planning our trip to the mountains."

"Now, that was a damn-fool thing to do if I ever heard a' one. Hiking the mountains in the middle a' the winter." When I looked at her innocently, she batted her eyes and added, "Long, cold nights with plenty a' time for the dirty deed, though. I gotcha," she said with a swivel of her neck. "And his birthday in October, so you just managed to get out a' buying your Mark anything for two holidays."

"Something like that," I acknowledged. "I think I would hate shopping at Puckey's Guns 'n' Things. What do you buy a man who loves hunting, dogs and cigars?"

"Something from Victoria's Secret."

I laughed, feeling the Coke tingle in my nose.

"He even know when your birthday is yet?"

"Nope. Never asked."

"He'll be mad you don't tell him."

I shrugged, uncomfortable.

"I got a picture picked out for over your mantel."

Grateful for the change of subject, I shook my head. "I have to pay off a certain jewelry bill first."

"You'll like it."

"Liking it isn't the problem. I always like whatever you bring me. But I'm flat broke."

"Next month?"

Stoney jumped into my lap, pressed his front paws into my leg. "Ouch. Listen, Stoney, you and I have to have a talk about this house and my person. No drawing blood."

"That cat think this house and your person is both his. You might as well give up and accept it. My guess is? He'll claim the bed and be sleeping with you inside a week. He a man. He'll take over. You tell me I'm not right," she predicted darkly. I had a bad feeling Arlana was right, but with Stoney purring like an unmuffled eight-cylinder engine, his fur warm against my fingers, I just couldn't seem to care.

9

I DIDN'T KNOW YOU COULD DO COUNTRY

Mark, green eyes hidden behind dark glasses, picked me up for the tent meeting at six-thirty Saturday, just as promised, idling down the driveway in his old, beat-up, farm truck. I had seen the truck the one time I toured his family farm. The dented, multicolored, patched and fenderless vehicle looked as though it wouldn't last another day. The sound of the engine suggested things might be a bit different beneath the hood.

I climbed in the unairconditioned cab, dropping my medical bag on the metal floorboard at my feet and propped an elbow in the open window. "Nice truck."

"Nice duds."

"Thank you, kind sir."

"I didn't know you could do country," he said slowly.

I looked down at my gray, hand-stitched cowboy boots, ironed jeans and plaid, sleeveless, cotton shirt, the recumbent lion pinned to my left shoulder. I took in his jeans, boots and dark T-shirt with a small round can in the front pocket. A cowboy hat rested on the seat between us. "I can do country," I said loftily. "No problem. I didn't know this truck could move."

"She can move." Mark gave the engine some gas and

it rumbled smoothly. "Believe me, she can move." He tucked a toothpick between his lips and chewed gently. He looked every inch the redneck country boy. The only thing missing was a rebel flag hanging in the back window of the truck.

"Perfect touch," I said of the toothpick.

He grinned happily, clenching the toothpick in his molars. "I thought so." A moment later, he shifted into gear and we backed down my driveway. "Who ironed your jeans?"

"The laundress."

"Just as a point of interest, redneck girls and PWTs don't have laundresses." Mark flicked the toothpick expertly to the other side of his mouth and gunned the old truck down Starlight Lane. "They go to the Laundromat." PWTs were poor white trash. Mark considered himself an expert on PWTs.

"You said I was going for country, not redneck. Besides, I look wonderful. Arlana said so."

The heat hadn't died. The vinyl upholstery was hot beneath my jeans, the strip of aluminum blazing beneath my arm, the air hanging humid and heavy. Early-evening sun heated the gold earring in my right ear and the lion pin affixed to my shirt. Engine rumbling powerfully, we joined a line of vehicles, most of them trucks and Jeeps and dualies, some ancient and dented cars. Ahead was the tent meeting, organ music blaring down the overheated asphalt.

"Well," he said finally, "mustn't argue with Arlana on the subject of rednecks and PWTs, and the proper way to dress at a country tent meeting."

Mark and I fit right in, though a big gun in the gunrack might have added to the authenticity. My ironed jeans didn't stand out too much in the milling crowd, and

Mark's hat and small round container of Skoll added to the reality of the moment. He beat the hat against his leg as we walked, my hands in my pockets, from the parking area.

It felt good to walk beside him. We weren't holding hands. Public displays of affection were not for either of us. But we were intensely aware of each other in the humid heat, the sun beating down on us like a hot-tempered child with metal spoons and a kitchen pot. We hadn't been close in recent months, the distance part his fault, part mine. Now it seemed easy again. Companionable.

Mark had killed a man saving me. If I had trusted him, if I had told him my thoughts and fears, Mark could have simply arrested the man. Instead, he had shot him to get me away safely. Since that time, there had been a space between us. A sort of vacuum. Like an empty darkness. For the first time, it seemed to be gone.

Smoke from the bonfire billowed around us, rich-smelling and spicy. People ran and walked and shouted. It was a bit like an old-time country fair. A special burning permit was tacked to a tent flap. Cozy.

From the corner of my eye, I saw Mark reach up and touch the can in his pocket. "You put any of that stuff in your mouth," I said casually as we ambled toward the big top, "and you can whisper goodbye to any thought of a good-night kiss."

"I'll consider myself warned," he said, lips twitching beneath the mustache.

We were supposed to be here incognito, so before we sat I wandered over to the ambulance crews sitting upwind of the bonfire, doors of the unit open, lawn chairs in the partial shade of nearby trees. Country music, turned down low, emanated from the ambulance unit.

Evan Yarborough, legs stretched out, booted feet crossed, nodded at me as I approached, and spoke when I was in range. "Mark. Doc. Almost didn't recognize you in people clothes. Last time I saw you, you were ankle deep in blood and amputated limbs, in the back of a wrecked van."

I placed the voice from the amputation only days past. "That was you and Buzzy helping in there?"

"Yep. We're all still talking about it." He shook his head as if remembering the hellish scene. "You did a good job, Doc."

"So did you guys. But I don't know how you stand it day in and day out, cutting people out of wrecks."

He pursed his lips. Evan was in his forties, balding, stout in a solid, weight lifter kind of body type. "I do okay until it's some little kid, and his mother or dad didn't secure him in a restraint. Then it's hard. Especially if the driver doesn't have a scratch on him."

"Yeah, I have to pull him off the occasional idiot. Howdy, Doc."

I turned at the fresh voice. It was Mick Ethridge, carrying cold Cokes and packages of Twinkies. He had sweated through his uniform, the fabric of the white shirt clinging to his thin frame as he settled and handed the snacks to Evan. "Evening, Cap'n. You understand that I was just joking. No EMS personnel would ever resort to violence at an accident scene. No matter how much they deserved it."

"Of course," Mark said, tossing the toothpick to the other side of his jaw. "Just like no cop would ever use unnecessary force in an arrest. No matter how much the perp deserved it."

"Right," Mick said, an amused gleam in his eyes. "Just like that."

I rolled my eyes. "Mark and I are here to see what's going on at these meetings. What do you—"

As if I had said something awful, Mick and Evan sat upright fast, but their gazes were looking past me. I whirled to see what had caught their attention.

A woman ran from the parking lot, screaming. "Help! Help me!"

The men were up and running, Cokes and Twinkies forgotten. I ran after Mick as Evan started the ambulance with a roar and slammed it into gear. Behind me, Mark shouted, "So much for incognito!"

Mick and I followed the pointing hands and shouts to a fallen man. He was on his back, hands clawing the ground at his sides, head thrown back, tendons and veins in his neck distended. Beneath a horrid red flush he was turning blue. He wasn't breathing.

Mick skidded into a kneeling crouch and bent over the man, immediately checking his airway. Settling more slowly, I tore open his shirt, sending buttons flying. I felt for the man's pulse at his throat. It was pounding and rapid, maybe 180.

"Nothing," Mick said. "No obstruction, no breath sounds."

The crowd pushed in closer, the woman's screams growing louder and softer by turns as she ran back and forth through the crowd in a panic.

Mark dropped to my side, thrusting my black bag into my hands. I hadn't noticed him detouring to his truck. With a snap, I opened the bag and tossed Mick the blood pressure cuff. Found my stethoscope and checked the man's breath sounds. I heard the unit pull up behind me. Heard Mark clearing the crowd back. But didn't hear anything from the man's chest except his bounding heart.

Mick was right, no air was moving in or out. I yanked the earpieces out of my ears.

"Anything?" Mick asked.

"No." I felt around the man's throat, my fingers probing quickly. It looked as though there might be external swelling of veins and tissues. The man's face was flushed a bright red while his skin was growing cold and clammy. His pulse was sky-high. Evan secured a mask and ambu bag over the man's mouth and compressed the balloon. Air made little burping noises as it escaped the mask's edges. The man's airway was totally compromised. "Blood pressure?" I asked as I tried three quick abdominal thrusts to remove any possible obstruction. Nothing came up. No food, no air.

"It's 280 over 120."

I made my diagnosis on what I had available, which wasn't much. "Get me an ET kit, large-bore IV with Benadryl and Epinephrine, and O_2."

"Yes, ma'am. You want the Epi through the endo tube, too?"

"Sure. Why not," I said as Evan tossed me the ET kit. I ripped it open and pulled the laryngoscope blade out, then nodded to Mick to move the man to the stretcher so I could get a good working angle. The emergency medical workers tossed the man to the stretcher as uniformed city cops, arriving on the scene a little late, ordered people back and gave me room to work.

"Pull him off the end," I said. The EMTs knew what I meant and pulled the patient up the stretcher so that his head was hanging off. Evan was starting a line in the man's arm, while Mick prepared to assist me. "Ready to apply pressure?" I asked, meaning to press on the man's cricoid cartilage in his throat.

"Ready when you are," he said, positioning himself

to lie across the man to restrain him if needed. It wasn't easy to tube a patient who was conscious, but I had no choice. Four minutes to brain damage. I estimated we were looking at two now. The man was gray, his motions becoming random and confused.

I pressed back a bit on the man's head, angled the blade, which looked like a hinged metal shoehorn, and inserted it between the man's teeth, through his mouth and said, "Now!" as I moved it down his throat. Mick applied pressure on the outside of the man's throat to keep the blade in place. The patient bucked as the blade triggered primal reflexes in his throat, which was swollen shut.

This was definitely anaphylactic shock, I decided as I hunted for the twin muscles that gave humans the ability to speak. "More," I said to Mick, who pressed harder. Finding the vocal cords, I eased the end of the blade through, reached a blind hand out for the plastic ET tube and glanced at it when it was slapped into my palm. Holding it up, I said, "Put some stuff on it."

Mick opened a small foil packet of lubricant and globbed the contents on. I bent back and inserted the tube through the small space in the laryngoscope blade down to the man's bronchial tubes. Even with the lubricant I felt tissue tear as the ET tube went down, yet everything looked good and I held the tube in place while I removed the blade. The patient had stopped bucking, unconscious from lack of air.

"Bag him, 100 percent O_2."

Mick nodded and pushed the ambu bag onto the tube end, attached an air line to the oxygen canister in the unit and turned it on. Pure oxygen hissed through the line and Mick pumped twice, quickly.

"One large-bore IV going, normal saline, wide open," Evan said.

"Benadryl."

"Going in now."

"Give it a minute and give the Epinephrine."

"I've got an Epi ready for the ET tube," Mick said.

"Hang on." I positioned the bell of the stethoscope on the left side of the man's chest. Good strong heart sounds. Two good breath sounds. Two more. Then the right side. Two good sounds, followed by two more. "Good tube placement. Give the Epi. O_2 sat?" I asked, wanting to know the oxygen saturation level of the man's bloodstream as measured through the skin and nail of a finger.

The woman, held back by a friend in the crowd, broke loose and threw herself across the man, screaming in breathless little bursts. "Belvin! Belvin! Oh Jesus, Belvin!"

"Sat is 83 and climbing. Eighty-five."

"Good," I said. "Get him to ER. Good work, guys." The woman ran for her car, still calling Belvin's name and breathing like a leaky bellows as Mick and Evan lifted the stretcher, easing it into the back of the ambulance.

"You, too, Doc. That was quick," Evan said.

"Oh." I stopped as a thought struck, and looked up at Mick, already in the back of the unit with the patient. "Should I have stood back and asked if you wanted my help? What's the field protocol here?"

"Protocol?" Evan asked. "I'd call it, 'He who can, does.' Help out anytime, Doc."

Evan slammed the doors and went to the front of the unit, revved the engine and pulled away from the parking lot. The hysterical woman followed them in her car, weaving and unsteady as she accelerated and braked. The crowd thinned and fell away, leaving Mark and me standing together in a dusty field, surrounded by trucks and cars and the blowing smoke.

I was sweaty and hot and more than a little dusty, having ruined the crease in my ironed jeans. Mark took the black bag and deposited it in the truck once more. As he returned, he grinned. "You do country better and better, girl. I think it's the dirt on your knees. Very authentic."

"Gee, thanks," I said, managing to put just enough sarcasm into the words to make him laugh.

The service wasn't what I anticipated. I had expected guitars, drums and an organ blasting old hymns, lots of heaving breaths and breast-beating and melodramatic tears, maybe a snake handler or two, repeated passing of a coffee-can offering plate and lots of drugs changing hands. I got something quite different.

The bonfire blazed hotly, strangely scented smoke billowing into the tent from fifty yards away, adding to the heat. Instead of a live band, taped organ music played, surprising me with Beethoven's *Ode to Joy*. No one danced in the aisles. No one rolled in the dirt. There was no breast-beating. An old man, skinny as a rail and bent like a staff, walked through the tent waving a smudge stick—a bunch of burning herbs. But the only smell I recognized was rosemary, the scent potent and cool in the broiling heat.

"Call upon the name of the Lord," he intoned gently. As he walked, the crowd quieted. "Call upon the name of the Lord." His voice rang, gravelly and rough.

"Lord, hear our prayer," a woman said softly nearby. The crowd picked up the phrase, inserting it between the old man's. "Lord, hear our prayer." The music died slowly, its volume dropping away, lost in the sea of voices.

Mark and I took a seat in the back and I looked around, studying the crowd. Congregation? Was it still a congregation if it wasn't in a church? They were all in hot-weather clothes—shorts, T-shirts, sandals, some jeans, some women in sundresses. No one was in a suit and tie or a Sunday-go-to-meeting dress and wide-brimmed hat. Some appeared to have come from work, discarding jackets and rolling up sleeves. Most were overweight by at least twenty pounds, many by much more, though that may have been simply a slice of Americana, not anything unusual. Some needed a bath and shave. Many, more than I could estimate, were sick. Wheelchair bound. On crutches. Carrying little green portable oxygen containers as they chanted along with the old man. "Lord, hear our prayer," they said together, looking expectant, hopeful, fearful by turns. As if this was their last chance for health and happiness.

The old man—I judged him to be about mid-fifties but unhealthy enough to appear much older, and in serious need of dental work—came back through, this time carrying a carved wooden cup, a bag hung on his shoulder. He was offering something to eat from the bag at his side, and something to drink from the cup. Lots of people were crowding around, asking to be fed, though it looked like a pitiful snack. After he fed each one, the old man gave them a sip from the same cup, wiping the brim between drinkers. It was clearly unsanitary. They grimaced as they swallowed, as if the stuff was bitter. I could hear the old guy speaking as they drank.

I had seen a similar ritual in Marisa's church. "Is that what I think it is?" I asked Mark in a whisper.

"The Lord's Supper," he murmured.

The old man neared, and I could hear him muttering, the words growing clear as he moved toward us from the front of the tent. "Body and blood of the Lamb. Body and blood of the Lamb. Call upon the Name of the Lord. Call upon the Name of the Lord."

"Yeah," I said. "Thought so." I figured everyone in this crowd was sharing enough germs to cause an epidemic. If anyone was carrying viral hepatitis the whole county would be sick. The man moved on without offering any of the food to Mark and me. We didn't complain. No one seemed to be enjoying it much.

The wind shifted and bonfire smoke blew in. I thought I smelled rosemary again, and oregano. Maybe a little basil. Something woodsy and dark, like mesquite and hickory. I liked the smell, and wondered how Mark's thick steaks would taste if cooked over that bonfire.

Suddenly, I knew what might have caused the anaphylactic shock in the man. Rosemary. Some people were deathly allergic to the herb and would react quite violently to the scent or taste. If the man were allergic to rosemary or some other aromatic herb, and it was put on the bonfire, he could easily have a reaction like the one we had just seen. I told Mark my theory and he sniffed the scented smoke, nodding. Most cops take a basic emergency-medicine course at some point in their professional lives and Mark was no exception. He understood what I was saying.

The pasture where the huge tent was pitched wasn't flat, but angled, and the altar or rostrum or whatever it was called was on the high end of the field, giving a sloped, easy view of the front of the tent where a small cubical of dun-colored material seemed to billow with the wind. I breathed deeply of the smoke-filled air, and felt oddly content to be in the crowd of people, with Mark.

The old man came by again. Surprising me, Mark elbowed his way to him and ate and drank. When he came back, he pulled out the Skoll tin and opened it, spitting the communal wine into the clean interior. I nodded. "Not bad."

"Oh, heck, it is, too," he whispered. "That stuff is rancid. Jeez." His face twisted in horror, as if his tongue were doing somersaults inside his mouth. I peeked at the wine. It was brownish and cloudy, a bit liked mulled wine, but it smelled astringent.

"Uh. There's something in this stuff. Wine can't possibly be that bitter," he said.

"Bitter herbs," a woman beside me said, smile revealing receding gums and long yellowed teeth. "The Lord commanded the Israelites to eat bitter herbs to remember their time as slaves." She nodded to add emphasis to her words, smacking her lips as if she still tasted the stuff and it was really great.

Herbs? Like drugs? Mark's mouthful might not be enough to test for biological additives. If he could claim a sample, so could I—communal germs notwithstanding.

I moved forward as Mark capped the bitter wine and tucked it into his pocket. Took the bite of fluffy white bread from the old man and swallowed. Nothing tasted odd about the bread. Leaning forward into the communal cup, I took my drink and felt my mouth turn inside out. The cup was nearly empty, the dregs heavy and acrid and vile. I jerked away so the old man couldn't see my reaction. Horrified, I lifted tear-filled eyes to Mark, gesturing to the Skoll container in his pocket.

"Sorry," he said softly, eyes full of evil mischief. "It's full."

I couldn't spit. I couldn't swallow. The taste grew in my mouth, vile green things and earth and old pine needles.

"And I don't have a handkerchief," he added, laughter dancing in his eyes like jade figurines. He had to be lying. All country boys carry handkerchiefs to wipe their sweaty brows while hunting or plowing or whatever country boys do. Almost gagging, I spat into my hand and shook the gunk onto the bare earth. Disgusted, I turned my head into my shoulder to hide my action and wiped my tongue on the back of my hand. Behind me, he was laughing softly. Even in the heat, I shivered from the awful taste.

I'd get Mark for this. Somehow. Returning to my place, I shot him a malign promise. He just laughed silently, mustache hairs twitching.

The chanting died. From somewhere in the parking lot, a bell began to ring, a deep, slow bell, like a church bell on a Sunday. And the curtains at the front of the tent parted.

A young woman emerged, tall, delicate as a dying breath, swathed in gauze that moved with the scented smoke. She was blond. Ethereal.

The noises of the crowd died. The bell stopped. The smoke from the bonfire stopped as if on cue.

She raised her hands and lifted her face. "There can be no healing of the body—no *real* healing of the body— until the soul is healed. Join me in crying out to the Lord for healing." Her voice was light, as faint as a breeze, yet I had no doubt that every person in the tent heard her. "Ask him to take your soul into his care. Come unto him for healing."

This was a far cry from the Reverend Lamb of God, the fake healer who was indirectly responsible for my weakened back muscles. There was no Hollywood in this woman's voice. No theatricality. "That's the healer?" I asked Mark, unable to keep the incredulity from my voice.

The woman beside us leaned in again, her face wreathed in sweaty ecstasy. "That's DaraDevinna Faith. She's the real thing. I seen her heal. I seen it with my own eyes." Beside me, she fell to her knees as if pulled to the ground by a great force.

As I watched, a young couple holding a tiny baby moved up the aisle and knelt at a bench I hadn't noticed before. DaraDevinna walked up to them and rested her hands first on the adults, her lips moving silently, closed eyes raised to the sky. Then she lifted something at her side and put it on the child, praying over him, too. And the three left the front of the tent. No one was slapped to the ground. No one shouted. No one said anything.

Others began to fall to their knees and the entire crowd began singing softly as if led by someone, though I didn't spot a song leader. "Amazing Grace." A song I knew from attending church a few times with Marisa while growing up, and from listening to Marisa start each day with a hymn while we were in medical school. It had driven me crazy back then, especially if I was trying to sleep in.

More of the crowd were on their knees, yet no one was shouting or beating their breasts or waving their arms in the air. A dozen people moved to the front of the tent, and were prayed over as the crowd continued to sing, each song progressing almost seamlessly into the next. "Amazing Grace" was a favorite, sung several times.

I was sweating all over, beads of moisture on my nose and upper lip, a thin film glistening along my arms. I found I was breathing with my mouth open to draw in enough air, yet I couldn't seem to care. Something was happening here. Something important.

I should have felt ill at ease in this crowd, uncomfortable, out of place. Instead, I felt strangely mellow, soothed by the sounds of voices raised in prayer and song. I knew Marisa would have been right at home, even in the down-home, casually dressed crowd standing on bare earth, smoky air wafting through the tent from time to time.

It was soothing. Calming. And over an hour passed as I watched and listened, one of the most pleasant hours I could remember in a long time. Later—much later—there was a commotion to the side and a wheelchair was rolled to the front. It was Venetia Gordon.

Stunned, I stepped into the aisle, almost by reflex. My composure vanished like the smoke from the smudge stick.

"You all know Venetia," DaraDevinna said in her soft voice. The crowd nodded and murmured, agreeing. "You have all seen the wondrous things that are happening to her through prayer and the power of the Lord. Join with me now in praying for her continued improvement."

I edged my way past several people and down the aisle to get a better look. DaraDevinna put the same thing on Venetia that she had been putting on all the people she prayed over. This time I could see the healer was dropping a single drop of some kind of liquid onto the girl's forehead, smearing it in a pattern and then covering the spot with her hand to pray. Anointing her head with oil?

As I watched, Venetia lifted both arms and gripped the healer's hands. The toes of her left foot were wiggling. Her right leg moved forward and her foot slipped off the wheelchair foot support, the limb dangling. But the hands were gripping.

Gripping.

A single breath seemed to groan through the crowd.

Something cold tingled down my spine as I watched. Standing there, frozen. In a tent in the middle of a field.

If black magic used fear and poison, what was this? What did religion use?

Then Almera Gordon turned and pushed her daughter's wheelchair off to the side and out of sight. The crowd starting singing something about "Praise Him, Praise Him, all the little children." I turned and moved away. Toward the car.

What was happening here?

I knew the answer. Somewhere in the back of my mind, I knew the answer to my own question. But I couldn't believe it. It went against everything I had ever been taught or believed.

Venetia Gordon was being healed.

10

LIKE FIRE THROUGH DRY GRASS

Mark parked at my back door, turned off the old truck and took my hand. Sitting in the dark, in the typical Southern night-heat, we enjoyed the silence for a long moment before he broke it. "I talked to Miss Essie today. About the book." His tone was strange, his words stilted, jerky, as if he didn't really want to talk about what he'd learned from the old woman but had to. "She said it was the worst kind of magic."

I nodded in the dark. I had figured that out already.

"I think someone was using those girls to practice magic on. I think they were sacrifices of some sort."

"And?" I asked softly when he seemed unable to go on.

"And I didn't tell you earlier because we hadn't put it all together till now. But we found tracks in the woods leading away from the van wreck. We got one clear footprint. Male, size eleven. I think whoever tortured them may have gotten away."

I sighed, the sound long and sad and full of something I didn't want to look at too closely. "Come on. Walk me to the door," I said, pulling my hand away and opening the car door.

Mark walked me to the stoop, our footsteps shushing on the driveway. My keys jangled in the night and I pushed open the door a few inches. Cold air rushed out through the crack as I dropped in my medical bag. I had left no lights on inside or out. Nothing marred the blackness.

We were silent now. The dogs groaned and whined twin welcomes. A faint breeze rustled leaves up high in the trees.

Mark took my hand in his once more, standing in the dark beneath the old tree. A nightingale called far off, and I lifted my head to the night sky, visible through the heavy foliage as patches of dark velvet spotted with glitter. Belle moved around our legs, asking for attention. I felt, rather than saw, Mark bend to offer a treat to each dog. He always carried something for dogs. Crunching followed.

Mark's hand was warm and callused. Safe. I didn't know why I suddenly wanted to cry. The bird called again, sounding lonely.

In the dark, his free hand slid from the head of a dog to my hip, up my spine, to tangle in my sweat-damp hair. His lips fell, gentle and soft on mine, his head blocking out the far-off stars. I leaned into him, sliding my arms around him. It was the first time we had kissed in what seemed like forever.

Mark was taller than I. A treat, because I was several inches taller than the average man. He cradled my head and bent me back, deepening the kiss. I sighed into his mouth and felt his smile, mustache hairs tickling. For an instant I remembered my anger over the communion-wine incident. So much for empty threats. I melted closer.

After a long moment, he pulled back just a bit, teeth

white in the black night. "G'night, country girl," he said, his mustache moving on my face.

"'Night, redneck."

Mark didn't pull away, his breath still warm on my overheated skin. "Some night you're going to invite me inside," he said, one finger touching my new earring, making the small loop move.

He hadn't asked to come in. He hadn't asked that in months, not since the day I was stabbed and he had killed a man. I understood that it was Mark who wasn't ready yet. Not really. "Do country girls do that sort of thing?" I asked.

"So I've been told. By the way, you look beautiful tonight." And he moved away.

The night closed in on me like a fist grabbing me from behind, my aloneness like sharp talons in the blackness. I was suddenly unable to breathe. Wanted to call out to Mark. I steadied myself on the rough brick at my side.

It was so dark, I could scarcely see him as he moved back to the truck and got inside, the interior lights broken, along with all the other unnecessary parts. Shutting the door, starting the engine, he pulled away through the dark, turning on his headlights only after he was around the bend.

Belle and Pup chased him for the length of the driveway and returned, settling on the porch. Finally, I released the brick, pulled the door shut and sat beside the dogs, the night breeze cooling, drying my scalp. Minutes passed as I heard the truck pull down the street and into his driveway across the street. He didn't come back. If he had, I knew I'd have asked him inside.

The stoop, shadowed all day by the huge oak, was cool beneath my thighs. I rested my head on the wall beside the door. Leaned my back into the brick. Silence punctured by night birds surrounded me. Slowly, the aloneness faded. Not loneliness, I assured myself. Just aloneness. I relaxed, stretching out my legs. No insects found me yet. It was comforting to sit with the dogs, listening to the sounds of night birds.

"Why didn't you ask him in?"

Belle came alert with a start. Pup barked and raced for the voice in the woods behind the house. I didn't move, though I couldn't have said why I wasn't startled. A splotch of white glided in from the darkness. Belle growled low in her throat before she caught the scent. "You always sit in the dark and wait on women to get home?" I asked.

"Makes me sound like a stalker. Down, boy." Cam moved from the darker dark of the trees at the creek into the lighter dark at the edge of the driveway. He was dressed in jeans and a white T-shirt, the fabric picked out by the inefficient moon.

"If Mark had seen you he'd have pulled a gun."

"If Mark had been looking at anything other than you he'd have seen me. You saw me."

"Actually, I didn't." Cam must have been waiting in the trees. Somehow I wasn't surprised to find him there. And I wasn't sure why that was so.

"Happy birthday. Well, in forty-eight hours and twenty-five minutes." He emerged fully out of the trees, moving like some mythical being of the night, his footsteps silent on the grass and gravel. Black hair, blacker than night eyes. And a heat about him that had nothing to do with August.

I felt Cam's eyes fasten on me. Slowly he lowered himself onto the small stoop, his arm brushing mine. Heat seemed to flow from him in waves. Belle whined and moved over. There was something dangerous about Cam tonight. Not the kind of danger that would set Belle into "protect mode." But the kind of danger most mothers warn their daughters about. And yet I let him settle, the sound of his movements like a sigh in the dark.

"Nice night," he said.

"Yeah," I agreed, looking back into the tree overhead, feeling my own ambivalence, my own aloneness. "I just came from a tent meeting where I saw a quad healed."

"No shit?" I laughed at his crudity and at the boredom in his tone. Cam wasn't interested in my night. "Why didn't you invite Mark in?" he asked again.

I wondered how much Cam had heard and seen, standing in the dark. "He isn't ready," I said.

"*Mark* isn't ready? *Mark?*"

I laughed and Belle shoved her nose at the sound. I stroked her silky ears as she settled her head across my legs like a heated, heaving blanket. "Okay. So it's mutual."

"I'm hungry. Got any sandwich stuff?"

"Bagels and turkey and cheese."

"Any fresh enough to be safe, or you still serving food moldy and stale?"

I stood, Belle moving with me, and entered the house. "Help yourself," I said. As Cam made himself at home in my kitchen, I went to the bedroom and put on music. I was feeling weird so it was an eclectic mix, Patti Smith, Tanya Tucker and Harry James, from the forties. Nothing soothing. Nothing romantic. I didn't think Cam needed any encouragement tonight. I didn't know what I needed.

Cam had sandwiches on the table when I came back, and had opened a bottle of wine, a Chardonnay I had picked up weeks before. I wasn't much of a drinker. Not with my mother's problem. But I took the glass he offered me, in the fine crystal I had from my broken engagement. He clincked his glass to mine and drank, a half-eaten bagel in one hand, a look in his eyes I didn't respond to. "Funky music," he said. "It's interesting."

"How's Shirl?" I asked. May as well put all the cards on the table.

"Moved in. Happy with her new place. Arlana's helping her decorate. Shirl was abusing her to rearrange the furniture and buy new stuff when I left." He ate most of the rest of the bagel with one bite.

"Shirl moved in today?" I put down the wine. I was supposed to help. It was supposed to have been a party with hard work, dancing and fun.

"Yep," he said without looking at me. "And then she dumped me. Cold." He reached past my wineglass and took another of the small bagel sandwiches.

"Ah," I said. Now I understood the energy coming off Cam in waves. And I understood what he was doing here, with me. "Dumped you."

"Like the garbage. Did you know only two women have ever dumped me in my life? My whole life."

"No," I said softly. But I did. Women didn't dump Cameron Reston. Women loved Cam. His bad-boy, reckless character, his dark good looks, his absolute love of women of all kinds, his total charm, attracted them like fish to an illegal lure. Cam went through women like fire through dry grass, and he didn't break up with women so much as simply move on to greener pastures. "Tell me."

He finished the bagel and finally met my eyes. "We've been dating for three months. I'd fly down to see her on weekends off. Twice she drove up to meet me. She was…different. You know?"

I nodded. Shirl was from the UK, the daughter of a rich man, with no ties or pretensions to royalty. Shirl knew who she was more clearly than any woman I knew. She wasn't about to let a playboy wreak havoc on her emotional life. My best guess was that Cam had seemed to develop shifty feet and she booted him out. "Shirl wasn't the usual little girl you date. She was a woman grown."

"Oh, yeah. And tough as nails." His mouth wrenched, a mood change I couldn't decipher. "Drink your wine. I'm changing that awful music."

"I thought you said it was interesting."

"It's fine if you don't want to dance. We want to dance," he said from my bedroom.

"I don't want to dance." I wasn't going to dance. Cam needed to talk about Shirl, and I was feeling too alone to dance with Cam Reston. The music cut off in midpeal.

"You dance fine," he called. "I saw you dance with John at some of those engagement parties his relatives threw for you."

Something wild and Latin filled the air. I hadn't heard it before, couldn't place it in my fast-growing CD collection. I quickly sat down at the kitchen table. No one can dance sitting down. The volume went up and Cam returned, taking the wineglass out of my hand. Gripping my wrists, he pulled me to my feet. I shook my head no, resisting, letting gravity urge me to the chair.

Cam tossed back his too-long hair and laughed. "Yes. Dance with me." His black eyes sparkled mischief and something warmer.

"No," I said, pulling away.

"Oh, yes," he said, not letting go of my wrists. Pulling me closer against him, both our arms around my body. "You know you want to. Dance with me."

Cam's feet and body moved into a rumba, his hips grinding close to mine, his hands leading me expertly across the small space. He stared down at me, his face so close I could taste the wine on his breath. Something dark smoldered in his eyes. Some painless and heated seduction that whispered and cajoled. That called to my aloneness and promised freedom from it.

I felt my resistance weaken, my muscles soften against his body. His hands slipped from my wrists, around my hips. My arms rested, one around his shoulders, the other at his waist.

The music was loud, the Latin beat strong and capricious as the steps to the dance. Cam's face was fierce and intent, the devilish grin gone. He seemed to draw me in with his eyes.

I hadn't danced in ages. And never like this.

For a moment, only a moment, I gazed into his eyes and moved into the beat, allowing him to guide me. As if sensing my acquiescence, he drew me closer, closer, whirling me into a turn and back into his arms. Our hips moved together. Arms, thighs intertwined in steps as intimate as loving. My breath grew shorter. Cam gathered me close and laughed low, like a growl. My heart rate surged as I followed his lead. My heart beat faster than the music.

The music ended on a violent note, Cam whirling me, his arms pulling me so tight against him, I could feel the steel of his chest at my back, his breath on my nape. His hands splayed across my midriff, thumbs resting just below my breasts. His palms gentled, fingers pressed close.

Tears I hadn't expected gathered in my eyes. I couldn't do this.

In the sudden silence, I stepped away, firmly pushed him back. Because if I hadn't stepped away, I'd have asked for more, asked him for what he wanted to offer. And I'd have been hurt. His eyes held mine, the heat there an echo of the heat throbbing through me as I backed away, my hands held up in warning.

I left him standing in the kitchen and went to the bedroom where I turned off the CD player. I was back in the kitchen before he could follow me. I didn't want Cam Reston in my bedroom with me tonight even for a moment. Ambivalence and near loneliness were a dangerous combination.

He handed me my glass. I shook my head.

"No?"

"No. Not even for you, Cam," I said, knowing the dance and the question were really about other subjects than dancing and wine.

"You let me cry on your shoulder after Marisa married Steven Braswell."

"And now I'm supposed to ask you into my bed because Shirl dumped you?" I said baldly, knowing I was being cruel. "Not my fault that you dated two intelligent women in your life and they both said no."

"Ouch." But he chuckled softly, ducking his head in that mischievous little-boy way he had. Cam was the single most charming man I had ever met. And for that reason alone he was dangerous to my psyche. Especially tonight, though I couldn't have explained why tonight was different. Or more correctly, why I was different tonight.

"Go back to Miss Essie, Cam," I said, emptying both wineglasses into the sink and turning him to the back door. "Let Miss Essie make you some mint tea and tell you bedtime stories. She'll make it all better."

"I'd rather you tell me bedtime stories."

"If any part of you were hurt except your ego, I'd consider it, but your ego can heal without my aid." I unlatched the door and opened it wide. Remembering his touch across me, so close to my breasts. Remembering Mark's hand, so calloused and warm. Fighting tears that I didn't understand.

"Maybe I'm ready for an intelligent woman in my life. Maybe I'm ready to settle down and I realized that my best friend in the world would make the best choice."

I almost groaned, the sound strangling in the small hallway. "Maybe your libido is in high gear and you want to get laid. Not me, Cam." I pushed him out on to the stoop. "Go home. Fly back to Duke."

"I can't," he said as I tried to shut the door between us. "The Cessna is in the shop for the next two days and I'm stuck here. It's just me and Miss Essie! Have mercy, Rhea!"

I shut the door. But not before I let him hear me laugh.

11

ALMOST IRRESISTIBLE

I slept hard that night, with pleasant dreams and no regrets. I wasn't the most introspective of people, but I understood why saying no to Cam was the wise move. And why I had kept Mark at arm's length. It wasn't that I hoped to avoid hurting one of them. I wanted to avoid getting hurt myself. Selfish is what I was. Utterly selfish.

In the Sunday predawn light, I rolled onto my stomach, shoved Stoney off the pillow beside my head and dialed Shirl's cell phone number from memory. After four rings I got her voice mail, and as the tinny voice told to me leave a message, I thought about what I wanted to say. I left a short message—"It's Rhea. Call me."—and hung up, dropping my face into the pillow. I didn't want to ask Shirl about Cam on an impersonal recording.

As I lay in the half dark, Stoney walking back and forth across my back, Belle snoring on the floor beside the bed, I remembered the vision of Venetia Gordon on the small stage at the tent meeting. Moving. Moving limbs that had been paralyzed only days before. A faith healer touching her, praying over her.

Marisa believed in prayer. What if Marisa went to DaraDevinna Faith and allowed her to put her hands on her? What if the woman really could perform miracles? The thought felt strange, bumping around in my brain like a blind rat in a maze.

I rolled slowly to my back, the cat keeping pace with the rotation, and stared at the ceiling. Stoney turned in slow circles on my stomach and settled, watching me with half-lidded eyes and purring. "I do not need comfort," I lied to the cat. He yawned hugely, his pink tongue curling up, sharp killing teeth exposed.

Pushing him off the bed, I crawled from the sheets and stretched for a run, pulling my sleep-frozen muscles gently at first, then harder as they loosened, paying careful attention to the place on my back where the knife had sliced muscle and nerve, leaving a weak place. It burned this morning, a deep, stinging pain.

Belle and Pup woke and stretched, tongues curling up toward the ceiling as if to mock Stoney, legs and toes taut and spreading. Recognizing my prerun stretch, they broke into twin runs, back and forth, up and down the hallway, yelping with glee as I dressed, adding a bottle of water and cell phone to my waistband. Together, we left the house, Belle at my side but free of the leash, Pup on the leash and tripping over his big feet. As the sun tried to climb over the horizon, we ran the last of the cobwebs out of my brain, both the sleep kind and the ones that were left over from the dance with Cam.

The sense of calm that settled on me as I ran let me know that I had made the right decision last night. Cam was almost irresistible. But only almost. And giving in to him would be a huge mistake. Having no family, I valued friends above almost everything else in life. Sleeping with Cam would destroy more than one of those friendships, as well as my relationship with Mark.

I remembered the feel of Mark's hand holding mine

last night as he walked me to my door. Steady. Warm. Comforting. Reliable. All the things Cameron Reston was not. And if some small voice whispered in my head, pointing out that the thought of Mark had intruded last night when Cam was making his pass, and that the cop might mean more to me than I had previously admitted, I was able to ignore it, and concentrated on my pumping legs and the dogs at my side. Mark wasn't ready for me. I had made the right decisions. All of them.

I got to work early and checked in with the ER crew. Wallace was still asleep, having pulled a twenty-four-hour shift, there were no patients, and I had time to kill, so I wandered up the halls to the medical floors, hands in my lab-coat pockets, looking in on the patients I had admitted. Because it was Sunday, the place wasn't exactly bustling with activity, or the expectant energy that signaled a new weekday, new problems, new emergencies. Today, nurses and technicians moved more slowly than usual, took more time to greet one another and talk to the patients. I nodded to the people I passed, able to call many of the employees by name.

The floors had been waxed during the night, and offered up a satiny glow. The wallpaper was a warm, pale shrimp color, fresh and clean looking. Someone had even cleaned the glass on the prints that decorated the walls. However, in three hallway openings weird symbols had been spray painted in various patterns, combinations of five or seven figures. The mad graffiti artist was still at work. I didn't think housekeeping would get the paint off this time. It looked well cured.

When I opened the door to Na'Shalome's room, the odor nearly bowled me over. The smell was beyond horrid: rank and sour, like dead meat. If the girl smelled that way, I feared she was having surgical complications. Quickly, I moved into the room.

While most patients were up, bathed and prepped for treatments or procedures, Na'Shalome was asleep, her mouth open, her doll perched on the bed beside her, its eyes staring at me. When I touched the patient, she was breathing fine, her skin was warm and moist. I sniffed her breath, and along her body. The scent was stronger here than near the door, but I couldn't pinpoint the exact source. I didn't understand the stench, and made a mental note to discuss it with Boka or the nurses. I backed from the room and went next door.

The other girl from the accident, still listed as Jane Doe on the nurses' notes, was awake, her eyes fixing on me as soon as I entered. I came into the room, pulled a chair close to her and sat. I hadn't noticed much about her as a person at the time of the accident. Now I saw that her skin was ashy and her kinky hair was dry and needed ''doing,'' as local people would say to describe the day-long process of washing, moisturizing, combing, and braiding.

''Hi. I'm Dr. Rhea-Rhea. How are you feeling today?''

She said nothing, her dark eyes in her dark-skinned face simply holding mine.

''I'm a doctor. I helped you when you had an accident. A car wreck. Do you remember the accident?'' *Helped?* The quiet part of my mind sneered. *You cut off her leg.*

Still Jane Doe said nothing, her face blank, eyes empty yet staring at me. There was so little emotion in there. So little reaction. I remembered the scars on her body and thought I could understand why. Someone had hurt this child badly and she had withdrawn from the world. ''Well, if you need anything, you ask for me. Okay? Dr.

Rhea-Rhea.'' Reaching forward, I attempted to pat her hand.

''No!'' she shouted, and jerked away, the motion violently reflexive. At last, there was emotion in her eyes. But it wasn't the comfort I had hoped to see. It was fear. Raving, mewling fear. Eyes wide, mouth open in horror, she shrank back from me to the far corner of the narrow bed, back pressed into the steel rails. Soft little sounds escaped her open mouth, sounds a kitten might make if it were being stung by killer bees.

Withdrawing my hand, I stood and left the room, Jane's strange, empty eyes on me as I walked away and closed the door.

It was nearing seven, the time I was to go on duty, but I made a last stop in Ronnie Howell's room. The room was dark and silent, the still form of Ronnie asleep beneath a thin sheet. Mrs. Howell was sitting in a chair in the corner, her eyes on her son. Bending over the boy was an unexpected sight. Dressed in jeans and T-shirt, hair in an untidy blond bun, was the woman from the night before. DaraDevinna Faith.

Her hands were on the boy's stomach, her eyes closed, her lips moving, soft words, almost a chant, whispered through the room. It was clearly prayer. As she whispered, she opened a small vial hidden in her hand and let a single drop escape onto her thumb. Without opening her eyes, she touched the thumb to the boy's forehead, drawing the pad down from the hairline to the bridge of his nose. Then she made a horizontal stroke, creating the sign of the cross on his forehead.

Fighting an irrational spurt of anger, I stepped back outside and pulled the door almost closed. What was she doing here? Who had let that quack in?

On top of my questions, I remembered Venetia Gordon, lifting her arms, wiggling her toes. My anger died, leaving behind some new emotion that I refused to examine. From inside Ronnie's room, I heard the cadence of the words change and could make out most of what was being said.

"I didn't take him to the doctor. I did this to him. It's my fault." Mrs. Howell said. I could hear the anguish, the guilt in her voice, the sound of her breathing loud with unshed tears.

"What do the doctors say?" DaraDevinna asked.

"They say they don't know. They got his sugar back under control easy enough, but he's got some weakness on one side. They say he could be..." sobs seemed to tear through her "...that he could be...permanently damaged. In his brain. And I...I did it." She cried, her breath like a bellows in the darkened room.

"Both forgiveness and healing are in the Lord's hands. Let me pray for you," the soft voice said. The cadence began again, the whispered words no clearer than earlier. After a moment, Mrs. Howell's breathing eased, smoothed out.

"Thank you," she said, and I thought she sounded surprised. "They gonna send us home today, but can we come to the meeting again so you can pray for my Ronnie?"

"Of course, but this time leave him on his insulin," DaraDevinna said, gentle admonishment in her tone. "I believe that with the medication, your Ronnie will be fine. The Lord will hear your prayer. Pray constantly," DaraDevinna said in that breathy, delicate voice.

Footsteps sounded close to the door and I checked my watch. I had a few minutes to spare. The door opened and DaraDevinna stepped out, met my eyes, and smiled as if she had been expecting me. "Hello, Dr. Lynch. Thank you for saving Belvin Stewart last night."

I hadn't expected the words nor that she would know my name. "Who?" I asked stupidly.

The woman touched my elbow, indicating that we should walk down the hallway toward the cafeteria. In the air I could smell coffee and the scent of hot bacon grease, and some clean shampoo scent that came only from her. She moved as if she still wore the diaphanous gauze of the night before, as if she might have been a dancer at some point in her life. "Belvin. The man in anaphylactic shock."

The memory of the man lying in the dust, his hands clawing the earth, unable to breathe, came back. I hadn't registered his name. "Oh. You're welcome. He's okay?"

"He's quite fine, thanks to you. He has allergies to dozens of things. One of them must have been on the bonfire last night." She smiled. "I did some research and I hadn't known so many herbs can cause such problems. We'll have to be more careful."

DaraDevinna smiled again, exposing crooked white teeth. She was almost painfully thin, and I wondered about an eating disorder or too much fasting. Were they the same thing? If religion was involved, did that make starving yourself okay?

"My father takes care of the bonfire and the smudge stick, as well as the practical aspects of setting up the meetings. We've had a talk about not using rosemary." She cocked her head up at me, the smile turning impish. "He wasn't happy. He says that rosemary is cleansing and healing. But he'll come around. Would you like coffee?"

"Actually, I would. I wanted to talk to you." I pointed toward the cafeteria. "DaraDevinna—"

"Call me Dara. DaraDevinna is for the pulpit." Her voice grew wry. "My father is a bit of a showman, and he chose my full name for the services."

"Dara, then. And I'm Rhea. I wanted to ask you about the kid you just prayed over. Ronnie."

"To ask me why his mother took him off his insulin." She sighed and opened the door to the dimly lit cafeteria. The smell of pork and eggs cooking was overwhelming, making my mouth water. "I tell all of them, all those who come for healing, that they must go to their doctor for confirmation, just as the Lord told the ones he healed to go to the temple for cleansing and thanksgiving. But some simply do not listen."

"Wait a minute. *You* tell them to go to a doctor?"

DaraDevinna handed me a disposable cup and took one herself. As she spoke, she poured hot water and added a tea bag. I poured coffee and added a packet of sugar and two creams. Coffee on an empty stomach didn't sound too smart today, but I wanted a caffeine jolt and the cream and sugar might prevent some irritation.

"I tell all of them. Unlike when the Lord was here, not all people are healed by touch. Some must be healed by medicine. And until stem cell research cures diabetes, I think that is one disease that needs medical attention. So, yes—" she turned solemn eyes up to me "—I told Ronnie's mother to take him to his doctor, but she didn't. And now there are two diseases in that room, one of the body and one of the soul. Diabetes and guilt."

I couldn't help it. I was impressed, and I didn't want to be. "Where did you learn about stem cell research?"

"Oh, it's my dream to be a doctor someday." She smiled shyly, as if admitting a great secret. "So I read anything and everything I can about healing. About medicine. About the human body and its relationship to the human soul." She sipped her tea, moving the bag around by pulling on the attached string.

"And the fact that stem cell research is done on human embryos doesn't bother you?"

"It's murder. Quite clearly," she said as we ambled back into the hallway. "But if the embryos were destroyed, or are to be destroyed anyway, why not use them for good?"

It was a practical response, quite logical, but somehow it didn't seem to fit in with most religious beliefs. I decided to play devil's advocate. "So when does life begin? I mean, if we can freeze embryos, does that mean that they aren't alive yet?"

"When someone is brain damaged and in a vegetative state, do they no longer have a soul? Are they no longer alive? The courts say that they are. Humans are given a soul by God and are protected by law. If there is the slightest potential that the embryos have a soul, should we not care for them?"

I shrugged. The concept of life in terms of religion was not something I wanted to respond to. I hadn't meant to get into some soul issue. I was talking about the medical aspect.

"The medical aspect and the religious aspect are one and the same," DaraDevinna said, as if I had spoken aloud. "If life begins at conception, and if human beings stand at the apex of God's creation, then the human being has a soul at conception."

"If," I said.

"Indeed. If." She smiled at me. "You find yourself torn. You want women to have control over their own bodies, to have the ultimate decision of what happens to them, yet that desire may conflict with the medical and spiritual question of when life begins."

I nodded, uncomfortable at being so transparent, and glanced at her eyes. They were gray-blue with odd golden flecks. Unremarkable from a distance. Pretty, up close. She smiled at me. Or more precisely, she had never stopped smiling, even when sipping her tea.

"What do you know about witchcraft?" I asked.

DaraDevinna stopped in the hallway and seemed to grow still, as if a small part of her soul were turning to stone. The smile left her face, and her gray eyes grew round. "There are many varieties of witchcraft. Some are intended for the good of humankind, though such practitioners walk a difficult and thorn-grown path." She ducked her head and resumed walking, the fluorescent lights throwing her face into shadow. A thick rope of hair slid from the bun and dangled across her forehead, though Dara didn't seem to notice. With the long slender fingers of her right hand, she pulled the tea bag around and around, its motion sluggish in the dark liquid. When she spoke, her thin, breathy voice was low. I leaned in to hear what she said.

"And then there is blood witchcraft. And that is a dangerous thing entirely. Frightening. Such witches play with powers that they think they can control, but the powers will overtake them."

This sounded a lot like what Miss Essie had been saying to me. And the weird thing was that both women believed this stuff. "Have you ever heard about a hub? A focus for blood spells? Or a gateway?"

The young woman's skin seemed to turn ashen. She lifted wide frightened eyes to mine and shoved the rope of hair back behind an ear. "Dangerous things. Perilous practice. *You* don't—"

"No way." I grinned, trying to bring a bit of lightness

back to the conversation. "Not me. I think all that kind of stuff is stupid…"

"I did not think I sensed such a path in your life."

I wasn't sure what she meant by that but I plowed on anyway. "We have a patient in the hospital with a weird kind of doll. A friend told me it could be a hub or a gateway."

Her nostrils flared. "Show me this doll."

I nodded back down the hall and we retraced our steps. But long before we got to Na'Shalome's room, it was clear that Dara knew where she was going. She headed unerringly to the door, stopped a few feet from it and stared as if she saw something in the varnished wood. Her hands lifted, the disposable tea cup tilting. Hot tea splashed over the back of her left hand and down her wrist. I grabbed the cup with my free hand, burning my fingers.

Dara walked the remaining step and placed her open hands on the door, palms flat. A reddish burn showed down the back of one hand where the tea had splashed. I heard her murmuring again, a cadence similar to the one she'd used when praying with Mrs. Howell.

Two nurses stopped in the hallway behind me and watched. "What's she doin'?" one asked.

"Beats heck outta me," the other said. "Doc?"

I shook my head and stepped back, not sure I wanted to be too close to Dara. This was religious mumbo jumbo of the highest order. "I'm not sure," I said. And then Dara lifted the vial she kept in her pocket and poured the liquid across the door in a single vertical line. With her thumb, she smeared it out in a horizontal line, forming a cross. Long ropy drops of thick oil ran down the door.

"Housekeeping's gonna have a fit," one of the nurses said. "First paint, now this."

Dara pocketed the vial and put her hands back on Na'Shalome's door for an instant. And then, moving fast, Dara opened the door. The rank smell blew out like a rancid fog as Dara stepped inside. The reaction was swift and violent.

Screaming, Na'Shalome leaped from the bed and crossed the room. In the dark, she was little but a blur. Hands like claws, she attacked DaraDevinna.

I thrust the cups at the nearest nurse and dived after Dara. Another nurse and I pulled the patient off the healer and pressed her back into the bed. A third nurse whipped a sheet into a long roll and drew it across Na'Shalome's chest, securing one end beneath the bed with a large knot. The other nurse secured the other end, effectively tying Na'Shalome down. The girl thrashed, and I saw that her pupils were once again pinpoint.

I stepped back, breathing hard. Wondering if the girl had torn surgical stitches, ripped something inside. Wondering what made her stink so badly. I wanted to gag at the stench.

One of the nurses dropped the doll back on the bed, facedown. The other found another sheet to further restrain Na'Shalome. It was only then that I heard the words she had been screaming. Like an echo, she now whispered them, eyes on the door.

"Hands. Hands. Hands. Hands. Found the hands. Found them found them found them found them..."

When I looked around, DaraDevinna was gone. Our cups, ditched by the nurse against a hallway wall, sent thin curls of steam upward.

I wasn't Na'Shalome's doctor, and really had no right to look at her chart, but I left the girl's room and went straight to the patients' charts behind the nurses' desk, pulled hers and went through the doctor's notes. Boka had ordered that the patient's room be sanitized, and blood cultures drawn in case the patient was septic. But I was looking for something else. Flipping pages, I found it.

A psych consult had been ordered for the girl, and according to the nurse's notes, had taken place the day before. But there was no preliminary report yet. Nothing to tell me what I had just seen. I had my own ideas, though—I thought she was having a psychotic break, total and complete.

Unhappy, I left the floor and headed to the ER and the long day that awaited me.

12

SECRETIVE CURVE TO HER LIPS

The day went by fast, several hours taken up with a patient who fell off his tractor and nearly severed his left arm. Farming accidents, crushing victims and people run over by trains are the worst thing imaginable to an ER physician and I had seen enough of each to make me hate them all. This was the third farming accident I had worked since signing my contract in Dawkins County. The first patient had been run over by a hay wagon, receiving a crushing injury to his pelvic region and right leg. The second had caught his hand in a hay baler. He was lucky the machine hadn't pulled him in, chopped him up and baled him along with the hay.

Today's victim had fallen off the tractor and been scooped around with a huge metal scooper used to push hay into rows for baling. By the time the farmer was able to crawl the half mile to the road and flag down help, he'd lost a great deal of blood.

Luckily, the first truck that passed was driven by a woman who had taken an EMS course and knew how to stop the bleeding. She had covered him in blankets, applied pressure to the arm at the armpit and sat with him in the back of her truck while her fourteen-year-old son drove the truck to the hospital. No one reported the kid for underage driving. In farming communities a fourteen-year-old kid had probably been driving a three-ton farming machine since he was seven. After that, what was a truck on empty back-country roads?

It took us two hours to stabilize the man. Because there was a slight possibility that microsurgery could save his arm, he was flown out to Carolinas Medical in Charlotte. As I worked to get the patient's blood pressure up and replace his blood volume, all I could think of was the girl in the room up the hall, Jane Doe. Yet even if EMS had been able to get her loose, she would have lost the leg. I knew that. A crushed limb was a far cry from a severed one, even one as mangled as the one I was seeing today.

I was pulling a twenty-four-hour shift and the patient load was high, with more critical cases than usual—a gastro-intestinal bleeder, his duodenal ulcer suddenly breaking loose and dumping half his blood volume out his rectum, the farming accident, a twelve-year-old burn victim with second-degree burns over 40 percent of his body, and three MIs. All that in between the usual PIDs, DFOs, OFWs, MVAs and UTIs—med-speak for myocardial infarction, pelvic inflammatory disease, done-fell-outs, old folks work-ups, moving vehicular accidents and urinary tract infections. I admitted one MI, shipped two for heart caths, flew out the farmer and the burned kid on medevac choppers to different trauma and burn centers, and handed out numerous drugs, prescriptions and work excuses. That was from 7:00 a.m. to 7:00 p.m., when the nurses changed shift.

I was pleased to find I was working graveyard shift with Ashlee Davenport, my favorite nurse, and with Coreen, the young newbie who had quickly proven herself.

Ash was a Chadwick by birth, a member of the county's famous—some might say infamous—multiracial family. She was mid-forties, pleasingly plump, a short woman with a dry sense of humor and ash-blond hair. We had time to grab a dinner prepared by Ash's nana, a great Southern cook who personally delivered the pot roast, potatoes, carrots, green beans fresh from the garden, and rice and gravy. We were just finishing when the night rush started.

"Dawkins County, this is unit 351, do you copy?" the scratchy voice came over EMS radio.

Ash glanced over her shoulder as she picked up the mike and said to me, "Unit 351 is at the tent meeting." Depressing the switch on the mike, she said, "Go ahead, 351."

"Dawkins, we have a sixty-two-year-old female with COPD and SOB. BP is 205 over 140, pulse 130. We have normal saline via small-bore IV and O_2 at four liters. Signal 45. Dawkins, please note, patient took herself off medications. Repeat, patient took herself off her medications. Meds on board. ETA four minutes."

All of that meant that the patient had a history of chronic obstructive pulmonary disease and now had shortness of breath and high blood pressure because she had taken herself off her prescription medications and substituted alcohol for the drugs. At least she had her medications with her and I would have an easier time deciding what to use to get her breathing again.

"Copy, unit 351. This is 414 clear." Ash sighed. "Well, ain't that just fine and dandy. Respiratory down here?"

"Yeah. We're probably going to need a breathing treatment."

The woman was the first of a horrible night. After the

morning's twelve hours, I was already exhausted, my thoughts scattered, my scrubs needed changing, and I was in need of a long hot shower. I got a cup of freshly made coffee instead and drank it down on top of the roast beef. The food and caffeine made me feel moderately better, which was a good thing. As I drank I heard another ambulance unit checking in with the EMT working extra ER duty tonight. Another hot time in the old town tonight.

"Dawkins, we have a thirteen-year-old male with insulin-controlled diabetes and Signal zero-three. BP is 170 over 88, pulse 130 and blood sugar 143."

I walked over and held out my hand for the mike, "Grand mal or petit?" I asked the EMT.

"Grand."

"Ativan on board?" I asked.

"Negative. We have Valium."

"Estimate of weight?" I asked as I pulled my reference book and checked a child's dosage.

"Maybe ninety pounds?"

I told him the dosage. "You got a history?" I added.

"Previously undiagnosed. First onset of epileptic activity."

"Understood." I nodded to the tech and listened as he signed off. "Ash, I need a Dilantin IV drip for a kid, estimate ninety pounds."

"Can do, Doc," she said.

"Keep respiratory down here in case we need to intubate him, and call the nursing supervisor as soon as we have a name, for an old chart and admission papers."

"You got it, Doc."

Ten minutes later, the unit pulled up and wheeled the patient in. It was Ronnie Howell, his slight body rigid with uncontrolled contractions.

Mrs. Howell, her eyes wide with panic, held on to the

stretcher railing, her auburn hair showing darker roots
that hadn't been there only days earlier. On the other side
of the stretcher moved DaraDevinna Faith, one hand on
Ronnie, one hand in the air, her mouth moving.

I slammed my lips together, controlling a flash of un-
reasoning anger and the words that threatened. Preachers
often came in with patients and prayed over them for a
moment. It was a comfort to both patient and family, and
not against the rules so long as no one got in the way.
But this particular preacher seemed to be part of the problem and I didn't like her being here one bit. Shoving my
feelings down and out of the way, I went to work.

Because my theory about the tent-meeting congregation involved the use of herbal drugs, I was careful in
my treatment of Ronnie. I had a urine drug screen and
blood collected for toxicology testing before administering anything stronger than the Valium. And I stuck with
Valium and Dilantin instead of other, more potent meds.
Not knowing what toxins might have contributed to the
onset of seizure activity, I wanted to move slowly.

There was a slimy smear of stuff on Ronnie's forehead
and chest, results of being anointed with oil. Below the
oil, Ronnie's eyes were rolled up into his head and a
bloody foam burbled at his mouth. The oil trickled down
toward one ear in jerky dribbles as Ronnie contracted.
Even in the ER in Chicago we had seen these practices,
and doctors were trained to be sensitive to the religious
needs of the patients. Usually it didn't bother me. But
this time it added fuel to my anger.

To give me something to do, I shoved my way into
the melee of techs and nurses at Ronnie's side and started
the Dilantin IV myself. When I was angry, it was best to
stay busy.

Within half an hour, Ronnie's seizures had abated and

he was as stable as I could get him in the ER. Dara and Mrs. Howell had held hands and murmured prayers from the corner of the room, both refusing to leave him. I tried to ignore them, but the incessant muttering was distracting and I was happy when Dara left my ER and returned to her crowd of worshipers.

In the next hour we got three grand mal–type epileptic-seizure patients who had never before had such attacks. Each of them had attended the tent meeting every night. My standing order was to collect specimens for toxicology testing so we could determine what they had ingested or been exposed to. We stabilized and admitted all four patients, using a variety of meds on the adults, and while it wasn't conclusive, I felt I now had enough empirical evidence to insist to Mark that the people running the tent meeting were somehow using drugs or herbal medicines on the crowd. I wondered what he had discovered from the mouthful of bitter wine he had collected in his Skoll container.

The memory of DaraDevinna praying over Ronnie and his mother seemed to refute the idea that they were using drugs on the crowd, but stranger things had happened. Or perhaps the connection to drugs came from the smudge-stick-carrying father, not the delicate woman. Either way, someone had to do something about the tent meeting. I found a minute to call Mark and warn him about the problems I was facing.

"Yellow," he said on the first ring, sounding cheerful and relaxed.

"What color is exhaustion and frustration?"

"Got to be orange or that weird color, puce. What color is puce, anyway?"

"Dark red, kinda brown. We got a problem with the traveling tent show."

"Whatcha got?" he asked.

I explained about the cases I had seen tonight, and told him the empirical evidence I had gathered. "Can't we get it shut down as a health threat or danger to the public or something?"

"I've been looking into the history of the tent meeting. There's stuff you don't even know about yet. Something'll be done. I'll let you know."

"You're going to drop hints about problems at the tent meeting and then leave me hanging? Unfair," I said, laughing.

"All's fair in love and war, babe. Later." The phone clicked off, leaving me wondering which he thought our relationship was, love or war.

At eleven o'clock, when the ER emptied out and the first break occurred, I was beyond tired. Unlike tonight, most long, difficult shifts are made bearable by periods of inactivity, and my brain was in serious need of a rest. I grabbed a Coke, called for Trisha to join me and went outside into the humid heat with the smokers. We perched on wooden picnic tables under a covered awning recently put up for outdoor eating and smoking, and I stretched my neck and back. The muscles gave slowly, and I moved gently to avoid tearing the injured ones. The heat was still oppressive at ninety-two degrees, August doing its dead level best to leach all the energy out of the South. Sweat, worsened by the humidity, beaded my face and arms.

Around us, the new X-ray tech, the on-duty lab tech, two respiratory therapists and Julio Ramos, the new agency nurse I had seen around lately, lit up and blew, scenting the air with burning paper and tobacco. It smelled wonderful, but lung disease was an awful way to die and it always amazed me to see medical personnel sucking down cancer-in-a-stick, especially as about half of all illnesses were a direct result of, or severely aggravated by, smoking, and these people saw that all the time.

"Trish, you don't smoke?" Julio asked.

"Not me," she said with a stern glance at the smokers, who waggled their butts back unrepentantly. "My only vice is men. And I don't date smokers."

"They aren't on her list of datable types," Kendrew said to Julio. Kendrew was the weekday third-shift lab tech, and I wondered idly why he was here on a Sunday. He supported his family on his lab salary while going to nursing school in the daytime, and thus was perpetually tired and sleep deprived. I tried to order only the most essential lab tests when he was working. Tonight didn't look very promising for him to relax. "No hunters, no fishermen, no heavy drinkers, no one too studious, too dumb or overly religious."

"No atheists, no smokers, and on and on," the X-ray tech added. "She's a mite picky."

"She sounds smart to me," Julio said, winning a grin from the nursing supervisor.

"Speaking of men, how'd the dancing go Friday night?" I asked Trish. When she looked puzzled, I added, "The good-looking fireman, shagging with a deejay at McDowries Bar and Billards Friday?"

"Oh." She smiled like a cat with a whole bowl of cream to herself. "That man can dance. I have yet to see if he can do anything more, but he can dance and dance well."

"Finally got you a new beau, Trish?" Kendrew asked. He was short, African-American and rotund, perched on the top of the picnic table, his rounded stomach pressed on his knees.

"Working on it. I think this one holds promise." She inspected her nails and buffed them on her collar.

"What about that military guy? He looked like a good catch."

"Got called to the Middle East."

"What happened to the cop you were dating?"

"Teddy? He moved in with his mama, started going fishing every morning, and informed me he had a son he was supporting up in Spruce Pines. Too much baggage."

"You'll never find Mr. Perfect, Trish," Kendrew said.

"So I should settle? I'm not old enough, ugly enough, bored enough or lonely enough to settle for a man who misses his mama."

"Ouch," the X-ray tech said, stubbing out his cigarette. "Now, that's cold."

"Company," Kendrew said, nodding to the driveway.

As we all turned and looked, a gray handicap vehicle pulled slowly up to the ER ambulance entrance and stopped. Recognizing the Gordons' van, I stood and walked toward the ER doors. The van was moving too slowly to be carrying an emergency.

When she saw me, Almera Gordon stepped from the driver's side, a secretive curve to her lips. "I was hoping it'd be you on duty tonight, Dr. Lynch. I got something to show you."

I stood aside, joined by Trisha and a smoke-blowing respiratory tech, as Almera opened the back doors of the van and punched the lift button to unload the specially made wheelchair Venetia used. The girl appeared slowly from the dark interior, the lift humming as it maneuvered her to the concrete pad. She too was smiling, and I saw instantly that her hands were gripping the padded arms of the chair.

"Let's go inside out of this heat. It ain't good for Venetia,'' Almera said. ''I won't leave the van here long. Promise.'' The secretive grin grew, but she turned her head aside and opened the door to the ER. Curious, we all followed the motorized wheelchair into the cool.

Once inside, Venetia spun the chair to face us and laughed up at her mother, the tone girlish and excited. Almera Gordon grabbed her daughter beneath the armpits and lifted. And Venetia came to her feet.

I felt the breath go out of me in a whoosh. The sweat on my skin, chilled by the air-conditioned air, seemed to freeze. A silence fell on us, deep and heavy, as if we were immobilized by a shock of lightning in our midst.

Almera stepped back, holding her daughter's hands. Venetia slid her left foot forward, her sock scraping the floor, sounding loud in the total silence. Her right foot followed more sluggishly, meeting the left. I could hear the grunting of her breath as she struggled. Her eyes were looking at her feet, her head hanging forward, hair straggling over her face. The left foot moved forward again. Venetia Gordon was walking. Two steps later, the girl's legs began to shake. ''Catch her,'' Almera said.

Hands shot forward and caught the girl. Babbling broke out.

''My God, what happened?''

''Did you see that?''

''Ease her back,'' Julio said.

''She walked.''

''Okay, on three.'' They sat her back in her chair.

I stood away from the group, watching.

''It's a miracle, is what it is. It's a miracle,'' Almera said. ''My girl is walking. And that healer praying for her is what done it.''

''What healer?'' Julio asked.

Someone started telling about DaraDevinna Faith and

her traveling tent meeting as the crowd grew around the wheelchair, the excitement drawing other employees to look and listen. Quietly, cold to my marrow, I walked away.

I had no idea what had just happened. I didn't believe in miracles. But…what if I was wrong? And what did it take to find that kind of healing? Faith? Blind ignorance?

Remembering the chart I had requested be faxed over, I went down the hallway to medical records where the doctors' boxes were. The door was locked, the knob resisting in my hand. Frustration welled up in me. I wanted to kick the door, bash in the little window beside it, maybe stomp my feet. I didn't believe in miracles. I didn't. I wouldn't. I took a deep breath, swallowed down the sense of failure, anger and yearning.

Feeling cold all over, I found a security guard to open the door, retrieved the stack of papers in my box and went directly to my call room. As I walked, I thumbed through the loose papers and found the envelope holding the faxed pages of Venetia Gordon's original ER chart. I closed the door to the room snugly and curled up on the bed, spreading out the chart and putting it in order. I had work to do.

Within an hour I knew what had happened to Venetia Gordon. By reading everything, beginning with the paramedic's report to the flight nurse's final exam after Venetia was medevac'd to Charlotte, I understood. Though Venetia was not ambulatory at the accident scene, when the first ambulance unit arrived, she did have sensation and motor function in her upper and lower extremities, but long before they got her evaluated, she was deteriorating into paralysis.

The emergency medical team put her in full spinal protocol, immobilizing her on a board with spinal collar and sandbags, restraints and blankets. By the time she reached the hospital, Venetia had lost all motor function and all sensation in her extremities.

According to the radiologist reading the routine lateral C-spine X ray, Venetia's films showed "distinct and uncharacteristic widening of the spinous processes of C4 and C5. This most likely represents a ligamentous injury at that level with instability of C4 and C5." The resulting CT scan, or CAT scan, showed "soft tissue swelling at the C4 and C5 area, but no fractures." The last diagnostic test prior to surgery was a spinal MRI, "displaying edema within the cord and tissue injury at the posterior interspinous ligaments."

I put the papers down and tilted my head back against the wall, staring at the ceiling of the call room. Venetia Gordon had central cord syndrome. Not a break—which was why she had motor function at the scene—but a hyperextension or hyperflexion of her neck that stressed her spine, causing contusion or bruising. Not a break. The fourth cervical cord segment remained intact.

Before she was went to surgery, Venetia had total quadriparesis, but with the presence of "sacral sparing." She could differentiate between sharp and dull sensations around the perineum, near the anus, and over other areas of the lower extremities. She had dense muscle paralysis and no spared muscle function.

I was fully aware that with the presence of sharp/dull discrimination, the prognosis was good for at least functional recovery. A few patients, perhaps two to five percent, eventually had virtually full recovery, though the majority tended to show a slow, spastic-type gait and permanent upper-extremity weakness.

I had not seen a miracle. Venetia's healing could be explained medically.

A pall of sorrow settled like falling mist in the dark places of my mind. Marisa could not be helped by this healer. Marisa would not be returned to herself. She would not be made whole.

Tears gathered along my lower lids. Until this moment I had not realized what I was hoping. What I was planning. Somewhere in the secret recesses of my thinking, I had thought about taking Marisa to DaraDevinna Faith for a little miracle of her own. Now that wouldn't happen.

I dropped the pages again and closed my eyes against the tears. Feeling frustration rise and constrict, as if a huge snake wrapped me in its coils, I banged my head against the wall, paused and banged it again, harder. The sound rang hollowly, in dual echoes.

I had never seen a miracle. Venetia wasn't a miracle. Just a decrease in pressure and a return of feeling to her extremities. It happened. Not all the time, but it did happen. That was medicine, not some arcane bit of mumbo jumbo with a God who loved everybody and made things right when they went wrong. I wasn't sure why that fact didn't bring me more peace or comfort. I had the proof I needed to keep my little medical world all neat and tidy. And it didn't make me happy at all.

Returning to the chart, I flipped through it again, quickly. There could be no mistake. Yet I realized that I couldn't find the final report from the neurosurgeon, Dr. Danthari.

Just to be absolutely certain, or perhaps to put a nail in the coffin of miracles I had been hoping for but never really believed in, I called the answering service of the neurosurgeon in Charlotte, North Carolina, who operated on Venetia the day she was injured. The sleepy woman who answered sent my call directly to Dr. Danthari's office voice mail. Feeling a bit stupid, I identified myself, told the machine what I had seen and asked for a return call. I left all my contact numbers with the automatic system before breaking the connection. I was feeling a bit silly by then, but at least I had covered all possibilities. For Marisa's sake.

Exhaustion claimed me, lulling me toward sleep, promising relief from the uncertainty and weirdness that surrounded me. Holding the pages close, I let myself slide into the darkness.

After what was surely only a minute or two, I heard a soft click and opened my eyes, focusing on the far wall. I jerked with shock. Something was painted on the mirror over my sink. The now-familiar shapes painted by the graffiti artist. In red, the color of blood. I clutched the pages against me.

I was certain I hadn't seen the red when I came in. Had I fallen asleep hard enough for someone to come into the room, draw a figure and leave? Easing my eyes away from the mirror, I checked my watch. If I had been asleep, it was only for a minute or two. Ten at the outside. No time for the mad graffiti artist to come in and draw. It could have been there when I came in. I was so involved with Venetia's chart I may not have looked up. But then, there was that sound I heard when I woke. The sound of my door closing? The air felt fresh, as if the door had been recently opened. Had someone been in my room just now?

Carefully, I looked around. Nothing else had been touched, so far as I could tell. Whoever had drawn this was no longer in the room. I eased off the bed and went to the sink to study the drawing. It was five figures, none of them from the English alphabet, all looking half-formed. They were not painted, but rather drawn with lipstick in drop-dead red. Not my shade.

The cold I had felt earlier at the sight of Venetia Gordon walking returned. Something about the arrangement of the five figures was half-familiar. They were grouped in the shape of a cross, three up, three across, the center space shared.

Suddenly, I knew where I had seen the shape before. In the dark, on a patient's bedside table.

In Na'Shalome's room.

I dialed the medical floor and got Ms. Scaggs, one of the agency nurses. I asked if Na'Shalome was in her bed, and if she had been up walking around. I was assured by the nurse that Na'Shalome was asleep, that she had not left her room. Less certain of my conclusions, I thanked her and hung up. Found myself staring at the bloodred cross.

I had once considered Na'Shalome as the graffiti artist, and discarded the thought due to her injuries. Perhaps I should have listened to my instincts. Sniffing the air, I could detect no trace of the rancid stench I associated with the girl. Yet I couldn't think of anyone else it could be. I couldn't prove it, but the graffitist had to be her.

I went to the door and pulled it open, checked up and down the lonely stretch of hall. No one was in sight. I shut the door and put a chair against it. If someone tried to come in, the chair would make a racket scraping across the floor that I couldn't sleep through. No one else would get into my room tonight.

The rest of my shift dragged by. There were no ER patients, the place empty, as if all the illness and accidents that could happen in one day had already occurred. But, it was after 3:00 a.m. before I could sleep.

13

LEAVING ME WANTING MORE

My morning wake-up call rang at six-thirty and I crawled back out of bed, fell into the shower and let the hot water steam the stiffness out of my body. I had fallen asleep in my dirty clothes, tangled in the sheets, shoes on my feet. Ready to run in case of danger? Silly of me. I was getting paranoid.

While I was drying off, my cellular rang, and I dug into my bag to find it. I knew it was Mark by the background sounds of the LEC. "Yeeellow, if the sun is up. Don't you ever sleep?"

"Not any more than you do." He yawned as if to prove his point.

"I feel sorry for you, then, because I didn't sleep three hours last night."

"I have info on the faith healer. Interested in breakfast?"

"Let's go for a run. You can tell me your news while we work up a sweat."

"What about your back? I don't feel like dawdling."

My eyebrows shot up at the challenge in his voice. "Dawdling? My back is fine, thank you. Meet you at the creek in one hour."

* * *

I was at the creek behind my house early, having stretched and warmed up, when he jogged around the side of the house, muscles looking pumped and loose, green eyes alight. Mark didn't look as if he'd been up all night working a case. I, on the other hand, looked like death only slightly warmed over. Point one to him.

Mark and I were strangely competitive, another of the many facets to our relationship that I had not bothered to analyze.

"Ready?" he asked as I gathered Pup's leash in hand.

Rather than answer, I moved off into the woods, along the creek, Belle looking back at Mark, Pup tangling around my legs in his excitement. We started off slow, but the pace was still faster than my usual warm-up. Mark moved beside me to my right as the path widened, and matched the rhythm of his legs to mine.

"So. Tell me what you learned," I said, managing to sound relaxed and conversational.

"Your faith healer's been on the road for over six months, stopping in little podunk towns all over the Southeast. She stays for a few days, creates a stir, then when people start to have health problems, she moves on. We've signed out a warrant against her and her crew. When the tent meeting opens tonight, she'll be arrested, everything will be confiscated. If we're lucky, we'll find what's killing people."

"Killing?" My breathing had been smoothing out, but that word made me tighten up again. I breathed in and out in long slow drafts of air to dispel the tension.

"In at least three towns in Georgia, there were several deaths following the meetings, beginning the day the Faiths pulled out. Some as late as four weeks later. Most involved seizures, neurological problems or breathing problems. We don't have the report back on the communion wine yet, but if we wait for the report, they'll be long gone. So we're moving tonight.''

"Do we have postmortems on the victims?''

"GBI is faxing them to us.''

"Beg pardon?''

"GBI. Georgia Bureau of Investigation. They've got one of the best criminal tracking systems in the South.''

"But they let the Faiths get away.''

Mark nodded cheerfully. He was always happy when he got to pick up the pieces dropped by another law enforcement agency. In the threat of a terrorist lifestyle, the Homeland Security Office had worked to make communication between agencies more effective. They still had a ways to go before the little boys with guns stopped their pissing contests.

We turned off the path by the creek and into the cow pasture of the farm bordering the north side of our neighborhood. I increased the pace, and Mark, who had been talking the most, fell silent to breathe. Point to me.

"Well, my news may sound a little dull and anticlimactic after that, but I'll share anyway. Remember the van accident at the ER?''

Mark grunted. Point two for me. I sped up just a hair more, even though sweat had broken out on us both, soaking through our clothes. When he looked at me in surprise, I showed my teeth in a grin. He rolled his eyes and added a bit more to the speed. But he was puffing.

"Too much coffee last night?'' I asked sweetly.

"Must be. Can't be the lack of sleep, or the weather, or the number of cases I'm working, or the stabbing last night.''

"Stabbing?''

"Out at a fishing hole by Prosperity Creek. Sergeant

Ralph McMurphy—remember him?—saw a light from the road. Literally walked up on the body. We sent it directly to Newberry for a post. Didn't make a much of a splash on the scanner.''

"I didn't hear. Messy?"

"Very." He shook his head as we rounded a curve in the path. "And it's the second one like it in the last week. Sheriff is thinking about calling in the state boys."

I knew from his tone that he was not going to offer any details in an ongoing investigation. But a county sheriff didn't cede control of an investigation unless it was something entirely weird or unless he found something on the National Crime Information Center that showed a pattern—something pointing to a serial killer.

I didn't like the direction my thoughts suddenly veered. "Mark…" I paused. I didn't expect him to answer but I decided to try anyway. "You don't think the murder is related to the Faiths and their traveling show, do you?"

Mark glanced at me from the corner of his eye and slowed our pace to make conversation easier. "That possibility just now occurred to you? For a smart woman, that was a bit slow."

I decided to ignore the insult in favor of information. "So the GBI said there were deaths and stabbing murders at the same time the Faiths visited their state, too?"

Mark grimaced. "Not exactly."

"Which means what?" I lifted a branch out of our way and ran beneath it as the cow pasture opened up around us. It was so hot the grass looked brittle and crisp. Off to the side was an abandoned piece of farm machinery, a tractor from the forties, rusted and decrepit, sitting on its rims. One of the rear wheel fenders was hanging by a metal thread. Tall grass grew up around the tractor, making it one of the typical rural views painters liked to capture on canvas and sell at craft fairs.

"The murders are a new wrinkle."

"And therefore may be unrelated."

"But it would be lots of fun if your case and mine were one and the same."

I almost said, *"Fun? You call weird murders and seizures fun? Cops are sick people."* But I was pretty sure I kept that thought to myself as we rounded a copse of cedars.

"The girl from the van wreck," I said, returning to my bit of news, "the one without the amputation—calls herself Na'Shalome—I think she's been painting graffiti all over the hospital."

"I heard about that," he said. "Stuff not in English."

"Right. No one has seen anything, nothing on the security cameras, as if someone knows where they all are and is avoiding them. I think it may be the girl. I think she got into my room last night. I found some graffiti on my mirror in red lipstick."

"Like blood?" Mark asked, drawing the same conclusion I had.

I nodded. "That could have been the intent."

"You taking precautions?"

Meaning, was I locking my door, keeping a chair under it while I was inside, keeping my cell phone nearby when sleeping? All the stuff I always forgot to do. I wasn't about to admit that I thought she got in while I was asleep with the door unsecured. "I hadn't looked at the mirror earlier, only when I went in to sleep. I'll take a new lock for the door tonight, just in case. And I made a copy of the graffiti to show Miss Essie later today. Maybe she can tell me about it."

"Good move," Mark nodded, and then, winded from

the effort of too much speed and conversation, we both fell silent, feet pounding a hard steady rhythm, dogs running beside us. The heat was rising, the air hanging limp and heavy even this early in the day. Birds were silent, squirrels too enervated to chitter at the dogs. It was a miserable August morning.

And it was only twenty-four hours to my birthday. Not that I was telling.

We were soaked through by the time we got back to my house, the dogs ducking through the doggie door in to the cool air and the full water bowl, leaving us alone. Mark grinned at me, showing teeth, just as I had done to him earlier. A predatory grin that warned me something was up. Yet, when Mark grabbed me, pulled me to him and kissed me, I was surprised. Our arms and mouths slid in the sweat, the heat of the day multiplied. He smelled of soap and coffee and that musky sweat-scent some men have that is both clean-smelling and arousing all at once. I felt a heat that had nothing to do with the humidity rise in me, and I kissed him back with an abandon that surprised me as much as it did him.

Mark pulled away and laughed low in his throat, eyes glistening like storm-wet jade. As suddenly as he grabbed me, he released me and turned for his house. Leaving me wanting more. And I was sure he knew it.

Point for Mark. Did that make us even?

Not that it mattered. I went in and stood beneath a cold shower for ten minutes. And not once did a thought of Cam Reston enter my mind.

I went in to work early, called in to help with a multiple shooting down in one of the old mill-villages. It was a poor neighborhood once supported by income from the Cooper Mill, now run-down and impoverished, the mill

in ruins. The McDonald and the Rainey families had reacted to the heat and the ennui with exploding tempers.
The story I got later from an amused cop was that Arkon
Rainey was sleeping with Hoover-Dub McDonald's new
girlfriend, Marlene, got her pregnant and gave her herpes.
Hoover-Dub, after a night of drowning his troubles in a
couple pints of cheap liquor, went to the Rainey house
at dawn to demand that the Rainey matriarch let him in
for a mano-a-mano confrontation.

When Big Mama Rainey refused, Hoover-Dub broke
in and yanked Arkon out of a deep slumber. Hoover-Dub
got himself shot three times by a small-caliber handgun
for his trouble. One round landed in his spine, leaving
him permanently paralyzed from the waist down. He'd
been flown out by medevac to Carolinas Medical in Charlotte, leaving his extended family to mourn and drink and
talk about the unfairness of life and law enforcement.

By the time the temps reached one hundred and two
degrees in the afternoon, tempers on the McDonald side
had reached the boiling point and they had gathered on
the street corner plotting what to do about the man the
police had not arrested. Twenty or so of the variously
related McDonalds converged at the Raineys', weapons
loaded, and demanded Arkon come out and make himself
accountable for both the pregnancy and the shooting.
When he refused, the McDonalds opened fire and pep-
pered the Rainey house with small-arms fire.

No one was critically wounded, but there were enough
injuries to require my help, and the presence of the
county's three general surgeons, an entire complement of
OR and medical techs, all the off-duty EMTs and every
cop in the county. The injured were patched up, operated
on and put back together. The uninjured were sent to jail,
the Raineys in one set of cells, the McDonalds in another.

By 7:00 p.m., when the tent meeting was to open, I had put in a hard day and was stretched out in the break room drinking a cup of coffee. The patients admitted from the tent meeting in the last few days were having almost continuous uncontrolled seizures. We needed to know what had stimulated the convulsions and I was eager to find out what Mark had discovered at DaraDevinna Faith's meeting.

Sipping fresh coffee, I listened to the scanner hoping to hear Mark's voice, my thoughts as much on his kiss this morning as on the faith healer. Instead of more excitement, all I heard at 7:10 p.m. was two clicks, followed shortly by the words "Dispatch, we are returning to the LEC." Mark sounded very frustrated.

Two clicks was the cop code for go ahead. They hadn't had time to shut anything down or arrest anyone by the time he called everyone back. The phone rang at seven twenty-two and I picked it up, expecting it to be him. I wasn't disappointed.

"ER, Lynch,"

"They're gone."

"The tent meeting?"

"Packed up and departed, every stick of tenting, every travel trailer. Gone." I heard what sounded like his hand hitting the steering wheel in anger.

Feeling my own sense of frustration, I said, "We sent toxicology screens off and the preliminary results show nothing. It'll be a day or two before we hear anything final, and meanwhile patients may start dying. We need to find out what they were giving people."

"You think I don't know that, woman?" Mark said, his voice rising.

I closed my eyes and tamped down my sense of failure. It wouldn't help this situation. Sighing, I said, "Sorry.

It's just that things are bad here for some patients and now we may never find out what caused the seizures.''

"The Faiths will turn up somewhere soon. They were making enough money off the locals in a voluntary offering at the end of each meeting to have developed a taste for it. We sent out a report on NCIC to warn anyone else about them. But—" He bit off whatever expletive he was considering, instead hitting the steering wheel again.

"Abusing county property?" I asked with a smile.

"I'd like to shoot something. Be glad all I'm doing is thumping on the car."

"Why don't we—" My words were interrupted when a security guard ran by, his radio squawking and blaring. "Gotta go," I said. "Something's happening."

"Later." Mark clicked off and I rose, going to the desk. "What's up?" I asked the night crew, gathered there.

"Ask her," Anne said, nodding to the form of Boka as she ripped open the ambulance doors and tore through the ER like a silk tornado.

"Boka?" I called.

"You want to help, come with me."

I shrugged at the nurses and followed, calling back, "Beep me if you need me." I caught up with Boka before she rounded the door at the Radiology Department and matched my pace with hers. "What's going on?"

"That crazy patient you admitted is trying to kill the Jane Doe."

"Any luck with IDing them?"

"None. Both are still totally uncooperative. And Social Services can't very well incarcerate them for no reason if they are over eighteen."

"Putting them in a foster home isn't exactly like jail."

I was in a devil's advocate mood. Multiple shootings do that to me.

"Tell them that. If you can get them to talk to you."

From the medical floor echoed the sounds of screaming and nurses shouting. I followed Boka into Jane Doe's room.

The lights were all brightly lit, the room filled with nurses, two security guards and the smoke of a dozen recently extinguished candles. The rank scent I associated with Na'Shalome underlay the haze of smoke like the tang of a mass grave. Jane Doe lay in the center of her bed, eyes dull and lifeless, a splatter of blood covering the sheets over her body. Her one good hand clutched the sheets in a grip so tight her flesh was gray from lack of circulation. The fist was the only sign that she was aware of anything amiss. The blood-painted doll stood on the foot of the bed, real blood splattered on it this time, its eyes on Jane.

I remembered Miss Essie talking about the effect of fear and drugs and how they related to blood magic. I moved past Boka into the room.

Crouched at the foot of the bed, her back to the corner, was Na'Shalome, bare bony knees drawn up to her chest, bloody hospital gown bunched between her legs. Boka began issuing orders to clear the room of unnecessary personnel, and have Na'Shalome returned to her room, restrained and sedated. As the room cleared and Boka started to look for the cause of the spray of blood, I inspected the doll.

It stank. Using my nose as my guide, I studied the doll at close range. The rank smell came from it. It was enough to make me gag, and anyone who survives medical school and its cadavers can stand a lot, smell-wise.

The doll had been secured to the traction bars with

bedraggled red ribbon, the knots tied so tightly they would have to be cut loose. With a pair of borrowed surgical scissors, I pried and pulled and cut until one knot came free. The motion as it gave jarred the doll and something fell onto the sheets. A panel at the back of the doll, in the general location of the buttocks and the tubing that was hot-glued in place at the anus, had dropped open, disgorging its contents. I bent and studied the thing on the sheets. Recognizing it, I felt the blood thump hotly in my head.

"Boka?" I said without moving.

"Yes? What?" She sounded distracted.

"Boka, look at this. Is it what I think it is?" I took a pencil from my pocket and moved the thing on the bed so we could view it from every angle.

The delicate woman bent beside me, her floral scent a fresh counterpoint to the smell of the doll. "It looks like…meat." But her tone had gone cold, and I knew she was thinking the same thing as I.

"Human tissue," I clarified softly.

"Yes. Perhaps."

"And do you think that scissors made these cut marks here?" I pointed with the pencil.

Speechless, Boka nodded.

I raised up and moved to the head of the bed and the staring girl sitting there. I didn't ask permission. I simply used my hands like a vise on her jaw and opened Jane Doe's mouth. Her tongue had been cut out. Beside me Boka gasped.

I checked Jane's hand. Her fingers were blood free. She hadn't done this to herself.

"Na'Shalome. She did this," Boka said softly.

I nodded. Boka jerked violently, banging her elbow on

the doll. Something else appeared in the crack of the doll's buttocks. A piece of plastic with something inside.

"Rhea?"

"I see it." Donning the latex gloves in my pocket, I lifted the plastic from the doll. It was a clear biohazard transport bag. Inside was a human hand, several days into decomposition. Maggots crawled over the surface. Boka covered her mouth in shock and said something in her native language. I didn't need an interpreter to know she had sworn.

On the far side of the bed a nurse stood, her mouth open. I hadn't even noticed her till now. "Go dial dispatch and ask for Captain Mark Stafford. Tell him Dr. Lynch asks him to get over here now. Tell him, and only him, what we have here. But you are to tell no one else what you just saw. This is a patient-confidentiality issue. Do you understand? I do _not_ want this blabbered all over this hospital."

She closed her mouth and nodded. "Yes, ma'am. I'll get him. And I won't say a thing."

"That goes for you, too," I added to the other nurse at the door. She nodded. I didn't believe her. Dawkins County was a small-town hospital and this was juicy news. But at least perhaps I could keep it from making the local paper. Patients deserved more privacy than these girls would likely get.

I didn't know how to treat the tongue and the rotting hand. One was a crime scene item more than a medical one. I turned the bag over several times to determine that the hand matched the one missing from Jane Doe. Not that I'd had much doubt.

"Na'Shalome cut off her hand. Cut out her tongue," Boka said.

"Yes," I sighed. "And it looks like Jane, here, let her."

At my words, Jane Doe blinked. And a single tear fell from her eye to trail down her lovely face.

Mark, crime scene team in tow, arrived about the time Boka finished taking snapshots of the doll, the hand and the tongue for the reports we would be filling out. Strange-occurrence report. Something weird happens, we have to document it, and in this situation, photograph it. Boka took an entire roll of Polaroid film with an old camera for her records, the patient's records and my records. Everything in duplicate, every i dotted and t crossed. Especially as the tongue had been removed on hospital grounds. There were liability issues, as well as medical and criminal ones.

For her own safety, Jane Doe would be shipped to another hospital and placed in a victim protection program. She would need the attention of a very skilled oral surgeon. We packed the tongue in saline-drenched sterile wraps and ice with the hope that it could be reattached. The hand was beyond help and would go to the SLED lab for analysis. The State Law Enforcement Division would verify by DNA analysis that the hand belonged to Jane Doe and estimate when it had been removed. Mark and his team worked fast. He had little time to get his evidence. Jane Doe's medevac was en route.

Administration was called in, and Rolanda Higgen-botham, dressed in dirty gardening clothes, made sure all the proper documentation took place. I went back to patients in the ER and missed most of the fun, though I knew I would have to give a statement eventually. I had, after all, helped discover the hand and tongue when I inadvertently opened the doll's backside.

Near midnight, Mark placed Na'Shalome under arrest and confiscated the strange doll, not that the girl even noticed. She was zonked out on the sedatives ordered by Boka. As he searched the girls' rooms, Mark found the tanned-hide bag I had seen and confiscated it, as well. On his way out the door, he stopped by the ER and showed it to me.

"This what you saw in Na'Shalome's room?" He had on his cop face, his voice professional and stiff-sounding.

I put on my doctor face and found my doctor tone. I opened the bag and poured the stones out on the table. "Yes, it appears to be the same bag. The stones look the same. Where did you find it?"

"Under the mattress."

Beneath the cop tone I could hear his amusement. Mark thought this was all funny on some slightly demented cop level. If this situation got out to the press, it would likely be from a police source not a medical one. I could tell he was bursting to talk about it. "Unique hiding place," I said.

"I thought so, too. I'm surprised we found it at all." His mouth twitched beneath the mustache.

"What are they?" The stones felt slick, polished and oiled from constant use.

"Runes."

"Say what?" I asked.

"Runes. An old alphabet, sort of pictorial, like Egyptian but different. Some people call them futharks. Lots of ancient peoples had their own version, the Germanic peoples, the Scandinavians. Even the Celts in England had a variety of runes. They used them for information and to tell the future. And in magic. These are what she's been painting all over the hospital. Or someone has. I have several nurses telling me that the graffiti artist can't have been Na'Shalome because she was in surgery or knocked out on sedatives several times when the pictographs appeared. But I think they nurses are mixed up about the time. It was her.'' He tossed a can of yellow paint, also in an evidence bag, onto the break-room table. The can bore traces of fingerprint powder. A final bag containing a pair of bloody surgical scissors followed.

"Under the mattress?"

"Yep."

"Clever, clever girl. How did you find out about runes?"

"I took an alternative-history course in Citadel. One that talked about Chris Columbus not being anywhere near the first European to make it to the West. Back in 1898, a farmer in Minnesota found a buried stone carved in runes. According to the runes, thirty or so Swedes and Norwegians made it here and were stranded in 1392.'' He shrugged, the ''have I got a story to share with the guys,'' look still firmly in place. "I thought it was interesting."

"So when I showed you the drawing I copied from my call room mirror, you knew what it was and you didn't tell me?" I didn't believe that. Mark would have shared his info and preened. It would have been part of the one-upmanship we enjoyed so much.

He flashed me a grin. "Not really. They looked familiar. But when I saw this, I had the LEC do an Internet scan for the symbols and they came back as runes.'' His eyes twinkled. "Then it all came back to me."

"Runes. Magic. Amputated limbs and tongues. Only in Dawkins."

Mark grinned happily. "Ain't it great? There's no place like home."

14

CURSE OF THE RUNES AND WHAT THE HECK IS HENBANE?

I was feeling out of sorts when I got off work, and refused to put it down to lack of sleep or general weirdness in my professional life. I also refused to consider acknowledging the loneliness that sniffed after me like a bloodhound. I missed Marisa, that was about all I wanted to admit. Instead of another run, I showered and dressed in long shorts and T-shirt—with bra beneath—and walked over to Miss Essie's, the dogs gamboling beside me, the Polaroids from the night before and a few papers in my pocket.

Cam didn't meet me at the door when I knocked, though there were signs that he had eaten breakfast with Miss Essie—two coffee cups, two plates drying beside the sink. Miss Essie put a basket of blueberry muffins on the table when she let me in and pointed to the Mr. Coffee. "Make them dogs stay outside. They been rolling in something. Pour you'self a cup and set down."

She dropped into a chair as I shooed Belle and Pup back out. I noticed that Miss Essie had put on a few pounds. She had become too thin in the last few months and I was glad to see the extra weight. It meant that she had been eating.

"Happy birthday," she said.

I shrugged, uncomfortable with the acknowledgement. To me it was just Tuesday, nothing special. Miss Essie changed the subject.

"That Cam," she said, her piercing black eyes on me, "already out to the airport. He mighty interested in gettin' out this town. You know anything 'bout his sudden need to go on back to work?"

I hid a smile and sipped my coffee. It was so much better than anything I got to drink at the hospital. Smooth and full-bodied. I told Miss Essie so.

She snorted. "Tell me all, chile'. I got to live with that man for another day or more."

"Shirl broke up with him," I said, my mouth hid behind my cup and two hands.

"That I know. My Arlana done call me and tole me all 'bout that scene." Her lips stretched knowingly. "And then he come to see you. Din' stay too long. Mad as a hornet when he come in. All twitchy like."

"He wanted me to help him drown his misery."

"Drinking or sexing?"

"Not drinking," I said wryly.

Miss Essie slowly lifted a hand and pulled my cup away from my face so she could see me clearly. "You turn him down?"

I nodded.

"Good. That boy is nothin' but pain for the woman who fall in love with him. And you always half in love with him anyway."

"We are friends, Miss Essie. Nothing more." I put down the cup, but kept my hands curled around it.

She snorted again. "That boy got two friends in this

whole world what are women. Me and you. Me, he uses to feed him and give him advice when things don' go jist like he want. You, he put on some tall pedestal and worship. You take that man to your bed and you break your own heart and destroy his soul, 'cause then you be jist like all the others.''

I took a muffin and broke it open. The blueberries looked fresh, the cooked dough fluffy and slightly blue. They should have been delicious, but when I crumbled one and put it in my mouth, it was tasteless.

''You gone be all right with this?'' she asked.

''I made the right decision.''

''Don't make it easier.''

''I'm his friend.''

''And Mark?''

I felt my face burn and I grabbed the cup to drink again. ''I haven't decided anything.''

Miss Essie just chuckled. ''So what you gone do for Cam when you see him again?''

''Take him to a movie.'' I looked at her over the rim of the cup. ''Remind him we're friends.''

She nodded. ''Now, what else you got to tell me?''

Thankful for the reprieve, thankful that I would not have to describe any more of my relationship problems, I pulled the Polaroids out of my pocket and spread them on the table. ''Do you remember the doll I told you about? This is it.'' Miss Essie pushed the photos around with a forefinger. ''What do you think?''

''Ain't a toy. Been used for something else.'' She pointed to the new drops of blood, scarcely visible over the red paint. ''Been used with blood. Sacrifice?''

''Sort of.'' I told her about the scene with Jane Doe, about the tongue that had been removed, and about the hand I had found.

"No circle on the floor or the bed?"

"Circle?"

"Drawn with chalk or made with salt."

"No. At least I didn't see anything."

"You'd a' seen this. It got to be thick enough to make it what witches call unbroken. And there no circle…" Miss Essie sighed. "I got to say that girl mus' be self-taught and full of hate."

The full-of-hate part I understood. "Self-taught?"

"Not been a part of any witch coven. Not trained under a witchy woman."

"You mean that she read about witchcraft, then practiced it."

"Made it up." She shrugged. "Play at bein' a witch 'til she believe it."

I laid out the drawing of the runes I had copied from the mirror in my call room. "And this? Mark said it looks like runes, but I can't read it."

Miss Essie pushed herself away from the table, taking her cup with her. "Come on. We find out."

In the study once used by Steven Braswell, M.D., Miss Essie sat in front of the dark computer monitor and moved the mouse. Slowly the screen came to life, showing an AOL icon minimized at the bottom. She clicked on it and signed on to AOL.

"Miss Essie? When did you learn how to use a computer?"

"Started when Miss Marisa talk 'bout gettin' that English woman to come be a nanny. Din have no use for them things afore. Got a computer class starting end a' the month. I do e-mail all right, but I still have trouble with some part of computers." AOL in place, she typed in *www.dogpile.com* and then typed in *runes*. Scanning carefully, she chose a site and clicked on the hyperlink.

It didn't take us long to find a page that showed the runes themselves, and quickly we discovered that all my runes were upside down—or reversed—which meant that of any possible interpretations, only bad things were intended to befall me. Miss Essie wrote the meanings on scratch paper as we discovered them.

The five runes were laid out in a cross, with the first three running up and down, and the two others as the arms of the cross. The position didn't seem to change the meaning of them, as far as I was able to tell. Either way they had been arranged, they would have been a curse. I had Uruz, Thurisaz, Wunjo, Hagalaz and Perthro, all reversed. I was being offered weakness, lust, sickness, obsession, violence, lies, hatred, malice, sorrow, alienation, delirium, suffering, crisis, loneliness, and addiction.

"Well, ain't that just dandy," I murmured.

Miss Essie frowned. It was her "you got to take this seriously" look.

"Not exactly a Hallmark card greeting," I said, still trying for levity. "Dang things don't even rhyme. How can she expect to get published if they don't rhyme?"

Miss Essie sighed hugely and closed down the Internet connection. "I 'spect you to pay attention to this. Someone is trying to cause you pain," she said as the monitor changed colors and Windows-blue reappeared.

"I do pay attention, Miss Essie. But I'm not a religious person, you know that. This is all just mumbo jumbo and I can't take it seriously."

"I pray for you, chile', every day and every night."

"And I thank you, Miss Essie." As the old woman stood, I put my arms around her. "You don't know what it does for me to know that you love me. And anyway, no curse is bigger than your God."

"That true, but you don' have to be stupid."

"I'll take care, Miss Essie."

She shoved me roughly away. "Come on back to the kitchen. That coffee getting cold, and ain't much worse in life than cold coffee."

"Cold hospital coffee?" I proposed.

"You win," she said instantly. "What else you want from an old woman you ain't gone listen to no way?"

"I need to know if there are any herbs that might have a psychotropic or mild hallucinogenic effect."

"Make people see visions, be agreeable to do things they usually wouldn't? Like that LSD and ecstasy?"

"Exactly." We settled back around the table and I poured fresh coffee from the carafe for us both.

"Them psilocybe mushrooms."

"Okay. Any others?"

"Near 'bout fifty or so, you prepare them right."

My mouth dropped open. "Fifty?"

"Hundreds if you count the ones that work on the body instead of jist the mind. And mos' them legal. You can buy them if you want to. I got some growing in my garden," she added almost grudgingly.

"You? You have drugs growing in your garden?"

"I cook with a type of sage that the Indians used to give them visions. Jist to name one. And every flower or herb garden got medicines in it, if you know how to use and prepare them and you is willing to take the chance with them. Dosages is difficult with herbs." Her eyes were hooded, and I didn't know if Miss Essie was trying to tell me something or trying to hide something.

"And these herbs...can they affect, say, the heart and blood pressure, too?"

"'Course." She exhibited her usual snort with more force than ordinary, as if to tell me that all my learning wasn't worth much at this moment. "You never hear of digitalis? That a flower. Used for centuries to help with heart trouble.'' Her head reared back and her nostrils flared, and I feared I had trespassed into an area of particular interest to Miss Essie. Like religion. Or cooking. Or the raising of children. Miss Essie had strong opinions, and I was suddenly on guard not to disagree with her or question what she might consider an ultimate truth.

I nodded and said carefully, ''I know most drugs are synthesized from plants, Miss Essie.''

'''Zactly. Where you think all them doctors find all they medicines? Already made up in the cabinet all nice and bottled? They take them from plants. Aspirin, blood-clot thinners, all sorts a' stuff come from plants. Heroin from a poppy and cocaine from a coca plant and marijuana, too, all plants give to us by the Lord for good, that man done take and make bad. Still, they got some good use in medicine, and if that FDA a' yours had a brain to deal with, they'd a made them good drugs available to the sick American folk what need them. Dyin' folk and such. And don' get me started on hemp and how them crazy FDA men got it on a bad-drug list and it ain't even a medicinal!''

I forbore mentioning that the FDA was not mine, and it never occurred to me to ask about hemp. I was getting better at holding my tongue. Sometimes. But clearly I was treading on delicate subject matter with Miss Essie, and that was like trying to cross a well-used cow pasture without stepping in offal, while blindfolded. I didn't know what question to ask next. I settled on, ''Can you make me a list?''

She nodded, ''I got a list made,'' she said, her eyes still filled with the expression I couldn't decipher. ''I'll update it for you. You want poisons, too? They still poisons everywhere in mos' gardens.''

"Yes. Thanks, Miss Essie," I said as I stood and made my way toward the door. "Can I pick up the list later today?"

Again she nodded, her eyes tightening in some subtle anger. "I e-mail it to you," she said, reminding me that she could use a computer. Remembering the omens and portents and the curse of the runes, remembering the nanny I had helped to find and who would surely displace some of Miss Essie's authority, I quickly left the house, after giving her my e-mail address. The heat and humidity hit me like an aromatic fist as I made my exit. The scent of herbs, some still damp with morning dew, was overwhelming. Looking around the raised beds, so carefully tilled and worked, I wondered how many of the plants were dangerous. And what Miss Essie did with them.

The dogs, lying in the shade of a tree, thumped their tails and didn't bother to rise until I was almost upon them. I looked up into the leaves over them and wondered if this was a medicinal herb, too. Or some poisonous tree I had never considered before.

Feeling odd, as if I had just discovered something about Miss Essie that had been there before my eyes all along, I walked briskly home, changed shoes and took off on a run, leaving the dogs locked up in the house with Stoney, who was asleep on my pillow. It was too hot for Belle and Pup to expend the kind of energy I wanted to blow off. Frankly, it was too hot for me, too, but I knew it and carried an extra water bottle and a towel with my usual running accessories.

I am a runner, not a jogger, but today I moseyed along in the heat, a half pace that left me coated in rivulets of sweat, my lungs burning and my legs not cooperating. I was exhausted, knees rubbery, before I made two miles, and I headed home along the neighborhood streets to cut the return distance in half.

I had a bottle of Gatorade in the fridge and drank the whole thing before showering off. The dogs thought I tasted delicious, and I had to push them away to keep from tripping over them. Following the shower and a nap that called to me from the rumpled covers, I turned on the computer and opened my mail. Miss Essie's was the first I saw. Her e-mail handle was herbgrower777. I didn't think Miss Essie was seventy-seven years old, so I figured the numerals were something religious. And her list was impressive—alphabetized and explained, with the Web site she suggested I visit at the top of the page. Her list went:

Aconite—sedative.

Adonis—cardiac stimulant, like digitalis. I don' like it, personally.

New England aster—used as smudging herb to awaken the unconscious. Is a pretty flower.

Bdellium—used in Arab tribal rituals. Don't got this one.

Belladonna—medicinal and can be a poison. Witches like it.

Bloodflower—works like digitalis, makes pretty red dye. My sister painted her nails with it when she a girl. Made a mess. I got some this, too.

Scotch broom—can regulate irregular heartbeat. Can cause respiratory paralysis.

Spanish broom—more powerful variety. I see I got mose these in my garden.

Catnip—promotes lethargy. That cat a' yours will like it. They lazy animals.

Cedar—can be toxic, but it smells nice and keeps

moths out.

Wild cherry—sedative. Good for furniture. You got a tree in your yard.

Codonopsis—improves breathing and dyspepsia and anemia.

Coltsfoot—used in relief of asthma.

Columbine—narcotic. This stuff dangerous. It used by root doctors. But it real pretty.

Oxeye daisy—relieves asthma and excitability.

Devil's claw—relieves rheumatism and arthritis.

Devil's club—medicinal and in rituals. Has magical properties. Or so they say. I ain't never seen none.

Ephedra, green—central nervous system stimulant. Dangerous stuff, it make a good tea.

Fo-ti—one a' them Oriental herbs. I got some growing. Good for high blood pressure.

Forsythia—lots a' uses medicinally. You and I both got this one.

Foxglove—now you know this one. I got whole beds growing.

Gardenia—helps insomnia, high blood pressure. Got some that smell great, too!

Heartsease—respiratory catarrh and sex stimulant. So they say.

Hemlock—poison. Causes nervous system changes and motor disturbances. Is an effective insecticide.

Henbane—causes convulsions.

I stopped reading. It had just occurred to me that the e-mailed list went on for another page or two. I was only at the "H's," but I had already seen several herbs that could contribute to convulsions, ending with the last two.

Henbane. What the heck was henbane? Copying the e-address to Miss Essie's herbal site, I started looking up the Latin names. I knew I would be busy for quite a while.

The day was long and boring and I finally ended it by driving out to the local airport to see Cam. Calling it an airport was too generous a description for the little concrete runway and grouping of ramshackle buildings. Even the windsock looked limp and faded, though that may have been the effects of sun bleaching, time, still air and humidity. I knew that the air currents over Dawkins County were renowned in the state by glider pilots, parachutists and pilots of small planes, but the vision of the airstrip was anything but comforting.

I parked my BMW Z3, crawled out of the AC into the blast of heat and found Cam, sweating like a shade-tree mechanic in the shadow cast by one building. Riding low on his hips were denim shorts that had once had longer legs. Now the left leg was just long enough to be considered decent, the front pocket hanging below the ripped hem, and the right-leg hem was cut at an angle with bleached-denim strings hanging from it. One leg was up on a strut, the position pulling his jeans tightly across his buttocks. He was shirtless. Slightly sunburned. Sweating. And had not an inch of body fat on him. A cold beer sat on a flat part of the Cessna, whose engine covering was bent open. Hearing my footsteps, he looked up as I approached and frowned.

"Lovely weather, isn't it?" It was the best opening I had, left over from etiquette lessons taught to me by Marisa's aunt, Miss DeeDee, so many years back in my youth.

Before he answered, Cam dropped his leg and lifted

the beer. His throat worked as he drank, skin glistening with the movement. He drained the beer and tossed the bottle into a crate nearby. The multiple clinks as it landed and settled let me know that this beer likely wasn't the first one.

"What do you want?"

"To ask you to a movie. I hear there's a great action flick in town."

Cam focused his eyes on mine. I could see the effect of the beer in his expression. Then he dropped his eyes and let them roam over me in a manner that needed no words to make clear. "And if I want to come in afterward?" His eyes returned to my face and his lips curved in a smile that had melted more debutantes' hearts than cheap wine. His voice dropped into a low rumble. "What if I try to...convince you into bed?"

I nodded, as if considering his questions. "I'll kick your nuts so hard you'll talk like Pee-Wee Herman for a week."

Cam laughed, the sound spluttering, his amorous expression fading to be replaced by something akin to relief. He wiped his wrist across his lower face and nodded, before licking the salt on his lips. "Just so I know where we stand. Still friends?"

"Always."

"What time?"

"Movie starts at seven-ten."

"I'll pick you up."

I nodded and walked back to my little car. Undulating waves of heat rose from the black paint. Sort of the way sex appeal rose from Cameron Reston. I got in and turned up the AC full blast, roaring out of the parking area like I was on fire. Maybe I was.

* * *

By seven I had accomplished three things. First, I had compiled a long file of herbs affecting respiratory and cardiac functions or resulting in convulsions. A twin file listed herbs with psychotropic effects. Altogether, I had around two hundred herbal names. There were probably thousands more, all legal, all available. Probably the average person could do little harm with herbal use, even if they were treating themselves for a mild or moderate medical problem. However, I feared that some herbs, in combination with others or with pharmaceuticals given in acute or severe chronic conditions, could do more damage than I could begin to comprehend.

And these things were common flowers, roots, leaves, stems. Anyone could go out into a garden and make a concoction that could injure or kill.

Even after all the work I had done, although all my fears were building, I didn't believe that only doctors of naturopathic medicine—doctors trained in the use of herbal medicines—homeopaths, and certified herbalists should be allowed to use them. I didn't think they should be banned. It was impossible to regulate Mother Nature. But I was frightened for the patients I had left behind in the hospital, many of whom were just now starting to respond to meds.

The second thing I had accomplished was restoring my friendship with Cam, who showed up at my door with a dozen salmon-colored roses in the midst of a bouquet of aromatic lilies, and a sincere apology for the pass he had made. The note on the flowers said, ''I'm an ass. So sue me.'' Almost amusing language from a doctor who cut on people's brains, not their backsides, and might be sued over anything.

The third thing I did was see a really great movie. Lots of gunfire where no one bled out or died slowly, lots of really cool "Make my day"—type lines, lots of popcorn and Coke, and even a box of Milk Duds that stuck to my teeth and made me talk funny.

The only problem was what I found when I got home.

15

FLATTERING AS HECK

Cam dropped me off in the driveway, told me, "Happy Birthday, gorgeous" and roared off in his rental car, no attempt to seduce me or even kiss me good-night, just his habitual jocular self. As I climbed the steps to the stoop, I heard the dogs inside, barking frantically, Belle's high-pitched warning and low-pitched threats, Pup's terror.

The dogs were still inside. That was wrong....

Instantly, I came alert. Felt myself chill in the muggy heat, tighten inside.

The dogs were running frantically through the house, their barking growing and lessening with distance and proximity. Belle's body thudded solidly as she threw herself at the doggie door. It didn't budge. It was sealed shut. Multiple strips of duct tape wound around the edges where the doggie door had been cut into the wood.

Below the sealed doggie door, something shined in the dim light of the porch. It was a clear, Ziploc bag; inside, a doughy-looking rolled shape. I started to lift it and realized, just before my fingers touched the bag, that I shouldn't. Bent forward at the waist, hand extended, I froze.

I turned slowly, staring into the darkness. My corner light was off. I had left it on. I was sure of it.

I didn't carry a purse. I didn't have my cell phone. I couldn't go inside safely. Turning, I sprinted down the driveway to Mark's, praying he was home. He answered my frantic pounding on the front door, a wicked-looking gun in one hand. Ignoring it, I shoved my way past him into the safety and darkness of his front hall.

"Rhea? What—"

"Someone has been to my house. They duct taped the dogs' door shut with them inside. They're going nuts. And there's this thing in a bag on the back stoop." I took a dozen quick deep breaths, aware only then that I hadn't taken a breath since Cam drove off. Sudden shivers gripped me.

"What, in a bag? What kind of bag?" he asked as he found a shirt and pulled it over his head, pocketed his cell phone, his police radio, and headed to the door. He never put the gun down. It was huge, black and dull chrome, with a matte sheen that seemed more threatening than any brightly polished weapon.

"Ziploc. I didn't touch it."

"The door locked?"

"I didn't try it."

"Key," he demanded shortly. I dropped it into his outstretched hand. "Stay here."

"Sure. You bet."

And he was gone. Shivers gripped me in the cold of the air-conditioned house. The darkness of the entrance wrapped itself around me as I watched through the glass of the side lights, my trembling fingers pressed against the casing.

Moments later, I spotted flashing blue lights as a marked county sheriff's department car pulled up the street, siren conspicuously silent. A second car pulled up just behind it. Both deputies disappeared into the darkness toward the back of my house.

Several minutes after that, a light went on inside. Room by room, the house lit up until it was blazing bright through every window. There were no gunshots. I figured it was safe. My heart rate began to slow. Gathering a sense of calm about me, I walked across the street and around back. The dogs were loose and darting all over the place, still barking, but now in joy and excitement. Both of them body-slammed me in happiness and I staggered before catching my balance, petting them and murmuring, "Good dogs, yes you are...."

On the outside corner of my house, a cop was standing on the ladder I kept inside in the hallway, his hands working on the light. As I paused in the shadows, it came on and he climbed down.

In the sudden illumination, I spotted Mark, standing at the stoop, staring at me. "Somebody unscrewed the bulb, but you left your door locked and the lights on. Good girl," Mark said, and turned his back to me.

I wondered at his tone and said, "Gee, thanks, Dad, I try. But it's hard since I have only half a brain. All these female hormones cluttering up my poor little thinking processes. Hi, Jacobson," I said to the cop putting the ladder back inside. Docs and cops. Dead certain that we'll know one another.

"Doc." He nodded, his mouth working as if he might be having trouble not laughing, and he turned away quickly, too.

"Someone tell me what's going on?"

"Later, Doc," Jacobson said as he and the other cop headed back around front. "Cap'll handle it. We got to

get back on the street.'' And as he walked away, I could
have sworn I heard soft laughter. *What was so funny?*

From above, I heard a mewling sound. In the dark
branches of the oak sat Stoney, visible only because his
tail whipped back and forth in agitation.

''You can come down now, cat,'' I said.

In reply, Stoney simply tucked in his tail, drew in his
body and grew still. I figured he'd come down when he
felt like it.

Mark was plying a flashlight over the back door, the
beam picking out shapes that had been painted on the
solid wood. ''More runes?'' he asked. He sounded angry
and I wondered what the heck I had done to this man
now. It was like trying to figure out another species entirely. And men said women were hard to understand.

''Looks like it.''

Tucking the flash under an arm, he opened a spiral pad
and pulled a pen from his shirt pocket. My pad. My pen.
From the kitchen bar where I kept them near the phone.
Right beside the extravagant flowers from Cam. I felt a
grin tug at my lips and let it come.

Mark was jealous.

He sketched the runes and flipped the pad shut. Still
not looking at me, he said, ''Jacobson will be sending a
crime scene tech to dust for prints around here.''

''And the thing in the Ziploc bag?''

''I'm not going to speculate. It's been turned over as
evidence.''

''Okay. That's what I thought. That you weren't going
to speculate,'' I said, trying to sound serious but hearing
the humor in my own voice.

Mark nodded and pushed open the door with his—
my—pen. ''Miss Essie came by the house with blueberry

muffins for me. She told me about the runes you translated. Let's go online and see what we can find.''

"Okay," I said, trying to keep the laughter from my tone. I must have succeeded, as Mark marched inside, right past the flowers, and went directly to the computer in the living room to boot it up. He'd have been most unhappy if he knew that I knew he was jealous, and was amused by it. It's a man thing. That much I understood.

Without my help, he typed in the address to the rune site. Leaving him to the work, I went to wash the popcorn butter and Milk Dud chocolate from my hands. Belle came in and sniffed at me, turned to Mark with questioning eyes and looked back at me, whining. I bent over her and whispered that he was being a silly man. Belle, who had much experience with males of her own species, settled on her bed and closed her eyes. She understood that men were silly. But I did notice that she stank, as if she had been rolling in something dead, and I remembered that Miss Essie had complained over the smell.

I went back to the living room and settled on the couch. Mark, his head bent over the computer, didn't look up. After a few minutes he handed me a piece of paper with the new interpretation. "When they're upside down, they are called merkstave. The meaning is opposite to the meaning when turned right side up, but with an attitude, making them worse. Both times all of yours have been upside down."

Again this time I had the cross-shaped placement of the runes, three up and three across, sharing the center space. All upside down. Hagalaz, Isa, Mannaz, Laguz, Raidho. Another curse so similar to the first that it could have been the same one. But after rereading the interpretation, I realized it had a slightly different emphasis. The previous time, the interpretation read like a general threat that could have been concocted for anyone. This time it seemed a bit more personal. I read sickness, suffering, crisis, egomania, plots, blindness, deceit, treachery, mortality, more blindness, "expect no help now," more sickness, suicide, despair, crisis, delusion and death.

To me, it read as if someone was calling me an egomanic who would make bad decisions because I missed something obvious, leading me or others into sickness, despair and death. A perfect curse for a doctor.

Oddly, I wasn't bothered by this one. I didn't look too closely at the fact that this time when I received a runic curse, I was not alone, but with a big, moderately burly, slightly jealous cop who carried a big gun. Or weapon. Whatever he called it. Without comment, I handed the paper back and shrugged.

"What? That's it?"

I lifted my eyebrows and waited.

"You've been threatened twice now and all you've got to say is nothing?" His green eyes slitted and his lips curled down.

I shrugged again and shook my head. I had nothing to say. Mark looked up at a knock on the back door. "Back here, guys," he shouted.

The "guys" were three crime scene techs, two of them women, one a man. All carried equipment, toolboxes and radios. All spoke to Mark and nodded to me as they were introduced. One of the women, Skye, was petite, brown-haired with blond streaks, and had green eyes that looked at me curiously, the way a woman might look at a possible rival. Interesting. I wondered if Mark knew she had a thing for him. If he had asked Skye specifically to be in this crew tonight because he did know. Or if he was oblivious.

I settled on oblivious. Especially after she called back

from the kitchen, "Nice flowers. Boyfriend?" in a tone that was more hopeful than curious.

I shouted back, "Friend from medical school," and noted with amusement that Mark's shoulders tightened.

The crew took their time, lifting prints on the back door, the outside light fixtures and my car. I hadn't thought about my car. What if someone had done something to it? Charlie, the male CS tech who did double duty on the county bomb squad and therefore knew me from a past hospital bomb threat, inspected it for signs of tampering and reported that it looked fine. He even took my keys and drove the toy-size car around the block to make sure. Of course, he may have just wanted an excuse to drive my Z3. It did a lot of downshifting as he roared off.

In poor rural counties like Dawkins, many police and emergency service workers did double duty in several areas, working in more than one specialty. Mark had taken EMS training, special courses in vice and homicide investigation; others might take training in the rescue squad to help put out forest or house fires in unincorporated areas and still work primarily in vice or as an investigator. Here, everyone knew everyone else.

Except for me. I was from Charleston. Unless the town decided to adopt me, I could live here for decades and would still be an outsider. By the same token, I could be away from Charleston for the same amount of time and still be a Charlestonian. After all, I was a *Rheaburn, of the Charleston Rheaburns,* whether I liked it or not. Whether the old Grande Dame Rheaburn liked it or not.

As I wandered my house and yard, watching the techs work, Mark stayed inside, at the computer in the living room, and in the kitchen, and on the phone, filling out paperwork brought by one group of cops or the other. He didn't talk to me except about business, and he didn't once look at the stupendous bouquet. The bouquet that had scented the whole house. The bouquet that took up the entire kitchen bar. The bouquet he passed a half-dozen times as he worked.

This was fun. If we were still keeping score, I figured I had lost points running to Mark like a scared rabbit. But that was his job, so the point loss was minimal. The points I was gaining as he grew more angry and more cold about the bouquet had to be a lot more valuable. When we next tallied who was ahead in the competitive little game we played, I could use this situation like a mortar and pestle and really grind his nose in it.

It was also flattering as heck.

Near midnight, Mark and the crime scene crew packed up and left, Mark saying only one line to me that might have been personal. "I don't think he got in," Mark said brusquely. "Your security system worked like it was supposed to. Lock your doors and call me if you need anything tonight." Then he turned his back again and walked off into the night.

He could have said call 911. Instead, he told me to call him. And he still never mentioned the flowers. That thought kept a smile on my face as I readied myself for the night.

I lay in my big bed, body crosswise on the mattress, sheets thrown off and cool air filtering down from the struggling AC. The blinds were open and moonlight swirled over me in strange patterns as the leaves outside were brushed by a faint breeze. I felt lethargic, relaxed, and still a bit wired as I let my body sink into the mattress in boneless rest.

Stoney, who had come down from his perch in the oak branches at some point, leaped up beside me, padded around in slow circles as he claimed the pillow beside my head. The dogs were in the kitchen, bellies on the cool floor, snoring in the darkness.

Staring into the shadows of the ceiling, I considered the two men in my life. I didn't know how to deal with men, never had. My father had died before I was born and I was an only child with no brothers to teach me. My male role models had been the distant, cool facade of Marisa's father and the jovial, drunken men my mother partied with and occasionally brought home.

I hadn't dated in high school, a time when most girls were learning about men and how to manipulate them. I was too gawky, too tall, too bony, too dull to interest boys. Because my mother had totally given in to the bottle by the time I was a teen, just as her Rheaburn trust fund ran out, there had been no money for clothes, makeup, sometimes not even for food. Boys weren't high on my priority list; surviving was. So I was at a distinct disadvantage when it came to men.

And then, during medical school, had come John. John Micheaux of a long line of physicians, blue-blooded in the Charleston tradition, living South of Broad in the same sprawling, three-story, antebellum house occupied by the Micheaux family since the original house had burned to the ground in the 1800s. Lineage, money, breeding, graciousness, and the most gentle man I have ever known. We fell madly, instantly, and I thought permanently, in love. Now John was dating Gabrielle-of-the-big-boobs-"Boopsie" Larouche and I was living in a little town in rural South Carolina, being half courted by a cop and hit on by Cam Reston. Life was weird.

Suddenly I remembered the bag that had been left on my back stoop, resting beneath a curse clearly meant for me. I hadn't looked closely at the bag, hadn't studied what might have been inside. Mark had refused to speculate, which had suggested to me that what I thought I saw was really something else.

It had looked like a human finger. Neatly severed. No blood. But a thick, possibly male, finger. Now *that* was weird. And even weirder was my own lack of reaction. What? Mark was there so everything was all right? Talk about needing to stand on my own two feet.

Suddenly I sat upright in bed, eyes wide in the moonlight. Rolling, I found the phone on the bedside table and dialed by touch and memory.

"Dawkins County Hospital," a tired voice said.

"This is Dr. Lynch. Put me through to the medical floor, please."

A beep, a few clicks and one question later, my false sense of calm evaporated.

Na'Shalome had not left the hospital. She was still in her bed, sedated and tied in place, with a police guard outside her room. She could not have painted the runic curse on my door. And that meant that several of my previous conclusions were incorrect. Na'Shalome may not have been responsible for the runes painted all over the hospital. She may not have been the one who came into my room while I slept and drew runes on my mirror. Someone else had cursed me. And I had no idea who.

On Wednesday morning, in the first hour of a twenty-four hour shift, I secreted myself in the dark cubicle that housed the MODIS equipment. The Medical Online Diagnostic Interface System was a glorified computer system that allowed doctors in participating rural hospitals to send digital photos, X rays, reports, charts, microscope photographs or any number of things to doctors, diagnosticians and labs at several large-area hospitals, in essence allowing real-time consultation on difficult cases. It was also an Internet service for research and a great way to get e-mail. What it didn't allow yet was instant messaging, except between certain hospitals and certain operating systems.

I sent Mark my list of herbs that might have affected any or all of the patients in the hospital. I got back a one-line reply almost immediately. "Narrow it down." No cute little sideways smiley faces, no endearments—not that we used them often, not even a signature.

"Well, sure," I said to the computer screen. "Now, why didn't I think of that?"

I sent back, "What a bright idea. Tell you what. You get that stuff in the Skoll container analyzed and I may not have to do guesswork." I hit send and closed down the system.

"Stupid cop."

My beeper went off before I got back to the ER and I found I had a phone call from Captain Mark Stafford. Before I picked up, I poured a cup of coffee, sweetened it, added a bit of cream, then a bit more, stirred carefully and sat in my favorite tall-backed chair in the break room. Then I scooted my backside around to see if I was comfortable. Making him wait. Sounding as sweet as I could, I picked up the phone and said, "Dr. Lynch. Can I help you?"

"If you'd a stayed at the MODIS, I wouldn't have had to wait," he said shortly.

"Really?"

"I thought it was a prank, a movie prop or something. I was wrong. It was a human finger."

The game suddenly seemed childish to me. I drank my coffee and steadied myself, remembering the Ziploc bag and the contents as I saw them in the moonlight.

"Rhea?"

"I'm here. There was no bleeding, no seeping. It wasn't freshly amputated."

"No. Medical examiner in Newberry says it was removed postmortem. Maybe several hours after death. Rhea, remember that body I told you about, the stabbing down by Prosperity Creek?"

"Yeah. I remember." I felt suddenly cold.

"Parts had been cut off it. The M.E. thinks this is one of that guy's fingers."

Because I needed something to do, I got up and poured more coffee. I wasn't sure where the first cup had gone, but this was looking like a multi-pot day. "Okay," I said, sounding steady and calm, totally unlike the terror-filled person I was inside.

"So you watch yourself." Mark took a deep breath. "I want us to talk again about what you may have seen inside that wrecked van when you dropped in." He paused, and when he spoke his voice was gruff, as if he was trying to hold in a shout. "And I want to know what the hell Cam Reston did that was so bad he had to send you roses."

Smiling with a warmth that was totally unexpected, I sat back in the chair I had vacated. "Been reading my cards?"

"Damn it, Rhea! Yes! *I'm an ass. So sue me.*"

I laughed softly and decided to tell him the truth. "Just so we're clear."

"We're clear."

"He got dumped by Shirl."

"Shirl's a smart woman. Why did he send you flowers and not her?"

"He came to cry on my shoulder and made a pass at me."

"Okay, so he's a smart man to finally see what's under his nose. For a noted Lothario, his timing sucks, though. And?"

"And I told him if he tried again, I'd kick him in the crotch so hard he'd be singing like Pee-Wee Herman for a few weeks. Or something like that."

"Good. You got a Feeb on the way over, out of the Columbia office. One you know. Have a good time." The phone clicked off. I was still smiling as I hung up. In fact, I was still smiling when the FBI agent, escorted by a hospital security guard, walked in to the ER and took the other seat.

"Special Agent Jim Ramsey," I said, recognizing the man from the South Carolina branch of the FBI assigned to the bioterrorist attack backed by the Reverend Lamb of God. He was tall, quiet-spoken. I had once identified him as low man on the totem pole, the guy in a group of three who was there just for show and to take notes. He had distinguished himself after the bio-attack and moved up fast for a Feeb in his mid-thirties.

"Dr. Rheane Rheaburn Lynch," he said, a twinkle in his eyes. He crossed his hands over his flat stomach and linked his fingers, relaxed and at ease with the interview. "Of the *Charleston Rheaburns,* as I recall."

"You recall correctly."

"So, how *is* your grandmother, the Grande Dame Rheaburn?"

Ouch. So, he wasn't going to be gentle. He was one of the ones who smiled while he committed torture. "I wouldn't know, Mr. Ramsey. I never met her, as your file on me surely indicates." I belonged to a city, not to a family. That much had been made clear by my grandmother to my mother on the day Mama was disowned for drinking, for marrying beneath her and for having me five months later. My mama was the black sheep of the Rheaburn clan. I was the refuse.

"It is the old biddy's loss, Doctor."

I raised my eyebrows. "Do you always play good-cop, bad-cop all by yourself?"

"One must work with the cards one is dealt, ma'am." But he was smiling as he said it. I could play this game, too.

"Is this interview being taped? If so, I must request that you turn off the recorder."

"Do you have a problem with being taped, Doctor?"

"Yes. I do. This is a hospital. Patient confidentiality could be breached by something you might accidentally overhear and tape in this place. That is against federal law. As I'm certain you know."

He smiled again, the twinkle in his eyes even more pronounced. "I am not taping this interview."

"Be so kind as to prove it to me."

"Emma Simmons is a bitch."

I laughed then, the sound loud in the quiet morning ER. Emma Simmons was Ramsey's direct up-line boss. "That was good."

"I thought so. Would you mind telling me—if you can do so without a breach of patient confidentiality—what you know of the seizures on the patients you received from the tent meeting?"

"Be happy to. And if there is some way to speed up the testing process of a certain sample gathered at the meeting, one collected by Mark Stafford, I would appreciate it. It might help treat them."

"I'll see if I can light a fire under the SLED boys." He grinned evilly as he said it. State Law Enforcement Division, the FBI and the local cops had a competitive spirit of their own. Sometimes it caused slowdowns in the solving of cases. Sometimes it sped things up. A challenge from the Feebs might help this time.

In layperson's terms, I told Agent Ramsey everything I knew, guessed and feared about the patients and their seizure activity. There wasn't much I could tell him about their conditions since admission, as other doctors had taken over their care, but I told him of the list of herbs I had compiled with the help of Miss Essie. I promised to e-mail him a copy of it by noon.

Agent Ramsey and I shared a cup of coffee as we discussed not only the patients, but the high pressure that had stalled hundred-degree temps over the state, and the chances of Charlotte, North Carolina ever getting another NBA team. Chitchat. Small talk. I had a feeling he didn't spend much time with doctors unless it was over an examining table or in the interrogation room. It seemed like a new experience for him.

Yet I knew he was cementing a relationship because it was one he might need someday, not because he particularly liked me. Typical cop politics. We had somehow formed an understanding in our last encounter. Not a friendship, but a wary, mutual respect. So I let him feel comfortable. Who knew, I might need a friendly Feeb myself someday.

Our coffee cups were almost empty when the overhead speaker blared to life. "Code 99 to the medical floor. Code 99 to the medical floor. Code 99 to the medical floor."

Someone had crashed. I stood, nodded and ran all in one instant. Ramsey sprinted beside me. "What's this?"

"Cardiac or respiratory arrest. Or someone pushed the wrong button. Everything or nothing. Why are you following me? Don't you have secret-agent stuff to do?"

"That's the CIA. I can pretty much do what I want

for an hour, until I get a subpoena for your patients' records. Mind if I tag along?"

"If I say yes, it ends up in my file, right? Marking me as uncooperative." I was only half teasing. Until recently, I hadn't known that the FBI kept files on ordinary people. I still was only half-sure it wasn't all a gag. "Come along. But don't expect to come into the patient's room."

"Patient confidentiality. I know. I know," he said, his hands up, palms out, in a gesture that seemed to ask for peace.

As I neared the room, my heart fell. It was Ronnie Howell's room.

The doors to all other patient rooms had been shut, and up and down the hall nurses ran, equipment hummed and rolled, and a state of determined panic reigned. Anytime a kid coded it was harder to live with. Pulling my stethoscope from my pocket, I entered the room.

Here was controlled pandemonium and space was at a premium. Boka was in the center, this time wearing a turquoise sari, her hair bound up in a single large curl of a bun. She quickly intubated the child and the respiratory tech took over breathing for him, pumping the ambu bag. The team had one IV going and nurses were pouring over him looking for another site, one nurse doing chest compressions, one taking notes. A lab tech was drawing ABGs, an X-ray tech was waiting to take a film for tube placement, and another nurse was administering Epinephrine IV, a drug to stimulate heart activity. Ronnie's mother crouched in a corner and wept until a nurse lifted her in her arms and half carried her out.

They did what they could for Ronnie. They worked the code for over an hour, pushing the boundaries into areas of brain death, as we always did when it was a child, hoping that the natural resilience of children might bring this one back when, for an adult, it would have been hopeless much sooner. I stood in a corner and watched as Boka gave that extra effort, no matter how futile it seemed after the first forty-five minutes.

They called the code at 10:08 a.m. Ronnie Howell was dead.

I left the room, leaning my back against the hallway's wall a moment to regroup, and spotted Special Agent Ramsey delivering his subpoena to the hospital administrator's office. Voices floated up the hallway, giving me clear access to their conversation.

Ramsey was being very agreeable, for a Feeb. He was willing to accept photocopies of the charts until such time as the patients were discharged. Rolanda Higgenbotham wasn't pleased, but there wasn't anything she could do to stop the agent. With the memory of Ronnie lying spread-eagle on the bed, his body full of holes and tubes, I couldn't care too much about what the agent was doing. Taking a breath to steady my nerves and clear my head, I turned back to the ER.

Sitting against the nurses' desk, her bony knees covered with her hospital gown, was Na'Shalome. She was singing a dirgelike tune, no words that I could hear, just soft minor notes repeated over and over. Her eyes were closed, she was rocking, and she looked half-dead herself. I walked up the hallway and found the police guard, dressed in the uniform worn by county detention center employees, sitting in the hall in a folding chair and flipping through a magazine, coffee cup at his side. The sight made me so angry I steamed, but when I spoke, my voice was soft.

"You always let your charges wander alone and unescorted through the halls?"

He looked up in surprise. "Say what?"

"I said. Do you always. Let your charges wander around? Alone."

"The crazy girl's in her room," he said, irritation with my attitude in his tone.

It wasn't smart to make a cop angry, even one that worked as a detention officer at the county jail, but I couldn't help it. I opened the door and shoved it back till it cracked against the room wall. Without looking in, I said, "Where?"

His expression changing, he stood and put a hand over his weapon and stepped into the room. It was empty. "Where is she?"

"At the nurses' desk, last time I saw her."

Without thanking me properly for fulfilling my civic duty, the cop sprinted down the hallway. At a more leisurely pace, I followed. He found the girl standing in Ronnie's room, at the foot of his bed, rocking herself and crying.

At the desk, Boka tried to comfort the mother, and I was glad it wasn't me who had run that code. I couldn't have been a comfort at all to the woman who had set her son's death in motion by trying to cheat medicine. All I wanted to do was sock her in the face. Not acceptable behavior for a medical doctor.

16

THE FBI WAS FOOTING THE BILL

It took me hours to get over the effect of Ronnie's death. I drank coffee and kept to myself, not interacting with the nurses, only offering the bare minimum of myself to the few patients who came in. I didn't eat. I didn't listen to music. I didn't go to my call room. I just sat in a chair in the break room, coffee at my side, a newspaper I didn't read opened before me.

I had wanted to do a lot of things when I went into medicine, the vast majority of them selfish. I had wanted to find myself. Had wanted to prove something to the rich-witch grandmother who had let me live in poverty when I was growing up because my drunken mother and I weren't good enough for her and her blue-blooded family history. I had wanted to make money. I had wanted to make Miss DeeDee proud of me. I had wanted to learn new things. I had wanted to help people.

That last part had carried me through the tough times in medical school. The impossibly long hours. The weary and unpleasant doctors who were my teachers. The poor pay. The shame over mistakes and the glory over successes. I had wanted to help people. A secret dream and desire. A secret need to do something for someone else, because no had done much for me in my life. Just help people.

And so every time something went wrong, every time I missed a symptom or a problem, every time I was unsuccessful in getting a patient to follow advice or care for themselves or their families, every time someone died, I had to live with personal failure. What did I do wrong or not strongly enough? Where could I have saved this patient? Sometimes it made me mad. Today it was something else.

I called it a case of the "if onlys." If only I had done this, or that, or the other, I might have saved this patient. While I grieved and went over my actions with a vicious and bloody conscience, I ignored the world, sat in my chair, eyes closed, and mourned. The nurses had learned to leave me alone after someone special died—special defined as someone who had once been my patient.

By lunchtime, I had a nice lengthy list of things I could have done differently to save Ronnie Howell. I could have called DSS, made a huge stink, and had him removed from his mother's care. I could have moved the kid in with me as a foster-care option. I could have called the cops on the tent meeting sooner. I could have rammed my car into the tent and ended the services. I could have stolen one of Mark's guns and shot Ronnie's stupid and irresponsible mother when she took him off his meds.

Anger roiling, coffee more than uneasy on my stomach, I sat, eyes closed, as the nurses talked about lunch. No one asked me what I wanted. They knew I wouldn't be eating.

Near 4:00 p.m., someone sat opposite me and dropped something on the table, on top of my newspaper. One eye cracked open and I saw it was a brown paper fast-food bag, grease stains oozing, and an extra large shake.

I opened my eyes all the way and saw Agent Ramsey sitting in the chair, his own bag open, a Whopper and fries on his burger-paper. While he opened little packets of ketchup and sipped his own shake, he talked, his eyes concentrating on the food.

"Eat. I called up here and the nurses are worried. Said you don't eat when a kid dies. Said you sit and grieve. That is stupid and you are not a stupid person, Dr. Rheane Rheaburn Lynch. You didn't kill that kid. You didn't put his mother up on charges of criminal neglect. You can't make the world perfect, and you can't be perfect. Now you eat, or I'll call your boss and tell him you are unfit to see patients."

"He won't believe you," I said. My lips cracked when I opened my mouth, and the feeling surprised me.

"I'll tell him you are drunk on the job. I'll tell him you haven't slept in three days and your judgment is suspect." Ramsey's eyes opened wide, as if he had a great idea. "I'll tell him you are acting like a puny little weak woman."

A half smile tugged at my stiff lips. "I'll pull your gun and shoot you with it."

"According to your boyfriend, you don't like guns." He took a big bite of his Whopper and chewed enthusiastically.

The scent of onions and grease wafted to me. My stomach made a little burbling noise. "There's an exception to every rule."

"Eat. I happen to know you love fat and grease."

"That in my file?"

"No. I asked the nurses."

I sat slowly upright and looked out the door. The chair seat creaked as I moved. My face felt inflexible, mask-like. Perhaps I had sat silent too long.

Ash was sitting behind the nurses' desk, blond head bowed, only the top visible. "Ash?" She lifted her head, her mouth in a stubborn line. "You been talking to cops behind my back?"

"Jim's a nice guy, Doc. We got to know each other when he was here last. He said he could get you to eat." She stood, her face firming. "And if you don't eat, I'll call my nana, who'll call Miss Essie and tell her. You have had, to my best count, three pots of coffee. Three pots! All by yourself." Warming to her subject, Ash moved from behind the desk and stood in the doorway. "That is thirty cups in one sitting. And you haven't been to the bathroom once. You are going to rot out your stomach lining and send your blood pressure through the roof and kill off your kidneys. Your hands are shaking and you look terrible."

I looked down at my hands. They were indeed trembling, and the skin on my fingers looked strange, slightly dried out. After a moment, I nodded. Opened the fast-food bag and took a fry and ate it. The taste exploded in my mouth, making my salivary glands dance for joy. But I wasn't about to tell her that. "Far be it from me to initiate the grandmother brigade. I don't eat and you'll have half the older women in this county bringing me food."

Ash nodded. "I will. There's no greater and stronger force than grandmothers in this county. You don't want them mobilizing except for a good cause."

I took another fry and ate it. "You and Agent Ramsey? Friends?" I looked between the two. Ramsey fought a smile. Ash pinkened slightly. "Just friends?" Ramsey shrugged slightly while Ash nodded firmly. "She likes the orchestra in Charlotte. You should take her to it."

Ash's face flamed in embarrassment. "Doc! Jim is young enough to be my...my...my nephew!"

I grinned in a "turnabout is fair play" manner and shrugged.

"I might do that," Ramsey said, unconcerned by my meddling. "You free Saturday night?"

Ash's mouth bobbed open and closed two times before she said yes, her face now scarlet.

"It's a date, then," he said. Breathless, Ash agreed before she turned and fled.

"Thanks, Doc. I owe you one," Ramsey said, still watching his disappearing meal. "Now eat. Stafford should teach you an acceptable way to get over bad things happening. Take you out to the gun range."

"I run. Usually. Today was hard." I unwrapped the burger and ate it. And it did make my stomach feel better. Almost as much better as meddling in Ash Davenport's life. She was a widow and datable men were fairly rare in this county. Besides, if the nurses were going to start meddling in my life, then they had to beware how I might retaliate.

It turned out that Ramsey had visited the ER for more reasons than to feed me and see Ash. He wanted info on the list of herbs I had meant to send him. After our meal, I saw two patients and made a few quick trips to the bathroom—too much caffeine—then Ramsey and I went to MODIS and I pulled up my list. He studied it over my shoulder while the list printed out.

"What we need here is a toxicologist with a subspecialty in plants and plant poisons," he said. "I've got a friend. You willing to talk to him?" I didn't know what I was getting myself into—the friends of cops were sometimes strange beings—but I agreed.

Less than an hour later, I was on the phone, talking to Dr. Noah Ebenezer, a specialist with doctorates in several areas. He seemed intrigued with the patient status and the fact that herbs might have been used to "induce adverse pharmacological and toxemic reactions in patients with chronic medical conditions." His words, not mine. He suggested that the ash pile at the site of the tent meeting might yield evidence of the species of herbs burned in the bonfire, and which therefore found their way into the systems of the congregation. It was an idea I hadn't considered but it made sense.

Dr. Ebenezer occasionally consulted with the FBI, and in his day job was currently involved in a research project identifying the active, medicinal ingredients of common plant material. Hence, fascinated by our little herbal problem, he agreed to drive down from Johns Hopkins, where he did his arcane research, to take a look and bring some of his equipment to test a few samples. I figured as long as the FBI was footing the bill, I would take all the help I could get.

I had finalized getting Dr. Ebenezer temporary staff privileges when the loudspeaker blared with a code I had never heard before. I unclipped my ID badge and pulled a laminated, printed card from the back to discover that the code was an "unexpected event." Basically that meant something weird had happened. I didn't know if that constituted a medical need, but I was bored, so I figured I would go stick my nose into whatever was happening.

This time, the weird event did have a medical need. The cop on duty outside of Na'Shalome's room was unconscious, lying on the hallway floor.

"Get me an ER stretcher and you nurses search for

Na'Shalome," I ordered as I gently shooed the RNs out of the way and bent over the man.

"She's not in her room, Doc. I'll alert security," Julio Ramos said.

"Call the cops, too. Tell them they've got a mad amputator on the loose," I said. I shouldn't have said it—doctors aren't really allowed a sense of humor, as it could be misinterpreted—but it made the worried personnel laugh, so I considered it permissible this time.

After ascertaining that he was breathing, I gave the guard a cursory check where he lay, my hands roaming over his body while the nurses did pulse and BP checks. I could find no bumps or abrasions on the man's head. He didn't look as if he had been socked in the jaw. No blood, no visible wounds. His respiration was slow, at about ten breaths a minute, and his pulse was faint and slightly erratic at 95, BP was decreased at 110 over 65. His heart sounded fine, no sounds of rubbing or clicking or signs of mechanical problems. His color was fine, but he had lost bladder function.

Easing my backside left to get a good look at his pupils without moving his head—I didn't know about spinal injuries yet—I spotted the cop's coffee cup. It was a well-used, six-ounce disposable cup with multiple dark brown rings all down the inside.

I carefully handed the cup to a nurse wearing a temp agency name tag. I remembered seeing her around for days, and though I couldn't remember her name, I made stern eye contact as I said, "This may have something in it. Don't let it get discarded or emptied out."

"Right, Doc," she said, and took the cup gingerly.

The stretcher arrived and we transported the patient to the ER for a full work-up and evaluation. His name was Gerald Chambers, age thirty-two, Caucasian, no pertinent medical history, a three-year employee with the detention center, no history of alcohol abuse or illegal drug use, married with two kids. Our work-up revealed no drugs in his system, no evidence of cardiac infarct; on the CT scan of his head there was no indication of an infarct—stroke—or bleed on his brain, no fracture to his skull. Nothing to indicate what had really happened to him. His blood pressure remained stable but low, his pulse and breathing rates unchanged.

We worked him up with cops everywhere underfoot. It seemed that Gerald was especially popular with the other cops, and was slated to go to police academy at the next session, before taking a job with the DorCity PD. Cops stayed with Chambers throughout the X rays and CT scan, through various injections and physical exams. They helped dress him and undress him, roll him and transfer him to different exam surfaces when needed. The only time they left was when the nurses inserted a catheter into his bladder. Apparently there are some things that are either too private for a cop to watch, or too gross.

With all the exams and tests, I could find nothing to indicate why Chambers was unconscious. The only thing I could think of was rupinol or ecstasy or some street drug that might not register on the lab's basic scan. I wanted blood, urine and the man's coffee sent to a reference lab, stat, for testing. When I suggested that, I had three off-duty cops willing to run the samples to the North Carolina line, with a promise that a North Carolina patrol officer would meet them there, transfer the samples to the North Carolina car for the trip to the reference lab in Charlotte. They had it all worked out.

The urine and blood samples we had, but the coffee cup couldn't be found. Neither could the nurse who took it. I didn't know if it was Murphy playing games or something darker.

I tried to remember the nurse's name, find a picture of her face in my memory. All I could recall was her ID dangling down toward me, with the blue stripe indicating that she was an agency nurse, not one of ours. When all the other nurses had been accounted for, it was deduced that the replacement's name was Susan Meadows, and that she had been on overtime to fill in for a nurse on vacation, but had finally been relieved and left for the day. While one cop lay comatose and a dozen others kicked their heels in frustration, the nursing supervisor tracked down Susan's phone number and called her. Susan claimed that before leaving work she had told her replacement about the coffee cup, placed it in a biohazard bag and secured it in the cabinet over the coffeemaker in the tiny makeshift nurses' station kitchen. But there was no biohazard bag in the cabinet. No coffee cup. The replacement claimed she was not told anything about the sample.

Nurses went through garbage cans looking for the coffee. It was nowhere to be found.

I sent Chambers's urine and blood on to Charlotte via emergency cop-transport for testing. And wondered who had discarded the coffee cup.

I turned Chambers over to his regular doctor for admission, and went back to more mundane tasks. This afternoon, that included patching up more McDonaldses and Raineys. The cousins and cousins-by-marriage had gotten involved in the feud and a knife fight had taken place. I had the familiar privilege of sewing them all up. It wasn't the first time. They were drinking buddies, fighting buddies, racing buddies, and shared sexual partners like free cans of beer. Things were always getting out of hand and adding to the folklore in the town.

In the midst of the bloody carnage of multiple lacerations, Mark Stafford walked in. I was aware of him instantly by the cadence of his boots. He parked himself in the doorway, standing hip-shot, arms stretched overhead, hands gripping the casing of the door's header, his torso stretched taut, ribs separated by pulling muscles, beige T-shirt and combat fatigues splashed with red mud and darker blood. His orange windbreaker with the word POLICE in huge letters was tied around his waist.

His green eyes settled on me as I stood, bent over a particularly difficult multilayered closure. "Every time I see you, you're buried up to your armpits in blood and gore and drunken, vicious bad guys. My kinda woman. Howdy, Wayne. See you got yourself cut up a bit."

"I ain't vicious, Captain Stafford. I jist got to protect what's mine," my patient said.

"Last time I saw you, you were telling me that you didn't have anything, Wayne."

"Well, I got me job as the midnight-shift manager down at the Gas-and-Go. I got a mobile home I'm renting and I'm making payments on my back child support. I'm gettin' my life in order."

"And now you're going to end up in jail and lose the job and the trailer, all because you couldn't keep your pants zipped."

"That Marlene was asking for it."

"Yeah, I know. They always are begging you for sex."

"Ain't that the truth. I'm a love god." Wayne laughed, the motion causing my work site to move.

"Hold still," I told him. "Can't you interrogate this

guy when I'm through?'' I asked Mark. Though I didn't intend to, I sounded irritable and exasperated.

Laughing, Mark tucked his hands into his jeans and vacated my doorway.

"Men," I muttered under my breath.

When I finally got the last guy stitched up and out of the ER, either into police custody or into the loving arms of family, I fell into my break-room chair, closed my eyes and sighed. My back muscles were twanging with fatigue, especially where I had taken the knife blade. I was tired, cranky and wanted a nap.

"Want a massage?" he asked, his voice pitched low.

"We'll start talk. It might get back to Clarissa," I said, my eyes still closed. Clarissa was Mark's mother, a local socialite, one of the white-gloves-and-girdle crowd. A flighty, slightly frivolous woman who had manipulated her deceased husband mercilessly, and now used her wiles on her son to keep him in check, Clarissa wanted grandkids. And, having found no local takers worthy of the role, she had decided that I was the perfect choice for her son.

"Dangerous," he agreed solemnly. "You hear back from the toxicology testing on Gerald Chambers?"

"Yeah. Not a thing in his system, or at least not anything we can test for."

Mark rubbed his hands across his face and up over his scalp, scratching with the pads of his fingers as he sighed. "Well, I've got news."

At the change in tone, I sat up and looked at him. "What?"

He dropped into the empty break-room chair and pushed the door partway closed. Voice soft, he said, "We finally identified Na'Shalome and the Jane Doe."

"And?"

"Both local girls. Four children in the family, different mothers, same father. It was a big case back a few years. Neighbor called dispatch, said a dog or cat was cater-wauling at a house down the street. Locked house, painted-over, locked windows with bars, fenced backyard full of old appliances and tires, and three chained, starving dogs. The home owner had been in jail for a week on assault charges, unable to make bail. Cop who answered the call said it didn't sound like a dog, and called for backup. They went in. Discovered the kids chained in the basement."

Mark stopped, his eyes on the far wall. I had seen that look before on the faces of cops, firefighters, soldiers—they called it the hundred-yard stare, where they looked into remote vistas, into realities that shouldn't be. His lips pursed and he laced his fingers together, as if to keep from saying something or doing something he ought to control better.

Needing to move, I got up, heated water in the microwave and opened cabinets, hunting for something soothing to drink. My stomach was suddenly unhappy with my previous coffee intake. "Want some tea?" I held up a Celestial Seasonings variety.

"Sure," he said without looking. "I wasn't here then. I read the reports today. Saw the photos."

I made tea while Mark talked. I was glad he had pushed the door partly shut. This wasn't the kind of thing that needed sharing.

"All the kids showed signs of torture, some of it fresh, some of it God-knows-how-old. They were malnourished, dehydrated and wild. They'd been kept there for years, hadn't been to school, hadn't seen a doctor. One, the youngest, could hardly talk, she was so traumatized and socially retarded."

"Jane Doe," I said softly.

"Mattie Duncan, best I can figure. Na'Shalome is Carol Duncan. DSS took them from the house. Made them disappear into the foster care system, with intense therapy, medical help, whatever they needed. I'm still trying to get access to the full records of them all, but it looks like they were kept together until the two oldest went off to school. The father's current girlfriend—who got three months of rehab to get off cocaine, and ten years suspended with two of probation—testified against the kid's father for the reduced sentence. I understand his time in the state pen hasn't been the finest experience." The last was said with a tone of utter satisfaction. The jail experience of child molesters was never good.

"Didn't get his law degree?" I asked, my tone wry.

"Not hardly. He's got advanced AIDS. He's dying."

I handed Mark the tea, a packet of sugar and a wood stirrer. He took them absently.

"I talked to their counselor by phone. The kids ran away a little over a week ago. Na'Shalome—Carol—is dangerous, deluded, sees visions when she's off her meds, which are about two yards long. The counselor is faxing the hospital a list of her prescriptions and a diagnostic summary."

I nodded and sipped my tea as Mark played with his tea bag, moving it around with the wood stirrer. The tea was too hot, but it tasted good, soothing on my tongue. I really had to give up coffee. I considered all that Mark had told me, knowing that cops only tell what parts they consider important. I found one component he had left out. "So when is daddy getting out of jail?"

Mark looked up.

"You said he was dying. He coming home to die?" Judges sometimes gave a compassionate medical waiver allowing a prisoner to go home to die. That was, if any-one would take him in. If he had family left.

"He married the girlfriend while in prison. He's at her place. Got there yesterday. Too sick to even register as a sex offender."

"And Na'Shalome knows he's here?"

Mark nodded and finally drank his tea. "That's what I think. The counselor and I figure the kids came here to kill him. That the person you got a glimpse of at the time of the accident was one of the other kids, maybe, and that one is the hospital artist. We have guards on the father's house, front and back."

"And the finger?"

Mark looked up at me, his face grave. "Some patients get fixated on their doctor. The less rational and more emotionally unstable they are, the more fixated they may become." He paused and I nodded for him to continue. "The counselor I talked to had been to the foster home they got away from. There were books stolen from the local library hidden under the mattresses. Books on witchcraft of all kinds. Spells. Sacrifices. These kids were planning something major for the old man when they took off for home. You may have gotten in the way. Or they plan to use you in some...manner."

"You avoided the question of the finger."

Mark leaned forward over his laced hands, his eyes intent, considering his words carefully. "The guy was killed in a ritualistic manner. Some important body parts were missing. Yes, it was his finger, but even with the print, we're having a hard time identifying him."

"Hands of evil maim and kill," I quoted, my words slow. "Hands of healing do Lord's will."

"Now you know as much as I do."

"I doubt that."

"Well, almost as much." He slanted his eyes at me. "Still want that massage?"

"Maybe later," I murmured as a nurse stuck her head in the door and summoned me back to work.

"Offer's always open."

17

BREAK PATIENT CONFIDENTIALITY—
A FEDERAL CRIME

Noah Ebenezer came by at 7:00 a.m. Thursday, just as I was getting off work. He was a tall man, but any further resemblance to literary Ebenezers stopped there. He was anything but cadaverously lanky, weighing in at over four hundred pounds, all of them loosely swathed in a summer-weight, brown wool suit. With a sweet face and a gentle smile, he asked me to join him for a brainstorming session at the bus station.

"I see you discovered the best breakfast buy in town," I said.

"Agent Ramsey turned me over to Captain Mark Stafford—fit young man, local boy—who made certain that I had access to all the resources in the county. And a man with my metabolism needs many resources."

"Mark knows his way around," I agreed, picking up my bag and lab coat, waving a casual goodbye to the nurses, and following the doctor's extremely ugly, over-size, green van through town. It was a seventies travel van, the kind that would sleep six in extreme discomfort, painted the original putrid green, a shade dubbed monkey-vomit-green by Marisa and me when we were in that gross-out-the-adults stage of teen life. The designation was more than apt.

At the bus station—which was not really a restaurant, but the actual Greyhound bus station with a grill in one corner, a diner-type bar and tall stools, and tables covered with plastic red-checked cloths—I ordered two pancakes with eggs and crisp bacon. Noah ordered and ate as if he was eating for an army: a stack of pancakes half a foot high, a plate of bacon, two omelettes and a serving bowl of grits. Instead of shoveling the meal in, though, he ate with quick dainty bites, talking all the while about herbs and toxins and ways to kill people with garden plants.

Noah was in his late fifties, as healthy as a man with his bulk can be, genial and balding and charming. He gestured with his utensils as he spoke, swirling with his knife at times, making a point with his fork at others. He was graceful in all his movements, like a conductor directing the strings in a concert.

Noah had driven down in the van, which was specially equipped with lab machines for the identification of plant material or whatever else he chose to test. He explained to me the steps necessary to identify the herbs used at the tent meeting. Not the kind of stuff I was usually interested in, but watching the utensil ballet made it all sound almost fascinating.

About halfway through the meal, Cam Reston stormed in, looking disgruntled and disheveled, as if he had just been pulled from bed. "You tell that boyfriend of yours that if I have to be stuck in this godforsaken town, then I at least get to sleep in." He threw a jeans-clad leg over a chair and ordered, "Coffee, hot and a lot," without meeting the waitress's eye.

My eyebrows went up. "Mark Stafford called you?"

"You got another boyfriend? Hi. I'm Cam."

"Dr. Reston?" Noah clarified.

"Yeah. Eggs and bacon and—" he said loudly, then looked up and caught Doris's eye. His entire demeanor changed instantly, as it always did when a female was present, even one as decrepit as the wife of the bus station's manager "—you got any of those great biscuits this morning, Doris?"

"For you, Dr. Reston, I'll have Darnel make up some fresh."

"That would be great. A real pick-me-up." The surly look returned, to be plastered on me. Except for a few notable occasions, Cam had never really seen me as female, so his irascible attitude toward me perhaps didn't count. "What do you want? Stafford explained it all to me and I still don't understand why I need to be here."

"Neither do I," I said calmly, but I had a good idea that Mark had gotten Cam out of bed for no other reason than to punish him for the bouquet. I debated suggesting that, and decided against it. Cam was acting ornery enough as it was.

While Cam waited for his breakfast, Noah and I finished ours and ordered more coffee. Feeling the onset of a massive caffeine headache from yesterday's overindulgence, I decided I would quit some other day.

Over dark roast with real cream and sugar, Dr. Noah Ebenezer shared with me what he had learned. Agent Ramsey had been able to goad the state lab boys into working on the communion-wine-Skoll-sample and they had identified several herbs.

From my own list, I recognized the Latin names for henbane, columbine, Scotch broom, Lion's ear, Lion's tail, Indian snakeroot, rue, scullcap and weatherglass. Mucuna and ololiuqui were two Miss Essie had not recorded.

Noah made suggestions about how the herbs might have interacted in the communion wine, contributing to the seizures in the patients we had seen. The active herbal compounds were varied and confusing, containing alkaloid compounds, steroidal precursors and other chemicals the human body had no idea how to metabolize. The herbal dosages would have been so small it was hard to imagine that they could have caused the massive seizures we had diagnosed.

"You understand that with the mass spectrophotometry-testing technique, we can only identify substances that have been previously identified, or which we have on hand to compare. And of course, our wine sample was limited," Noah said.

"I tried to get more but was unable to," I muttered, remembering the trick Mark played on me with the bitter communion wine. I had forgotten to add that prank to the total of our competition. I figured he would think we were about even.

"And, dear doctors," Noah said, looking back and forth between us, "if we indeed had a larger sample and dozens more herbs on file—say, the entire list—we would only have this particular batch, and not the wine that was given to each group. That may have been different every night."

"And then there was the bonfire. It smelled harsh, with the scent changing several times, as if new things were added to it. And the smudge stick…" I sighed. The people at the tent meeting had likely utilized many different methods to administer their herbal drugs. People were breathing smoke all night every night.

"Did you notice a drinking fountain at the meeting?" Noah asked.

"No. I didn't think about it. But I did see Porta Potties, so it's likely that they had water."

"Captain Stafford tells me that there were concessions, as well. Is it possible that they sold the communion wine in larger quantities?"

I felt more than slightly unobservant. I hadn't noticed concessions, and shrugged helplessly.

"I still don't know what I'm doing here," Cam grumbled, breaking open the first of the specially prepared biscuits and slathering on butter. "I'm a neurosurgeon, not a neurologist. I cut on people, I don't diagnosis obscure brain function abnormalities. And if that mechanic can't get to my plane today, I'm having the engine taken by flatbed truck to Charlotte. I can't stand this place another day."

"Indeed? I find the bucolic pace of life restful. Just the sort of locale I might retire to someday," Noah said.

Cam rolled his eyes. I knew he was irritable not because of the pace, but because he had no willing female to hop into bed with. It must be a new experience for the boy. Of course, if he stayed around a day or two longer, he could have his pick of the local beauties. Doris's daughter Trellie was standing at the counter now giving him the eye. I figured Doris had called home and ordered the girl up posthaste so Cam could see her. A doctor in the family was always desirous, and matchmaking was practically a religion to most Southern females. Trellie was a homegrown beauty of marriageable age and mama wanted the best for the girl.

"In fact, rather than drive directly home when my work here is complete, I believe I shall visit a Realtor and discover if there might be a small farm for sale in the district. One where I might grow herbs for the burgeoning medicinal market. Always a dream of mine,'' he confided, gesturing with the coffee cup.

''Well, it's been fun,'' Cam said, dropping a ten on the table. ''Hope you find a place, Noah. Later, Sunshine,'' Cam said, and departed as breezily as he had entered. I narrowed my eyes at his departing back. Sunshine was a nickname from grade school. I hated it. ''Rhea-Rhea, Ray of Sunshine,'' the kids had chanted, or sung that awful song about Ray of sunshine on my shoulders making me happy. Not the worst thing they could have said, but since it was directed at me, it had seemed particularly horrid at the time.

I gave Noah my Realtor's name and number, my unlisted home number, my cell number and my e-mail address, and told him to call me anytime if he needed help. Then I went home to the dogs, took a long slow run and cut my hair, which was driving me crazy in this heat. I used a pair of surgical scissors when my bangs got too long and tendrils in the back started tickling my neck. I hated that feeling.

Finally, sluggish with exhaustion, I fell into a long deep nap. I blamed the lethargy on the cholesterol in the breakfast, and not even the gallon of coffee I had consumed in the last twenty-four hours could keep me awake.

I had only twelve hours off, and the last two sped by at dinner with Miss Essie and Arlana, who wanted me to get a professional haircut and harped on how I looked like a shaggy dog. I hated getting haircuts. I had better things to do in life than sit in a swivel chair beneath a plastic bib and have a stranger snip at my locks. Arlana informed me that I had uneven bangs and a hole in the hairline in back. I informed her that it no longer itched. Stalemate.

I also knew that there was a ward secretary on ICU who had been to beauty school and who would even up my head for five bucks while on her lunch break. By 2:00 a.m. I would be uniform and neat.

Long before 2:00 a.m., however, I had seen the return of DaraDevinna Faith. And she wasn't well.

"Dawkins County, this is unit 252."

Unit 252 was currently stationed on the far western side of the county, about twenty-five miles away, and handled everything and anything that went wrong for over ten square miles of back-country roads and isolated dwellings. One trip in they might bring a person with a fishhook stuck in a finger, the next trip in they might bring a massive trauma. Because the place was dead, I waved off the nurse and took the call. Leaning into the mike, I depressed the talk button and spoke to the EMT. "Dawkins County here. Go ahead."

"Dawkins, we are en route to your facility, code three, with a twenty-four-year-old female, possible signal 45 and seizure activity." He was shouting over the noise of the siren and the roar of the engine, but his tone was calm, which was always a good sign in a code three—a real emergency. "We have a line established with normal saline. BP of 170 over 90, pulse 125 and tachy, respiration 18. Temp is 99.2 and O_2 sat is 96."

"Unit 252, is the patient on antiseizure meds? If so, do you have the meds with you?" I asked.

"Unknown, Dawkins. She was found by a neighbor in the driveway. A newcomer to the area, and no family, according to the neighbor. We have discovered signal 45 on her person. Do you wish to administer any meds en route?"

"What kind of signal 45? Pills?"

"Negative, Dawkins. Plant material."

Plant material. Marijuana. I wondered if it was home-grown or something imported that might have been spiked with other drugs. "What is your ETA?"

"About seven minutes. But she's in constant seizure activity. No abatement."

I debated giving antiseizure medication in the field when I hadn't personally evaluated the patient and she might be smoking strong marijuana—possibly laced with other drugs like cocaine—versus not giving anything and having the patient die for lack of treatment. "Estimate how long the seizures have been taking place?"

"Neighbor says she spotted her about seven-fifteen, called 911. We got here at seven twenty-seven. Witnessed seizure activity for over twenty-five minutes at this point."

That meant the patient was in status epilepticus. I'd have to treat and hope for the best. "I've been informed you guys don't carry Ativan on board. Is that correct?"

"Correct, Dawkins. Valium on board. You want us to administer five milligrams?"

"Affirmative. Five mils, IV. And if there is no abatement in five minutes, administer five more Valium. You should be here by then. Keep her airway open. Monitor her. If her O_2 sat starts falling, bag her and let me know. If her heart rate or rhythm changes, let me know."

"Will do, Dawkins. Unit 252 out."

I looked up at the nurses, happy it was Ashlee and Anne. Two good nurses to back me up, if we had to shut this patient down totally and put her on the ventilator in order to stop the seizures. "Get some more Valium IV push ready. Get someone from respiratory down here. Lab, too. And get a Dilantin drip ready." I gave orders that prepared medications and equipment for use, and then stood back and let the nurses work. I had learned back in medical school that a good doctor not only listened to the RNs on duty, but let them do their jobs. A good doctor often asked the crew what they would suggest in difficult situations—after all, a dozen well-trained heads was always better than one.

Ten minutes later, the doors to the ambulance air lock blew open, letting in the EMT and paramedic from Unit 252. It was Gus and Carla, pushing a stretcher on which a frail young woman twitched and bounced, her facial muscles pulled back in a spasm.

"It's that faith healer who was doing the tent meetings here in DorCity," Carla said. "And her O_2 sats are dropping. Down to 82." She quickly updated me on the most recent BP and pulse readings, all the while wheeling the stretcher into place in the cardiac room and moving the woman from the ambulance gurney to the ER stretcher.

"How much Valium?" I asked.

"Ten mils."

"Give five more," I said to the nurses. "ABGs and rainbow her. Let's get the vent ready. The drugs you found?" I asked.

Gus lifted a gallon-size Ziploc bag from between the patient's legs and tossed it to me.

"Dang. She selling and preaching, too?" Anne asked.

I opened the bag and sniffed. "Doesn't smell like dope," I said. I sniffed again. "Smells like menthol and—" I drew in a deep breath "—maybe rosemary and sage?"

"Cooking stuff?" Anne asked as she took over bagging Dara.

"Not with that menthol smell in it. But it might be a batch of the stuff they put in the communion wine. Ash, call dispatch and tell Mark Stafford to get the herb specialist out here stat. Tell him we may have found something. And give him the name of our patient.''

''Ma'am?''

I had just told a nurse to break patient confidentiality— a federal crime.

''There's a warrant out on her. Do it.''

''Valium in,'' Ash said as she lifted the phone on the cardiac-room wall and dialed out. Maybe it was sad that ER nurses knew every emergency number by heart. But it was useful.

Twenty minutes later, we had Dara on the ventilator, her seizures under control, though not stopped entirely, her doctor on the way and a roomful of cops underfoot. Obtaining her address from the EMTs, Mark sent a sheriff's unit out to look for Dara's father, called in for a series of search warrants, and was performing a simple test on the bag of herbs to determine if marijuana or cocaine were present. They weren't.

The bag was both the possible answer to the seizures suffered by the patients from the tent meeting and evidence, and Mark and I wanted to know what was in it pronto. There wasn't time for the SLED lab to dillydally.

Noah Ebenezer and his magical van of tricks was the answer to our needs, and Mark sent a third car to the site of the tent meeting to bring the doctor in. It took a while to get him to the hospital, and I had bought Mark and the nurses dinner from Pizza Hut long before Noah arrived. Unfortunately, I didn't buy enough to feed the good doctor. There were only six pieces of cold pizza left when he arrived.

Noah in a pair of white work overalls was a sight to behold. Knees and rubber work boots were muddy and ash covered, elbows dusty, and a long ash streak crossed his upper thighs as though he had leaned up against something to rest. In the white jumpsuit he looked like a hot-air balloon, yet he still moved as gracefully as a dancer and smiled like a well-fed cherub as he dropped into a vacant chair and helped himself to the remaining pizza, gesticulating with his slice-of-the-moment as he talked.

Noah had spent the better part of daylight on his knees at the tent-meeting site, collecting samples. "I discovered half-burnt twigs, leaves and flowers," he said, taking three quick dainty bites. "Perhaps two dozen different varieties of herbs. Some I recognized instantly, others I'll need to run through my equipment. Very exciting, all this, and I'm ready to start analyzing my samples tonight."

Several quick bites later he continued, after wiping his pursed lips with a paper napkin. "I assume I can use the hospital electrical system as my power source. I have a gas chromatography system and a model 5100 mass spectrophotometer used for biological analyses, and a liquid spectrophotometer just out on the market. It's one of the finest systems available, with an enhanced data system...." Finishing off the pizza, Noah droned on, content and happy in his three passions—herbs, machines and food.

The nurses drifted from the room as he talked, finding paperwork that needed to be done and pills that needed to be counted. Mark's eyes glazed over, until he was saved from ennui by a call—code three—on his police radio. Happy to be heading to blood, guts and possibly bullets flying, he left at a run.

I had nowhere to be and simply tuned Noah out. I had worked in a lab to help put myself through medical school, but the fascination of some medical people with technical devices was beyond me. They could sit and debate the relative merits of equipment companies, machines, testing methods, even power supplies and water purity. It was boring—necessary, I suppose, but boring.

While he talked and delicately inhaled the leftover pizza, I motioned for Ash to call security. We would need a guard to determine the best placement for Noah's van and help set up a power source for the mobile laboratory. Stuff I could easily delegate and did.

Noah and the security guard parked his ugly green van beside the permanently moored mobile home that housed the CT scanner, and snaked three thick cables through the door into the hospital proper. The van started to hum as power flowed to it.

Standing in the almost oppressive heat, I peeked into the old, oversize van. I was stunned at the amount of equipment in the small space—equipment ugly enough to rival the ugly van. Nothing matched. The casing for each piece of equipment was its own vile color, ranging from a yellowish-stone shade, to a deep olive-green shade, to an orange so bright it would have shamed a pumpkin. There were exhaust hoods, air-conditioning vents, cables, wires, computer screens, monitors, knobs, readouts, graphs, something that looked like a flame casing and a miniscule workspace where Noah had placed the contents of the bag found on DaraDevinna Faith.

There was just enough room for Noah to turn around, his bulk scraping both sides of the van as he moved, his gestures as elegant and smooth in the tiny space as they were in more open areas. Above the workstation were hundreds of small drawers, nooks and crannies, where he had secreted known substances for comparative testing and calibration of his equipment. Noah worked to find samples as he fired up his machines.

Finally, he looked up. "Dear Lady Doctor, I suggest you either close the door or step inside. The van AC isn't equipped to cool the entire parking lot."

Blatantly I looked around the nonexistent floor space.

"Precisely my point," he said gently.

"Ah." I closed the battered door to the ramshackle van and walked back inside. I had been politely asked to leave. Even Miss DeeDee would have been impressed with Noah's tact. "Precisely my point." I'd have to remember that one.

As I walked back to the ER, an ambulance pulled up and my beeper went off. I didn't need to look at the beeper screen to know I had a major problem. As the ambulance doors opened, a trail of blood ran out. Someone screamed, an angry, terrified sound of agony that was suddenly cut off in a breathless grunt.

"Doc!" he shouted. "This one's bad!"

Mick Ethridge was splattered with blood.

18

PASSING THE BUCK

In an instant I took in the patient. A young man was strapped to the ambulance gurney, his clothing and skin slimed with blood. Eyes wild, teeth pulled back in a death-mask rictus, he clawed one-handed at the restraints. His head rolled in an unnatural arc as he fought. A blood-soaked field dressing beneath a six-inch Ace bandage circled his torso and left shoulder, starting just below the cervical collar.

Mick's bloody, gloved hands were applying pressure to the dressing at the jointure of the neck and shoulder. He adjusted the position and the patient grunted. I heard him suck in a breath. Blood dripped steadily off the end of the gurney and onto Mick's shoes.

Behind me, a DorCity police car roared up and screeched to a stop. Fumes and engine noise swirled around us as Mick shouted vital information.

"We got an avulsion to the left side of the neck, six inches long, deep enough to put my hand in!" In a single motion, Mick and Sam Tooley jerked the gurney from the back of the ambulance unit and slammed its wheel-frame to the ground. "Last BP was 80 over 40, pulse 160 and tachy, respiration 36! IV Ringers via large-bore

Jelcos in both arms, O_2 at three liters via nasal cannula!"
One of Mick's hands was still at the patient's neck, holding pressure and keeping the man immobile while shoving the rolling bed forward with his hips.

"You got arterial blood?" I shouted back.

"Negative. But I'd say the jugular is at least nicked.
Clavicle shattered, bone fragments all down inside. Exposed muscle tissue. And he lost a gallon of blood!"
They hit the air-lock doors and propelled the ambulance
gurney inside. It wasn't level but slightly inverted, the
patient's head lower than his body. Mick was bent at an
unnatural angle to hold the dressing in place.

I glanced back into the unit as I followed the guys in.
They would have to take a hose to the ambulance. "He
on drugs or just panicked?" I asked.

"Panic is my guess, Doc!" Sam said, his voice loud
and harsh, his breathing rough from exertion.

"What happened to him?" I asked as the doors
whooshed shut, sealing out the engine roar.

"I saw the whole thing, Doc!" the city cop beside me
spoke, his voice breathy and stressed. "I was making
rounds. He was standing on a corner with a group a'
guys. And this little bit of a girl, naked as the day she
was born, come out of the shadows with an ax and just
hit the sumbitch with it. His friends scattered like they
was shot."

He huffed again, trying to keep up with the pace of
his words, then bent forward to rest his bloody hands on
his bloody knees, dropping his beer gut down between
his arms. "If I hadn't a' been there, he'd be dead." The
cop finally drew in a deep breath of air. He was in distress, but I had more immediate concerns with the patient.
He was still screaming, writhing on the gurney.

"Girlfriend?" I asked.

"His friends said not. White girl. Crazy white girl."

I followed the gurney into the trauma room. "I need Statler, two units of O neg, ABGs, H&H, stat," I said to Ash. "Cross-match four more units, and get respiratory down here. And I need some bodies!"

Statler was the surgeon on call. The rest was blood, lab tests and personnel I wanted. I watched the patient's head loll. Out of control, all the motion to one side. He had muscle and tendon damage, as well as the jugular problems. But it wasn't completely severed or he'd be dead by now.

"We're going to have to fly this guy out," I decided. "Get medevac on the phone. This is too much for us to handle here."

Ash nodded and fled for a phone, her face tight with tension.

The EMTs flipped the releases on the gurney restraints and lifted the man to the ER stretcher. The sheets beneath him were soaked scarlet. "I need that blood *now!*" I said to the lab tech when he stuck his head in the door. Trish slid in beside me. "Get me another line going." She nodded and went to work. "Get the stretcher in Trendelenburg." Someone changed the level of the ER stretcher, dropping the patient's head below his body, allowing gravity to help keep blood where it was needed.

The patient grunted, Mick's hands accidentally pressing on his larynx. Mick adjusted, and the patient began regular grunts in place of the screaming. But the accidental pressure had the effect of calming the man somewhat. His eyes met mine.

"It's okay," I said. "We're going to take care of you." He grunted again in reply and licked his lips. The movement of his tongue didn't look quite right, though I may have been mistaken.

"I want a BP, pulse and O$_2$ sat." No one replied as they worked to stabilize the patient, but I knew they heard me.

"I got a good look at her. Had yellow and red sh—ah, stuff, painted all over her body and face. Like letters. Dangdest thing I ever seen in my life." The cop dropped into a chair and bent forward, then reared back and threw out his chest, tossing his head back, trying to get a breath. His face was crimson, his lips slightly ashen. He flattened a hand to his sternum as if trying to relieve pressure there.

It was Bobby Ray Shirley, a good-ol'-boy cop in his forties, balding, stout, and it looked as if I wasn't going to be able to put him aside for the moment after all. Still watching the action on the stretcher, I took Bobby Ray's wrist and estimated his pulse. Irregular, about two beats per second. Near 120.

The EMTs were using leather restraints to tie the bleeding patient to the bed. His left arm was already immobilized against his chest with a secure sling and his head kept rolling to the right. As he struggled, the dressing over his neck was exposed for a moment. The bandage was supersaturated. It wasn't doing anything to stem the bleeding.

"BP 60 palpated," a voice said.

I was losing him. "Get me hemostats and suction! Both IVs wide open. Pressure to the neck, Mick! Ash, I need people!" Mick replaced his hands on the patient's dressing. Blood oozed out beneath.

"On the way," Ash said, looking up from the phone. "Statler's on the way, too. Amanda, blood?"

The lab tech drawing blood said, "Kendrew's getting it." With a single glance, the tech said, "It's here. Sign for it?"

Someone had to sign a release whenever uncrossmatched blood was given. I slashed my signature across the bottom of the sheet. The buck stopped here. If the patient died of a blood reaction then it was on my head, not the lab tech's.

I glanced down at Bobby Ray. The cop looked worse.

Trish was on her knees starting a third IV line. "A third line going now," she said. "Fourteen Jelco. Give me a unit," she reached up. Someone stuck a unit of O negative blood in her hand. Trish shoved the unit into a pressure cuff to speed the blood into the patient.

"Get Bobby Ray some oxygen and check his pressure," I said to a passing nurse. "Heart monitor. Bring me a strip." She nodded and handed off three syringes in individual paper packets to another nurse.

The respiratory therapist had hooked up a pulse-oximeter to the patient's right index finger. I glanced at it. Nintey-two percent. Probably because he was still fighting and breathing like a bellows. It dropped to 90 as I watched, and he started shivering hard as he lost fluids and body warmth. "Hot blankets," I said to another nurse. "Rectal temp. And get me a blood pressure. Heart monitor?" I pressed a nail bed on the patient's right index finger. The return was sluggish.

"Strip running now, Doc."

I glanced over at the monitor and saw a sinus rhythm at 150. At least the guy had a good heart and lungs. But his respiration was slowing down even as I watched. He was struggling to breathe. His eyes were getting that glassy stare than meant either he was passing out or coding on me. The blood seeping from the neck wound was paler now, a cherry red that was nearing pink. He was exsanguinating before my eyes. "I need those hemostats!" I said. As the patient's head lolled, I added, "And some piano needles if you happen to see some. But don't spend any time looking for them.''

''What?'' a voice asked.

''Piano needles. Or something similar so I can secure his tendons if I get the chance.''

The patient slowed further, his waving right hand snatched from the air by a nurse and tucked into a restraint. I finally had my extra bodies. The patient's heart rate on the monitor slowed, as well, but his rhythm still appeared normal. And then he was out. Unconscious.

His breathing continued to change and I didn't like the sound of it. Elbowing my way in, I stuck my stethoscope to his blood-soaked chest and listened. The right side sounded normal. The left not so normal.

I concentrated on the sound of the man's breathing. The left lung had diminished breath sounds. His lung was probably filling up with blood and air.

''Get me a portable C-spine and a chest X ray. I want to see if the lung was nicked. We may have a hemopneumothorax. Get me two thoracotomy trays ready. And clean him up. I want to make sure there aren't any more injuries.'' A nurse slammed down a dozen hemostats onto a tray.

Someone opened and shook out a blue paper gown with a plastic backing and held it for me. I stepped into it, pushing my arms through. It was tied behind me. I opened and pulled on a pair of sterile gloves, but I may as well have used plain ones. Nothing about this scene was sterile.

''Face shield,'' a voice said, and I ducked down, allowing one of the faceless crowd to slip it over my head.

''Open them,'' I said, nodding to the hemostats. The same hands reached in and opened each of the clamps, leaving them on the still-sterile packaging.

"Get ready with a fresh dressing," I said to Mick, "and support his cervical collar in case something hit his spine. Anne, I'll need suction. Move the light so I can see. And step back, people. I need space."

Bodies moved back away from the table a bit and I squeezed into a space near the patient's head. "Suction?" Anne, also dressed out in blue paper personal protective equipment, held up the plastic suction tube to indicate her readiness. "Okay, Mick, peel back the bandage a little at a time, starting at the front and keeping pressure on the back. Go."

The bandage rolled back, exposing the huge wound. One heartbeat later, fresh blood filled the space. Anne stuck in the suction tube and vacuumed it up, exposing the jugular for an instant. It had a ragged tear. Between beats of his heart, I slipped the clamp on above the tear and tightened it. I then clamped off the vein below the tear.

I nodded to Mick. He rolled more of the bandage back. A tiny bleeder shot a spray of blood at me. With one hand, I applied pressure on the small artery and with the other I clamped it off. Anne suctioned blood out of the way. No more arterial blood appeared. Now I could work. I heaved a deep breath and heard Anne do the same. Spotting another smaller vein, I clamped it off. It had been severed by the blade of the ax.

I noticed the severed end of a tendon and, and though it wasn't my primary concern, I asked, "Piano needles?"

"None."

I nodded to Mick and the bandage rolled back all the way. Behind me, I heard someone curse at the sight. It was a nasty injury. Finding a last blood vessel, I clamped it off and stepped back.

"Now," I said to Mick. He slapped on a wad of gauze

dressing and Sam Tooley wrapped a fresh bandage across it, then up over the man's shoulder and down under the other arm, securing it in place.

I glanced up at the amount of oxygen the patient was on. He was receiving 100 percent O_2, yet his oxygen levels were still dropping. "Bag him," I told the respiratory tech. "We may need to do a trach. Use your best judgment and tell me if you think I'm missing it."

"Yes, ma'am."

A lab tech held a strip of paper in front of my face. ABGs. When they were drawn, he had been in respiratory alkalosis from breathing so hard, so fast. "I want another set in ten minutes. What's the H&H?"

"It's 10.8 and 30.2."

Not normal values, but not life threatening. Also not efficient signposts of his current condition. The test had been drawn several minutes earlier and the patient's hemoglobin was surely lower by now. Just looking at his blood I guesstimated the hemoglobin at five. I ripped off the bloody gloves and tossed them onto the dirty instrument tray. The face shield I handed to a passing nurse.

"Doc, his blood pressure is dropping."

"Are all the fluids open wide?" When Sam Tooley started to check, I said, "Open them up. Replace the hot blankets. How about another IV site? Anybody see anything promising?" I wanted blood and fluids flowing as fast as possible. My patient was in classic shock. And I wanted another IV site for giving more blood and keeping his volume up while he was in surgery.

"Not with his pressure dropping."

"Start him on two grams of Ancef," I ordered, knowing the antibiotic was essential to keep this man from going into sepsis later. *If* he survived my tender ministrations. "Get me a central line kit." The portable X-ray machine hummed in behind me. I was grateful to see the tech was Dora Lynn. She was fast. "Let's get a C-spine, just in case, and chest. I'm looking for a hemo-pneumothorax," I said.

"Yuck. Nasty," she replied. "Who'd he tick off?"

"Naked white woman, according to the cop on the scene," Mick said. He lifted the patient beneath the arms and helped Dora Lynn position the X-ray film behind him.

"We got any history on this guy?" I asked. "Name? Age?"

"His pals followed us in. Probably have half the city out there by now," Sam said.

"Everybody out who wants out," Dora said. "I'm ready to shoot."

"I'll check with the crowd outside," I said, leaving the room. I didn't have specific plans to have a kid, but why ruin my equipment, just in case?

The crowd in the waiting room was large and agitated. Alcohol fumes, traces of cigarette smoke and reefer hung in the air. A security guard was standing in a corner, watching. "Any family here?" I asked him.

"Mother on the way," he said, not taking his eyes off the milling crowd.

"Let me know when she gets here."

"Will do, Doc." I retreated to the relative safety of the ER. The X ray was done, Dora Lynn off to develop the film. I stood in the trauma room and watched.

"Dr. Lynch. What do you have?"

I turned to see Dr. Statler, one of the county's few general surgeons, standing in the doorway, lab coat pushed back, hands in his pockets. I quickly filled him in and finished with, "I've called medevac to fly him out. Ash? What's medevac's ETA?"

"They haven't called us back. Doc, his pressure is dropping again."

"The IV in the left arm," Statler said. "If the axillary vein was compromised, we may be getting fluid into the chest. Let's put in a femoral line and cut that IV down low. Good evening, Ash. Aren't you supposed to be off?"

"Overtime, Doc."

I eased back, out of Statler's way, letting him take over the case. Statler was old school. Proper, stiff, very much the take-charge surgeon, proud of his credentials, and with the bedside manner of a mannequin. But competent. Unfortunately, he also had the reputation of throwing bloody surgical instruments when things didn't go to suit him in the OR. Rumor had it, he'd been reprimanded more than once when a tech was injured during one of his tirades. So I was surprised as heck when he looked back at me and suggested that I might want to put in the femoral line while he put in the chest tubes.

"Sure. Ash?"

"Both kits right here," she said, and I went to wash up.

I directed that my kit be set on an adjustable table and pulled to the right side. A nurse opened it and I checked to make sure all the equipment was there. The days of a doctor having to ask for everything by name was gone, as hospital-supply companies created specialized kits for every kind of procedure a doctor might face. Of course, not all kits were perfectly filled, but luckily this one was. Pulling on the sterile gloves provided, I started swabbing the patient's groin area with a Betadine swab.

Out of the corner of my eye, I watched Statler look over the patient's chest X ray, the developed film held over his head. He moved to the side of the bed where I stood and held the film to the light overhead. "What do you think?"

I glanced up. Found the place where the patient's clavicle used to be. Now it was a mass of shards and broken bone. "I think there's a good chance one of those shards hit the lung, and maybe one lodged in the axillary, just like you thought. The start of a hemo-pneumothorax?" I questioned, pointing with a finger to the upper tip of the lung. "Air here? Blood here?"

"Agreed. The C-spine looks fine. At least he won't be paralyzed. Let's get rid of the cervical collar and do those chest tubes. Ready, Ash?"

"Yes, sir. I just heard back from medevac. The chopper is in Charleston on a run. You want me to try Columbia?"

"Yes," Statler said shortly. "And if they can't be here in half an hour, get an OR crew in. We may have to do this here."

I looked up from my kit. I wasn't about to question the good surgeon in front of the ER staff, but this patient needed a vascular surgeon at the very least. He had severed muscles and tendons, a damaged jugular. A nicked lung. Embedded bone fragments. This was going to be a dicey repair job. Statler must have sensed my discomfort because he glanced up and met my eyes. "I can have an OR crew in here in fifteen minutes. A trip to Richland Memorial is half an hour, plus time for evaluation, plus time to surgery. Add that to the time in this ER, and this man may not have the time to fly anywhere."

I nodded once, fast. "You're the surgeon." I know how to pass the buck as well as anyone. And I was glad that particular decision would not be mine.

19

TRYING TO KILL HER?

"Doc, you got a minute? Bobby Ray's EKG." A nurse thrust a slick, graphlike page into my hand. On the red graph, in black print, was a twelve-lead EKG, and with just a single glance, I knew it didn't look good.

The cop had first-degree AV block and elevated ST segments on his cardiogram. In other words, he had both a major blockage of one of the arteries that feeds the heart and signs of infarction. A heart attack. And a big one.

"Get me a cardiac work-up and retavase ready." I turned to Ash, who was hooking up another unit of O negative blood. "You ever hear back from Richland medevac?"

"They're at a bus accident. It'll be at least an hour. We got an OR crew on the way. Why?"

"Get me an ambulance unit to transport. Bobby Ray's going to Richland. He needs a heart cath."

"When it rains, it pours," Ash muttered. She looked at her nursing partner, Anne. "You got it in here?"

"Anne and I will be fine," Statler said as he made the first incision in the wounded patient's upper chest, beneath the arm, and inserted a gloved finger to test the depth of the cut, feeling for the lining of the patient's lung. Eyes closed, he concentrated on the sensations inside the chest wall. For a surgeon with his reputation, he seemed almost jocular tonight. "Ahhhh," he breathed, opening his eyes. "Got it."

The tech nodded and adjusted the fit of the blue plastic mouthpiece and ambu bag that would seal over the man's lower face and force oxygen-rich air into his lungs. As the techs worked, Statler shoved a stiff plastic tube into the man's chest. Positioning it with delicate movements of his fingers, he ran a large needle and thread through the man's skin and around the tubing, anchoring it in place. Moved his feet out of the way so that another tech, kneeling at the floor, could hook the tube end to the dry-suction chest drain—the unit that would apply negative pressure, drawing off the fluid and air that was filling the lung, allowing the lung to reinflate. It was a painstaking and skillful dance. I couldn't have done better myself.

A moment later, bloody liquid began flowing from the patient's chest cavity into the collection chamber on the floor. Moving with practiced ease, I finished tying off the femoral line and opened the IV fluids up wide.

Counting ribs, Statler felt lower on the man's chest for proper placement of the second tube. Waving to the nurse, I mimed going next door. Anne nodded and indicated she would call if Statler wanted me. Bobby Ray needed me more than the unnamed avulsion patient.

"Time to bag him," Statler said to the respiratory tech. "His O_2 sats look a little low."

I entered the cardiac room. At Bobby Ray's side stood a city cop, taking down his statement. Around the two, nurses and a lab tech worked. Bobby Ray had two IVs running, oxygen via nasal cannula, a continuous lead showing on the heart monitor. His color was better, but he still caught at his chest and gasped when he spoke.

"She was painted in red and yellow. The yellow glittered, like that fancy nail polish my wife wears. Red looked like blood. Blond and long-haired, all matted and braided. Five foot two or three. Maybe ninety pounds. Skinny as a rail."

"And the stuff she was painted with looked like what?"

"Like letters. Like them Greek letters at the fraternity and sorority houses." He clutched his chest. "Oh God. Help me."

"Get him two mils of morphine. Turn up his O$_2$," I said loudly enough to make the questioning cop turn to me. I used his body movement to insert myself between the two men and eased the cop away from the bed as I placed the bell of my stethoscope on Bobby Ray's chest. I listened to him breathing, listened to his heart beating.

"You on any meds, Bobby? Got any allergies?" I asked. Bobby Ray shook his head. "You have any heart problems?"

"No. Healthy as a horse, Doc."

"Except for smoking, drinking beer, chewing tobacco and eating junk food while he's on duty." I glanced around. It had to be Bobby Ray's wife. Red-haired and slender, she wore skintight black jeans, a short-sleeved red silk top, a ton of gold jewelry and enough makeup to last me a year. Glittery gold was everywhere—shadow on eyelids and polish on inch-long nails, cerise lipstick and mascara, all flaked with gold, finished off the look.

"You his wife?" I asked just in case. There had been times when I guessed wrong.

"That's me. He's having a heart attack, ain't he?"

I hadn't yet told Bobby Ray that. But I nodded and

turned back to the cop on the stretcher. "Looks like you are having a heart attack, Bobby. We need to get you to Richland where they can do a heart cath."

The wife, who had elbowed a nurse out of the way, slapped Bobby Ray hard on his stomach. "I been telling you! You got to clean up your act. You die on me and I'll never forgive you. It's been too hard gettin' you trained right."

"Anything else you can give me, Bobby Ray?" the cop asked, laughter in the tone. His position was now at the foot of the bed, effectively being shut out of the action. He stood flat-footed with his thumbs hooked into his heavy-duty leather utility belt and holster.

"She was yelling. Crazy stuff." Bobby opened his eyes wide. "Ahhh," he moaned. "That's better. Just a little bit, but better."

"That's the morphine," I said. "Nitro?" I asked the nurse.

"Three. Relief on the third."

"Good. Give him four baby aspirin."

"What was she saying?" the cop asked.

"She was saying it's time to leave," I said.

"'Hands of healing.' I remember that. 'Hands of healing.' And doing God's will. Crazy stuff."

I stopped in surprise, the bell of the stethoscope on Bobby's chest forgotten. "'Hands of evil maim and kill. Hands of healing do Lord's will,'" I quoted softly.

Both cops turned to me. "The things painted on her body are runes. Magical symbols." I pulled the earpieces out of my ears and tucked the stethoscope into my pocket. "She calls herself Na'Shalome, and thinks she's a witch. But it's more likely a case of full-blown psychosis."

"That girl who was here in the hospital? Drugged Chambers and left him on the floor?" Bobby Ray asked.

I nodded. "You know who you're looking for now. My patient needs rest." I glanced at the door to the hall, a silent command.

"Yes, ma'am. And thanks."

"You're welcome. Call Mark Stafford for her real name. I've forgotten it but he knows."

"Oh." A twinkle of humor glinted in his eyes. "So *you're* Cap'n Stafford's doctor girlfriend." He glanced down at my legs and nodded in approval, as if he saw what Mark saw and liked it. My eyebrows rose in irritation. I wasn't anyone's *girl*friend. "Happy to make your acquaintance, Doc."

"Out," I pointed at the door.

He grinned and sauntered out, turning in the doorway. "You take care, man. We'll be up to see you tomorrow."

"Sneak me in a bag of Redman."

"You sneak in a bag of tobacco and I'll skin the hide off you," the wife said. The cop and I both knew she meant it, too.

He shook his head. "Sorry, man. I'll come visit, but no chew. Tanya's too mean to tangle with."

"And you best remember it," the wife said, tossing her long red hair.

By the time the transport ambulance unit was ready to roll out, Bobby Ray had already responded to the meds. Retavase was a fast-acting clot buster. Combined with three nitroglycerine tablets and a second shot of morphine, his pain had decreased from a level ten—the worst pain the cop had ever felt—to a level six. He was also breathing easier, his pulse was at a normal rate, and his blood pressure had been cut from 243 over 149, to 180 over 100. Still high, but much more manageable.

Bobby Ray was facing a heart catheterization and maybe surgery. He was going to have to make some life-style changes that included giving up fat, beer, smoking and fast foods, replacing them with vegetables, fruits and regular exercise. Tanya was telling him all this in no uncertain terms, so I didn't have to. Lifestyle changes and a bossy wife to make him stick to them. Purgatory for a good-ol' country boy. But he was smiling as he pulled away from the ambulance ramp, and he offered me a wave.

Statler was in surgery and the nurses were mopping up. Housekeeping had gone home early and left things a mess. In a small hospital, RNs do everything that needs to be done, from changing sheets and mopping up blood to administering drugs and CPR.

I looked at the charts that had stacked up during the multiple emergencies, and placed them in the order I wanted to see them. Two kids with fever were first, sore throat third, laceration last. Quiet tonight, numberswise, and a good thing. There had been times when I had a couple dozen patients waiting following a crisis.

I tested, treated and sent the fevers home with Tylenol, the sore throat went home with a penicillin prescription for a strep infection. The laceration took a bit longer only because it was a jagged cut. Seven stitches and a tetanus shot. I was almost through when the next crisis hit. They always come in threes, so I wasn't really surprised.

"Code 99 to room 112. Code 99 to room 112. Code 99 to room 112," the loudspeaker blared." Room 112 was DaraDevinna's room.

I tied off the last stitch, shouted to Anne, "Dress it and give him wound-care instructions." To the patient, I said, "Stitches out in seven days. Keep it clean and keep antibiotic ointment on it.'' And I turned and sprinted up the hallway.

Most of the time, doctors can get away with running in the halls. Anyone else would have been reprimanded for the dangerous speed. In my case, the security guard I passed merely lifted an eyebrow and made a tsking noise. I flashed a guilty grin his way.

"Don't report me!" I said, half begging, half demanding.

"I see nothing. I hear nothing."

I flipped him a wave and disappeared into 112. Inside was pandemonium. Dara was arched up in a seizure so strong I was afraid her spine might be damaged. She surely would have torn muscles. She was bleeding from the mouth where she had ripped out her ET tube and chewed on her tongue. Her eyes bulged, her face was a mask suitable for Halloween. The smell of vomit was strong on the air.

Boka, wearing only a skintight Lycra running bra, leggings and sneakers, hovered over the head of the bed. A glance told the tale. The silks were wadded in the sink.

I sniffed at the stuffy air in the room. Beneath the smell of vomit, there was a scent I didn't recognize, harsh, acrid, yet with a sweetish undertang, though there was no smoke hanging in the air.

"Give it to her. Now!" Boka said.

"A dose that strong will shut her down," the nurse warned.

"So noted. Do it. Respiratory?"

"Here, Doc," a voice said as the nurse who'd questioned the dosage slowly shoved the plunger of a syringe, emptying the contents into Dara's bloodstream. Boka pressed a button, raising the bed to a level comfortable enough to work, should it become necessary to reintubate the patient.

I glanced over at the nurse who was keeping notes on the code. In urgent situations, no doctor could be expected to remember all he or she had ordered, so a nurse kept track of what was done when and how often, a running record of every move made by every person present. I could see that Dara was on Dilantin, phenobarbital, Ativan and Valium. She had a busload of meds in her and was still seizing. Not good.

"Get some help," Boka said to the RT. "I'll need one therapist to bag her, the other to get the vent set back up while I intubate her."

"I can do that," I said, pointing to the ambu bag.

"Yes, ma'am. Thanks."

The RT tech and I changed places and I found myself at the head of the bed next to Boka. "Nice underwear," I said as I took the rubber ambu bag in my hand and began pumping oxygen-enriched air into Dara's lungs.

Boka snorted delicately. "Thank you. My Calvin Kleins. The sari may never be the same again."

"I have an extra pair of scrubs in my room. She starting to abate?"

"Looks that way. Finally." Boka reached back and twisted loose hair into her braid. "Trish went to surgery for a pair of scrubs. And I'd never get these hips into anything that fit you. Thank you anyway."

"What do you think is happening?" I asked as Dara's limbs grew relaxed, then flaccid, her features almost calm.

"I suppose it could be febrile, but I did an LP earlier," she said, referring to a lumbar puncture—the careful insertion of a needle into a patient's spine to remove a few cc's of cerebral spinal fluid. "CSF is clear, protein in normal range. I'm leaning toward a toxemic reaction or some bizarre form of withdrawal.''

''We've got Dr. Noah Ebenezer on the premises,'' I said.

''The plant specialist?''

''Yep. In a panel van out back, electrical cords leading to the van. Want him to take a look?''

Boka spotted a nurse in the corner. ''Get security to ask Dr. Ebenezer to come for a consult.'' The nurse nodded and slipped out the door.

''My biggest concern is that someone may have slipped her something. Two of the nursing assistants saw a man come out of her door. When the nurses entered, there was smoke so heavy they could hardly breathe, but no sign of flame anywhere. I'm thinking cause of seizures by ingesting or being injected with something, perhaps. She became markedly worse again following the visit. Extubated herself,'' she pointed to the bloody ET tube on the floor. ''Security searched the grounds and called the cops, but they found nothing. I've got pre-Valium urine set aside for a UDS here and a more comprehensive work-up for biological toxins at a reference lab.''

The remnants of Dara's seizure suddenly stopped. Her spinal muscles relaxed and she eased down toward the mattress. ''How long since the LP?'' I asked, concerned that seizures soon after a puncture might lead to complications.

''Not long enough to suit me. If she leaks, we'll deal with that later. But I have to get her stabilized and relaxed first.'' As she spoke, Boka pulled on a pair of mismatched scrubs, worn green top and new purple pants that tied at the waist. No one seemed to notice or care that she was dressing, or that she had been underdressed until now. Something about working in a medical environment makes self-consciousness evaporate fast.

The door opened, and the nurse who had gone to find Noah entered, the doctor on her heels. He smiled widely as his eyes settled on the patient and recognized her. Before I could speak, he held up an admonitory hand and sniffed the air, slowly, the way a perfumier or a chef sniffs to determine the content and origin of a scent. Finally, he nodded at me.

"Seizures of unknown etiology," I said, "worsening after the appearance of a strange man and smoke in her room. Maximum dosage of Valium administered." I turned back to Dara. "And now this…" I let the words trail off.

"Interesting," he said. "How wonderfully interesting."

I wanted to disagree, but could see his point. Dara's posture since the seizure had eased was bizarre. Most postictal patients are lethargic and unable to focus. They lose control of bowel, bladder and swallowing reflex, have slow pulse and often show signs of motor control difficulty, with delayed reaction time to stimulation.

DaraDevinna Faith was fluttering her eyelids, flexing her fingers, pushing away the face mask and ambu bag, swallowing relatively easily and breathing fine. She seemed to be suffering no ill effects of the heavy dose of Valium. Any other patient would have been practically comatose. Paralyzed. On the ventilator.

Dara seemed revitalized.

Noah stepped lightly around the medical personnel and pulled a tiny Maglite out of his pocket to check Dara's pupillary reflexes. She pushed the light away, blinking in irritation. Noah persisted, finally pocketing the light before applying pressure with his fingers to her jaw to force open her mouth. "Bet that's going to hurt," he said of her tongue. "She chewed it up rather badly. Needs a suture or two to control bleeding and put a flap of tissue back in place. You might want to restrain her now while the Valium is in effect and do that."

"No," Dara said, the word only slightly slurred, her hands pushing his away again.

Noah ignored her, pulling out a reflex hammer and testing her response time on both sides all the way to the soles of her feet. As he worked, he inspected her skin for signs of injection marks in veins and into nail beds. Everything looked normal to me. Which in itself was definitely not normal. Not after the seizure I had just witnessed.

"Let's get her tongue stitched first. And make it fast," Boka said.

"I've got a suture kit here, Doc."

"Restrain her."

In the hall, while Dara gurgled and fought on the other side of the door, I asked Noah, "What do you think it is?"

"No track marks, no physical signs of drug addiction, but with the purity of heroin on the market these days, it can be smoked, effectively hiding any obvious physical signs of prolonged drug use." He pulled at his lower lip with thumb and forefinger, leading me down the hall toward the cafeteria. The place was dark, but Noah pushed through the doors and went directly to the Coke machine. He purchased one for each of us, popped his open and drank deeply. I followed suit, recognizing that he was thinking things through.

"Yes, I think she is heavily addicted. The smoke is the biggest part of it—did you notice the slightly sweet scent on the air? But I believe that someone must have injected her with something through the IV line.'' He pulled again at his lips.

"Trying to kill her?'' I asked.

"Or unexpected results to a drug she takes often. Or the street drug wasn't pure and she reacted to that with which it was cut.'' Noah stepped to another machine and purchased two packs of powder-sugar doughnuts. Holding the packets and the can, he stared up at the dark ceiling. "No. That theory doesn't feel right, somehow.'' Sitting at a table in the dark, he opened a pack and ate two before speaking again. He offered me a doughnut and I ate one, sitting opposite him at the small table. I needed a sugar-caffeine boost, too.

"Oh...perhaps the girl has seizures, started them at an early age, say, and someone has been controlling them with herbal medicines.''

"The packet she was found with?''

Noah nodded, popped another doughnut and chewed thoughtfully. "I am only now starting on the contents of the Baggie, and after what I just witnessed, I expect to find some particularly strong herbal medicines in the mixture.

"In which case, I imagine she was extubated, then given something to drink—a strong infusion, perhaps, instead of an injection. And herbs were burned to augment the effect. But before the herbal remedy could take effect, she started seizing. Then when she was given Valium, the same herbal drugs were able to counteract the effect of the sedative.''

"What have you found with the testing you were doing on the bonfire scraps?''

"A little bit of everything. Some of it innocuous, some of it quite medicinal. I'm surprised you didn't have a number of heart irregularities and breathing problems from the amount of digitalis and Scotch broom, codonopsis and oxeye daisy, just to name a few. The strange thing I'm finding is a high percentage of hallucinogens like *Datura inoxia* and *D. stramonium, Trichocereus pachanoi*," he said, lapsing into Latin. "Very dangerous herbs, those, if not used with discretion."

"So, we've got a person who knows how to grow and use herbs but not the smarts to use them wisely."

"A very dangerous person," he said ruminatively. "Very dangerous."

20

PRETTY SAD AND HEADLESS SQUIRRELS

Blinking into the Friday-morning light, I walked across the parking lot to my car, listening to the birds sing, trying to keep my eyes open. A night of no sleep had left me dull and tired, and I stumbled over my own feet. There would be no running this morning, just a long day's nap. I tossed my overnight bag over my shoulder, one hand on the door handle of my car. Already it was hot enough to warm the metal and it was only ten after seven in the morning.

"She's in danger!"

I whirled at the sound of the whispered warning.

A bent old man stood near me, too close. His body odor clubbed me in the face, unwashed, pungent with sweat and smoke. He stepped closer. Threatening. I released the handle, jerked away. Unwittingly into the lee of the building. Cutting off my own retreat. He closed off my escape. My hand came up to block him. A sudden rush of adrenaline swept through me. Fear.

His pupils were pinpoint. Drugs?

I needed to run. I'd have to go through him. I dropped my bag. My breath caught in my throat. A shout strangled there. Suddenly dry-voiced, I couldn't scream.

''She's in danger.''

''Wh-who,'' I whispered, wanting to bellow, but fear-reduced to quiet dialogue.

''Dara. Grave danger.''

And then I recognized him. Mr. Faith. The man who controlled the herbs at the tent meetings. The man who gave out tainted communion wine. Recognition eased the fear a notch. I struggled to breathe.

''Someone is trying to open a doorway. A doorway into darkness.'' His skin was pale, sallow, diseased-looking. Huge black pores mottled his nose and cheeks. ''And evil will come through. Vile evil.''

I finally caught a breath, my lungs expanding painfully. A security guard appeared in my peripheral vision, looking away. I lifted a hand. Faith caught it in his clawed ones.

''Dara is pure. It is she they will want, she they will take.'' Foul breath blasted me. ''She will be sacrificed as they rent the final opening. *Save* her!'' His grimed nails dug into the flesh of my hand. I jerked away, the thick talons dragging weals along my skin.

''Call someone who can help her. Find someone who can save her!''

The security guard glanced my way, stopped and stared. ''Get away from me. Get away!'' I said, my voice achieving enough volume to communicate my panic. The guard whirled at the words and trotted toward me.

''You have to save her!''

The guard lifted his radio and spoke into the black plastic. Increased his speed. Another guard appeared at the ER doorway.

''She's in danger!'' Faith gripped my hand again. I let him hold it, his skin greasy on mine.

''We're doing everything we can for her,'' I said, finding words and clear thought now that help was coming. "Are you the man who was in her room last night?"

His head lifted, his odd, drugged eyes focusing on mine with an intensity that shocked fear back through me.

"Did you give her something?" I asked, needing to know.

"She was having fits again. The devil fits."

"Yes," I said. "Fits. Seizures. Did you give her something?"

"Holy water and wine. Just as always. To drive out the devil."

Behind him, a shoe scraped on the asphalt. "You save her!" Faith commanded. Spinning, he placed one hand on the hood of my car and leaped. Rotating in midair, he cleared the small BMW and sprinted around the building. I dropped to the ground, trembling.

"You okay, Doc?"

"I'm fine," I said, looking up into the face of Jessie, a seventy-three-year-old guard. "Watch where he goes. See that someone catches him." Jessie trotted off, his gait surprisingly spry for his age. Still, there was not a great lot of good Jessie was going to do in the face of Faith's strength. If I had to guess, Faith was on PCP, probably mixed with other drugs. The medicinal thoughts were calming, putting reality back in its proper place. In the distance a siren wailed. Police to the rescue. Still shaky, I stood and waited for the cops.

Though they searched for an hour, and even called out the search dogs, no trace of Faith was found. His trail ended beyond the hospital grounds in the winding roads of a cemetery. His handprint was the only evidence left behind. Hospital security made certain a good print was picked up by Charlie—the county crime scene tech on duty—who went to work with amused good nature when he was called to the scene. Doctors who wanted to work in a small town were hard to find. Administration didn't want to lose one by neglecting her safety.

Exhausted, too tired to think, I stumbled into my house by nine and into my bed, asleep before I got my clothes off, before I hit the covers, before I pulled down the comforter. Face first into dreamless slumber.

Eight hours went by before I moved or woke, eight hours of good, hard, uninterrupted rest that I desperately needed. I woke to find Stoney curled up and purring on my back. Waking me to tell me it was time to feed the pets. Not a bad alarm clock. Comforting, in a way.

Groggy, I showered, dressed for work and tried to straighten the comforter so Arlana wouldn't notice I had neglected to climb under it before sleeping. Arlana had pretty strong opinions about where a person was supposed to sleep—in bed and under the covers. No dogs, no cats, no shoes. I didn't figure I would fool her, but I tried, even picking long cat hair off the pillow beside mine.

Double-checking that I was wearing a sufficiently supportive bra, I fed the animals, gave them fresh water, grabbed a pack of Snowballs for breakfast and headed to the door as I opened the pack of frosted cupcakes and took a bite. Delicious.

But when I tried to open the back door, the dogs stood in front of the doggie flap and wouldn't let me past. Whining. Belle growling that low growl of warning. Remembering the crazy man at my car this morning, I paused, went to the kitchen window and studied the backyard. It took a few minutes to find the stationary squirrel sitting on the trunk of the oak tree.

Another second to realize the squirrel was headless. Nailed to the trunk. The sudden shaking that took me was totally unrelated to the super-sweet cupcake.

My eyes swept the backyard and the edge of the woods, remembering the severed finger in the slim plastic Baggie. And the man who was axed by a naked girl. My stomach tightened. The squirrel hadn't bled much. And the blood was old, clotted brown. Surely whoever had nailed it there was long gone....

Belle, sensing my awareness of the problem outside, pawed her way up my thigh and put her snout in my stomach, still whining, still soft-growling. Holding me in place. She didn't want me to go outside. I shoved her down and she immediately jumped back up. Braced her back paws. Stopping me. If there hadn't been a headless squirrel nailed to my tree, I might have smiled at her worry.

"It's only a squirrel," I told her. But she nosed me hard in the stomach, her claws holding me down. "Okay, girl. I'll stay inside." Fondling the dog's silky ears, I picked up the kitchen phone, called Mark at the LEC and told him about the squirrel. "You think I'm okay to leave the house?" I finished.

"No! I do *not* think you're okay to leave the house," he said, making it sound as if the question was a really stupid one. "Stay put. A squad is on the way and so am I."

"It's a dead squirrel, not a dead person," I said, exasperated and feeling a little foolish now that I had put my problem into so many words. Feeling even more foolish that I had let the dogs stop me. "I should have just gone out and gotten a shovel, pried it off the tree, buried it and forgotten about it. This is stupid."

A siren blared in the distance. Belle hopped down and

ran for the back door, tail wagging. "I hear the squad. Later," Mark said, and broke the connection. Slowly I put down the phone.

It was pretty sad that my dog knew the sound of sirens and associated them with help on the way. It said something about my life I didn't want to look at too closely.

The police used a claw hammer to remove the dead squirrel, bagged the rodent and took it for evidence. Evidence of what, I didn't know, but perhaps it went with all the questions they asked, none of which I knew the answer to.

"Did you see the perpetrator? When did it happen? Did you hear the hammer? Did the dogs bark? Did you hear a car? Motorcycle? Did you see *anything?*"

"Nope. Not a thing. Slept through the whole event."

Giving a police report is a useless endeavor when the witness was snoring as the dirty deed was done. But it made Mark happy to be doing his job, so I pretended to be cooperative until the cops were satisfied that the squirrel was the only evidence on the property and drove off.

Mark left me with the warning, "Be careful, woman. Something hinky is happening around you." Like I hadn't already figured *that* out for myself.

The dogs were happy and didn't seem concerned that Mark had left me alone to deal with any squirrel murderer who might have been watching from the woods. Together, two hours before dusk, we walked through the woods, over the creek and into Miss Essie's backyard, hot daylight sucking the energy out of me like a sponge.

The old woman was sitting on the deck waiting, her purple shawl tossed over the back of her chair in honor of the heat, feet bare, housedress spread to allow for air circulation. Sweating tea glasses and fresh-baked bread waited on a tray with blueberry jam. "What happenin' over your way?" she demanded. "True what I hear 'bout you got a dead rat nailed to a tree?"

"Squirrel, not a rat," I said, not even bothering to feel surprised that she knew already. "Head cut off. Mark figures it's a warning of some kind, like the runes." I settled into the chair offered me and drank the wonderful tea. I couldn't make tea as good as Miss Essie's. I had tried and failed.

"That man sometime got a way a' pointin' out the obvious."

I stuffed a slice of bread slathered with jam into my mouth and nodded both my appreciation of the food and her words.

"What he doin' 'bout it?

"He took a report," I said past the dough and sugary sweet. I had left the Snowball on the kitchen counter, uneaten except for the first bite. I'd have to take the left-over to work. Midnight snack, breakfast, it was all the same to me. I swallowed hard, the bite too big to be polite. "Miss Essie, a lot of strange stuff is happening and I need your take on it."

"I'm listening. Drink some tea and slow down. You gone choke you eat so fast."

"Yes, ma'am." I drank the tea, ate with proper-size bites and told Miss Essie all that had happened in the last few days. She listened silently, nodding her head, eating now and then of the cooling bread. Her face was creased with concentration, *figurin',* as she called it. When I told her about Mr. Faith and the words he'd said, Miss Essie nodded as though I had given her a final puzzle piece, sat back and crossed her hands over her middle. "What do you think?" I asked.

"What you think?" she countered.

"I think we have two different situations about to collide. I think we have a psychotic young woman on the loose and an addicted woman in the hospital. The psychotic woman may know about Dara and be after her next."

Miss Essie nodded slowly again, the fingers of one hand tapping on the back of the other hand. "That partly right. You got facts, but you leaving out good and evil. *That* what 'bout to collide. Good and evil. Spiritual and scientific, they 'bout to collide, too. And you is the central theme, 'cause you don' believe in *nothing*."

Thoughtfully, Miss Essie reached into a pocket, pulled out a folded piece of yellow paper and handed it to me. It was warm from the heat of her body and folded so many times it was no larger than the size of a nickel, creases deeply worn. "That woman comin' to see you tonight at the hospital. You be ready."

I opened the paper, smoothing out the creases. In purple ink were written three words in Miss Essie's crabbed hand. Sister Simone Pier.

"Simon Pear," Miss Essie said. "Like Simon Peter, only a woman. She got the Spirit. She know things. And she a woman of power. You listen to her. She help. Help both them young womens. Help you, too, if you let her."

"Simon was a disciple of Jesus?" I asked.

"That the one. Became Peter. The Rock. Leader of the first church. The sister jist like him. You see."

This was stupid. The whole thing was stupid. I was stupid for going along with it. "Miss Essie, I don't believe in weird stuff."

"Time was, folk didn't believe the world round, either. That didn't make it flat."

I sighed, refolded the piece of paper and tucked it into a pocket. "Okay, Miss Essie. But no prayer meetings in the ER. I don't want to get fired or have a security guard toss her off the property."

"Sister Simone Pier take care of herself jist fine. Take care of you, too."

That's what scares me, I thought. But wisely, I didn't say it aloud.

Just before dusk, I moved from the empty emergency room to the smoking area with Trisha Singletary and Fazelle Scaggs. The sunset was brilliant, golden and peach clouds against a lavender sky. Swallows dived and wheeled in the air above the hospital, banking off heated air currents rising from the extensive roof system. In the distance, a car engine revved and hummed, downshifting hard. I don't know how I knew who it was, but I did, even before the convertible came into view.

"'Scuse me, ladies. I have company." I said, rising from the concrete bench seat where I had been sitting.

"Sure, Doc," Fazelle said, her voice curious, neck craning to see where I looked. Trish simply sighed, her eyes on the sky, her thoughts probably on men.

Walking slowly, I entered the doctors' parking lot, happy I was wearing a lab coat so I could shove my hands in the pockets. I needed somewhere to put them all of sudden.

The bloodred Porsche, top down, roared into the hospital driveway with no regard to speed limits, downshifted again and squealed into the doctors' lot. It came to a stop beside my little BMW, and its engine went silent. I ambled over, palms sweating slightly. Shirl watched me come.

As usual, her multiple red braids hung limp on her shoulders, wilted from the high-speed drive where they whipped like Medusa's coiffure on methamphetamines.

Even in the dusky light, I could see the storm clouds in her eyes, and so opted for classic etiquette as a greeting. "Good evening, Dr. Adkins. Lovely weather we're having." Miss DeeDee would have been proud.

"Sod the bleedin' weather. What's that wanking, misbegotten son of a rutting goat done now?"

I knew who the son of a rutting goat was. Cam. Natch. But I had embarked on this perilous conversation with good manners and I was sticking to them. "I beg your pardon?"

Shirl muttered something beneath her breath, levered herself up and out of the seat with both arms, swiveled her legs over the door and dropped to the asphalt. She was wearing three-inch heels, skintight jeans and a sleeveless Lycra shirt that exposed mounds of cleavage. She had lost some weight in the weeks since I last saw her, and she looked both thinner and younger than I remembered. Both fisted hands went to her hips. In the heels, she had to tilt back her head only a bit to look me in the face. I didn't think the choice of heels was a lucky accident. Her gaze was like frozen steel.

I backed away three steps and pasted a smile on my face. "Hi, Shirl."

"Bugger that."

"Ah…yes, well…" I was really erudite tonight.

"You left a four-word message on my voice mail. *At dawn!*" She crossed the three steps to me and back to the car, to me and back to the car, pacing. "That bloody minger Cam left a dozen much more verbose messages, the Moaning Minnie. And on the eighth and ninth, I could swear he was bladdered as a kerb crawler."

"Bladdered as a…what?"

"Bladdered! As a whore!" she shouted. "Rat-arsed, pig-eyed, legless, pissed, sozzled." Her voice went up another notch as she whirled and came back toward me, her fists rising from her hips into a boxer's stance, her mouth sucking in a deep breath of air. I backed up another step or three, but she wasn't done. "Drunk!" she screamed.

I had seen Shirl this mad only once, when a doctor—a very important doctor—made a pass at her, one so crude she couldn't ignore or shake it off with a laugh. I had thought she might decapitate him in the elevator. Now that anger was directed at me. Cam Reston drunk. I remembered the clink of beer bottles that day I went to see him at the airport. I bet the idiot had just called her. Gently I said, "And?"

The breath whuffed out of her. "And he kept mumbling about how sorry he was and how he'd made a mess of everything. How he'd lost me—which he *should* be grieving over, as I'm the best thing that ever happened to the wanker—and how he'd lost his best friend in all the world. Which is *you!*" she accused. Her fists went back to her hips and I felt moderately safer. Until she added, "The bloody wanker made a pass at you, didn't he!"

I managed not to flinch. "Shirl, um, does wanker mean what I think it does?"

The sound that whistled from her nose could have been laughter, but I wasn't betting on it. "Most likely. Answer the question."

I'd never been very good at fine etiquette, and gave it up now in favor of honesty, which might be the only thing that would save my friendship with Shirl. "Well...sort of."

"Sort of!" she shouted again, her voice almost squeaking. "Sort of? Codswallop! Cam Reston never 'sort of' made a pass at anyone in his life! Do I look like a blathering idiot? When Cam makes a pass at a woman, it's a damn good one!''

I laughed. I couldn't help it. Shirl was jealous. Cam was miserable. This situation could be fun. Besides, if Shirl really did hit me, the three-inch heels would work in my favor. I figured I could rock her on her backside in about a half second. I dropped back against the still-hot car and propped my palms on the hundred-dollar wax job. ''You have a point,'' I said, my laughter still ringing on the air. ''It was a really good pass. The best one I've ever had, to be honest.''

Shirl's eyes blazed in the falling dark. She drew herself up to her five-foot, four-inch height, tossed back her braids and speared me a with a look I knew she must have learned at the queen's knee. Imperious would have been a good description. This time when she spoke, her voice was icy. ''Elucidate, if you please.''

''He met me on my back stoop near midnight, invited himself in, made sandwiches, poured wine, changed my musical selections to some wild Latin theme and pulled me to my feet.''

''He danced with you.'' The tone was even colder than a moment past. Very precise. Very British. Very deadly.

It was a good thing Shirl's clothes were so tight. There was no chance she had a weapon on her person. And since I had gone from good manners to egging things on, I was very glad of that fact. ''Yep. A rumba. And that man can dance, let me tell you.''

''I am fully aware of Cam's dancing ability. And of that ability's effect on women.''

I nodded, fighting back the grin. ''It heats the blood, I'll say that.''

''Did you...'' For the first time her words faltered. ''Did you and Cam...''

I thought a moment. "As I remember, we finished the dance, and then I sent him home to Miss Essie and a cup of her herbal tea."

"Without…"

When Shirl couldn't find the words, I just grinned and said, "Without."

The breath shot from her. She turned away for a moment, shuddered and spun back quickly. "Damn that man. Damn! Damn, damn, *damn!*" she whispered, her voice sounding broken in the dark. When she sucked in a breath, it whistled just a bit in the back of her throat.

"He only made a pass at me because he knew I'd say no. He only made a pass at me to get back at you. And so you would find out about it."

"Balderdash. He made a pass at you because he's half in love with you and always has been. You're his best friend."

I disagreed, but didn't know how to object without sounding like I "doth protest too much." Cam just wanted to get laid and get back at Shirl. I was handy. *Men.*

Shirl shuddered once more and tossed back her hair, sending the braids arching like cowboys' lariats. Her fists opened into palms, and I started to relax. One-handed she pulled me from her car. "Don't smudge the bleedin' shine, if you please. How did you resist? Cam on a dance floor is enough to send a dead woman into heat." Her voice sounded almost normal.

I shrugged and focused on her pale face in the now-total dark. "Some relationships mean too much to me to screw them up—pardon the pun—with a quick roll in the hay."

"There's nothing quick about a roll in the hay with Cameron Reston."

"Trying to make me have regrets?"

Shirl giggled, the sound ragged, one hand flying to her mouth. I realized she was crying as the security light caught the glimmer of tears on her face.

"What did he do to make you cut him off?" I asked. "He's miserable. You're miserable."

"You might not have noticed, but Cam is a bit of a wanderer. In my estimation, he was beginning to scan the horizon for his next conquest. I found one for myself instead."

"So you ran him off to keep from getting hurt."

"I did." Shirl was always honest. Sometimes brutally so.

I took her elbow and led her to the covered ambulance bay and the lights, pretending not to see when she wiped her face with the back of her wrist. "I think you should consider taking him back."

"I might. Once he's more miserable than simply brokenhearted."

"You want him ready to die for missing you?"

"I want him with bradycardia, diaphoresis and total apnea. Positively paralytic with fear."

I pushed open the ER lobby doors and she entered beneath my arm. "You are a cruel woman."

"Thank you most kindly. This cool air is splendid." She lifted her braids off her neck to let the cool reach her nape. Unexpectedly, she asked. "Was I one of the relationships you didn't want to screw up?"

"Want a Coke?"

"Diet, please."

"Yes, you were," I said as I bought us both colas.

"Good. Well, I'm off."

"You're leaving?" I wasn't sure I had dodged this bullet, and didn't want her to go until it looked more certain. But she whirled on the three-inch heels and headed back into the heat. There was no way to hold her unless I tied her down. I followed more slowly.

"I am. I have a date with a surgeon. About which I have been most careful to let Miss Essie know."

"You were jealous. Of me." Okay, I just wanted to hear her say it.

"Positively green-eyed."

"Come back down when Marisa gets home for a girls' day out?"

"She'll leave the ankle biters with Miss Essie?"

"We'll take her for a manicure and facial. She'll agree to leave them home."

"Let me know when. I'll arrange to be available." Shirl sat on the Porsche's door and swiveled her legs over and into the driver's side. With a roar the racing engine came to life. "Cheerio!" she called and wheeled the car expertly back, around and out of the lot. And she was gone, leaving me oddly comforted.

21

WEIRD STUFF. I HATED IT.

By midnight, my thoughts still full of Shirl and Cam, and the confusing intricacies of intimate relationships, I had come to the conclusion that I would have made a great monk or hermit, or whatever. Shirl's game of one-upsmanship with Cam seemed infinitely more perilous than the games Mark and I played. Where we competed for being the strongest or the fastest or the most important, Cam and Shirl competed with issues of the heart. Dangerous, to my way of thinking.

The ER was dead, as if the world were trying to make up for yesterday's wildness. The nurses, finally caught up on paperwork and pill counting, were sitting in the break room studying for certification or reading a novel. Nothing happening and there was a sense that nothing would.

I sat alone, outside in the smoking area, my feet on the bench beside me, arms curled around my knees, head back, still, and listening. I loved nights like this one. Balmy temperatures, a nearly full moon, a security guard roaming the grounds keeping me safe from crazy old men.

Nights like this reminded me of vacationing at Myrtle Beach, the breeze fresh and slightly salty, the moon so

bright it outshone all the security lights and cast shadows
that moved and wavered. There was something innocent
and harmless in the air. Like the time Marisa and Miss
DeeDee and I went to the beach for two weeks, staying
at a gated beach resort. Late-night walks on the smooth
sand, good food in great restaurants, girl talk, boy watching, shopping. Innocent, ingenuous fun like most teenage
girls have, fun that had been so little in evidence in my
young life.

A bird called, sounding oddly like a seagull.

Suddenly I wasn't alone.

I hadn't seen her walk up. No cars had driven by. The
shadows hadn't moved. But she was there, in an instant,
between one blink and the next, sitting opposite me, a
shadow beneath a white head covering. She was dressed
in black, three crosses on chains around her neck picking
up the moonlight, her eyes black on white and watching
me.

I didn't move. Wasn't startled or afraid. Instead I
smiled. "Sister Simone Pier."

She nodded her head, the crosses tinkling, the white
scarf moving regally. She was dressed similar to Muslim
women, or maybe nuns—I didn't know enough religion
to know the difference—her dress long and layered, with
slits for her arms to move through. She looked old. Older
than Miss Essie. Older than any woman I had ever seen
before, her face creased in thousands of soft folds, her
flesh covering bones fragile as a bird's. But when she
spoke, her voice was young, liquid as moonlight on water.

"You the child Essie sent me to see. Why? You not a
Christian. You not in danger." She cocked her head.
"Except peripherally. Danger swirl around you, some-
time inside you. But you walk through it like a stone

through smoke. You don't need me. Not yet. Maybe not ever.'' There was the faint hint of an accent in her voice, but I couldn't place it. French, perhaps?

"She sent you to answer questions," I said. "And to talk to DaraDevinna Faith."

"The young healer," the sister said, nodding.

"She needs help. According to her father, she needs protection. I agree."

"Tell me about her."

I tilted my head. "Are you the woman who helped Miss Essie drive out the root doctor over twenty years ago?"

"I am. You going to tell me what I need to know to help?"

Nowhere does federal law give a doctor the right to discuss a patient with anyone else without that patient's written permission. I hesitated a moment, but only a moment, arms crossed around my legs, night breeze blowing in the moonlight, the strange sound of a seagull breaking the quiet now and then. Then, without another thought, without concern, without the slightest reticence, I started talking.

"Our best guess is that she's an undiagnosed and previously untreated epileptic. And she's addicted to some kind of herbal drug," I began. I covered everything, from the accident where Na'Shalome came into my life to the uncontrolled convulsions of DaraDevinna Faith and the people who attended the tent meetings. Sister Simone Pier sat still as a statue in an old graveyard, only the slight movement of her breathing proving her other than a painted Madonna.

"I want to see these herbs she have on her body when you find her. I want to see this doll. I want to see this healer, so young and epileptic. So full of the Lord. You have the doll?''

''I have a picture, in my bag in the break room.''

''Good enough, for the moment.'' She blinked.

I stood and stretched and found the sister standing beside me. Again I hadn't seen her move, and again I wasn't surprised. I felt strangely lighthearted, as if nothing in the world could touch me or hurt me. As if someone had slipped me a really expensive street drug that left me peaceful and contemplative. I grinned at her and she grinned back, white teeth perfectly bright as the moon.

Noah's oversize van was still parked in the lot, though no electrical cables ran to it, and it was silent and dark. I knocked before I opened the back door, then entered and found the gallon bag of herbs in plain sight. I handed it to the sister.

''Come. I need light for this,'' she said.

Together, we entered the ER and as I searched for the Polaroid in the depths of my overnight bag, the sister cleared the small round break-room table of its half-empty cups of cold coffee, cola cans, pastry wrappers.

The sister sat and took the photo obtained by Boka from my hands, studying it for long moments. As she stared at the photo of the weird doll with its metal, wood and wire limbs bedecked with flowers and ribbons, her hands began to shake, to tremble, as if she had just realized her own age and was being overtaken by the years. She started to mutter, the words so soft I couldn't make them out, but it sounded like chanting. Dropping the photo on the table, not taking her eyes from it, the sister reached into the depths of her robes and pulled out two vials. Uncorked them, she poured a few drops from each onto the photo, still muttering under her breath.

Her concentration was so complete, I could have stripped and danced naked on the table beside the photo and she would not have seen me. She placed one hand over the photo, her palm covering the doll completely, closed her eyes and fell silent. I assumed she was praying, the way I had seen patients anointed and prayed over in the ER in the past, but I thought it was weird to pray over a photo in the same way.

Five long minutes later, Sister Simone Pier opened her eyes and met mine. Carefully, holding my gaze, she lifted the photo, tore it in half. Shock raced through me and I almost reached out to stop her from destroying the Polaroid. But I paused. Why should I stop her? I couldn't think of a single reason.

The sister tore the photo into small strips and made a pile of them before gathering the pieces into a small, white silk drawstring bag. My eyebrows rose as she swept every small scrap away and drew the bag closed. Disturbed, but unable to say why, I sat back in my chair and broke the strange stare.

"Later, I will dispose of it," she said, tucking the bag and the vials out of sight in her clothes. "This is a thing of power. A gateway into another place. A thing of vengeance, created for death and pain. You say the creator of this thing has seen you and the young healer who is so sick?"

"Yes. Both of us. And she acted strange both times. Not that I think Na'Shalome ever acts normal."

A hint of a smile touched the sister's lips. "You were correct. The girl who made this needs hands, healing hands, to make it active. She may have wanted yours. May still settle on yours, if she can't obtain DaraDevinna Faith's hands."

"Well, that makes me feel all warm and cozy inside," I said, my tone as wry as I could make it.

The sister lifted an admonishing finger. "What it should make you feel is cautious. Wary. Prepared for trouble."

When I didn't respond to the warning, Sister Simone Pier opened the Ziploc, spread the contents out. She began making small piles of herbs, crinkling some, sniffing others, tasting minute bits, arranging them according to color and size, taste and smell.

As she worked, the three crosses swayed back and forth. One was gold with a ruby on each end of the cross. One was silver, the cross made with pointed and jagged ends, like lightning. A single diamond glittered in its heart. The third was wood, blackened as if it had been burned, shiny as if it had absorbed all the oil from thousands of fingers holding it for centuries.

After a while, Sister Simone came upon something in the bag that caused her to pause. It was gray and crinkled, and she studied it for a long moment, turning it in her dark-skinned fingers. She looked up at me. "You should get that plant doctor out here. This something I bet he never seen before, this one."

I hadn't thought about Noah Ebenezer, and wasn't sure how he would react to this woman plowing through his herbs. Wasn't sure how he would feel about me entering his van and walking off with his stuff, either. I lifted the phone on the wall and dialed his room number. Noah had taken an extra call room, bunking down near the Respiratory Therapy Department. He had fluttered his fingers to me on his way to bed. Though it was one in the morning, he sounded wide-awake and I heard Conan O'Brien's late-night TV voice in the background. "Yes?"

"Noah, this is Rhea. I have a, a wise woman in the

ER. I gave her the bag of herbs. She says she wants to talk to you about them.''

There was a slight pause. ''You gained access to my van?''

''It was unlocked.''

''No. It wasn't. I'll be right there.'' The line went dead.

I looked at Sister Simone Pier. ''Weird stuff. I hate weird stuff. I don't believe in weird stuff.''

She grinned again. ''You can't fear what you don't believe in. If it don't exist then it can't hurt you.''

''But if I fear it then it must be real?'' I wasn't sure I liked the sister's logic.

''Fear makes all things real, child of Essie's heart. So does faith. But faith stronger. Faith give you access to power that uses you for God's good. Fear take power from you.''

I sat silent, watching the dried herbs as their little piles grew.

Noah appeared a little over five minutes later, a billowing white robe like a parachute swirling around him, yards of beige pajamas fluttering. He stopped at the door and stared down at us, his face a thunderhead of anger. The sister tilted back her head and smiled at him, an otherworldly smile that might have given me the shivers had the night not been so strange already. ''Sister Simone Pier,'' she said in her lilting young voice.

''Sist...Sister *Simone*.'' His face altered in an instant, the anger melting, replaced with something else. After a second I realized the expression might be reverence. Or excitement. Or awe. Maybe all three. He dropped into a chair as his legs gave out. The air exploded from the cushion, the chair wobbled beneath his bulk. ''Sister, I have been hoping to meet you for ages. Trying to get in touch with you.''

She nodded again. ''I was aware. But the time was not right till now.'' She indicated the piles of herbs, some of which had whirled in an eddy when Noah sat. ''This is the proper time. The proper need. What have you discovered?''

''Indian snakeroot, opium poppy, diviners sage and grape-scented sage, lobelia, ololiuqui, mucuna, maikoa, among others. Powerful stuff.''

''*Rauwolfia serpentina*,'' she said, interpreting to the Latin without missing a beat. ''*Papaver somniferum, Salvia divinorum* and melissodora, *Lobelia inflata, Turbina corymbosa, Mucuna pruriens,* Brugmansia species, I see two of them here. And yes, this is powerful medicine. But what do you make of this one?'' She held the odd wrinkled gray thing over to the doctor.

''I tested that one, but can't place it. It looks like a species of fungi, but I'm unfamiliar with it.'' Noah's eyes were gleaming, his gaze locked on the sister, his pudgy hands fisted on the arms of his chair. I might as well have been on the moon as far as he was concerned, but at least he wasn't PO'd at me for trespassing in his van. It seemed he had forgotten it entirely.

''I don't know what the ancients called it. I have found no certain references to it anywhere. But I call it ram's apple. It is a tiny fungi that grows in the tight crevasse of a barren and shaded apple tree, where two branches come together forming a tight-fitting shelter. I have found it nowhere else, and in no quantity at all.'' She held the gray thing out to Noah, a silent command to sniff. He breathed the scent in with short bursts of air. The sister held it out to me and I too sniffed. The fungi did have a vague apple scent.

"It is a highly addictive sedative, with hallucinogenic properties. And this bag is full of it." She pointed to the pile of wrinkled gray things. Noah took a small sliver from the pile and put it on his tongue, swirling it with a bit of saliva and holding it there, eyes closed. Sister Simone narrowed her eyes at him, the expression becoming one of approval when Noah removed the sliver and simply held it, waiting for something to happen.

Noah's eyes popped open. "Ahhh," he breathed. "Interesting. Delightful." He twirled the sliver in his fingers and, almost regretfully, placed it back on the table. "I see what you mean about its addictive qualities. I do indeed." He licked his lips.

Sister Simone shook her head. "You are too fat to test things in the old way, Noah," she said gently. "You spoil the herb's effect on the body. You should fast for several weeks, to begin the fat removal, and go through a purification process to remove the toxins accumulated beneath your skin and in your organs."

"I would be honored to have you teach me, Sister Simone. Would you let me work beside you?"

"I don't mean to interrupt all this New Age hocus-pocus, but I have two questions. One—Noah, you were looking for Sister Simone?"

He nodded, his eyes on the old woman, almost possessively. "For about two years now. I have spoken to her granddaughter and her younger sister. Left messages with several cousins. She never called me back. I had hoped to do another search for her in this part of the state when my work here was done."

"Okay. I don't believe in coincidence, but okay, I'll pass on that one. Two—what does that stuff do? And how can we help Dara if she's addicted to it?"

The sister laughed. "Always the impatient one. It is

her strength—'' she glanced at Noah ''—and her weakness. First, there is no coincidence in God's world, child. Second, give fluids, lots of fluids. Sedatives, Valium. You are doing the proper things. It will take time to remove the ram's apple from her system. And then you will have to deal with the seizures.''

I pursed my lips at her ''coincidence'' reply, keeping my response to her comments between my teeth. I didn't want to be either unflattering or rude, knowing I'd hear back about it from Miss Essie. Instead I said, ''So you think this stuff was controlling seizures in Dara-Devinna?'' When the sister nodded, I went on. ''So, why so many seizures in others?''

''Addiction. If the ram's apple were thrown on the bonfire in quantity or offered in the communion wine, it would have taken only a few sips over the course of several nights, or a few nights breathing in the fumes to prove addictive for the susceptible. Then, when the fungi was removed...''

''They have seizures from withdrawal. And if the Faiths were selling this stuff as communion wine, and people were taking it home in quantity, then when they run out, we're going to see a deluge of seizures.''

The sister nodded. I wanted to curse. And all we had to treat patients was what we had before. Time and fluids and sedatives. Great. Just freaking great.

22

DID ANGELS GET ANGRY?

By 3:00 a.m., Noah and the sister had talked their way through more Latin names than I had heard since medical school and covered a staggering range of individual symptoms—not to mention what might happen when the herbs were given together—all of them contained in the bag found on DaraDevinna Faith when she was picked up by the ambulance. After sitting silent for two hours, I understood that treating Dara, and the patients I could expect when the communion wine ran out, was going to be difficult. As much art as science.

Withdrawal from any addictive substance was dangerous. It could result in hallucinations, acute anxiety, paranoia, violent behavior, convulsions, cardiac irregularities and a host of other symptoms. Most were short-term and could be dealt with in a hospital setting. But sometimes, long-term damage could result from both the addiction itself and the physical and mental stress of drying out. It was up to the doctor to find a way to make the process as gentle as possible on the patient.

There were three ways a doctor could treat withdrawal. One was to give a small amount of the addictive substance through an IV and slowly wean the patient off the drug. This method was once used to treat alcoholic patients suffering from D.T.'s. A doctor would have the pharmacy mix up a diluted alcohol IV and give the liquor through the IV line. The second was to administer medication that would substitute for the missing drug, a treatment used most commonly for withdrawal from cocaine, alcohol and abused street drugs. The third was to treat for symptoms only, which was dangerous and usually used only as a last resort or when the addictive substance was unknown. Like now.

While the two plant specialists were still talking, I made some calls to prepare the hospital for problems to come over the next few days or weeks. I left a message with the mental health professional on call, called the Department of Social Services, DHEC—the Department of Health and Environmental Control—and left messages with the administrator's voice mail and the medical chief of staff's emergency call number, as well as Boka's answering service. No need to be waked up, but they all needed to know as soon as possible in the morning. We had a public health situation looming and needed to be prepared.

I came back in the room to hear Noah inviting the sister to come meet DaraDevinna. "She is the most charming young woman. I have been in her room several times tonight, playing chess. Remarkable girl, though her short-term memory seems to have been affected by the withdrawal. Seems to affect her memory of information provided, not people. Interesting effect. Temporary, I hope."

"Does she know she may be addicted?" I asked.

They both looked up at me and I had the feeling I had missed something important but didn't know what. "Is it necessary—absolutely necessary—to tell her?'' the sister asked.

''I think it is. There's an important distinction between giving herself drugs and being given them by her father. We don't yet know how the herbs came to be in her body. In fact, we don't really know *if* she ingested herbs or *if* she's addicted to them. All we have is speculation.''

''Pish,'' Dr. Noah said, wagging his finger at me. ''Empirical evidence suggests she's addicted. And that girl would no more give herself drugs than poison.''

I wasn't sure there was a difference but kept the observation to myself. I was getting pretty good at keeping my mouth shut these days and simply shrugged, proud of my restraint.

Noah lifted the phone and dialed the medical unit, spoke to the nurse, then dialed Room 112, spoke to Dara and hung up. Smiling, he said, ''The young woman is awake and willing to see us.''

''Come.'' Sister Simone stood and moved down the hallway as if she knew where she was going, Noah close on her heels, a slight figure followed by a massive one, their robes billowing out behind them like DaraDevinna's tent in a strong wind.

I followed more slowly, moving almost against my will, pointing to my beeper, and making sure my nurses knew how to find me. The sister's weirdness had faded after a time, but I had experienced enough of the spirit world tonight, and wanted to stay put in my nice safe ER. Yet I felt I had to be there. Not because of medical instinct, but woman's intuition, which I hated. Just really hated.

Outside Dara's room sat a cop in an uncomfortable folding chair, a paperback open in his hand. It meant that Dara had been charged with something. I wondered if she knew, if she remembered. The cop wasn't Gerald Chambers, the officer who had been drugged. Chambers may have been discharged from the hospital. I hadn't checked on him since his admission. I nodded to the cop and moved on, stopping to speak with the nurse at the desk and ask after the patient's condition. Having information meant I was both forewarned and forearmed in a hospital setting.

Entering room 112, I found Dara sitting up, the head of the bed at an upright angle, the covers tight under her arms. She looked very young and lost in the harsh lights behind the bed, her orbits bruised, the veins clearly visible beneath her pale waxy skin, her undernourished body a slight hump beneath the covers. She had two IVs in her left arm, tape securing them both in place, and a nasal cannula was looped over the head of the bed, ready should she need oxygen. A bedside phone and a Coke rested on the adjustable table nearby, with a folded-up board game that might have been chess. It looked like any old, ordinary room.

Until her eyes stopped me at the door. They blazed with an anger so hot it seemed to heat the air as she stared between Noah and the sister, and burned their way to me. The silence in the room was sharp and cutting. I was sure I had missed something important again. When she turned those eyes to me, I was sure I should have stayed away.

"Are you going to tell me why I'm here?" she demanded in her breathy voice, the one that seemed to carry across a tentful of worshipers with little or no amplification. "And what that officer is doing outside my room? And what is going into my arm?" She lifted her arm, displaying the IV sites. None of the phrases were actual questions, but demands for information.

"Um," I said, cleverly stalling, "cop?"

She cut her eyes at me and I felt as stupid as my question. Her irritation decided me on the truth, brutal as it might be. "Okay. I'll tell you." I studied her expression a moment. "You may not like what I'm going to say."

"I'm quite certain I'll not like what you're going to say, but it seems my right to hear it." Her breathy voice cut like steel. And she had a point.

"You were found on the side of a road having a grand mal–type seizure. You have been having similar seizures ever since. You were given Valium and now have a Dilantin drip to control the seizures, but you appear to have an atypical reaction to the medication, which should knock you out but seems to leave you wide-awake, conscious and alert and oriented to time, place and person. You don't remember being told any of this?"

Dara shook her head no. The look of determination in her eyes faded a bit into uncertainty, but her gaze remained on mine, direct and penetrating.

"According to the nurse at the desk and Dr. Noah, here, you are displaying signs of short-term memory loss. They have explained all this to you several times, but you keep forgetting it. I suggest your nurse write down everything and leave it on your bedside table. After a few times reading it, you may begin to remember.

"In addition to the Valium and Dilantin, you are also being given fluids to flush your system of a possible herbal and or chemical dependency. The herbs the EMTs found on you are dangerous and addictive. Many could result in seizures themselves if misused. Are you getting all this?"

Dara nodded, her gray eyes growing heavy as clouds

full of rain. Sister Simone turned her sharp eyes on me, but I kept mine focused on Dara, ignoring the old woman.

"The cop outside is there because of what happens to the people who attend tent meetings once you leave town, and sometimes while you are still there. They start having seizures like the ones you had."

Dara's lips slowly parted. Tears gathered in her wounded eyes. "Seizures...are they all right?" she whispered.

"Not all of them." I paused, uncertain now. But Dara lifted a hand and encouraged me to continue. "A few have died."

Dara flinched slightly, as if my words stung. Sister Simone shook her head slowly and turned back to Dara, her hands folded in a position of prayer.

"Do you take drugs, Dara?"

"No. Never. Not even aspirin," she breathed.

"Do you take herbal medicines?" When she didn't respond, I asked more gently, "Does your father give you herbs? Like in the communion wine?"

Dara's eyes slipped from mine to the covers over her legs. A single tear slid down one cheek and fell. The transition from anger to tearfulness was sudden, but, with the drugs in her system, not unexpected.

I softened my voice. "Does he, Dara?"

She nodded slowly. "In the wine. Every day. He says it's good for me."

"And you don't have seizures?"

She shook her head no again, the motion so slow it looked as if it might cause her pain. "Never before. Never that I remember."

"And is that the same wine he gives as communion wine at the tent meetings?"

"Yes. The same." She raised her head. "People...died?" Her face, her voice, were full of horror.

After a moment I answered. "Yes. They died," I said. "And the police want to question you about it. Your father, too."

Sister Simone's shoulders jerked, and she looked at me with such rancor I wanted to duck my head, but I didn't. I kept my eyes on Dara, who was crying openly now, her frail form shaking with quiet breathy sobs.

The sister whirled and went to the window, staring out into the graying sky, her hands on the warm glass. The posture made her look as if she had wings. An angry angel. Did angels get angry? And when they did, were they dangerous? I'd have to ask Miss Essie. Or Marisa, when she got back. I had a feeling Marisa would be the safer one to question. I had a feeling Miss Essie wouldn't be happy that I had ticked off the good sister. She might not be speaking to me anytime soon.

Dr. Noah Ebenezer shook his head as he watched Dara try to understand all the alterations in her life. The changes, the new way of seeing old things, and the new knowledge that would surely change her vision of herself. I ignored him, too.

"So—" Dara took a shuddering breath and met my eyes again "—I am a drug addict and a murderess."

I almost recoiled at the words. They were unbelievably brutal. And they had come from my mouth first. I swallowed down the repellent taste of them.

"Thank you for telling me the truth." Dara lifted her head, exposing her tear-wet cheeks. "No one else has, or I would have remembered it, I'm sure. Please inform the police that I will work with them in a totally honest and open manner. But I don't know where my father went. He always leaves following a tent meeting, to find the next place and get us set up. Then he returns for me. This time he stayed gone too long, I suppose."

I had no reply to that and so remained silent. It was clear from the reflection of Sister Simone Pier's malignant stare through the window glass, that I had said way too much already. Maybe I still needed to work a bit on reticence.

Still, there was one thing I needed to ask. "Dara, does your father drink the communion wine?"

"No," she said. "He takes his herbal tea. It's different from mine. I've seen him make it and it has different herbs in it."

Sister Simone reached down and twisted the window blinds shut, closing out the dark. But not before I saw something move outside, just beyond the reach of the illumination of the room. A form. *Someone was out there.* The sister turned to me and said briskly, "Go out. Leave me with this child. She needs no more of your heartless words. She needs prayer."

Obeying, I nodded and walked out, Noah behind me. I left not because I had said too much already. I'd have to be dumb as a box of rocks not to know that. I obeyed not because of her words, but because of the message in the sister's eyes. *Get the cop. Send him outside. Now!*

Weird stuff, I thought as I told the cop about the form outside the window. I hated it.

Two marked cars arrived out front of the hospital, and two bored deputies, hoping for a bit of excitement in the dull night, made a search, hands on weapons, huge flashlights scanning. But it was over quickly. No one was seen outside Dara's window, no footprints were found in the dry soil or mulched beds. After a short consultation with the officer on duty and Jessie, the security guard, the marked cars pulled off and went back to patrolling the sleepy county. The cop went back to his paperback. Noah and Sister Simone left together for the parking lot and Noah's van, heads bent close, robes still surging like a heavy surf. I wondered if Noah even realized he was wearing his pj's.

I forced away my guilt about shocking Dara with the truth, knowing that the truth was usually the best policy, and that lies and prevarication simply delayed matters, didn't fix them. Back in the ER, I checked in, then found my pal, the hairdresser, ready and willing to trim my wayward locks, and sat for a quick clipping before hitting the sack in my call room. Dull night. Dull, dull, dull. I loved it, sleeping for close to five hours before it was time to change shifts. Far as I was concerned, it was a perfect night.

Saturday morning dawned cooler, with cloudy skies. The locals were hoping for rain for thirsty crops, as the effect of the storm the week prior was long gone. The Southeast had been in the grip of a devastating drought for several years, with a cumulative rainfall loss of more than thirty-six inches. A major storm the past spring had helped a bit, and fostered hopes that the drought was over, but the summer had been even drier than the one before. Local water tables were dropping, making rural wells run dry, lowering the level of lakes, ponds, streams and the Catawba River that ran through three neighboring counties. Rain and gardening uppermost in my thoughts, I headed home through the beautiful day.

While I made coffee and played with the dogs, I let a sprinkler run on the unused beds shaped for me by the lawn-care crew in the spring. Then, with a huge insulated mug at my side and the dogs trying to help dig, I went to work in the yard. Surprisingly, it was a satisfying morning. I hated housework, but sticking my hands into moist soil and digging around as I set plants produced an entirely different feeling from that of cleaning and dusting and mopping. This was soothing. Relaxing. And the effects could be measured instantly by the change in the yard. I decided I liked yard work. I liked it a lot.

Belle and Pup liked it, too, alternately digging up what I had planted, digging new holes, playing tag, and bowling me over as part of the intricate game they played. It was fun for all three of us, though the dogs got a stern lecture about digging in the beds.

Lunch was brought over by Cam and Miss Essie, who both thought it a rare treat to see me dirty, muddy, industrious and happy. We picnicked on the front porch, eating tomato and basil sandwiches topped with melted goat cheese, iced tea and leftover spicy bean soup.

Miss Essie gave suggestions on bed preparation and bulbs that would like various locations, perennials and annuals that would like others. I memorized the plant names and took her up on her offer to root flowering plants from her garden. Cam lounged on the broken tile porch, silent, watching me, an amused and platonic glint in his eyes. Until Miss Essie changed the subject.

"Now. While I got you young people's attention I got some things to say. This house been attacked by forces a' darkness and Sister Simone and I prayed over it. It clean now and protected from evil. Won't be no more them runes put on it, and no more threats of any kind. Not here. You safe."

Cam winked at me and rolled his eyes.

"You kin stop making eyes at Miss Rhea. I know how you feel about religion, Cameron Reston, but it a power to be reckoned with jist the same. I pray for you, too, even if you don't appreciate it none."

"I appreciate it, Miss Essie. Really," Cam said, fighting a grin, amused and perhaps slightly embarrassed at being caught making fun of her. "I guess I need whatever prayers you offer for me."

"That the truth. You jumping in and out a' beds with so many women. Shameful life you leading till you settle in with Miss Shirl. Jist shameful."

That one hit too close to home and Cam bit his lip to escape replying. I looked away to keep from laughing. Miss Essie was on a roll and no one was going to stop her saying what needed to be said. I had tried in the past and knew better. And I was always oddly comforted by the prayers she said. It was nice to know she prayed over my house. I didn't know one could pray over things. I figured prayer was only for people.

"My Miss Risa comin' home in a few days. That English-nanny woman comin' by New Year's, 'less I can change her mind. Cam, you and Shirl be made up by then, and I 'spect you both to be here two days after the Lord's birthin' day to celebrate."

"Shirl?" Cam sat up straight, his amusement forgotten. "Shirl told me to get lost."

"And you gone call her up and apologize to her for being ten kinds a' fool. You been thinking 'bout that ever since my Miss Rhea tole you no, and it the smartest thing you could do. This time, Miss Dr. Shirley gone answer the phone. You call her," she demanded.

Cam's black eyes spit at me and I shook my head, laughing. "Don't blame me. The woman knows stuff even when no one is around to tell her. She said you came home acting itchy." Cam's eyes narrowed and I could have sworn a blush settled on his cheeks.

Miss Essie disregarded us both and plowed on. "I had my doubts 'bout that relationship from the first, but Miss

Shirl seem to have her head on straight and seem to know how to keep you going in the right direction—a difficult thing when a man as good-looking as you. I think you perfect for each other, so you gone call her and make it right.''

''I am not.'' Cam sounded like a stubborn little boy and I laughed aloud at his tone.

''You is, too,'' Miss Essie said, her eyes stern. She tossed back her purple shawl in preparation for the lecture she was warming up to. ''Afore' you fly outta here, you gone call her and tell her you shamed a' the way you actin'. *Make nice.* You been wantin' to, and now you is.''

Cam crossed his arms, a mutinous expression on his face. I was delighted to see Miss Essie sticking her nose in someone else's life besides mine. It was a treat. I rolled back on my elbows, knees bent up to watch them both better.

''And when you bring my Miss Risa back from that rehab place, I 'spect you to act like a man grown and not a little chile' ain't got no sense. Time you was growin' up and actin' like a man who want him one woman and not like a little boy got to see how many ladies he can stick himself into.''

Cam's face flamed. He opened his mouth and closed it fast, having thought better of whatever he was going to say. Miss Essie in a dander was a force stronger than the ocean.

''That plane a' yours fixed?''

''Yes,'' Cam said, the word grudging.

''Good. Missy Rhea?'' It was my turn to cringe. The ''Missy'' was a sure sign she was going to lower the boom on me now. ''You gone make fine with that Mr. Mark so him and Miss Clarissa join us for our celebration. And you gone see that my Arlana and her man available and doin' right to join us, too.''

''Mark I can maybe handle, but—''

''Mark you been runnin' from for near on a year. You got to be decidin' and lettin' him know you want him. And soon, or some sweet thing who know her mind gonna get him and leave you sittin' in the cold.''

Cam laughed at me, his blush fading in my discomfort. I lifted my chin at him. ''I can do that, Miss Essie.''

''You can?'' She didn't have to sound quite so surprised.

''I can. I can even stick my nose in Arlana's love life if you want me to. But I'll warn you. I have no practice with things like that.''

''You do jist fine. But another thing you got to do may be a mite harder.''

''Oh, no.'' I sat up quickly on the broken tile.

''You got to call your man John and make things right with him. Too much left undone and unsaid between you two and it cause problems in the future you don't get it worked out and said all proper.''

''No.''

''No?''

''No, *ma'am*. I am not calling John Micheaux. He made a decision and I—''

''Then what you gone do when that man come callin'?''

''John would never come here.''

''Yes, he would. I sayin' so. It up to you, 'course, but you bes' beware a' the possibilities what come from runnin' away from the altar.''

''I didn't run away.''

''Uh-huh.'' Miss Essie stood and folded her shawl back around her shoulders before gathering up the dirty paper plates and cups and packing them all away. There was a conspicuous silence as she worked, and Cam and I avoided looking at one another.

"I sending the good sister back to the hospital tonight to deal with the problems there. Mr. Cameron, you help an old woman back across the creek and then come back and say your goodbyes to Miss Rhea."

Cam stood and moved off with Miss Essie. I stared out over my front yard and tried not to think about John Micheaux and Mark Stafford and Christmas.

23

REASON IN THE FACE OF HOCUS-POCUS

Saturday afternoon was a full moon. Full moons were when witches and warlocks and genies in bottles came out and did their dirty work. Or was that vampires? Werewolves? I'd have to do an Internet search someday and see. I was just glad it wasn't Halloween or the shortest day of the year. Devil-out-among-us days. As I drove to work at six-thirty, hours before dark, the silver-white face of the moon peeked at me between the heavy August foliage, keeping pace with me like a taunting bully.

I had a steady shift in the ER to keep me busy, with two MIs at the same time—one with no insurance—and a postsurgical infection that looked as if the woman had squeezed ricotta cheese into the space between the surgical staples. Nasty stuff. I was betting on a multiple-antibiotic-resistant organism with major complications. The decades of antibiotic misuse had come back to bite us all in the collective butts. Once again, people were dying from simple bacterial infections gone haywire.

Doctors once gave out antibiotics for viral infections and treated bacterial infections before the body had a chance to do some fighting of its own. It was easier than dealing with the results of a mother gossiping at a bridge game that the doctor had refused to treat little Tommy's flu or cold. Easier by far to just scribble off a prescription and be done with it. Little Tommy would heal on his own and the antibiotics wouldn't hurt anything. Or so the prevailing medical wisdom went.

Now we knew better. Now it was too late.

After doing full work-ups on each, admitting all three, and seeing the intervening coughs, sore throats, rashes and sprains, it was near midnight. I was hungry, irritable and tired of being a doctor when all I could do was diagnose and slap a Band-Aid on it, all the while arguing against a system uninterested in finding a way for a sick man to pay for urgent health care. Bummer.

Close to midnight the overhead speakers blared. The "unexpected event" code, followed instantly by a security-alert code. The ER was too busy to leave unattended, but I figured I was expected to make an appearance. Waving to the overworked nurses, Coreen and Anne, I trotted off. I could always stop by the empty cafeteria for a Coke and a frosted bear claw if I discovered I was not needed.

As I neared the medical floor, I heard the cries and increased my pace. There was a ruckus in one of the rooms. When I realized it was DaraDevinna Faith's, I broke into a full run and rounded the corner. On the floor outside her room lay an overturned chair; beneath it, a deputy lay unconscious, a trickle of blood easing its way across the floor near his temple. I bent and felt for a pulse. He had one, strong and steady. He was breathing fine. A nurse knelt beside him. "Get him into a cervical collar and to ER. Full spinal protocol."

She nodded and took over, casting curious glances at the room where the shouting came from. A clot of people blocked the doorway.

I shoved into the room and stopped cold, trying to take it all in. Candles glowed in the darkness. Dozens of them. My eyes, accustomed to the sharp hospital lights, struggled to focus. The air in the room was frigid, the AC turned up all the way, flickering the candle flames. I moved through the nurses, pushing my way in. At the far corner of the room, an uneven circle had been painted in red on the floor. In the center of the circle were three figures.

Dara, her hospital gown streaked with red, hung limply in the embrace of another. A third figure lay at their feet.

The doll was on the tile. The doll that should have been locked up in police custody. Na'Shalome stood holding Dara, the healer's body draped forward, hair falling across her pale face.

I wasn't amazed to see Na'Shalome, her naked body painted in a smooth layer of glistening gold paint, overlaid with painted red runes. I had halfway been expecting her to make an appearance. But the wicked blade she held at Dara's throat was a surprise.

Long and slightly curved, the blade was streaked with red. Dara was bleeding profusely; the red streaks on her gown were not paint. It took another instant to realize the circle was also blood.

Blood dripped steadily down Dara's arms, off her fingertips, splattering on the doll, pooling on the floor and running in a thin trickle around and beneath the feet of the huddled girls, sliding toward the window. I tried to calculate how much blood she had lost. And my mind slid sideways just a bit.

Blood on the doll… She had been trying all along to get blood on the doll.

Na'Shalome was chanting softly. The blade was sawing slowly back and forth. Candlelight glittered on its honed edge.

"Get out," I said softly to the nurses. "Get out and call 911. Call Statler, get him up here. Boka, too." When no one moved, I murmured louder, "Go."

Na'Shalome looked up at me, her blue eyes black in the lambent light.

The room emptied behind me. The blade slowed, but continued to saw.

"You don't have to do this to stop your father," I said, pitching my voice low.

Na'Shalome blinked, the motion drowsy, as if she hadn't slept in days, her lids heavy with fatigue. Dara's fingers flexed, the gesture faint, an involuntary quiver. Was she coming to?

"He's dying," I said, trying to add the melody of persuasion and truth to my tone. "The spells you already cast did their job." The blade slowed almost to a stop. "He's dying. Your father is dying."

"Vengeance," she whispered.

"Yes. Your vengeance worked. In prison, the other men...did vengeance for you. They...hurt him. He's dying now."

Dara moaned. Her hands twitched, exposing slashes down her lower arms. She had been cut.

"Healing hands do Lord's will," Na'Shalome said.

"Yes," I said. "They do."

She nodded, her movement and her eyes hypnotic. "Hands of evil maim and kill," she chanted, her voice singsong, "Hands of healing do Lord's will." Na'Shalome's eyes bound mine, her lips barely moving. "Tooth for tooth and eye for eye, cut out tongue and slay the lie. Head and hands and heart all three, bring forth death that will not flee. Blood and breath and power mine—''

Dara flinched. Raised up in Na'Shalome's embrace. Lifted a hand to the knife hilt to stop the sawing movement at her throat. "Angels and spirit now minister to me," she whispered. "I call you by name—"

"I am a woman of power," a voice said from behind. "A virgin and a healer." I turned a fraction of an inch. Sister Simone Pier stood there, hands held out. "Take mine. Take me. Not the young healer. Allow her to fall from the circle you have made."

"Hands of evil maim and kill," Na'Shalome said. "Hands of healing do Lord's will."

"I call you by name. Raphael, Asa, Kallum, Jeriah and Rohan, I call you to defend and heal," Dara said, lifting her bloody hands.

"I am a woman of power. I offer myself to you to save the young healer."

"Your father is dying," I tried. Hoping for reason in the face of hocus-pocus. A wind blew through, fluttering the candles. The cold air grew icy.

Just the air-conditioning, I assured myself, my eyes on the embraced pair. Just the air-conditioning. I felt myself tense as if with fear. Cold prickles broke out on my arms.

"A willing sacrifice is far better than a struggling one," the sister said.

"Draw your swords. Defend me!"

Na'Shalome jerked DaraDevinna closer. The blade twisted up for a vicious downward slash.

The window behind the women exploded. Glass blasted in. A boom rocked the room, sharp and cracking.

A sharp sting in my temple. My hands came up to cover my face.

Dara and Na'Shalome slammed to the floor. Blood

spurted in an arc. I fell prone, dropped by the sound. The sister tumbled behind me.

Someone had shot at us.

A second shot shattered the window remains. Screams came from everywhere. A hot wind blew through. The candles fluttered and died.

Holes appeared in the far wall, visible by moonlight through the window opening.

The sister pulled me beneath her as if to shield me with her body.

A third boom sounded, closer. The room fell totally dark.

An inane thought flashed in my mind. *People are always shooting at me through windows.*

Silence descended, broken by sobs and screams. My ears ringing with a buzz, damaged by the blasts of sound.

I shoved at the sister and she rolled off me.

"You okay?" I half shouted.

"Yes. By the grace of the Lord. You?" I could see her mouth move, but heard no words above the buzz.

"Just freaking dandy," I said. The sister laughed.

Together, we crawled across the floor to the two women. The sister kicked at the doll, sending it out of the circle of blood. Rising to her knees, she grabbed a form in the tangle of bodies and pulled it across the room toward the hallway light. I grabbed the other body and followed, scooting and crawling, keeping my head down. Something hot and wet drenched my torso to the hips as I moved.

In the hallway, my eyes stinging from the bright light, we rolled the women to safety. Someone else pulled the downed deputy after us. A trail of smeared blood tracked our progress. We ended up behind the nurses' desk.

Three wounded and too many frightened personnel, some still screaming.

"Did someone call 911?" I shouted, my voice sounding dull and tinny to my injured ears.

"Yes. They're on their way," a calmer voice answered.

"Get pads and dressing! Hemostats! Someone start an IV on all three patients. *Triage!*" I demanded, wanting to get them all back working and thinking like medical people and not victims. Reason and training over fear.

My hands were shaking. Smudged with sparkling gold body paint. Forcing a breath into my lungs, I rolled the body I had dragged from the room over on its back.

Na'Shalome, her mouth open in grunting screams, had been hit by one of the blasts. Her right upper chest had an exit wound in it that I could have put my fist into, just below the collarbone. The wound was a deep cavity of bone and ruined tissue. Rifle shot, not shotgun, or more of her chest would be missing. Gouts of arterial blood spurted with each beat of her heart. Something major had been hit. "Where's that dressing! Gloves!"

Someone opened a pack of sterile four-by-fours and held it to me. Someone else a handful of gloves. Snapping on the latex gloves, I pressed a wad of sterile gauze into the wound and covered it with a bigger pad of nonsterile gauze. I had to get the bleeding stopped so I could see the artery and clamp it off. I leaned my body weight into the wound.

"Airway, breathing, circulation, people," I said, reminding them of the proper order to triage the severely wounded. Someone bent over Na'Shalome and checked her airway. Another took a pulse. "You. Hold this," I said to a nurse. He bent and positioned his hands over mine. "I'm gonna need suction, hemostats. I can't do this one here. She's got to get to the ER fast. I want Ringers IV, large-bore needle.''

I lifted the shaking form and checked for other damage. The bullet's entrance wound was in back, centered on the right shoulder blade. Probably had punctured the lung on its way out the front. I settled Na'Shalome back to the floor. I could hear her low-pitched cries now, soft groans of shock and pain.

Anne settled beside me. ''I can take this one,'' she said. ''I brought a stretcher for the cop.''

''Good. She's got a bleeder. Axillary may be hit. Looks like it may have hit the lung. Move her as soon as you get her stable. I want three IVs, chest tube kits, and if we didn't give her tetanus on her first admission, get one now. Cross-match times two. Do whatever else you need till I get there.'' Anne, cool and professional under fire, nodded.

Dara was bleeding profusely from lacerations at arms and neck. Nothing arterial, nothing urgent. Nurses were slapping dressings on everything that bled. Dara turned huge wounded eyes to me, her mouth opening and closing with horror. No screams. No tears. She was breathing, she had a pulse, the carotid beating fast in her neck but not spurting blood. Thank God. I didn't want to have to handle two massive bleeders at one time.

''I want labs on all these guys.''

''I can help with that.''

I looked over to see Kendrew and Lita, the lab tech and his venipuncture tech, blood-collecting trays at their sides. I gave a list of labs on each patient, added X-ray orders to Anne, who nodded, committing them to her phenomenal memory.

Someone had put a cervical collar on the deputy. He was still breathing and had a strong pulse. The wound on his temple might mean a subdural hematoma, but his pupils were equal and reactive. A good sign.

Sirens sounded in the distance, seeming to come from the dark room. Through the missing window.

"Did someone call Statler and Boka?"

"They're on their way."

"We got a name on this one?" someone asked.

"It's that weird patient who escaped. Anyone remember her name?" someone else said. Then instantly asked for a liter of fluid.

"Na'Shalome will be in the hospital computer. Cross-reference it," I suggested. "And get her to the ER first. She's our primary concern." At some point, I had stopped shouting orders and returned to a calmer tone of voice. My ears seemed to be working better, too. Reason and training over fear. Works every time.

The sister, her dark robe splattered and smeared with blood, joined me with Na'Shalome. Her white scarf had been knocked off at some point and I was surprised to see that Sister Simone Pier was completely bald, her scalp crisscrossed with ancient, gnarled, dark blue veins.

"The gurney can be pulled over here." She pointed, directing a tech pushing the ER stretcher. It squeaked into place as two nurses half rolled a sheet lengthwise and placed it near Na'Shalome's back, turning the patient onto it. Then, seven workers grabbed the doubled edges and lifted her to the stretcher.

We trotted at double time to the ER, gurney wheels squeaking horribly. Somehow Sister Simone ended up at the head of the stretcher holding Na'Shalome's dressing. When she saw me looking, she said, "I had nursing training in World War Two. Red Cross."

"I see you still remember a thing or two." I grinned at her, and she nodded back. We rounded the hall to the

ER and the supplies I needed to save the psychotic gold-painted girl.

Na'Shalome reached up, took the sister's wrist in her hand and held on. Sister Simone Pier smiled down into the girl's face, the crosses she habitually wore swinging between them. Na'Shalome's eyes filled with tears and she cried, the sound one of emotional agony rather than physical pain.

"I am here for you, little one," the sister said. "I am here."

Statler stood in the hallway, his arms crossed over his chest, a frown on his face.

"Got another good one for you," I said as we ran the stretcher into the trauma room, locked the wheels into place and dropped the head of the bed down into Trendelenburg. "GSW—entrance wound back right shoulder. Probably rifle, given the size of the exit wound in the upper right chest. Arterial bleed, possibly axillary, unable to see it at the scene. My guess is the round shattered the scapula and took out the top part of the lung. No other injuries noted."

"Festive girl. She's painted gold all over, why?" he asked as he slipped into a paper apron and clear plastic face shield.

"Witchcraft. Something she cooked up herself."

"Just curious. You do offer me such challenges, Dr. Lynch."

"My pleasure, Dr. Statler."

"Suction, Anne?" he said, taking over.

"Ready, Doc."

"Soon as this bleeder is clamped, I'll need two chest tube kits and an X ray. Blood gases, cross-match times two, and H&H."

"Lab already drew blood at the site."

Statler said, "Good. Tell me what happened."

I left Statler and Anne to stabilize Na'Shalome, taking the sister with me to the cardiac room to check on DaraDevinna. The young healer needed a healer herself, preferably one with surgical skills. She was bleeding profusely from a ragged laceration to her neck. The muscle was cut, the avulsion deep enough to need surgery. Not as bad as the patient who had been axed, but bad enough. There were multiple lacerations down her arms, as well, but they were more shallow. Most would just need closing. Only in a few places would I need to do a deeper layered closure.

"Who's on backup call for surgery?" I asked Coreen.

"Dr. Derosett. You want I should call him in?"

"Yes. And tell him to step on it. Then get me an H&H and let's see how much blood she's lost. She looks a little shocky—get her warm and turn up the fluids. I want another IV, ancef and tetanus if needed."

"Will do." Coreen lifted the phone on the wall between the two stretchers and dialed out. As she spoke, the deputy was wheeled in. Even from a distance, I could tell that one pupil looked different from the other. I stepped to his gurney and did a pupil check with my trusty little Maglite. The pupil on the side nearest the wound was sluggish; a change in pupillary reaction was an ominous sign. "I need a head X ray and CT scan on this one," I said as I turned his fluids down. Last thing this guy needed was more blood volume; if his brain was swelling I had to know fast and get him flown out of here to a neurosurgeon. Too bad Cam had finally gotten his plane fixed and left; he still had medical privileges here and could have helped assess the cop. That man was never around when you needed him. "Might as well get a C-spine, too, while X ray has him."

"Rhea?"

I looked up and saw Mark standing at the door. He was wearing his off-duty uniform of jeans, boots and POLICE windbreaker, his shoulder-holstered gun hidden beneath. I smiled.

"You wear that look well," he said.

I looked down and saw the blood that covered my arms and torso. Remembered the feel of arterial blood hitting me in the dark after the blasts.

Dismissing the mess, I said, "You catch the guy?"

"Oh, yeah. We got him."

I walked over, gesturing to the break room, indicating a need for privacy. "And?"

"DaraDevinna's father, Joshua Faith. He was still just standing there in the dark, holding the gun. Like he was waiting on us. Put down the gun. Came all peaceful-like. He's being processed now. Crime scene guys are working the site outside and in. Lots a blood in that room. Looks like someone slaughtered a steer. Like maybe you."

I smiled at his comment. "There was a ring of blood on the floor. We had to crawl through it and then drag the girls out." I turned on the water in the sink and started rinsing the blood off my arms.

"You know anything about the doll? It was in lockup in the evidence room at the LEC. Then it was here. Now it's gone again."

"Na'Shalome's doll?"

"Yeah. First time I put it in evidence myself. This time, I papered it, gave it to one of my men, and he put it in the CSI truck. Now it's gone. Again. And no one saw anything."

"Not me. I have no desire to touch it. Maybe a witch flew by and took it for a souvenir. Or it got up and walked away. That would be cute."

"The witches I've met don't claim to be able to fly. I'll be back up in an hour or so to take your statement."

"It's not like I'm going anywhere. And it'll take an hour to get things settled, so I'll still be up."

"If you've gone to bed, can I come to your room and wake you? Pretty please?"

"No," I said, my tone amused. "You may not. You can get me in the morning."

"Promise?" he said, teasing, taking the word at another meaning entirely. I ignored him and completed my rinse.

Mark dropped into one of the upholstered chairs. Sounding almost innocent, he said, "Can you spare a tired man a cup of coffee? ER coffee isn't quite as potent as LEC coffee, but a small jolt'll hold me till I get back."

Mark was asking me to wait on him like a girl in home ec class waiting on the football jock. More competition stuff. Wryly, I said, "The little woman will be glad to bring the big tough he-man a cup." I patted dry, poured a cup, added two creams and two sugars and handed it to him. I could do the little-woman routine when needed. Our fingers met around the cup and held.

"You sure you're okay?" he asked, green eyes serious with disquiet.

"I'm fine."

"Then why are you bleeding?" He reached up and touched my temple, high on my cheek.

I remembered the sting in the dark, touched it, as well. Fresh blood trickled through cracked and dry blood. "I'll see to it in a few minutes. Got hit by flying glass, I think."

"Take better care of yourself, woman."

"I try."

"Like heck you do," he said, laughing. "Like heck."

* * *

An hour later I was done, and Mark was finished with my statement. I was drinking my third cup of coffee and sitting in the break room, eyes closed, resting and thinking. Dara and Na'Shalome were in surgery, and the injured cop, who had been beaned by something hard enough to crack his parietal bone, was waiting to fly out of here. The place was dead. The mental health people had been notified that Na'Shalome was back and needed their services posthaste. They were getting a room ready for her in the state hospital, a nice dull room with plenty of guards, no windows, no sharp corners and lots of padding. It was my guess that she'd be there for years.

I should have known Miss Essie's omens and portents would converge on the full moon. And now? It was over. I was sure of it. Miss Essie's omens and portents were finally over. In the movies, didn't all bad things end with the full moon?

After the wounded cop was flown out, I was wired and unable to sleep, even though there were two hours when the place was quiet. Wide-awake, I sat in the ER, fingers tapping, my brain working overtime, trying to put the time sequence into better perspective. Sister Simone had just appeared. At midnight. Of course, at midnight. And offered herself as a sacrifice. Blood circles and sacrificial dolls. Candles. Spells using body parts.

Weird stuff. I hated it.

My mother had been into weird stuff several times in her life. At the end it was TV preachers, crying and moaning and shouting religion and asking for money. Not that we had any by that time. She had drank it all away. But earlier, during happier times, she had been into Ouija boards, horoscopes, a bit of spell casting, most of it directed toward my grandmother. Mother wanted the old woman dead. I just sat and watched as my mother chanted and burned incense and stuck pins into a voodoo doll. Stupid. The whole thing was stupid. Even as a kid I had known that. The old bat Rheaburn had outlived her anyway. But I kept thinking about omens and portents and Venetia Gordon able to walk. I didn't get any sleep.

24

WITH WHAT? A TANK AND A HOWITZER?

In the morning, I changed clothes and crawled out of the hospital, so tired I could barely walk. I needed sleep almost as much as I needed air, but I drove around the hospital to the crime scene. The broken window had been sealed with a sheet of plywood and duct tape, yellow crime scene tape cordoned off the area, including a tree and hedges, some flowering plants that looked like daisies from a distance. No one was there.

Off to the side, about a hundred yards away, in the woods, was another roped-off area with the crime scene truck, a police car and Mark's dark-green Jeep. I parked and got out, stretching in the dawn heat, intending to invite Mark to breakfast at the bus station. He had to be as beat as I.

As I walked up, I saw Skye, the petite, pretty crime scene tech, laugh and hand Mark something. Her other palm lingered on Mark's sleeve for a moment too long as Mark shook his head and said something to her. She cocked her head, doing that expose-the-neck thing flirty women do, as he spoke. I could hear her answering laughter on the wind. It tinkled.

Something odd twisted deep inside and I contemplated

turning around and heading back to my car. I had never fought for a man. Didn't know how. Didn't want to learn. If Mark wanted Skye he could have her. But I'd been seen. I couldn't leave now.

Skye waved at me and turned to Mark, leaving her hand on his arm too long again. The strange thing inside me made another half turn. An image of Big Boobs Boopsie Larouche standing with John Micheaux popped into my head.

Miss Essie's fortune-telling was suddenly explained. If even I had seen Skye's interest in Mark, it was likely public knowledge by now. Skye's laughter tinkled again.

I laughed like a horse. And I didn't know how to flirt. I forced my feet forward to the couple standing inside the yellow tape. Skye said something else and Mark laughed, moving forward to meet me. I put aside the twin images of men I cared for involved with women I didn't, stuck my hands in the pockets of my jeans and walked on.

A horrid smell hit me as I crossed the health run that circled the hospital grounds and I understood why the crime scene tape was over here. Something was decomposing nearby. Something large.

"Morning," I said when we were close enough to speak. "You up early or still up from last night?"

"Still up. Want breakfast? Skye and some of the guys and I are going to the bus station for a cholesterol fix before we crash."

Together? a little voice whispered in my mind. *You want us both together?* "No, I'm beat. Just wanted to say goodbye," I lied. I wasn't joining Skye and Mark for anything. "Place stinks."

"One of the guys found this spot last night while they

were finishing up the scene around Faith's window. Said
his nose led him right to it.''

''And?''

''Two bodies, male and female. Been here awhile.
Both bodies were pretty well putrefied. Was a mess getting them into body bags.''

''How long?''

''Coroner says several days at least, by the maggot and
beetle count. Major infested.'' Heat was also a contributing factor in the process of decomposition, and it had
been a typical August. I was glad I hadn't gotten off work
earlier and had missed the body transfer.

''Your mad stabber again?'' I asked, my hands still in
my pockets. I didn't quite know what to do with them.
Mark might be oblivious to Skye's interest, but Skye
wasn't oblivious to my discomfort. I was sure of that. A
little smile curved her mouth as she turned back to work.

Mark reached the tape just as I did and spoke more
softly as he answered. ''Looks like it. No hands, no
heads, ritual placement of the bodies. Sheriff has called
the state boys. And the press is already lining up to be
pests. Come to breakfast with us,'' he added for my ears
alone.

''Skye wouldn't be pleased.'' I nearly shriveled up and
died as the words left my mouth. I wanted to melt into
the earth.

Mark's eyes glinted green in the rising sun. ''Skye has
a schoolgirl crush on her captain. Her captain doesn't
reciprocate. Couldn't reciprocate even if he wanted to,
which he doesn't.''

I struggled not to show my reaction to his words. Was
pretty sure I kept the delight inside until he added, ''It's
against regs. Come with us. I'd like the guys to hear what

you saw in the room when you dragged Na'Shalome out.''

So much for my delight. He wanted to talk shop. ''No thanks. I'm too tired for a party, and hearing the recount of the process of stuffing icky bodies into body bags is a surefire appetite destroyer.''

''Is that a medical term? Icky?''

''You want me to bore you with Latin?''

''No thanks. Actually, you could be a help at breakfast. It was a bad night all around. These bodies weren't the only ones. Had to call out another crew.''

''Oh?'' I tried to sound interested, but now that my silly girlish worries had been exposed, I wanted to sleep.

''Henry Duncan and his new wife made a successful murder-suicide attempt last night.'' Mark propped his foot on a tree stump around which the crime scene tape was wound. It didn't look as if he was going to let me leave till he finished his spiel.

''Who's Henry Duncan?''

''Father of Mattie and Carol Duncan.'' At my blank look he said, ''The father of Na'Shalome and your Jane Doe. He's dead. Looks like it took place after midnight.''

''He killed her?'' I asked, feeling stupid. *Midnight?*

''No. She killed him, then herself. Used a filleting knife. Cut his throat. Took three slices. When he stopped screaming she used the knife on herself. Neighbor called the police.''

I didn't like the timing of this. Not at all. It was just too creepy. I shifted my weight and shoved my hands deeper in my pockets. ''So what you're telling me is that at midnight, while the attempted blood sacrifice was taking place in DaraDevinna Faith's room, the man Na'Shalome was trying to kill died.''

"No," he said, surprised. "I said after midnight. It was 4:00 a.m."

"Oh."

"You're acting kinda odd. You weirded out by all this?"

"You ever trick-or-treat?" I asked by way of answering his question. When he raised his eyebrows and nodded, I said, "At my house, for a few years, trick-or-treat came every day. My mother was into seances and voodoo dolls and she and her drunk friends would sit around in these silly filmy costumes and chant. Weird, I've seen. And what I've noticed is that weird usually has a human component and a little bit of coincidence."

"Like last night."

"Like last night," I agreed. "Long as it didn't happen at midnight I can live with it."

Mark grinned. "So, come to breakfast with us."

"Nope," I said, sticking to my guns. "I'm going to Miss Essie's. She needs to hear about all this. And then I'm going to hit the sack."

I tried to be true to my word. After parking my car and dumping my bags inside my house, I pocketed my cell phone and took both dogs to Miss Essie's for breakfast, but we never made it out of the woods. As we came across the creek, I saw through a break in the foliage that Miss Essie wasn't alone. She and another woman were standing in the yard, close enough to whisper to one another. The other woman was Sister Simone Pier, her white mantle fluttering in the warming breeze. Something about their postures looked strange.

I grabbed Pup's collar and quietly called Belle to me. Moving more slowly, I found a better view while I kept us hidden in the woods.

The two women stood in the back corner of the yard, far from the herb and vegetable beds. On the ground at their feet was a candle, a silver bell on a coiled silver chain and three earthenware bowls from Miss Essie's kitchen. Before them was a pile of dried brush and deadfall tree limbs. On top of the tree limbs was a heap of Miss Essie's fresh herbs. Even from this distance, I could see spikes of rosemary and the pale-green oblong of sage leaves. On top of the herbs, just above knee level and facing the sky, was the doll. The sister was pouring something on it, the sound of her murmur like a soft chant.

Mark would be livid. The doll was evidence. The doll was important. I needed to stop this, whatever it was. I needed to call Mark, tell him I had found his missing doll.

The scent of rosemary reached me on the warm air. The soft chant followed, as if it rested on the same breeze. I pulled the dogs closer, taking Belle's collar in my other hand.

I didn't reach for the phone clipped to my pants. And I didn't know why.

Miss Essie, her back to me, picked up a bowl, lifted her hands and poured a clear yellow fluid across the doll. A sweet scent reached me, like attar of roses.

The sister bent and lifted another bowl and slowly poured it, too. A moment later I smelled something new, like patchouli. Together, the two women lifted a candle from the ground. I hadn't noticed it was burning. They bent forward, hands together, and held the candle to the doll. After a moment, the scent of smoke reached me, warm and sweet, green and potent. The breeze died. Smoke swirled up into the morning sky, making a little tornado pattern as it rose, straight up into the heavens.

Sister Simone lifted the bell, holding the silver chain

near the flames. With a small silver rod she began to ring the bell slowly, the tone deeper than I expected, a clear, strong sound over and over again. A rhythm of almost once a second, the chime pure and clean on the silent morning. The steady chime almost matched the beat of my heart.

I didn't call Mark. I stood in the edge of the woods and watched as Miss Essie and Sister Simone Pier burned the evil doll into slag.

Not until the pile of brush and plastic was nothing more than ashes and pink sludge did I think about the county burning ordinance the two women had violated. There was a watch out in the county fire towers. Someone should have arrived, lights and sirens flashing. No one came. The morning was still and quiet, as if the whole world slept except us three women and the two dogs.

Finally, I slipped away, taking the dogs with me. I fed them, gave them fresh water, ate a pack of Hostess Twinkies for breakfast while debating with myself what to do. Deciding to ignore the blinking message light on my phone—it could only be more problems—I finally called Mark. Propping my feet up on the clean kitchen table, I dialed, and Stoney jumped up into my lap, purring happily. I stroked the long-haired cat as the phone rang. Mark answered at the bus station. Before he spoke, I could hear Doris call out an order to Darnel, her husband, working at the grill. "Scrambled and crisp!" An order for eggs and bacon.

"Yeeeellow."

"Actually it's sorta flesh-colored."

"That sounds interesting. What's it wearing?"

"A coat of paint, ashes and oil."

"Even more interesting."

"Interesting only if you want to arrest Miss Essie and Sister Simone Pier."

"I'd cause a riot in this town. Why is it flesh-colored?"

I took a deep breath. "This is off the record."

"Why off the record?"

"Because if you want to hear what I have to say, it's off the record. Say yes."

"Okay, it's off the record." I heard the background sounds fade, and knew Mark was walking away from his cop buddies.

"Miss Essie and Sister Simone just burned your missing voodoo doll into recycled plastic."

"What!"

"Keep your voice down."

"They burned it? How do you know? How did they get it?"

"Yes. I saw them. And I don't know," I answered in order. "But I would hazard a guess that the good sister stole it last night."

"Where did this take place? When?"

"In Miss Essie's backyard, just now. The dogs and I watched through the trees."

"Tell me."

"You can't make a report."

"Oh yes, I can."

"You can't. Because there's only me to prove it and I'll not testify against them. I'm only willing to talk to you off the record. Remember?"

"But that doll is evidence!"

"Tell me, evidence of what?"

Mark was silent on the other end. Fuming, no doubt. Thinking. I knew he'd reach the same conclusion I had.

"That girl, Na'Shalome, what chance does she have of a recovery?" he asked.

"To stand trial? None. In my opinion, she's had a full psychotic break. With her history, she'll never recover enough to stand trial. Best hope I have for her is a halfway house someday. By the time she gets out, your witnesses will be impossible to find, evidence will be scattered, lost."

"Burned."

"That, too."

"You watched them burn it?"

"From the woods. They didn't see me."

"Why didn't you stop them?"

I laughed. "With what? A tank and a howitzer? You're dealing with forces of nature here. No way I'd have any luck stopping them. You would have had to shoot them to stop them. Only reason I'm telling you is so you don't waste time trying to find who took the doll. It's gone."

"I'll have to talk to Miss Essie."

"You can't mention my name. Off the record."

"Woman—hold on." Mark broke off whatever he was about to say and turned the phone to his chest. It wasn't a good seal, little sound was blocked out.

I heard Skye's dulcet tones in the background. "Some of us are going to Puckey's Guns 'n' Things for a bit of shooting. You want to come?"

"Maybe next time. I'm beat. You guys go have fun."

"You need some time on the range, Cap'n."

I heard Mark sigh. "Yeah, I do. Okay. I'll meet you. Half hour?"

"Sounds good. See you there."

I didn't know much about the byplay between men and women, but I'd bet good money no one but Skye was heading to Puckey's. But then, what did I know? It might all be legit. For once I kept my mouth shut and didn't say the first words that popped into my head. *Mark, this is a date. She's setting you up.* No, not me. I said nothing. "Okay, where were we?" he asked me a moment later.

"We were no place. I'm going to bed. I'm beat." I almost cringed as I unwittingly used his phrase.

"I should do that, too, but I got some things to handle first."

More than you know, kiddo. But I said, "See you later, then."

I finished the Twinkies, lifted Stoney to the floor and hit the sack. I didn't move for hours.

25

DON'T LET THERE BE SNAKES AND SPIDERS

It was dark in my room when I woke. Rolling stiffly, I cracked open my eyes and found Belle's nose an inch from my face, dog breath being blown across me. There were worse ways to wake up, I suppose. Pup snored in the bedroom doorway. Stoney was nowhere to be found. Forcing my eyes to focus on the clock, I found I had slept almost ten hours. The answering machine was blinking with one message but I ignored it, my brain too sleep-fuddled to care what happened while I slept.

Crawling out of bed, I made my way to the shower and let hot water draw the stiffness out of my bones. I needed a run, badly. After the shower, I pulled on a semi-clean jogging bra, a sleeveless, long, white T-shirt and a dirty pair of jogging shorts—clothes just rank enough to be tolerated against my skin one more time, but not so rank they were ready for the laundress—and stretched slowly. Very slowly. My muscles felt like old elastic—crinkly, brittle, ready to crumble into dust.

A little more alert, I hit the play button on the message machine and listened. The call was from an exhausted-sounding Dr. Danthari at Carolinas Medical Center in Charlotte. I couldn't place his name until about halfway through the message. Venetia Gordon's neurosurgeon. His voice was precise, British-Indian accented. "Dr. Lynch, you must be mistaken about Venetia Gordon. You are surely speaking about a different patient. There is a one-in-a-million chance that she would some day develop limited upper-extremity sensation, but she is never going to walk. The damage to the cord was extensive. Nothing from C4 down was working. She had comprehensive flaccid paralysis and no deep tendon reflexes. I at first attributed it to spinal shock, but when she didn't come out of it in the first three months, I had to deduce there would be no improvement. Forgive me for being blunt, but there has been a mistake."

He left contact information with me and closed his statement with, "Please return my call to my office number this afternoon before two, as I am going out of town. I have a conference in Baltimore and won't be back until after the weekend. If this girl so much as lifted a finger, it is a miracle."

Miracles. Hocus-pocus. Omens and portents. Well, the good doctor was mistaken. Venetia was indeed walking. I had seen it with my own eyes.

Feeling punch-drunk, I saved the message. Stared at the steady red light. It was way after two. I couldn't call for days. *If this girl so much as lifted a finger, it is a miracle.* Boneless, stunned, I flopped across my comforter and dropped my head into the downy softness of my pillow, staring up into the ceiling. *If this girl so much as lifted a finger, it is a miracle.*

Marisa needed a miracle, a quiet voice said inside my head.

My breath came in unsteady gasps. A pain was building in my chest where my diaphragm rested against my ribs. *If this girl so much as lifted a finger, it is a miracle.*

Stoney padded in and jumped up beside the answering machine. Tail twitching, he batted at the red light before turning flat uncurious eyes to my face, staring. *If this girl so much as lifted a finger, it is a miracle.*

An empty place opened up inside of me, exposing shadows and vacant barren spaces where there had once been the certainty of training and science. I could hear Miss Essie's calm voice telling me that just because people once thought the world was flat didn't make it less round. *If this girl so much as lifted a finger, it is a miracle.*

Stoney jumped across my face, landing on the pillow beside me. As his body leaped, stretched-out and lithe, the doctor's voice intruded, calm and reasoned. *You are surely speaking about a different patient.* I sat up slowly. *You are surely speaking about a different patient.* My breathing steadied and I took in a deep, satisfying draft of oxygen. The pain eased. I would call Danthari back next week and we would clear up the misunderstanding.

I ignored the vision of Miss Essie's deliberate sigh, the slow shake of her head when I didn't see things as she did. It had to be a misunderstanding. It had to. And if it wasn't, then…well, I'd deal with that later. Once Marisa was home and could tell me what she wanted. After all, this was her body I was thinking about.

Rolling off the bed, I added my water bottle and cell phone, though I had seen no rabid animals all season, and leashed Pup before heading out. The dogs were frisky and wanted a fast run in the late heat, but I started slowly, still feeling stiff from too many hours in bed. At a slow jog I headed into the woods along the creek, hoping that as dusk fell, temps would cool. Off to the west, the sun was a glowing ball only inches above the horizon, gilding treetops and slicing through trunks with an occasional stab of glare. Above me was the moon, still looking full in the dull, near-dusk sky. Behind me, I heard other runners, voices carrying to me through the trees. It was a good evening for a run. I had plenty of time to get back before full dark.

Belle ran ahead of us and back, whoofing in that special way dogs have that means "Let's play!" Pup strained against the leash, which I coiled tightly around my left wrist. As I neared the pasture where Mark and I ran last, I increased my speed. Belle barked once, a joyous yelp that sounded a lot like "Finally!", and fell into place beside Pup as we stretched into the run. The other runners behind us fell back, their pace too slow.

I ran through the pasture, passing the old tractor, an abandoned building whose walls were splayed out and roof was caved in, and jumping over the trickle of creek leading to a cattle pond. Cattle mooed softly as they headed back to the barn on the other side of a swatch of trees and the pond. I always avoided cows. This was their territory and I was the interloper. I didn't feel like hiding out in the dilapidated building while a mad mama cow ran all around snorting with rage, hoping to get a chance to pound me with her hooves in protection of her calf. Not a fun way to end a run.

As I ran, I felt the stiffness finally slip away. Felt muscles frozen with sleep and the strange phone message loosen and begin to move fluidly. Felt my heart smooth out in a steady pounding rhythm that matched the rhythm of my legs and lungs. I ran for forty-five minutes, pausing only twice when the dogs needed water, and even then I kept my legs moving in a stationary jog.

The sun was setting when we started the slow turn back, shadows long and dark against the red earth, the rare call of a hoot owl echoing over the pasture. The scent of a campfire burning somewhere close, despite the ban, added to the ambience.

I loved running at dusk. Always had. There was something so solitary and soothing about the feel of night air brushing my sweat-damp skin. If it weren't for the swarms of mosquitoes, summer-night runs would be perfect. The mild concern over West Nile virus took some of the fun out.

When I felt the first feathery brush of mosquito wings across my skin, I turned the dogs directly toward home, taking a path straight across the last open pasture to the woods.

Between one breath and the next, I caught the faint scent of cigarette smoke. Saw a shadow moving in the shadows. Rising up and falling. *Toward me.*

I jerked left and stumbled over Pup. He yelped in surprise. Twisted sharply away. Something scraped down my right shoulder and landed at my feet. Pup jerked the leash. I was off balance. Struggled to compensate, ankles twisting. Fell toward Pup, hitting him hard in the side with my knees. He scrambled and writhed, whining. We ran.

Belle growled low and menacing from just ahead. Someone cursed.

Flames appeared through the trees. I was off the path, turned around. Disoriented.

Belle, blacker than the twilight, roared. Rose up in front of me. Collided with something. With someone. They fell, Belle sounding vicious, deadly. A voice screaming and cursing.

Pup whimpered. A blast rang out. A dog screamed. Pup twisted in midair and fell. I tripped across him and dropped, rolling in the dark, a bruising somersault. The leash stopped my tumble and I swiveled my wrist, releasing it. Pup was a pale blur on the pasture grass. Still. Silent. Rolling to my feet, I ran into the night.

Behind me I heard more cursing, cries. Belle's mad growls.

"Get it off me!"

A horrid thump. Belle fell silent.

I sobbed, unable to find breath. Shook my head. A single thought repeating in my mind. *What? What is it? What is happening?*

"Get her!"

I sobbed again, trying to breathe. Trying to stay upright. Running. A tight pain stabbed at my side. Footsteps sounded on the packed earth behind me, then vanished, sounds absorbed into the pasture grass. I finally sucked in a breath. Another.

Someone was after me. Someone had hurt my dogs. I bolted hard left, into the darkness.

I heard a crackle and searched to my right. Flames, visible through a spit of trees. The woods on the other side of the pasture were on fire.

Glancing down I saw the white blur of my T-shirt and ripped it off, tossing it at a low cedar tree. I had to get help for my dogs. Fast.

Orienting myself by the radiant red luster of the sun, I snaked my body right. Then left. Deeper into the dark. Pulled my cell phone, still clipped to my shorts. My water bottle was gone in the tumble.

"What is it?" someone asked.

"Her shirt," another voice said.

Two. There were two of them.

They cursed, the sounds glottal and growling. "I'll gut her alive."

I punched speed dial for Mark. Being gutted alive was not how I wanted to end my day. A titter of hysterical laughter rumbled from my lips. I bounded behind a copse of cedars, the phone at my ear. Mark answered.

"Yeeeellow," he laughed. I heard a noise in the background. Unfamiliar.

"They hurt my dogs," I gasped out.

"Rhea?" Surprise in the tone. That sound again. I almost placed it. A giggle?

"Shut up and listen," I said. "I'm in the pasture where we ran the other day. At least two people attacked me. They hurt my dogs!"

"Are you hurt?" Mark, all business now.

"No. But I think they shot Pup and hit Belle with something. I got away. And there's a fire between me and my house."

"There she is!" Behind me. To my left.

"Get her!" To my right.

"Brush?" Mark asked.

"Yeah. But it's in the trees, too."

"Where are you? Exactly."

"I'm not sure...wait." I veered hard right again. A dark shape loomed up before me. "I'm at the old tractor. The abandoned one."

"Gotcha."

"They know where I am."

"We're on our way. But don't hang up. Keep the line open."

I gripped the phone in my teeth. Ran to the rear of the tractor. Ducked down and shoved brush aside. "Please, God, don't let there be snakes and spiders. Please, please, *please,*" I whispered past the phone as I shoved my way beneath the belly of the machine. There was a clear space directly underneath, the grasses pushed and matted down. The daytime sleeping space of an animal?

I squatted. Easing the cutting pain in my side. Gasping

for breath. I dropped the phone to my lap. Breathed, mouth open. My legs ached at the sudden lack of movement. A soaring screeching pain that clawed up my thighs. I breathed hard, pulling in oxygen. Needing the water bottle. I could hear Mark's voice. Calling me. I pressed the phone to my breasts, stopping the sound.

Mosquitoes buzzed angrily, hungrily, around me. Sweat slicked my skin, advertising a tasty meal for the little bloodsuckers. They settled on my exposed back and thighs, flew at my nose and mouth. I covered my face to breathe without them being vacuumed into my lungs. I couldn't afford to cough. Couldn't let myself groan or scream with the agony of my overheated body suddenly stilled.

Voices came closer. Feet beating softly on grass. Passing by. Slowing.

"Keep going," I whispered. "I headed into the woods. Into the woods."

From far away, I heard a dog whining in pain. I had to get back.

The running stopped. I could hear them breathing. Quiet conversation. Voices calmer.

They were coming back. The dog whined again.

I needed a weapon. Clipping the phone to my waistband, I reached forward. Hands moving slowly, I searched. Patted the grass around me. Nothing to the left. Sharp grasses to my right, cutting my little finger, a razor of pain.

I stuck the digit into my dry mouth. Blood flooded it and the moisture of saliva followed. The taste exploding. Salty and slippery wet. I sucked until the pain subsided, still searching with my other hand. Mosquitoes dive-bombed my eyes, my nose, swarmed my mouth, stabbed at exposed skin. I touched something solid. Metal. Cool in the dark. Resting on the grass to the side.

Using both hands now, I explored the surface. It was curved, with one rounded edge where the metal was rolled under, making a rim. The other edge was rough. Rusty. And sharp along one side where fresh metal was exposed.

Suddenly I remembered the rear-wheel fender I had seen hanging by a metal thread, the big curved scoop of steel shaped vaguely like a human shoulder blade. I tried to lift the thing. It was heavy. Cumbersome.

The voices were closer. A draft of smoke reached me. I could hear the crackle of flames. Too close.

I gripped the fender.

Footsteps moved closer. One on the left of the tractor. One on the right. A click. Another. A flame of light brightened the world just beyond me. A lighter, illuminating a hand. A face. I knew that face.

Julio Ramos.

His blue eyes, dark in the night, found me. He smiled.

I raised the fender. Threw my body forward. Rising. Shoving with my legs in a single massive thrust.

His mouth opened.

The tractor fender caught him in the jaw, ripping the flesh of his smile wider.

I jerked the fender hard right. Came to my feet.

Julio screamed. A gurgling sound. He dropped the lighter. It flickered. Went out. He gasped. Retched.

I whirled and moved in a crouch around the tractor. The darkness was complete. My legs protested the near squat, my back fighting the stoop. I moved slowly toward the other form, bright in the moonlight.

"Zayvee?"

It was a woman's voice. I hadn't noticed that before.

She was just ahead, wearing a filmy white dress that hung on her form, the hem bunching on the grass. The dog whined again. Smoke swirled around me.

"Zay?"

He writhed on the grass, rustling. Gurgled, the tone a warning.

Her hand came up. Even in the dark, I could see the chrome gun. Small, but deadly in the moonlight. I eased on, lifting the fender. My arms objected. I ignored the pain.

My foot came down on something. It snapped. The woman whirled. I launched myself at her. Caught her just below the arms, across her chest.

The gun fired.

I body-slammed her. My breath huffed out of me. She went down. I went after her.

Slicing with the fender. She screamed. I sliced again. Ripping the jagged edge through her clothes. Her flesh. She was beneath me. Screaming. Raising up, I brought the edge down on her upraised hands. The gun was gone. Dark streaks marred the pristine whiteness of her gown.

My breath was coarse and rough. I looked up. Around. Julio was crawling toward us. The nearly full moon caught his face. His mouth was a black gash in his olive flesh. I looked back to the woman. She was blond. Mouth stretched wide with fear. I had seen her somewhere before.

She was curled on her side. Whimpering.

"If you've killed my dogs," I said, finding voice, finding breath, "I'll come back and finish you both."

Slinging the heavy tractor fender to the side, watching where it landed, I moved away, back toward the path. Toward the sound of my injured dog.

26

BEEN THROUGH THE WRINGER

I had no light. The sun was gone, the moon was not directly overhead, hidden by a small hill feathered with cedars, but I spotted Pup by his movement. He was struggling with the leash, trying to get at something on his back.

I slid to a stop at his side, knees skidding across tough grass and several stones. "It's okay, boy," I said. "I'm here. Easy."

When I reached forth a hand, he snapped. I jerked back. "It's okay, Pup," I soothed. "It's okay, boy. It's just me." I maneuvered upwind of him, letting my scent reach him along with my voice. "It's just me. Easy, now."

Pup's struggles slowed and he whined, the sound breathy and pained. I eased my hand forward to him and let him sniff my palm. Slowly I placed my palm on his head. Stroked down his neck. Again. And again. Found his collar. It was cruelly tight around his neck.

I remembered my fall. The final jerk as I got my hand free. "Easy," I said as I traced the collar down and found the hook. The leash. Unsnapped it. The collar loosed beneath my fingers. "That's a good boy."

Pup whined. Pain foremost in his tone now that he could breathe and his panic was subsiding. I moved my hands gently down his body. Back up. A sticky wetness met my hand. Blood. Cool in the night air. I followed the blood trail back up, fingers probing only lightly. And found the origin. A matted mound of hair and tissue. The hole was small. The blood only minimal. Either it was not much of a wound, or the bullet was deeper inside, causing internal bleeding.

Gently, moving slowly, I probed around the mounded wound. No broken bones. Little swelling. Inches away, my fingers hit something. A hard knot was just beneath the skin. The bullet.

"Small caliber," I said to Pup, fingers moving back to the hole. "On the surface. Looks like it may have bounced off your hard head and stopped cold. Good boy." I hugged him, putting my face down where he could lick my chin. "Good boy." Relief rested uneasily on top of my fear for Belle, and I cuddled the huge dog close, slapping his side firmly, the way he liked. He panted, his inch-long canines showing in a doggy-grin.

Moments later, I eased away. Pup whined again, licked at the air, clawed the earth toward me. "I have to find Belle. Stay." His head dropped to his paws and I heard a tail thump as I moved into the darkness.

"Belle? Where are you, Belle?" Unlike Pup, she would vanish into the darkness, her coat a part of the night. I moved in a bent crouch, feet sliding forward over the grass, hoping to find her with a toe. The aches in my body grew worse. Incipient cramps tightened my calves.

I stubbed a toe on something in the brush. With a hand, I patted until I found it. My water bottle. Opening the spout, I took a long squirt. Swallowed. Resealed it and moved on. I needed a lot more water than that, but Belle might need it, too. "Belle? Belle?"

The wind swirled. Smoke blew at me. Strong. Pungent. Flames suddenly crackled just ahead. To my left, a cedar. Tall dark feathery form. It exploded into flame. Hot air whooshed past me. Drying the sweat on my body in a single instant. Scorching my face.

"Belle!" I screamed.

Something touched my thigh. I flinched. Pup's head bumped me. I gripped his collar. *"Belle!"*

Pup pulled me toward the cedar. Into the heat of the flame. And I saw her. Lying beneath the burning tree.

Sparks shot out as the heat torched the heart of the dry tree. Branches fell, showering me. I jerked back, forced Pup to sit. He complied, but his dark eyes never left the black form on the ground.

I opened the water bottle and dumped it over my head, drenching my hair, shoulders. And ran under the flames. I grabbed Belle by the front legs, backed out, dragging her with me. Back. Across the grass. Stopping ten yards from the tree, I rolled her in the grass to make sure her coat was not on fire. My hands found several hot places and I bent and rubbed my wet hair into the spots. Singeing my scalp.

Another cedar burst into flame. Totally engulfed in an instant. Heat slammed into me. A wind was surging in, feeding the flame. Little tufts of burning grass and smoke flamed up around me. The pasture was going up any second now. A single conflagration. I had to get to the pond. I squatted and picked Belle up in my arms. Threw her across my shoulders.

"Pup! Come!" I turned and ran away from the fire. Toward the water. Pup assumed his position at my left thigh. Loping with me.

I spotted the pond through the trees. Fire had ringed the pasture. Flares of heat shot up and out as the grassland caught in patches and exploded upward. The pond was just beyond the stand of trees and I raced to it.

At the top of the slight rise, I tripped. Fell down the hill, rolling with Belle. Into the water. Pup stood at the top and whined, his eyes on the water, curious.

"Come!" I demanded. Pup yelped and dived for me. I dodged and he hit the water with a huge splash. I grabbed Belle and followed Pup into the cool, slightly slimy water. Mud sucked my feet down. I slogged deeper.

Cattle watered here. It couldn't be clean. But it was wet. Pup paddled over to me, a water dog happy with the unexpected swim. He had temporarily forgotten his pain. I pulled Belle even deeper into the water, holding her head above the surface.

Down in the pond, I had little light to assess her with, but she was breathing. I could feel the movement and scent of dog breath on my cheek. Around us, the woods, the scrub brush and the farmer's pasture burned. The smoke was awful, but heat rose, and somehow, there was enough clean air for us to breathe. Pup swam for a few minutes, happy with the new experience, then tired and came to me. I moved deeper into the pond, where I could almost stand, and held him, too, his front paws on my knee.

My back muscles jerked in a spasm, a twisting spiral of wrenching pain starting at the weak place where the scalpel had sliced through muscle and nerve. Leg cramps, staved off by adrenaline and movement, struck. I sobbed with the pain. Tried to find a way to twist to relieve my back, to massage the bunched muscles. Tried to relieve the agony by shoving my feet into the muck beneath me. Nothing helped. I screamed with the misery, and Pup licked my face, his big eyes tender. I needed to get out. Needed to walk. But I stayed in the water. Held the dead weight of Belle. And cried.

What seemed like hours later, I heard sirens, far off. Much later, voices. Odd sounds. An engine. A tractor roared closer. Then away. Back again. I understood someone was plowing a passage near the pond. Plowing the fire under.

"Rhea!" Mark's voice.

"Here!" But it emerged as a croak. Pup shoved away from me, his nails raking my thigh, and bounded out of the water, to the top of the rise. The big puppy barked joyously. Mark appeared beside him, a black shadow against the flame's brightness. Tiredly, I slogged my way out of the pond. Fell at the edge, sinking into mud. The movement eased the spasms in my back and legs. I swiped at the tears streaking my face and pulled Belle onto my lap. Mark slid down and knelt beside me, Pup at his side.

"You okay?"

I nodded, but when I spoke, my voice was raspy, as if I had been screaming. "Yeah. Sorta. Got a flash?"

A light clicked on and Mark extended it to me.

"You hold it, please. That woman hit Belle with something. Must have hit her head."

Mark trained the light over Belle and we found the lump just behind her ear. I didn't know much about dog brains, but in a human, that would be near the brain stem. A dangerous place for a hematoma. I looked up at Mark, cleared my throat. It felt raw. "I need to get her to a vet."

He nodded. "We can get you out of here soon."

"How did you find me so fast?"

"Your cell phone. You shouted nonstop. Helped us

figure out what you were doing, mentioned the pond about a half-dozen times. We followed the dialogue until you dropped into the water and shorted out the connection." He smiled at me, his lips not quite steady. "You scared the ever-living hell out of me," he said softly. "You have to stop doing that."

"It was Julio Ramos and Fazelle Scaggs. Nurses from the hospital. Did you get them?" Resting Belle's head on the mud beside me, I swiveled, pulled my calves up and started massaging them. The pain was unbearable and I groaned. Turning off the flash, Mark took over one calf, his fingers warm and strong. When he finally answered, his tone was strange.

"Oh, we got them. They're on their way to the hospital and then to jail. Well, that is, if and when they can be jailed." When I looked at him quizzically, he added, "They need surgery first. A lot of it."

"Oh." I didn't know what to say. I remembered the look of Julio's mouth, the gap ripped back to his ears. Remembered the blood on Fazelle's hands and clothes.

"When you told them you'd be back to finish them off, if they had killed your dogs, you were serious. Weren't you?"

I shrugged. I had meant it at the time. I don't think I'd have gone back. Not really. "I was kinda PO'd," I said finally.

A voice called from the top of the rise and a man appeared. "You all right, Cap'n?"

"I'm fine. We need a ride outta here, though. The doc can't walk, and we have a hurt dog."

"Farmer says you can use his truck to get back to the farm. Fire is still burning over toward the creek. We got some houses in jeopardy, so it'll be a while 'fore you can go that way."

Mark stood and lifted Belle into his arms. Her large amber eyes were slit, her tongue hanging out of her mouth. I forced myself to my knees and tried to stand. Pup, as if sensing my distress, ran to me and stopped, his body turned at just an angle I could use. I braced myself on his back and made it to my feet. The pain was pure agony, my calves like rocks beneath the flesh. But with the big dog's help, I made it to the top of the pond's rise.

In the pasture, grass scorched and trees burned to rubble, I spotted three fire trucks, one nearby, lights flashing yellow and red, hoses spread all over. As I stood there, wobbly and unsure, a county rescue squad volunteer dropped into the hole of the pond, a hose braced on his shoulder. Pup turned and watched him go. I could feel the vibration in Pup's limbs as he thought about joining the firefighter in the water. I'm sure to Pup it looked like fun. But he was working, and stayed stationary beneath my hands. I was glad. I might have fallen without him.

I watched as Mark placed Belle in a secure place in the back of the pickup truck. Putting aside my own misery, I moved forward on lead feet to the truck. Climbed into the back with Belle, Pup beside me. Mark said nothing about my not riding in the cab with him. If it had been his dog, he'd have been in back, too.

The engine roared to life and we moved across the bumpy pasture toward the two-lane, rutted path leading to the farm. I cushioned Belle's head on my lap. Pup stared into the night, scenting all the new and unusual smells. Happy. Twice he jerked his head back as if something was stinging his neck. Otherwise, he didn't seem aware he had been shot.

I could hear Mark's voice through the open windows as he radioed for a car to meet us. The sounds of the firefighters fell away. The scent of burned cedar and grass wasn't unpleasant. The feel of the metal slats bumping beneath my legs was. But I didn't move until we got to the farmhouse except to stroke Belle's head.

A marked car met us there, lights flashing blue. Without looking to see who had met us, I eased my way down to the ground. Pup jumped after. Mark took my place in the truck and handed Belle down to me. She weighed a ton. She smelled of wet dog. But she still breathed. I buried my face in her fur and hugged her to me.

"You look like you've been through the wringer."

I looked up at the voice. It was Skye. Dressed in off-duty jeans and cowboy boots, her hair pulled back in a ponytail. Makeup fresh. Pretty.

"Your hair burned off?" She sounded incredulous.

"Belle was on fire," I said, thinking back. "I put it out with my wet hair. Is it bad?"

"It's awful."

"Skye!" Mark said.

I laughed. Snorting into Belle's fur. I knew I had to look like death warmed over—charred to burnt toast, covered in mud, smelling like smoke, cow pond and dog. And I just didn't care. If Mark wanted Skye, he could have her.

"Well, it is."

"Come on, Rhea. Let's get Belle to the vet." Again Mark eased Belle away from me and settled her in the back of his marked car. Pup and I joined Belle behind the steel mesh, and we pulled away from the farm.

Belle woke up on the way to the veterinarian and snuggled her body close to mine. She whined only once, as if to make sure I knew she was hurt. I stroked her ears and told her she was wonderful, letting the tears come. Once there, we had her X-rayed and gave her some fluids, IV. She was groggy, and a little loopy, unsteady on her feet, but the X-ray film was negative and Dr. Aycock let me take her home. Pup, too, once the doctor removed the .22 round from his head and cleaned and bandaged the wound.

Mark, stripped down to his undershirt and jeans, bathed both dogs in a deep sink to allow Dr. Aycock to check for other wounds. There were none, and the vet prescribed rest and seven days of antibiotics, Pup's meds to be taken internally to fight infection, Belle's topically for the burned places on her body. The wounds weren't bad, but I wasn't taking chances.

It was near eleven when Mark's cruiser pulled into my driveway and he cut the ignition. He didn't ask to come in, simply opened the cruiser's back door and lifted Belle in his arms, carrying her to the door. I had locked my house and fished around in the stack of plastic pots beneath the oak tree for the spare key.

Opening the door, I let Mark go first. Pup leaped after him and I followed, closing the door and locking it. Mark placed Belle on her pallet, and pulled it into my bedroom, beside my bed. Then he brought water and food and placed them nearby. Pup curled up beside his mother and put his head down. Sighed. They smelled of medicinal soap and a little of smoke. No. I sniffed again. That was me. I stank.

"Mark, I need a shower."

"Go ahead," he said. "I'll fix you some soup and a sandwich or something. Glass of wine?"

"Oh, yes. Please."

I stripped in the shower, under the hot water, letting the blast of heat rip the stench from me, cleanse the burns and tears in my flesh. I didn't need medical help, other than what I could do for myself. No stitches. But I could feel the blisters in my scalp when I washed my hair. So much for the new do. I found other blisters on my palms and the backs of my hands. On my forearms. I had packets of Silvadene in the medicine chest. I'd be fine.

I let fresh tears come then. Slow racking sobs. I had wanted to kill a woman. Really wanted to. If I had succeeded, I wouldn't have mourned the death, only the desire in me to cause it. I had almost lost my dogs. If I hadn't gotten back just when I did, the fire would have burned Belle to death. Too much. It was all simply too much.

When the tears subsided, I blew my nose in the stream of water and soaped, the water running from me, muddy and sooty black. Massaging my aching calves, I stretched to ease the overworked back muscles, then shaved my legs, turned off the water and oiled my skin from toes to nape, checking for other places that needed attention. I was in the shower a long time. Maybe half an hour. Maybe longer. I knew Mark would wait.

As I worked on my body, doing all the girlie things I so seldom did these days, I realized that I wouldn't have found Belle except for Pup. Pup found her. Pup saved her, saved me, too. Pup wasn't a puppy anymore. He needed a grown-up name suitable for a grown-up dog. A very special dog.

In fact, he would make a great service dog for Marisa when she came home. I'd see about getting specialized training for him. There had to be someplace in the state where he could be taught to be a special-needs dog. Tears came again. I rinsed them away. Enough of this. I didn't cry. I wasn't a whiner.

Out of the shower and dried off, I treated the burned places on my skin and scalp and popped four aspirin to stop the pain of the cramps in my legs and back. Applied a smear of lipstick and combed my ragged hair. It looked funny with the white cream oozing out of it. I sprayed on a bit of perfume to conquer the last of the smoke and wet-dog stench. Dressed in soft slacks and a pullover shirt. Clothes I hadn't worn in over a year. Silk with a texture like suede. Nice stuff. Low black slippers instead of socks.

Belle watched as I dressed, an understanding glint in her eyes. "Okay," I whispered when I realized what I was doing. "So I'm not going to just let her have him." Belle grunted in satisfaction and closed her eyes, slipping into easy sleep. I rested my hand on her side, listening to her breath sounds, feeling the beat of her heart. Belle was safe. Tears prickled. I forced them away. Stroked her ears. She breathed deeply and evenly, more than content at the attention.

Just before I left my bedroom, I shoved Stoney off my pillow, sat on the edge of the bed and played my messages. There were four new ones. One from Shirl informing me she had taken "that scamp Cam back." One from the hospital asking me to come in to work. Fat chance. One was from Miss Essie telling me to call her when I got in, if I got in by ten. The fourth message was from Mark, telling about the two bodies found near the hospital. They were the real Fazelle Scaggs and Julio Ramos. Which meant that the people taking their places in the hospital were impostors. To call him.

Thoughtfully, I put on music. Some CDs by Carole King and Enya. Soft, romantic stuff. Belle sighed in her sleep. Pup snored. It had been a long day.

When I entered the kitchen, there were candles lit. Two bowls of soup were on the table, steam rising from each, sandwiches made from bagels and cream cheese and sliced smoked turkey. A chilled Chardonnay in my good crystal. I didn't have any white wine in the house. Mark had been home and back. He half smiled at me from across the room, that easy, glinting smile I saw sometimes in my sleep. His hair was wet, his clothes were fresh, clean jeans and button-down blue shirt, the sleeves rolled up to show his forearms. Mark had exceptionally well-defined forearms, covered with a feathering of long dark hair.

I slid into my seat and smiled at him. He sat opposite me. "No business. Just eating and talking," he said.

"Before we agree to that, the two people who attacked me. Who were they? Do you know now?"

Mark nodded. "Zavon and Esmerelda Duncan."

The names meant nothing to me. I had never met them. Never heard of them.

"Na'Shalome's older brother and sister. The ones who left to go to school. Turned out they went to technical school. Both were licensed practical nurses," Mark said, his green eyes solemn, the smile gone. "They quit their jobs two days after Henry Duncan got out of prison. Disappeared."

I put two and two together, did a little guesswork and said, "They wanted me to finish whatever they had in mind all along?"

"Yeah. They didn't know Henry was dead. We found the source of the forest fire. A campfire in the center of a white circle. Various knives. Sharp knives." He paused. "Butcher knives. Skinning knives. Oils in little brown bottles. Some other stuff." He took a deep breath and let it out, his eyes hard on mine. "I have an idea what it was all for because I saw the last two victims. They were laying in wait for you. Had probably been waiting there for you since we ran the last time."

"They wanted my hands."

"At the very least."

I nodded, shook out my napkin and spread it across my lap. Tasted the wine, which was bursting with flavor and slid down my throat like nectar. I was dehydrated and needed water. Lots of water. The wine would go straight to my head. And I didn't care. "Soup looks good."

"So do you."

I reached up and touched my burned hair. Mark caught my hand, his eyes intense. "You look beautiful. Even if you burned your hair off bald, you'd still be beautiful."

I ducked my head, embarrassed and pleased. To cover my reaction I lifted my glass and held it up as if in a toast. Mark held his up, as well, and waited.

"To Pup for saving Belle. To Mark for saving me. Again."

"You saved yourself. I just drove you home afterward," he chided, "but I'll accept the praise. Just this once. It's good for my manly pride." He clinked my glass with his and sipped. I smiled and joined him.

Mark's cell phone rang, the sound little chirps. Our eyes fixed on it, lying on the table. It rang again. And again. I lifted my eyebrows, my eyes still on the phone. "You going to answer that?"

Mark sighed, put down his wineglass and lifted the phone, touching it on. The chirping stopped on the sixth ring. "I am off duty, damn it."

I laughed softly and put my wine down, too, in favor of the water. Ice clinked as I drank. Mark never cussed in front of ladies. I'd have to remind him of that.

"How many?" He paused. "Why me?" Another pause. "Hell, yes, I have plans." A longer pause. I started my soup. It was canned but delicious, some kind of chunky tomato. I finished off my water while Mark listened and sighed.

"Okay. Send her to pick me up." His voice sounded weary and angry and distinctly frustrated. He put the phone down.

"Back to the fire?"

"It got away from them. Wind came up. We have an entire neighborhood in jeopardy. Forest fires aren't exactly common in this area." It sounded as if he was quoting, but his eyes settled on me, saying much more than his words. "They're overwhelmed."

"Eat your soup first. You'll need your strength."

Mark took several spoonfuls of soup before looking up again, his eyes like jade in the flickering light. "I had hoped to need strength for other things."

I sipped my wine, considering. Trying not to sound coy or silly. "I'm not going anywhere. I'm off tomorrow. There's a key on the kitchen counter."

"I might be late." He lifted his bowl and drained the last of his soup. Wrapped three of the small sandwiches in a paper napkin.

"I might be asleep."

He stood and moved to my side, bent, kissed me gently. "I might wake you," he said against my lips.

"I certainly hope so."

The kiss deepened. And then he was gone.

___ Author Note ___

About Dawkins County:

Most doctors who commute to the small county hospital where I work, are scheduled for weekend coverage of the ER. Upon hearing of the small population in the mostly rural area—about 50,000 people—they expect to experience a restful weekend with a rare car accident and perhaps a sore throat or earache. Instead, they find an incredibly high incidence of alcoholism, drug use, teenage pregnancy, sexually transmitted diseases, heart and liver disease, unvaccinated children with childhood diseases not seen in this country in decades, diseases acquired through contact with wildlife, farm animals and poor water quality in the few well systems in outlying areas, farm and industry traumas, people hit by trains, and on and on. Most leave feeling shell-shocked. Longtimers like me just grin and say, ''Wait till next week. it'll be worse!'' An often-heard phrase in the ER is, ''Oh, honey, I could tell you some stories...''

About the doll:

I am often asked how much of what I write is based on my life, and certain events in this novel are true. The doll is a real doll, brought to the ER one night at 2:00 a.m. by a nurse, Dan Thompson. His son had acquired the doll in New Orleans, over Mardi Gras, and shared the strange thing with us. I did change one arm of the doll, and added the cavity in the back, but all other parts are true to life! The doll now graces Dr. Jason Adams's living room in Florida.

About Rhea:
So many of you have fallen in love with Dr. Rhea-Rhea Lynch. I love her, too! For me she is as alive as I am, as full of angst and energy, pathos and joy. Though Rhea and I are nothing alike, and she is fully fictional, I would recognize her if she walked into the room. I have heard the same comment from many of you.

For those of you who have asked, Rhea ages one year for every three books. After book three, she will permanently be listed in her mid-thirties. And no, I don't yet know how her romantic life will turn out! I am as ambivalent as Rhea about the two men in her life! And then...there's that small problem of John, the ex-fiancé...

Thanks to your help, Rhea will be around a long time! (And yes, I pronounce her name Ray, like a ray of sunshine—though she would hate that comparison!)

About medicine:
Our knowledge of medicine is evolving so fast that even the finest doctors have a hard time keeping up with the changes. When you read any medical novel, many of the procedures used by the characters will quickly become

outmoded, outdated, and be put out to pasture! I hope you will keep this in mind when you read about Rhea Lynch, M.D.!

The torture of the two sisters and the incident of the woman's tongue were all based on real-life situations, though I changed all the particulars, locations, all names, and drew primarily on newspaper accounts of the incidents to protect patient confidentiality. I have often said real life is much more horrific than fiction.

About the author:

If you wish to learn more about me, please come to gwenhunter.com or go to my author's page at mirabooks.com. I will answer any letters that come via e-mail quickly. Any letter that comes by snail-mail through the publisher will simply take longer! And if you don't send me a return address, it won't be replied to at all!

Thank you all!
Gwen Hunter

In the high-stakes world of power and politics,
everything is worth the risk....

RACHEL
LEE

Two seemingly unrelated murders—an elderly nanny and a
young exotic dancer—are linked together. Tampa homicide
detective Karen Sweeney discovers that a U.S. senator,
and presidential contender, is the only connection between
the two women. Did he commit these crimes? If not, then
who is trying to ruin him?

Karen is drawn into a web of lies and hidden motives that
she must unravel before the senator, his children and
Karen herself become the next victims.

WITH
MALICE

MIRA®

GWEN HUNTER

66916	PRESCRIBED DANGER	___	$6.50 U.S.	___ $7.99 CAN.
66803	DELAYED DIAGNOSIS	___	$5.99 U.S.	___ $6.99 CAN.

(*limited quantities available*)

TOTAL AMOUNT	$_____
POSTAGE & HANDLING	$_____
($1.00 for one book; 50¢ for each additional)	
APPLICABLE TAXES*	$_____
TOTAL PAYABLE	$_____

(check or money order—please do not send cash)

To order, complete this form and send it, along with a check or money order for the total above, payable to MIRA Books®, to: **In the U.S.:** 3010 Walden Avenue, P.O. Box 9077, Buffalo, NY 14269-9077; **In Canada:** P.O. Box 636, Fort Erie, Ontario L2A 5X3.

Name:_____
Address:_____ City:_____
State/Prov.:_____ Zip/Postal Code:_____
Account Number (if applicable):_____
075 CSAS

*New York residents remit applicable sales taxes.
Canadian residents remit applicable GST and provincial taxes.

MIRA®

Visit us at www.mirabooks.com

MGH0203BL